CAR TROUBLE

A Cassidy Callahan Novel

by
Kelly Rysten

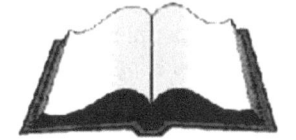

CCB Publishing
British Columbia, Canada

Car Trouble: A Cassidy Callahan Novel

Copyright ©2010 by Kelly Rysten
ISBN-13   978-1-926918-03-7
First Edition

Library and Archives Canada Cataloguing in Publication

Rysten, Kelly, 1960-
Car trouble : a Cassidy Callahan novel / written by Kelly Rysten.
ISBN 978-1-926918-03-7
Also available in electronic format.
I. Title.
PZ7.R98Ca 2010   j813'.6   C2010-905194-7

Cover artwork by Kelly Rysten: www.kellyrysten.com

Publisher: CCB Publishing
               British Columbia, Canada
               www.ccbpublishing.com

*Special thanks to Allen and Brandy K. for sharing
their experiences in Police Academy and Search and Rescue.*

*Thanks also to Paul and Donna for their patience,
hard work and dedication in helping me put my stories into print.*

Other books by Kelly Rysten

Triple Trouble

Read about Cassidy Callahan's first
tracking adventure with trouble at every turn.

Published 2009 – ISBN 978-1-926585-41-3

Chapter 1

The white monster truck appeared out of nowhere. I was winding through the narrow mountain roads of the Angeles Forest when it came barreling around a corner. I yanked hard on the steering wheel, pulling off to the side of the road to let him pass. My dog, Shadow, standing on the front seat, yelped with surprise as he lost his footing and hit the passenger door. The white truck barreled past in a cloud of dust. My first thought was the driver hadn't seen my vehicle in his haste, but then I saw his face as he drove by. The guy was laughing at me.

"Wimpy little Jeep Wrangler," he seemed to be saying, "stay off my road."

As his tailgate disappeared behind the billowing dust I hopped from the Jeep to survey my situation. Shadow watched intently as I looked down the embankment. The mountain fell away in a three-hundred-foot drop with only the tall pine trees returning my gaze. One wheel hung over the precipice, one was deeply embedded in the soft shoulder, while the other two were hanging to the very edge of the solid roadbed. I switched the Jeep to four-wheel drive and gently got back in on the uphill side. I cranked over the engine, eased up on the clutch, down on the gas pedal, gently, easy does it. I felt the Jeep move slowly forward. As the shoulder gave way, the Jeep slowly twisted downward and I felt the passenger side tip a little more. Okay, better stop. Shoot, how many times had I needed a winch on this thing then forgotten all about it the next day? Too many times to count. Maybe I should paint notches on the fender or something to remind me. Cass, you know this is the umpteenth time you've done this. And there I was at umpteen and one.

I grabbed my daypack from the back of the Jeep, found Shadow's leash and stuffed it in the pack.

"Come on boy, we have a long, hot walk ahead of us."

I looked in the pack. Two days of backpacker food, a plastic bag with trail mix, a hunting knife, a change of clothes and a couple of pieces of beef jerky. It looked like the standard stuff for this pack. The backpacker food wouldn't be used because I didn't have my stove, but the trail mix and jerky might be greatly appreciated by the end of the day. I found a couple water bottles rolling around on the floorboards and added them to the pack. I tended to take off like this a lot and there was no telling when some water would be needed, so I kept a small stash in the Jeep at all times. I looked for more bottles but only found the two.

"Okay, if that's what I've got, that's what I'll make do with," I said even though no one was around to hear me. I added my wallet and car keys to the pack and then shouldered it.

"Shadow, heel," I commanded. He took his place to my left and followed me down the road. The command wasn't really necessary. I was sure that he would stay with me but it was good for him to hear anyway. He understood that this was work, not play, and would listen better now that he was in work mode.

I set my feet to a steady pace and headed downhill. "Just pretend this is the Marines," I told myself. "Just keep the pace and eventually the hike will end."

It would have been a pleasant day for hiking except for the heat. It was slightly cloudy but this was Southern California in the summer and it was hot. I walked and kept my focus on the woods around me, hoping to catch sight of the light green paint of a ranger truck or for any other signs of movement. Movement meant animals and I always enjoyed taking a break from these hikes to stalk an animal through the woods.

This was not a new situation for me. My name is Cassidy "Trouble" Callahan; tracker, cowgirl and general all around trouble magnet. I was only called Trouble by my family, which also included the employees of my father's quarter horse ranch. However, the tendency to get into trouble didn't always stay at the ranch. It followed me around. Sometimes it snuck up subtly and sometimes it came barreling towards me. Sometimes it meant a hike to civilization and sometimes it meant fighting for my life. So this little episode was actually quite a relief compared to what could have happened. This little bit of trouble was more of an inconvenience. A five-mile hike to the road and a ten-mile hike to a telephone were annoying, but not something to get upset over. I could probably flag down a ranger once I reached pavement.

I soon decided the day was too hot. The animals were sitting in the shade waiting for the cooler part of the day, just as I should be doing. My problem however was an appointment I needed to keep and I didn't want to be late. I wasn't sure what the appointment involved but it was with Rusty Michaels and somebody he wanted me to meet. Rusty was a detective I had met during another trouble attack in which I'd been carjacked. After Rusty had helped me to escape and arrested the carjacker we had kept in touch. However, recently it had escalated into more than just keeping in touch. If I was late Rusty would worry. He knew I was generally early to these things but he also knew how often I was delayed by trouble. If I was late, he'd start looking for me. He'd call the house. He'd call my cell phone. He'd call Paul, the ranger at the station I visited frequently. I got out my cell phone and looked at the screen. No reception here. The mountains blocked it. I tried calling Rusty just in case it worked. I got a ring and he answered but I couldn't hear anything and I doubt he could either. I continued speaking to him in the event he was able to hear me.

"Rusty, I don't have any reception here. I wanted you to know that I'm having car trouble and might be late. If I don't show up, don't worry about me. I'm walking to a phone and I'll call back later." I made it sound routine, which unfortunately it was. Shadow followed along, tongue hanging, drool dripping. I shared my water with him but we didn't have a bowl so he lapped it from my cupped hand. Shadow was good for the long haul. He'd been backpacking with me a number of times, this hiking was just a little more open than usual.

Five miles later we hit pavement, the Angeles Forest Highway. I clipped on Shadow's leash. Now it was just ten more miles to a telephone. I looked at my cell phone again. It was already five o'clock and maybe Rusty would be off work soon. I headed down the highway but this was tougher going than the long dirt road. There was very little shoulder and cars whipped around us making their commute from L.A. to Joshua Hills by way of the long, scenic route. This scenic route could be faster or slower, depending on the freeway's conditions. A mile later another bar appeared on my phone so I tried again. Sitting on the side of the road, I punched a few buttons and there he was.

"Hey," I said, "It's me. Did you get my other call?"

"Yeah, where are you? And where were you?"

"I was up in the mountains and I'm still up in the mountains but now I can talk. Did you really need me to meet you at your office? I don't think I'll make it back to town by six." A particularly loud car whipped past. "I need to find a place where I can meet a tow truck or a taxi and I don't think that's going to happen for about ten miles."

"Why don't I just come get you? You sound like you can use a ride."

"Yeah, a ride would be nice. I already got my exercise for the day. I'll find a pullout and wait if you're sure it's not an inconvenience."

"I'll call Lou and reschedule and then I'll head out. Can you give me directions?"

"Take the 14 to Angeles Forest Highway and follow Angeles Forest Highway until you see me. There's a lot of traffic up here so I'll try to walk on your side of the road and find a pullout. If you get to the turn off for Mount Pacifico you've gone too far. That's the road I just left."

"Okay, gotcha."

We disconnected and I followed the road downhill, always downhill, until I came to a large pullout overlooking the forest. I wasn't going to sit and wait, though. Pullouts were great places to read tracks. There were many different kinds of people who pulled over and it was like reading the newspaper to walk around and see who had been there. It was also good practice for honing my tracking skills.

I found a spot where a car had been parked, probably a van, because about six people got out. I found the footprints of a woman with small feet. She was heavy and the sides of her shoes overlapped the thin soles. From the driver's side a man had stepped out, also heavy. He shuffled his feet as he walked to the overlook, and then stood smoking cigarettes as the kids ran around. There were four children ranging in age from six to teens. The teenagers didn't move around much. It looked as if they only left the van to escape the heat. The younger ones ran out to the lookout and jumped around on the railing that protected them from the drop off beyond.

I went to another parking space and found the tracks of a young couple who had walked along the railing, stopping several times. The guy would stand really close to the girl and I pictured him with an arm wrapped around her, pointing to different things in the scene below. I looked out on the expanse and saw a hawk circling. Maybe he'd been pointing out that same hawk. Maybe he knew what kind it was. Maybe the girl was actually interested. I hoped she was.

I could go on doing this for hours. It just felt right to me, reading the ground. It was all I knew how to do well. I also found a parking place where a couple with a toddler had stopped. When they removed their son from his car seat and set him down he immediately ran towards the road and the dad chased after him. It was a big pullout but he didn't get far. The dad carried his son but the boy didn't want to be held. The dad's footprints kept shifting this way and that trying to still the squirming child. He had finally given up and set the boy down again, holding his hand to keep him close.

I walked around reading all the news in the sand until I eventually noticed Rusty's dark blue Explorer parked at one end of the pullout. He was smiling, amused that he'd snuck up on me and knowing the reason why I'd been so preoccupied. He enjoyed watching me work because only then was I so at ease. I think he could feel the rightness of it the way I did. Giving me a patch of sand was like giving a mathematician a problem or an athlete a physical challenge. I jumped in and it was like pulling teeth to get me to stop. I walked towards the Explorer and he pulled forward to save me a few steps.

"I was wondering if I was going to have to honk the horn before you'd see me," he said.

"I'm sorry, I was reading and I lost track of time."

"I know, I just think it's funny." His sandy brown hair always looked slightly windblown and his blue eyes usually smiled at me. I loved those eyes, so warm and expressive. I had certainly seen my share of emotions in those eyes. Guess that's what comes from being a trouble magnet. He had helped me through many tough things in the short time we'd known each other. As usual, he was dressed in brown slacks with a sport coat. He'd taken off his tie and seemed at ease.

I placed Shadow in the backseat and then hopped into the front.

With a serious look he asked, "Okay, where's it at this time?"

"Mount Pacifico."

"And what happened?"

"I got forced off the road by an overzealous road hog."

"Do you want to pull it out?"

"Do we have time? You'd be proud of me. I didn't lose it over the side and I didn't bury it axle deep. It just seemed a little risky to keep trying, so I started walking instead."

"I was a little worried when you called me the first time. You know, we need to come up with a rating system or something. I never know if 'I'm not going to make it back to town by six' means 'I'm going to be late' or 'I'm fighting for my life out here and if I survive I'll probably be there after six.' So I want to drive up there and see just what you got yourself into and I want you to tell me how serious this was in your eyes."

"Okay. So is a one a mild situation and a ten an extreme emergency?"

"If that's what works for you."

"Okay, then this was a two."

We drove up the highway a mile or so and turned off onto the road to Mount Pacifico. He drove the five miles to where my Jeep was hanging off the mountain and pulled over.

"A two. You rate this a two?"

"Sure. No danger, food and water in good shape, five miles, easy walking. Sounds like a two to me. If you change one of those factors, the number changes a lot though. If I didn't have water I would have called it a three, and if it was five degrees hotter it would have jumped to a four."

"So what would a ten have been?"

"The Jeep would be down there," I said pointing over the precipice, "And I'd have no water and the temperature would be five degrees hotter. I guess that would make it a ten, if I was down there with the Jeep. If I was up here and the Jeep was down there I'd make it a four again."

"Cassidy, what am I going to do with you? You wouldn't have called at all if we didn't have an appointment set up, would you?"

"I would have flagged down a ranger or a police car and gotten a ride to town and called a tow truck."

"And what would you do if somebody else stopped and offered you a ride?"

"I doubt I'd accept it. I'm not very trusting and the walk wasn't too bad."

"You'd walk ten miles in the hot sun before you'd accept a ride from a stranger?"

"As long as I had water."

He shook his head, although he seemed relieved that I wouldn't accept rides from strangers.

"As long as we're here we might as well pull it back up onto the road."

I took the towrope from the back of the Jeep, latched it to the bumper and handed him the other end. Rusty attached it to his Explorer, and then pulled the Jeep gently from the edge and back onto the road. The Jeep sat crooked across the narrow dirt road so I got in and straightened it to let other cars pass.

"I better drive it home. You know what'll happen if a ranger finds it here. Kelly or Paul would have a fit." Kelly and Paul were the two rangers I knew best: Paul worked at the station I checked into on my many treks into the wilderness, and Kelly was Rusty's friend. I'd tracked him down when he went missing in the spring and we kind of kept in touch through Rusty.

"Thanks for the ride," I said to Rusty, "I swear, tomorrow I'll go buy a winch for the Jeep."

"Then when would I see you?"

"Very funny, you can see me whenever you want."

"Then how about going out to dinner with me?"

"Sure, what kind of dinner?"

"I don't know. Surprise me."

"Surprise you?"

"Yeah, surprise me."

"I can't surprise you. Nothing ever surprises you. The only thing that would surprise you would be if I wore a dress."

"Okay, don't surprise me. Wear that dress you wore for your birthday party."

"You want to go out for *that* kind of dinner?"

"I don't care about dinner. It's just a side of you I don't get to see very often."

We got into our cars and he followed me back to town before splitting off to return home to change. I didn't know what he was going to change into. He was already wearing a sports coat and slacks. I, on the other hand, was covered head to toe in mountain dirt and sweat. And he wanted me to go out to dinner in a dress? I wondered if he knew how much he was asking.

Asking me to put on a dress was like asking a wrestler to wear a tutu in the ring. There was only a handful of people I'd dress up for and even fewer occasions. Dinner was not one of them, unless Rusty asked.

I rushed home, brought Shadow into the house and took a quick shower and shaved my legs. I put on the evil panty hose and the dainty slip and pulled the dress over my head and felt the slightly slinky, clingy material settle into just the right places. I looked in the mirror at the stranger that looked back at me. I curled my hair and put on make-up and wore the matching pumps my mother had made me buy. I put on a little lip gloss and then paced nervously. I could fight. I could wrestle skittish horses. I could hike to the ends of the earth and back, but put me in a dress and I was a nervous wreck.

The doorbell rang and Shadow barked at it excitedly. I opened the door timidly and Rusty stepped in. He had changed to a different suit and he'd put a tie on. He was always so confident and sure of himself.

"Rusty, why do you do this to me?"

He smiled, amused by my uncertainty. "No matter how much mountain dirt you manage to get on you, you can't hide that beautiful woman I see. I'm just hoping someday you'll feel as beautiful as you look to me."

Over dinner we started talking. "So, what was this important appointment I missed out on? You never did tell me. Since it was at the station, I assumed it was work related."

"It was, in a way. I wanted you to meet Lou Strickland. He's the commander of the local search and rescue team. You seem to need some work to do and occasionally he has need of a good tracker. I just didn't know if you would work with a team, and you'd have to if you worked with him."

"Would he even consider me? You know the first impression most people get of me. He'll think I'm more of a liability than an asset."

"If he gives you a trail and sees you work, he'll know you're a natural. I told him about the times when you tracked Silva and Kelly. I didn't fill in all the details but he knows you followed a week old trail to find Kelly. I told him about other times I've observed you tracking and that it is a natural talent you have. Not many people have that talent and it's even rarer when someone with the talent actually has a chance to develop it. He may ask you to go out with him and give him a demonstration, but it wouldn't be anything you couldn't handle."

"Okay, I guess I can at least talk to him. Why do you want me to do this?"

"You wanted a way to contribute. If you got into this, you would be doing some good, doing what comes naturally to you, in an environment that you enjoy, and it would be safe. You'll also learn a thing or two along the way."

The food was excellent and the atmosphere was pleasant. Rusty had chosen a more formal restaurant and the waiters were all dressed in suits and opened wine bottles for diners. They tended to bow a lot and poured a little taste of wine into the goblet so you could smell the aroma and taste the wine before they filled the glass half full. The tables all had starched white tablecloths and silver trimmed dinnerware. I wasn't used to formalities. I felt like I could shake out my own pepper and sprinkle on my own Parmesan cheese. I tended to frequent do-it-yourself type restaurants. Rusty seemed to be at ease no matter where we went.

He dropped me off at home late that night and we set a new appointment for two o'clock the next day. I'd stay in town so I'd be sure to be there, a little early as expected.

When I got to Rusty's office the next day Lou Strickland was already there. I peeked in the window of his office and Rusty rose and opened the door with an appraising look. He hadn't told me what to wear to a tracking interview and I hadn't known either. I finally decided not to push the combat look. He'd see through it and he'd assume I was trying to prove a point if I dressed like that. I wore blue jeans, a cute little sleeveless blouse, and my moccasins. I carried a real purse, not the daypack I usually hauled around. I did my hair and makeup. If I had to prove my worth I was going to do it from a woman's point of view. I wanted my skills to count, not my attitude.

Lou Strickland stood with a bemused expression on his face. He looked like a combination of my grandfather and a drill instructor in the Marines. He was in his sixties; silver hair cut short, almost a buzz but long enough to spike a little. He was tall, wore twill khaki slacks, a navy blue polo shirt, and casual shoes. The edges of a tattoo showed under his sleeve as he ran his hands through his hair, wondering what in the world this meeting was going to lead to. He shot Rusty a knowing look. That look told me more about Rusty than the past few months did. I was a little alarmed by it but I didn't let it show. I squared my shoulders and entered the room.

"Cassidy, this is Lou Strickland. Lou I'd like you to meet Cassidy Callahan."

"A pleasure, I'm sure," Lou said politely, "Michaels told me he had a tracker for me to meet. He didn't tell me much more. I have to admit I'm a bit surprised."

"That's okay, most people are," I answered.

Lou Strickland took the far chair in front of Rusty's desk so I slipped into the closer one scooting it over so I could watch both men.

"How did someone your age gain enough experience tracking to get noticed by the local police?"

"I guess you could say it's just been a lifelong habit. I can't remember when I didn't notice tracks. I grew up on a ranch, and it was easier to track people than look for them. I was doing easy tracking when I was six. Then, when I was old enough to go off into the hills I'd track animals, people, anything that left a trail. The tracking isn't something I advertise. The police wouldn't know about it at all except that I got carjacked last spring. The guy that carjacked me was a bank robber and Rusty was assigned to his case. When Silva got away from the police I knew how he had escaped from my yard so I tracked him down to a mobile home park and he was caught. Tracking comes very naturally to me. When Silva got away, it was the natural thing for me to do, find the tracks and track him down. I think it was easier for Rusty to accept the tracking because it was forced on him in an emergency. He didn't have time to question it."

"An emergency, the easy way?"

I looked at Rusty. "Most people don't take tracking seriously. If I actually tell someone I'm a tracker they never believe me. But the situation I found myself in when I met Rusty called for some quick tracking skills and so I kind of forced the concept onto him. What do you think? Was it easier to accept me as a tracker when you saw it first hand and had no choice but to follow?"

"I never really thought about it like that," he said, "I was thinking more along the lines of how I was going to keep you from getting your head blown off."

This seemed to amuse Lou, too. At least he seemed like an easygoing kind of guy. I was sure when it came right down to it, though, his serious side would be extremely evident.

"Look, you can ask me all the questions you want, but what it really boils down to is, can I follow a trail? Give me a trail and I'll read it for you and you can decide for yourself."

"As a matter of fact I do have a trail for you. It's two days old, through varying terrains. It's just out of town." He looked at Rusty. "You want to go? If you'd made the appointment yesterday the trail would have been fresher."

"Sorry," I apologized, "I had car trouble. I was stuck up on Mount Pacifico and had to hike out."

He gave me a look that said, 'Why was a little kid like you up on Mount Pacifico all by yourself?' I was used to that look. I couldn't help it if I looked like I was fifteen. In fact I looked a lot like Skipper, the well-known little friend/sister of Barbie. Throw in a little G.I. Joe and that was what I looked like. When I was up in the mountains I wore camouflage pants, khaki t-shirts, moccasins. Yep, Skipper meets G.I. Joe, that's me.

And, as usual, I asked myself, 'Why is it I couldn't do anything without surprising guys? What's a girl supposed to do if she gets stuck somewhere? I'd still be up there if I'd waited for some camper to pull the Jeep out.'

We piled into Lou's red Suburban. Knowing guys like to be as close to the driving experience as possible, I automatically got in the backseat but Rusty got in the backseat too. We rode a short distance out of town and Lou turned down a dirt road. He pulled over about a half mile down. I opened my door and looked at the ground before getting out. I wasn't going to fall for the obvious trick that I expected him to pull on me. A beginner would automatically assume the trail took off from the passenger side of the car but I wasn't assuming anything. The passenger side was just the easiest way for a person to go.

I faced the back of the Suburban, took ten paces behind the vehicle, and then began a wide circle. Just as I had suspected, I picked up the trail on the far side of the road.

"How much do you want to know? Do you just want me to find the end of the trail? Or do you want to know details along the way?"

"Some observations would be nice, but unnecessary. Just do what you feel comfortable doing."

Just in case, I marked the start of the trail and walked down the road to see if there was more. I'm glad I'd walked up the road because he'd started with a simple trail but further down had set up an elaborate scenario that mimicked a real emergency. Maybe they had held a drill out here and he was wondering how observant I was. A beginner would have just tracked the simple trail assuming that was test enough. Assumptions. You can't go with assumptions, especially in search and rescue. One assumption and you could endanger someone.

I looked at the road and it appeared as though a car had collided with a motorcycle. The car came along the dirt road and the motorcycle had suddenly appeared from the desert, crossing the road and hitting the car. The deep gouge through the mound of sand on the side of the road told me the motorcycle had been traveling fast when it hit the car. The car ended up sitting diagonally across the road and two people had gotten out.

"Okay," I said reading the ground. "We've got a crash here involving a small car and a motorcycle. The biker was riding through the desert and came up the bank and ran into the front fender of the car. The car came to a stop diagonally across the road and the motorcycle ended up on its side over there," I said pointing. "Two people exited the car. A man exited the driver's side. He was small for a man. Maybe five-five, a hundred and fifty pounds. He has a short stride. He came around and opened the passenger door and a woman got out. She looks like she is heavier. She just stands there like she doesn't want to move. She could be just shaken up by the accident. She's leaning back on her heals a lot like she's off balance. Maybe she's pregnant. The guy fusses over her and then trots off to check out the motorcyclist." I followed the footprints to where the motorcycle had lain. There was real blood on the ground. Shock immediately replaced my study of the ground. I turned to Lou. "You didn't set this up. This is real."

"You're right, the first trail was the one I set up. But this is telling me more than any trail would have."

"Why are there no tracks from police? Firemen? It's like these people just crashed and went on their way again. But the motorcyclist was injured. There should be more to this than what the tracks show. There's one set of car tracks over the accident scene. It must have happened earlier today. There's not a whole lot of traffic on this road." I went back to the man's footprints. "He walked up to the motorcyclist and knelt down. The guy on the motorcycle was lying next to his bike and had rolled around a bit. The motorcycle dude got up. The two men stood here talking, the motorcycle guy bleeding. No sign of a struggle. I'm guessing these two parties knew each other. The neighbors out here live far apart but they do know each other. Most of them have been in these same houses for thirty years. Looks like the occupants of the car got back in and took off, and the motorcycle guy headed down the road." I followed the track of the motorcycle down the road. "He isn't doing too good. He can't even ride the bike straight and he's still bleeding. He followed the road and then cut into the desert again. He almost lost it on this bump."

I looked into the distance. There was a house about a half mile off the road. I followed the track, came over the top of a small hill and almost stumbled over the motorcyclist lying face down in the dirt, his leg pinned under the bike. That was the least of his worries, though. He was really banged up. I turned away, bumping into Rusty and Lou. Rusty took one look and whipped out his cell phone. Lou knelt and felt for a pulse. He assessed the situation and fired the information to Rusty. A half hour later a rescue squad appeared on the dirt road followed shortly by a black and white and an ambulance.

As he was being carried on the gurney to the ambulance the guy briefly opened his eyes. "You've got to be the luckiest man on earth today," Lou told him. They loaded him up and drove away, siren wailing.

Lou walked over to me, hands in his pockets, a pensive look on his face. "Tell me what you thought when you saw the guy laying there. Why did you turn back?"

Rusty looked quickly in our direction. He'd heard the question. He knew why I'd turned back.

"I'm sorry," I said, "I'm a bit shell shocked. Has Rusty told you what has been happening with me the past several months? I've seen more than my share of violence. I've been carjacked and hunted by drug dealers and I watched as a man was gunned down by police right in front of me. When I saw that guy just lying there... I'm not a doctor. If you're looking for someone who can step in and save a life, I'm not that person. If you're looking for someone who can follow a trail and lead others in to do their job, I'll be glad to help."

"You saved that guy's life. A few more hours out here and he'd have been gone." He paused. "Come over here. Read this trail just to get your mind off the accident."

I went back to the start of Lou's trail. It was hard to concentrate but maybe that was part of the test too. How would I work after I got rattled?

Rusty stayed behind to help the officer figure out the accident scene.

Ten paces into the tracking I turned to Lou. "You didn't make this trail either. This trail was made by a shorter man." I followed the tracks into the desert. "He is just walking here, strolling through the desert." The tracks turned. "He's looking back at his car, probably planning the trail, wondering how far he wants to go, how he will get back to the car from wherever he ends up.... His footprints lean in that direction. Of course I don't know what he was thinking but he stands here long enough, his footprints move around a little like he was thinking that. I guess it's what I'd be thinking if you asked me to lay a trail for somebody. He continued on, concentrating on his trail now. He is trying to find ways to trip me up. He's walking more softly." I slowed. "He's gone into what I call stealth mode. He's trying to walk as softly as he can and not leave sharp edges to his tracks. He's using hard pack a lot but since the hard pack here doesn't happen very often I know he's going to follow it. And I could tell quickly if he left it. Here's a scuff. There's a bent branch." I continued following the tracks. The man had walked in stealth mode for another quarter of a mile. He was obviously trying to hide his tracks but that tipped me off to look for ways to hide them and made things easier in a way. He came to a bush big enough to make a shadow and then sat in its shade. I pointed out the flattened dirt area to Lou. It was a fairly easy trail of footprints to follow. I had to stop a time or two to figure out the guy's thinking and I had to get down to ground level once to examine the tracks from an angle. The tracks led in a rough circle and came back to the road a quarter mile down from where they started.

As we were walking back up the road to the Suburban Lou said, "Tell me about the guy you just followed. What kind of a person do you think he is?"

"Well, like I said, he's shorter than you, lighter. He wears those funny looking sandals made out of nylon webbing and Velcro and he shouldn't have worn them in the desert because the sand gets in them and makes walking uncomfortable. He's got a fairly serious personality. He doesn't joke much. He didn't try any funny tricks on me. Everything is very straightforward with him. I get the impression that he isn't a real neat dresser, he's right handed."

"How could you tell he's right handed?"

"When he was sitting under the bush he'd picked off little pieces of the branches as he cooled down. Almost all the branches on the guy's right hand side had pieces broken off. Then he'd tossed the pieces to his left."

"Interesting," he said, "Have you been to tracking school?"

"No, tracking is just something I have always enjoyed doing. I've tracked animals, people. I like to go stalking in the woods. I track an animal and then stalk it until I'm as close as I can get to it. Tracking people is a lot easier than tracking animals. I doubt Rusty will go to the beach with me anymore because I read the footprints in the sand until it drives him nuts."

"Oh, I bet you can get him back there, no problem," he said with a wink. "Look, I'm going to have to talk to Rusty before I make a decision. You indicated that he seems to know a lot of history that I should probably be aware of. I can see you have an incredible amount of talent in tracking but there are demographics involved in this. If you don't hear from me in a while don't be concerned. I'll let you know in a week or so what you can expect."

"Why talk to Rusty about it? I'm willing to tell you what happened."

"If you wish to be there, by all means, you are welcome. We don't want to talk about you behind your back. I think Rusty can see things from my point of view, so I'd like to hear it from his point of view. That's all."

"One of the things you will learn is that I refused to work with a team when I tracked down Kelly Green. Since then I've come to see it in a better light. So don't go thinking I won't follow orders or work with other people."

I'd decided that Rusty would be more comfortable if I had other people around me and maybe getting out with a team occasionally would take care of my wanderlust. I'd get to help people and contribute.

Back at the station I left the guys to talk about me behind my back, knowing Rusty would fill me in later. I was convinced Strickland was ready to use me if he thought I'd fit in with the team. I wondered, though, if finding out about all the crazy things I'd been through would cause him to back down and question my readiness for this work both emotionally and psychologically. I had to admit I was still bothered by nightmares but I'd come to accept them and I didn't stay freaked out when they happened. I left the matter in the hands of the one person I trusted and put the matter aside.

Chapter 2

Strickland didn't call back for a week but when he finally did, it wasn't what I had been expecting. It was obvious that he was calling from Rusty's office and he sounded rushed, but something was definitely wrong.

"Cassidy, how would you like to try your hand at a case that could involve tracking?" Strickland said.

In the background I heard Rusty say, "I'm telling you Strict, she's not going with you. If I have any say in this I will not let her on that helicopter."

"You don't have a say in this. It's her decision," Strickland replied.

"Give me that phone," Rusty demanded. Whenever his voice grew angry it sounded like thunder rolling through a canyon. He could control it, but as it rose I sensed the power behind it. I didn't want that anger directed at me.

"Hold on," Strickland said before covering up the phone. I could still hear them speaking but their words were muffled. "Michaels, I'm telling you she will do fine. It's a clear-cut case. A passenger missing from a crash. It's a classic case for her."

"That's not it," Rusty said. "I know she can find the guy. Just don't take her to the site. I can't ask her to do something I couldn't do. She isn't ready for it. This is the one thing I'd keep her from. I'd rather she go back against Peccati than go out to that site." And then I understood. It was a plane crash. This wasn't danger he was worried about. It wasn't a physical challenge. It was an emotional thing. And I wondered, too, how I would react when I got there. But this had to be done. If someone was missing, then my feelings were of little consequence. I wouldn't risk someone's life just to spare myself the anxiety.

I'd seen Jack's crash site. The officials knew I'd go out there even if I had to walk so they arranged an escort. I was sure the military had hidden things from me. Technically I wasn't allowed out there at all but they knew who they were dealing with, how stubborn I'd be and I think they might even have been sympathetic about my situation.

When I stepped out of the Jeep to view the site, all I saw was flame-blackened rubble. It was hard to tell that it had once been an F-15, and when I saw the impact site I knew there was no way anybody had survived that crash. At that moment my whole world had turned upside down. My husband Jack was gone, just like that, and it had happened so fast.

"You aren't asking her, I am," Strickland said, "and I think she's the person for the job. Cassidy?"

"I'm on my way and I'll take care of Rusty. Give me ten minutes."

I hustled, gathering my wallet, keys and pack. I jumped into the Jeep and took off for the downtown police station. With green lights the station was only seven minutes away but the lights were rarely green. Ten minutes later I pulled into the station parking lot. At the counter inside I asked to see Detective Rusty Michaels.

"I'm sorry Miss Callahan. Detective Michaels can't see you right now."

"Okay. Can you just tell him I'll go wait by Lou Strickland's car and I'll see him when he has the time?" There, that ought to bring him out.

I went outside and found Strickland's red Suburban. At least he drove a recognizable car.

It didn't take Rusty long to get outside.

"I heard the whole conversation you had with Strickland. What's wrong? Why don't you want me to do this?" I asked. He was beside himself. This was a side of Rusty I had never seen before. He was struggling to find an answer. "It's a simple tracking case. A passenger's gone missing from a crash. I won't have to deal with the crash. I'll have someone with me when I find the missing passenger. They will do all the medical stuff. I just have to find the missing person. So what's the big deal? There's something you're hiding or there's more to this than Strickland is telling me. Which is it?"

"Cassidy," he said and I knew he was really struggling. He only used my whole name when he was serious. "I just can't. I can't let you go."

"Because it's a plane crash? Is that why? Rusty, a crash is a crash. It's not like they can take Jack away again. He's gone. But this missing person isn't. If I can find them I need to try. You can't toss aside someone's life just because of my feelings. That's selfish. You have to let go. We'll deal with whatever comes up and it'll all work out."

I looked around and Lou was sitting on a planter observing. Watching me verbally stalking my goal. He seemed impressed. Guess he didn't have a daughter. If he had a daughter he'd know the power we hold.

Rusty knew my logic was good. He knew I'd make it through this. But something was eating at him. I sensed fear, but what would frighten Rusty?

"Look at me," I said. "We have a mission here. What's the goal?"

No answer.

"Rusty, what's the goal in this situation?"

He only said it because he knew it's what I wanted to hear, "To find the lost passenger."

"And what do we have to do to achieve that goal?"

A big sigh. "Lou can find someone else. It doesn't have to be you."

"Nope, Lou wouldn't have called me if he had someone better. So what do we need to do?"

He almost didn't say it. "I've got to let you go look for him."

"Okay, so are we on the same page now? Are you going or staying?"

"Lou won't let me. He says this is your ball game. He says we both have to face our own challenges."

"Is he right?"

"I don't know." Long pause. "I promised myself I would always be there for you."

I swallowed a big lump in my throat. I spoke with as much compassion as I could find. "You did? But… you can't do that. You know there's things you can't control. You know you were bound to run into one of those things eventually. And it's not very fair to me. Here I lead this jinxed life and you are trying to make yourself responsible for the outcome of it? You are *not* responsible for what happens to me. If you are, then it's my fault if you get hurt. You need to ease up. This is a simple tracking case. How old is the trail? Not a day old. Plane crashes are sudden things and they require sudden action. So it's not a day old. I can find this guy. I won't dwell on the crash scene. Remember, it's like a puzzle. I take the pieces that I need and I figure them out. I don't need to figure out the crash site. I just have to find a trail and follow it."

He stood there looking defeated. I hated doing that to him. I'd have to make it up to him later but right now I had a helicopter to catch.

"So," I said, "I'm going to go with Lou and you're going to *let me* go and I'll call as soon as I get back."

I gave him a big hug and felt the familiar chin on top of my head. I felt the sorrow as he struggled and then reluctantly let me go. I pictured the punching bag in the barn at my parent's house. When I got frustrated I'd go punch that bag. I imagined the punching bag at the station might get a workout this afternoon.

Lou came up behind me. He clapped Rusty on the shoulder and gave him an "it'll all be okay" look. He steered me away before Rusty could change his mind. Gee, I hated doing that to him, but I was really curious why this had affected him so strongly.

I grabbed my box of tracker tools from the Jeep, stuffed them in my daypack and followed Lou. I carefully kept track of the route as he drove to the helicopter pad. I might have to find this place on my own next time. When we got there five people stood around waiting for us looking like they had spent the entire last week at Starbucks. They were ready to roll. I felt bad for holding things up. Strickland parked the Suburban and we both got out.

"You're late Strict, but I can see why. I'd be late too if I was you."

"Ease up guys. This is Cassidy Callahan. She's our tracker today. I know what you're thinking, but I've seen her work. You will show her the respect she deserves. She's proven herself to me more than once. Lanksy, you went after Kelly Green. Cassidy found him, and called in a team from L.A. to come retrieve him. You'll be glad to know he's back home and doing fine. Cassidy, this is Roscoe Lansky, Landon Wilson, and Victor Gomez, EMTs. This is Thez Brockman, all around good guy, and Gordon Thompson, county coroner. Guys, Cassidy Callahan, tracker. Now let's get going."

Everybody else seemed to know exactly what their job was. They leaped into action and gear was stowed. This was a routine run and each piece of gear had its assigned place on the helicopter. Each person slid things into place like a well oiled machine. I was the loose cog and they knew it.

Everybody already had their favorite places staked out on the helicopter. I climbed in and found an empty spot. The helicopter clattered away, lifting us into the sky. I watched out the window as the ground faded below me.

"First time in a helicopter?" Thez Brockman asked.

"Nope, been there, done that. Reading the ground is just a habit, doesn't matter how far down it is. It's readable from up here, too."

"Gotta be awfully big tracks to be seen from up here. What are you looking for? Big Foot?"

I decided I'd be better off studying the inside the copter. I had to work with these guys. I bet I could learn a thing or two before we touched down. I studied the men. Roscoe was intense and focused. I had the feeling that being rescued by him was more like a forklift operation. He was big, well muscled and very quiet. He preferred to be in the background. Landon was more easy going. He was lean and had a friendlier look to him. He would be the one talking to victims, calming them down while Roscoe tended to the real threat. They would make a good team together. Victor Gomez was all business, right now, but I suspected he hid a quick wit and a sharp eye. He looked like someone I could identify with. Not much slipped by him. He took things in and contemplated how things fit together, and I bet when he finally did speak, people listened. I was guessing, if Lou had one of these guys laying my test trail, Victor was the guy. He fit the tracks and his manner fit the way the trail had been laid out. Thez was the odd man out. All around good guy. What did that mean? And what kind of a name was Thez? He was tall, just a hair shorter than Lou, and it was because Lou had hair on top of his head. Thez was beginning to bald on top. He talked with his hands a lot. He was animated and alert. Gordon Thompson was older. He had been at his job a while and he was seasoned to it. He knew what he was getting into. He looked like a stabilizer for the group.

"So, Cassidy, what got you into our rag tag motley crew?" Thez asked.

"Mostly Rusty Michaels. He thought this would keep me out of trouble."

"Oh yeah? You're kidding. *Out* of trouble?"

Lou broke in. "Thez, if you knew what she's been through you'd think so too. I talked to Michaels. Nuff said."

"I don't care if they know. Rusty would think they *should* know since they have to work with me. So much has happened, though, I wouldn't know where to start."

This got looks. Oh boy, were they going to have fun with me. Thez seemed to be the group social director so he started it off.

"Okay, well, since this is to keep you *out* of trouble, tell us the scariest thing that's happened to you."

"The scariest? As in fear or as in most dangerous?"

"Either. It's just a question to get you going so answer whichever you want."

"Well, the car bomb in Afghanistan was right up there, but that was years ago. Recently, I was hunted by drug dealers through the Angeles forest. It was dangerous because I had to follow a trail and it was wide open to sharp shooters. See, when Kelly Green disappeared it was because he ran into drug dealers up in the mountains. They shot him and dumped him over a cliff. So when I tracked him down I ran into the drug dealers, too. I lucked out. They dumped me over the cliff, *then* shot at me so it wasn't so bad for me. After the rescue crew hauled Kelly off to the hospital I went back to do some surveillance on the drug lab. I didn't know it, but they knew I was there and so they were looking for me. They caught up with me on the trail and it turned into a hunt. They were supposed to bring me back to their boss and I knew he'd kill me if I went back, so I wasn't cooperating. They were hunting me with these high-powered rifles through the woods and I had to cross this big bare mountain. That was pretty scary, I guess. Yeah, dodging bullets is never fun and kind of scary. Actually the scariest thing I have *felt* was when I thought Rusty was going to stop me from going after Kelly. He didn't want me to go alone and I couldn't *not* go. I couldn't leave Kelly out there if there was a chance I could find him. So really, that was the most scared I have ever been."

"You went after Green alone?" Lansky asked.

"Yeah, I'd never worked with a team before. I've always been kind of a loner in the woods."

They were all quiet. They looked at Lou for confirmation. All he had to do was nod.

"Have you been on any other rescue runs?" Thez asked trying to keep things going on a safer level.

"Not organized ones like this. I have done a little tracking for Rusty. I found Manuel Silva after the police lost him. That just kind of happened by accident because Rusty didn't know I could track at the time. Once I found a lost boy scout but I just happened to be nearby and heard he was lost, so I asked for a starting point and tracked him three miles through the Angeles Forest. Then there was the time I rescued my nephew when the drug boss kidnapped him. He was pissed off at me for messing up his drug lab in the Angeles Forest. I guess the police went in later and closed it down and he blamed me. He was nutso, wanted to hunt me like an animal, took my gun away and turned me and Patrick loose. It was run or die so I ran, hid Patrick where searchers could find him and then I had to bring Peccati in without any firearms. I tricked him by leading him into a trap and he lost his rifle in the scuffle. I ended up in a boxing match with him until I could find his rifle and hold him for the police. I guess that was another one of my scarier moments."

Silence again.

"So," Thez said, "Does anything *normal* happen to you?"

"Only for short periods of time."

My stomach did a little flip flop as the helicopter descended and then settled on top of a hill. Everybody hopped out and gathered in a group away from the blades. We hiked down the hill for a short distance until the noise level decreased.

"Lansky, Landon take care of the plane. The radio call into the station said a small plane spotted one passenger making his way northeast from the crash site. Why he went northeast I have no idea, the area is rocks and buttes. Seems to me like he'd head downhill, looking for a road. Victor and Thez, stay with Cassidy. Cassidy, stay on the passenger's trail."

I followed the group down and around the base of the hill. Lou was sticking to me like glue. I think Rusty must have told him about Jack. He wanted to gauge my reaction. He also needed to keep things under control. I meant to keep my feelings under wraps but I still felt a wave of nausea when we rounded the corner and saw the plane, debris scattered over a couple of acres of land. The tail section was intact but the cockpit had crushed into the main body of the plane. The debris was mostly the wings, having been sheared off by some small trees dotting the landscape. I stood silently until the nausea had passed and I could clear my head.

Focus on the job, Cass. Find a trail leading away from the plane. Don't look at the cockpit. It's not your job. I set my mind to the task at hand and trekked around the hill. Casting around on the ground, it wasn't hard to find the tracks. One man had left the plane. One man… and something else.

I looked at Lou then started for the plane but he stepped in. He knew I wouldn't go to the plane without a reason. He stopped me, understanding that it was something Rusty would have done.

"What is it Cassidy?"

"I need to see something...Okay, I don't *need* to see it. I need something confirmed."

"What is it?"

I showed him the tracks I found in the sand. Huge dinner-plate sized cat paw prints.

"This isn't a mountain lion," I said. "I've seen a few mountain lion tracks. Never seen a mountain lion. The tracks come from the direction of the tail."

"Thez, look in the plane. Tell us what you see."

Thez trotted over to the plane and glanced in. He crawled in through a gaping hole in the side. There was a short wait and he came out with two rifles and handed one to Lou.

"Those aren't ordinary rifles." I observed. "What did you see, Thez?"

"There's a big cage back there, empty."

I checked the rifle over carefully. "These rifles are loaded with tranquilizer darts. I hope our missing passenger thought to bring one of these with him."

Lou got on his radio to talk to the guys in the cockpit. "Heads up guys. We've got a large cat on the loose. Keep your eyes open."

"Okay," I said, "the passenger first. The cat second."

"Cassidy, if there's injuries we're leaving the cat. We can't risk people's lives for the sake of a cat. We'll call in animal control once we know what we're dealing with."

"I know, just prioritizing. This cat is too big to bring back anyway."

I found the passenger's tracks again and picked my way along, reading the sign. This was going to be tricky because he was heading into the buttes and buttes meant rocks and rocks meant poor tracking conditions. I took mental notes as I went along. Smallish men's boots. Looked like hiking boot tread. Could be a woman but the walk looked more masculine, the gait firm and determined, focused. This guy wasn't looking for help. He was either hiding from something or looking for the cat. I couldn't yet tell from the tracks if the person was injured. So far so good on that count.

The area around the plane was grassy, which wasn't great for tracking but the trail was fresh so it wasn't a problem either. It just slowed me down a little. This brittle yellow grass was much easier to read than other kinds. I wanted to take my time with this track. I had a feeling I needed to know something about the man I was tracking. This operation was not making any sense. Who would be transporting large cats in small planes across California? Was it legal? When things don't add up I become cautious and piece things together trying to make sense of it. I take in all the subtle, little clues I can read.

Thez followed along, rifle in hand. Victor was behind him, calm, just waiting for his turn to act.

"Make yourself useful," I told them. "Keep an eye out for movement, man or animal, doesn't matter. If you see movement point it out to me." Thez took his eyes off the ground and started looking around more.

I followed the tracks up into the bluffs and the terrain became rocky with sandy spots where the rock had eroded away. The guy's trail became more erratic. He would walk and stop and his footprints would stay in one place for a bit, as if he was looking up into the rocks. He would then continue forward. I was convinced he was looking for the cat. He knew how dangerous it was with the animal being loose. I wondered whether his intentions were to shoot it or tranquilize it. If he was hunting the cat he must have a weapon of some kind. A tranquilizer gun or a rifle. Surely he wouldn't just tranquilize it. That would only be a temporary fix for a very dangerous animal and there was no way one person could transport an animal that large back to the cage. If he found the cat he would be forced to shoot it. Why he didn't just follow the cat's tracks was a mystery to me, but many people just don't think that way. They forget there are clues all around them and will just go by their gut reactions.

I'd followed the guy's footprints around the bluffs in a fairly predictable pattern until suddenly I noticed that the man had knelt down on one knee. The weave of his pants was still visible in the dirt. This had happened very recently. I looked up at the rocks in the direction his leg had been pointing. I tried to picture what he was seeing and doing. Pictured the shot, pictured the casing falling. I looked back to the ground near the place where he had knelt. Finding the casing confirmed something in my mind. The guy was trying to kill the cat.

"Hey, guys, what do we do with evidence?" I asked. "I've never done this before but I know we ought to collect it in case this turns out to be a shady operation gone bad."

Victor produced a plastic bag from a pocket and picked up the casing with a stick. It was a big casing. He then deposited the casing in the bag and we were on our way again. The passenger started into a kind of stealth mode. He wasn't hiding his tracks but he was hiding from the cat. He would crouch behind brush and then inch forward. He was in a kind of defensive pursuit. It's just what you do if you are hunting something dangerous. Been there, done that, too. Sheesh! I was too young for all this.

I continued tracking and reading sign until I felt Thez stiffen and draw back to my left and slightly behind me. I sensed the tenseness from several yards away and I wondered how it was that silence shouted so loudly.

"What is it?" I asked quietly.

He crouched down and pointed. Movement. White movement. What would be white and be out here? Then it disappeared.

"Thez, is that dart gun loaded?" I said quietly.

Another motion and suddenly a shot went over our heads. I slipped into stalking mode heading for the shooter.

"Take it easy," I called out. "We're just search and rescue." Another shot, this time lower. "If you're within shooting range you're within hearing range. Are you hurt? We've got medics. Just come out and we'll get you patched up."

I was staying on the guy's trail, staying low so he wouldn't shoot me. I was trying to close in on the situation when I saw the cat's tracks cross the man's tracks. Maybe he wasn't trying to shoot us. Maybe the cat was close. The hair rose up on the back of my neck knowing how quiet a cat could be, how close it could come without being heard. It could also be stalking our rescue party. Now I was trying to keep track of four things. Where was the shooter? Where was the cat? Where was Thez? Where was the track leading? I looked back for Thez but couldn't see him.

"Thez? You still there?"

No answer.

"Victor, where's Thez?"

I backtracked to where Thez's trail had departed from mine and followed until I found him sitting at the base of a large boulder.

"What are you doing here? We have work to do!"

"Did you see it?" he gasped nervously.

"No, but it doesn't matter, we still have work to do. You've got the rifle but any of us might need it too. So we have to stick together here. You're not going to leave me without the rifle are you?" He gave me a scared look.

"How long does it take a dart to work?" he asked.

"I don't know, a few minutes, maybe?"

"We could be dead in a few minutes. That cat is huge!"

"We've got to find the passenger from the plane. He's got a rifle. If we find him we'll have more of a defense. We better our odds by finding him, so follow me. Let's go get him."

Thez stood and followed me reluctantly. I found the man's trail again and followed in a crouch. I knew he couldn't be far away. If his shots were reaching us he had to be close. I noticed the cat's tracks following the man's footprints. I really needed a rifle. I'd feel so much better with a real rifle. I had Thez with a dart gun and Victor with a pistol, yet I didn't even know if he could shoot. I hurried forward. It looked like this situation could become intense real fast.

Quick and quiet, Cass, I told myself. You don't want to startle the cat or the shooter, better to see them before they see you. I read the tracks and came to an open area. Finally there was the passenger standing with his back to the bluff, rifle aimed at a large white tiger. He was shaking. I turned and stopped the search party from advancing. I held a finger to my lips in the universal *hush* sign, and signaled for everyone to stay low. I took the tranquilizer gun from Thez. Victor appeared as if he wanted to take it from me but he didn't know the situation yet. I looked at him seriously.

"EMT or sharpshooter?"

"I passed the test."

"Thez?"

Nope, I thought, not Thez.

"I've got a plan," I said, "wait here."

"Cassidy…" Victor said trying to stop me.

"I'm no EMT. We need you after I take out the tiger. I can shoot it if I can just get the rifle."

I looked again into the clearing. The passenger was shaking so bad there was no way he could possibly hit the tiger. He stood there in big game hunter clothes but it appeared to be more of a costume than a uniform. He was scared spitless. I stalked around to the side of the clearing getting closer to the man. *He* might not be able to hit the tiger, but I could. I didn't want either of them to see me until just the right moment. This had to happen quickly and the less distance the more chance of success. I came as close as I dared, raised the tranquilizer gun and fired into the tiger's shoulder.

"Toss me the rifle!" I yelled. The man looked at me, stunned. "Throw it!" The tiger took a step closer and the man shot at the tiger missing again. "Throw me the damn rifle!" I yelled again. "I can kill it!" He didn't trust me. I raised the tranquilizer gun and fired again. "Look," I said. "I hit it twice. All I need is a real bullet!"

He heaved the gun unsteadily. I snatched it from the air but catching it brought me several steps closer to the tiger. The tiger swung in my direction. It stared me in the eye and let out a low, rumble of a growl. It took a step closer. The passenger took off running. The tiger's muscles rippled as he prepared to leap. I squared off, raised the rifle, found the tiger's heart in my site and squeezed off a shot.

The tiger dropped with a soft *whuff*. How could such a large animal fall so softly?

I looked at the man before me. He had been bitten by the tiger but not mauled. I suspected he'd tried to prevent the tiger's escape. His left arm just hung there, the muscles torn. He had a gash on his head and cuts and bruises all over his body. All in all I thought he came through his ordeal pretty well.

"Thez, Victor, get in here," I called.

Victor moved in, assessing the man's condition. Thez joined him after walking a wide circle around the huge cat. The man was still shaking from his standoff with the tiger.

"Hey," Thez said, "relax, it's over. Don't you know the old line? Cats in planes fall mainly on the plains? Too bad it's not raining. Cats in planes fall mainly in the rain sounds better. Relax. You'll be back in town before you know it."

Thez continued reassuring the passenger while Victor patched him up. We then helped him back towards the other group with his left arm in a sling bound tight to his body. He refused the stretcher so Thez and Victor carried it back empty. I watched the man's footprints and despite being off balance from the sling they remained steady, if a little bit shaky.

As we rounded the side of the bluff and caught site of the rest of the group, Lou smiled and waved like we were returning from a picnic to a big family reunion.

"One safe passenger and one dead tiger," Thez reported.

"Who shot the tiger?" Lou asked.

"Cassidy did," Thez said.

"Cassidy wasn't supposed to be armed."

"Well, maybe you should arm her," Thez replied. "She's a decent shot."

I looked at him, pleading. "We won't tell Rusty about this, right?"

"You better. Things like this tend to get around the station pretty quick."

As the helicopter settled back at the pad an ambulance pulled forward and whisked our passenger off to the hospital.

"Meeting on the 15th. Everybody got that? Cassidy?"

"Yup, I'll be there. I'll need details later."

"You need a ride to the station, anyway. I'll fill you in."

"I doubt if I need a ride. I bet Rusty pulls up before we get a chance to leave. I promised him I'd call when we landed."

Lou handed me a sheaf of papers. "Welcome to the club. There's a form for everything you can imagine in there. Have fun." I helped people pack up any way I could, carrying, holding things while they unlocked their cars and trucks. I pushed a few buttons on my cell phone and Rusty answered on the first ring.

"Hey," I said, "It's me. I promised I'd call when I got back. How are you?"

"Relieved. You sound good. Guess you found your man?"

"Yeah, and a little more but we'll talk about that later."

I disconnected and turned around. Lou was waiting for me.

"I guess Michaels survived your day," he said amused. "You're lucky you did. What made you go into that clearing?"

"It was the only way to get a real rifle. I used the dart gun on the tiger twice but I was afraid he'd charge the guy before I got a bullet into him."

"What would you have done if the guy hadn't surrendered the rifle?"

"I'd have fired the rest of the darts hoping they did their thing fast. But I know that isn't what you want to hear. Look, if you're worried about me carrying I won't carry a gun. We didn't expect to need them for this case but we were lucky some came our way. I *can* shoot, though. In the Marines I went to sniper school. I grew up on a ranch. We did plenty of hunting, and we did a lot of target practice. You can ask Rusty. He's seen me shoot; he's seen me clean rifles. I don't take them lightly. I don't like having to use them, but I'm glad I was able to today. That guy was shaking so bad he couldn't have hit the tiger if it had been the size of an elephant. His shots were going every which way. I thought he was shooting at us at first but all the shots were from missing the tiger."

"Which brings me to my next question. Why did you advance when you thought someone was shooting at you?"

"Well, that's a tougher one. I was really torn on whether to go forward because I knew the guys were following me. If it had just been me I wouldn't have had a problem going in. I know how to stay out of sight. But I'd told Thez to stick to me because he had the tranquilizer gun and I knew he was the one authorized to use it. So I couldn't advance without him but I couldn't advance because of him. While I was battling that out it became apparent that the shooter was just desperate and that I needed to close in, gun or no gun. Thez wasn't budging. He'd seen the tiger and he was scared of it, too. We needed Victor's medical experience so I took the gun and went forward. I figured there was no use fearing the tiger until it went after me. As long as it was focused on something else I was safe. The guy saw me standing there but he didn't trust me to be able to shoot the tiger so I shot it with a dart to prove I could do it. He didn't throw me the rifle until the last second and I just did what I could. One shot right to the heart. I was lucky the rifle was built to take down a tiger."

"Did you get a bruise out of it?" Strickland asked as he pointed to my shoulder.

"Any rifle built to take down a tiger is going to kick, but I knew what to do. I've shot bigger weapons than that. I wouldn't want that gun for regular use, but it did the job."

"Did you know I was in the background while all this was going on?"

"No, and you're pretty good at it if I didn't know."

"The guys at the plane knew their job. They weren't threatened in any way. I started closing in as soon as I heard shots fired. You almost didn't get your shot at the tiger. Next time I won't send you out with Thez. I didn't expect trouble on this trip. I chose Thez because he is good at normalizing situations. You know how every hairdresser you go to you're comfortable with because they talk about everyday things, and they don't mind hearing the same stories over and over again?"

"Yeah."

"That's Thez. The chatter on the way out to the site? If he hadn't been there everyone would have been tensed up. They would have been suspicious of you, but Thez has a way of toning those things down, smoothing them out, without really trying."

"Why do they call him Thez?"

"Because he's an actor. A thespian. Used to be a cop, and a firefighter. I think now he's got his own business. But he's useful occasionally. Thanks for helping out today. I'm glad it turned out well. Our passenger is getting patched up and I'll send someone out to collect the tiger. I hope it doesn't hit the news. If it does, we can expect the save-the-tigers foundation to jump on us but I know and you know we did what we had to. Meeting, on the fifteenth. I'll call with the details."

"Thanks."

Rusty pulled into the parking lot and swung into a parking place. He was almost out of the truck before he shut off the engine. He stood there for a second and then came over, wrapping me in a big hug, the relief clear in every movement. He didn't speak for a long time. He let me go and stood me at arm's length looking me over. No black eyes, no bruises, no bullet grazes, no cuts… I was still in one piece. Considering what I usually came home with, it was a miracle.

"You'll never guess what I did today," I said. Might as well get it over with right at the start.

"What?" he asked, knowing it was going to be a doozie.

"I went tiger hunting. And I bagged a big one."

"Okay, this I've got to hear. How about Zeke's? I think I might need a beer to go with this story."

When we were settled at a table in Zeke's bustling pizza place the atmosphere returned to its former somber mood. I had tried to sound glib about the tiger but Rusty wasn't fooled for a second. He understood how much I loved animals and knew that I would never have shot the tiger unless things were very close. He was also aware that I'd not been armed. He concluded that things had come up unexpectedly, so I continued from a different point of view.

"Why did Lou give me all these forms? There's one for everything, every step of the whole operation. How am I supposed to know which ones are for me and which ones I can ignore?"

"Welcome to the club. The boring part of search and rescue. Lou probably gave you all of them this time because he wanted you to see what it entailed. You'll have to file a general report and the one where you explain why you fired the gun."

"What do you do if you fired someone else's gun? Guess I'll have to go into some detail. I hope these forms have plenty of writing space. There was a tranquilizer gun and a rifle but the tranquilizer darts didn't seem to work. I couldn't tell if they had any effect on the tiger."

"I think you better start at the beginning."

I began by taking care to mention that Lou had followed us and had been prepared to act if needed.

"And so this guy was standing there shaking so bad he couldn't have hit *anything*. The tiger was slowly getting closer and the guy didn't trust me to be able to hit it. Guess I wouldn't either if I saw me standing there. The guy was lucky he gave up the rifle when he did. I brought it down with one shot. I didn't want to. You know I hate to shoot animals. But if I hadn't, the guy would have had a heart attack or gotten mauled."

Rusty looked on in disbelief. "I know you're not making this up. If anything you toned it down so I'd feel better."

"You know these calls aren't always what they sound like at first. Nobody knew there was a tiger on board that plane. I bet there will be a big investigation about why tigers were being transported that way in the first place." I paused. "Rusty, why were you so against me going on this call? I've never seen you so worked up before. This was different for you somehow and I don't understand it."

He looked at me closely, obviously assessing something. He then bowed his head with a defeated expression on his face.

"Tell me about when you saw the crash site," he said. "Was it rough?"

I knew he had worried about that. Still, his feelings were too strong for this to be all there was to it.

"It was really bad for a very short time. When I first caught site of the wreckage I felt sick inside. But it passed quickly once I focused on the job. Lou was watching out for me. When I saw the tracks of the tiger I headed towards the plane, to check for any evidence that they had been transporting a large cat. Lou stopped me and sent Thez instead so I wouldn't have to look." The relief was written in every worried line of Rusty's face. "Once we knew the situation it was time to focus on the job. I was okay as long as I kept my eyes off the plane and only on the ground."

"You know, if you stick with this you'll have to get some training. Are you ready for that?"

"What kind of training?"

"First will be reserve officers training. Then comes EMT training. If you are the first one on the scene, you need to be ready to take charge. Many times search and rescue gets there first, especially in your line of work. Tracking will take you where ambulances and fire trucks can't go. Right now you are just finding people but eventually you will work as part of the team and you will be expected to know what to do."

"That might be good for me," I said. "I've got a good start with my Marines training. I just don't know if I have the right mindset to do this from a medical point of view. I don't faint at the sight of blood or anything but..."

"I know what you mean and it does take a certain mindset. If the idea appeals to you though, start the training. Lou won't send you where you can't be used for your own talents. If it turns out to only be tracking then he'll just call you when he really needs a tracker. If you turn out to be good at something else he will be glad for those skills as well."

"Rusty, you have to know, even though Lou stopped me from going into the plane, I was willing to go. It was my job. I'd have done it. I let him stop me because I knew it was something that you would have wanted. And I'm sorry that I stood up to you this morning. Did it make you look bad in front of Lou?"

"No. Lou is amazing. He reads minds or something. He knows what was going on. And you were right. You had to go. It was just hard to let you."

"Maybe I'll go to police academy, too."

"No!" he said, suddenly alarmed again, "Level Two. Shoot for a Level Two. It'll give you the skills you need without scaring me to death. And it'll make it so I can call you up for cases, too. But please don't join the force. I couldn't handle that."

Chapter 3

One night a few weeks later I was restless. City life was confining and I needed to get out for a while. I went to the gym hoping a workout would still the call of the mountains. If training for search and rescue was in my immediate future then I needed to get into better shape. I was already fit from going to the gym several times a week. I also jogged regularly and would hike whenever I was overpowered by a feeling of wanderlust. I was usually in the gym during the morning and I could see the nighttime crowd was different. I went through my normal routine purposefully, then hopped on a treadmill to jog. I was into my second mile when Rusty wandered out of the weight room. I'd never seen him at the gym before but since he didn't have time for a morning workout it made sense that we'd never run into each other previously. Like every other woman in the gym I watched him while he wandered from machine to machine. He would sit to begin his work out, but he didn't change the weight settings on any of the equipment. After several repetitions and never having adjusted any of the settings he'd select another machine and continue his workout. It appeared as if he was killing time and cooling down from the weight training. No matter what tension the machines had been set to, he didn't seem to have any problem with them. He turned towards the treadmills and noticed me jogging. As he neared I slowed the machine so I could talk easier. Every woman in the gym gave a collective and disappointed sigh when he approached me. I could see their ears pointed in our direction wondering what kind of pickup line he was going to dish out. Should I wait to see what it was or come up with my own and see what happened?

"They should pay you to work out here," I said.

"Oh yeah?"

"Yeah."

"Why?"

"These women are in better shape than the morning crowd. They come to the gym when you're here and they stay until you leave. How long have you been working out?"

"Two hours."

"You can't do that! The newbies will kill themselves in two hours here."

He smiled. "So what are you doing here?"

"You mean besides watching you? I usually come in the mornings. But I needed to work something off and I was hoping this would help."

"Anything I can help you work off?"

I blushed. "It was either the gym or the camp and I thought I better start running if I was going to try that academy. How far do they make you run there?"

"Till you drop."

"Okay, so I'm training for a marathon here."

"Want to race?"

"That's no fair. I've put in 3 miles and *now* you want to race?"

"Okay, we won't race."

He selected a treadmill, hopped on and set the speed to a jog then kept at it. I upped my speed to finish my last mile and then I weighed in. I was more worried about losing too much weight than gaining any. I tried to stay above a hundred and fifteen pounds. Once academy started it was going to be a constant battle.

I sat in a chair beside the lobby and waited, suspecting Rusty had more on his mind than simply working out. I also knew that he'd never talk about work at the gym. He finished his work out and then walked towards me.

"I'll be out in a minute."

I glanced around the room and was met with evil stares from twenty women.

"I don't think we should leave together," I replied. "I'll track you down tomorrow."

"That's appropriate. Come by early, dress for tracking. Desert."

I shot him a questioning look. "Okay, I'll see ya."

I left the gym wondering what was up. I felt the eyes on my back until I got in the Jeep and drove off. His eyes, making sure I got homeward bound without mishap, and all the women looking on with jealousy.

Uncertain what Rusty's definition of *early* was, and considering we'd be tracking in the desert, I thought it best to begin in the cool of the morning. I was also unsure what he wanted me to wear. He said I should wear tracking clothes. He might prefer me to dress the part in the event there were other police officers there. I dressed in camouflage pants, a tan t-shirt, and moccasins. In the garage I dug out my Camel Pack and added my tracking tools. If this was desert tracking I'd need plenty of water. I fed Shadow on my way out the door.

I drove to the police station and checked in at the front counter. Although everyone knew me, it was standard procedure to always check in. I made my way to Rusty's office and peeked in though his door's little window to make sure he was alone. I preferred not to barge in on meetings. It was always a peek through the window, two gentle knocks, then I'd crack the door and look in. He was sitting at his desk typing on the computer so I took a seat and waited for him to finish. He wasn't dressed in his usual slacks and sport coat. He appeared ready for a day out in the hills. His hiking boots poked out from under the far side of the desk and his clothes were meant for hiking.

"Before we go, I want to talk to you, make sure this is something you want to do."

"Okay, although I can't imagine why I wouldn't want to go out tracking."

"These cases are not a pretty sight. And it involves carjacking. These people were not as lucky as you were. Do you still want to go?"

My heart sank. Sure, I'd go, but I remembered vividly what it felt like to be carjacked. And this was worse. These were murder scenes.

"Yeah, I still want to go."

"There's some things I want you to know before we go. Some of it you might find useful in the tracking. Mostly I want you to be alert when you're alone. This guy is dangerous and he doesn't seem to have any problem finding victims."

"What's his MO?"

"He hangs out in bank parking lots. He waits for someone to use the ATM, in the process of robbing them he forces them into their car and it is later found in some remote location. He has also been known to find unlocked cars and hide in the back seat. Whenever you go anyplace, no matter how short a time, lock your car. I know you're observant but be extra careful around banks, even if you aren't at the bank itself. Remember Silva."

"Yeah, I remember Silva."

"If he carjacks a large vehicle, like the one we will go look at today, the body is found in the vehicle. If it's a smaller car there's no sign of the suspect or the body. Get the picture?"

"So you want me to help you figure out what happens after the murder took place."

He looked at me seriously. "You still want to do it? I can get guys from the station to go out there with me. I just have better luck with you... um, tracking-wise."

"Speaking of which, I was lucky to get out of that gym in one piece. You need to do something about your little fan club."

"My fan club?"

"If you had gone in the dressing room and left me out there waiting for you I would have been interrogated. If you want to race come in the morning, six AM. I'm not competing with that nighttime crowd."

"Babe, you're not competing with anybody."

We left the station in an unmarked car and drove out of town. The country around Joshua Hills is bleak and barren to say the least. Joshua trees are the tallest things around and the view to the horizon is an endless sweep of dry desert. Not even cactus like it out there. It is a hostile land. Rusty drove down one nameless dirt road after another until we reached a place where a white van had veered halfway off the road. Two wheels were buried in the deep mound of dirt left by the last bulldozer and the other two were off the road.

"This is it?"

"Yep, one white van, a couple of footprints, then nothing."

"Any other car tracks on this road? He couldn't have gone far out here. He had to have wheels. No normal person could hike more than a mile or two from this spot without roasting. How long ago did this happen?"

"Yesterday."

"Someone was getting killed out here yesterday?" No need of an answer there, Rusty's look said it all. "How could I have just been having a normal day when someone was out here getting murdered?"

"Now you know a little of what I was thinking when you were with Silva."

I looked carefully at the tracks exiting the van. A large man's shoes. I measured the track and sketched it as well as I could. The sand was deep here and shifted a lot so it didn't leave a lot of details.

"Why would he exit the van from the driver's seat with all those big doors in the back? Can you open them?"

"You don't want to see back there. This is a work van. I'll just say there were tools back there and he made use of them."

"The man who got out of the van climbed over the front seat facing the door and landed with both feet." I looked in the van. Bloody smears verified he'd grabbed the steering wheel on his way through, and confirming what Rusty had said, I didn't want to see the back anymore.

I studied the footprints just outside the van again, then followed them around to the front of the van, where they vanished.

"No wonder your officers had trouble with this trail. This trail has trouble written all over it."

"What do you mean?" he asked.

"This guy is good. The ground is hard here, bad for tracking. But not only that, this guy knows how to hide a trail. This is going to be rough. Are you ready to try it? Did you bring plenty of water?" I dug around in my pack and pulled out a very used and folded hat that I only wore in extremely hot and sunny hiking. I looked ridiculous wearing it but there were times when necessity forced me to look ridiculous.

"What about you? Are you ready for this?" I asked Rusty.

"Yup, just say something *before* you pass out from heat stroke," he said.

I looked at the ground where the footprints had faded into nothingness. Boy, this was a puzzle. This would be slow going. Not many hints to start out with either. A man with big feet, work boot tread. That's it.

It's bad news when I have to get down in the dirt on my belly right from the start but that's what I had to do. Studying the ground from a low side view revealed a slight indentation and I traced beside it with my finger. The slight curve was the only visible part of the track. Tracking someone with knowledge of how to hide a trail is rare in tracking. Most people never consider their tracks when they walk. I wasn't used to someone planning ahead.

Now that I could see the line, I could barely make out the track and it pointed just a few degrees west of north. The next track was discernible now that I found the first one. I was hoping he'd tire of this type of walking because I was going to get tired of this type of tracking. I measured from the heel of the first footprint to the heel of the second one. This would give me an idea of the man's stride. I followed the direction the footprints pointed and found the next step and the next, sometimes having to do the side view thing and sometimes finding faint scuffs where rocks had turned in his passing. After an hour we could still see the van and the day was heating up.

"Cass, are you sure you want to follow this to the end? It's okay to back out."

"I'm not quitting unless we have to. If the sun gets to be too much for us or we run out of water we will have to quit. Other than that I am good to go. I'm hoping he gets tired of hiding his tracks. I think after he decides he's gotten a safe distance from the van he will quit trying to hide his trail. He is either testing us or hiding, but eventually I expect him to relax and his tracks will become more readable. All we have to do is stay on this faint trail till he changes modes."

It was hot. It was arduous, but we picked along examining the ground minutely until I finally noticed his attention to detail was slipping. I took a break sitting in the little bit of shade offered by a scraggly mesquite tree and drank some water. I also brought out my ever present Ziploc bag of trail mix. I dusted off my blistered hands, offered some to Rusty and we both dug in.

When we hit the trail again it was much easier. I could see faint tracks now and the man we followed was walking normally, just being careful. The ground was still hard but there were clues. I started a mental profile of the guy. He had survival training. He'd spent a lot of time in the desert. He was shorter than Rusty, taller than me. I could get a better feel for his size if I could find some tracks with good impressions to them. I was also hoping for enough tracks so I could get a feel for the way the guy walked. That would tell me a lot about his stature and his attitude. That break didn't come, though, until we tracked him to a hill. As we came down the other side there was a shack standing in the middle of nowhere. As the suspect came into view of the shack his pace had quickened. As he closed in on the structure with determination I was able to read more from the tracks and form a mental picture of his gait.

Finding the shack was good news. A road led up to the shack and the tread from a vehicle was clearly visible in the deep dust. It was a larger vehicle with oversized tires. We examined the shack first because the suspect had made a point of leading us here. It was made of rock with a simple wooden roof added. No ceiling. No glass in the single window. No door. Just rock walls and a dilapidated roof. The shack had phrases spray painted all over it. One said, *the hills have eyes*. Another said, *you won't catch me*. Rusty quickly checked inside the shack, his gun in hand. Then, when we knew there was no one lurking, he started casting around, picking up evidence with a gloved hand and photographing the painted walls.

I walked around avoiding the tracks, trying to get a feel for the way this guy was thinking. I wandered into the shack and an angry, whirring rattle instantly caught my attention! It was dark inside and I couldn't see a thing! Where was the damn snake? I started for the door but it was too late. I couldn't get past and this was one angry rattler. I kept my eyes focused on the dark floor, willing my eyes to adjust to the dim light.

"Rusty!" I yelled. No response. "Rusty! I've got a Level Six Situation in here!" The snake lunged. "Level Eight!" I shrieked. I heard footsteps. "Don't come in! Don't come in! Just shoot the damn snake!" The snake lunged at my leg and I leaped to the side, my heart pounding. The snake had me cornered. Its head bobbed and weaved while its tail kept up the incessant warning rattle. I was heeding the warning but it would be easier to back off if I had some place to go.

"I can't shoot it! You're standing behind it! Even if I hit it I'll hit you too."

Okay, Cass, think, think. I looked around. What could I use to get out of the way? The snake lunged again but I jumped aside. I looked up into the rafters of the shack. I believed they were low enough to jump up and grab them.

I told Rusty the plan. "I'm going to jump and grab the rafters and haul myself up there and while I am up there you shoot the snake."

He looked at me like I was nuts. Would the shack hold up? Would the aged wood hold me? Hell, I didn't know but it was all I could think of.

"Ready?"

"Ready," he said grimly removing his sidearm from its holster. He aimed his gun at the snake's head. The tip of the weapon moved as he tried to follow the snake's head. It was a very small target in very poor lighting.

I leaped up, grabbed the rafter then hauled for all I was worth. My feet rose up. The snake lunged and its fang hooked on the seam of my moccasin. I pulled the rattler up into the rafters with me. Shit! Now what? I shook my foot and the snake just dangled. I shook it harder, no luck. I took a moment to think, the snake thrashing around, dangling from my foot.

"Okay," I said nervously, "Clear out. I need a clean shot at the door."

"What are you going to do?"

"You don't want to know, just give me a clear path. Any more snakes down there?"

"Nope." Rusty said, looking around. He backed up.

I brought my foot carefully to my hand. Rusty's eyes got big.

"Cass, no, don't do this," he said nervously. I grasped the rattler firmly, directly behind the head so it couldn't reach me with its fangs. I pulled up and felt a *snap* as the fang jerked loose. I dropped from the rafters and dashed out of the shack dragging the hapless serpent with me. Rusty stared at me, astonishment clearly written on his face.

"Now I'm scared to let it go!"

I couldn't just set it down. The rattler was mad and was thrashing all around. It was all I could do to keep a firm hold on it. I tightened my grip behind its head. If I just let go, it would attack me instantly. I needed more leverage than my arms offered to throw the dumb thing. I started spinning around and around, building up enough momentum to launch the snake away from me. I made sure my release point was well away from Rusty then released it, watching the snake sail up and away into the desert. It landed with a *whump* in the dirt. Backing away from the area, I sat down in the dirt, in shock, waiting for my heart rate to slow down. I studied my hands, examining them for any tiny scratches I might have received when throwing the snake. Rusty came over and took my hands, turning them palm upward. I didn't see any scratches, but he saw the blisters.

"How'd you mess up your hands like this?" he asked.

"The sand was hot. It'll be okay. It'll heal fast. It's just part of the job."

"Not when the job is for me." Then, remembering the snake, he said, "You are totally nuts. I don't know of anybody who would grab a rattlesnake by the head with their bare hands and throw it into the desert. Nobody."

"Well, what was I supposed to do? I wasn't going to ask you to do it! And the snake was stuck. It couldn't have bit me."

"I still think it was a crazy thing to do."

"Well, it worked. Let's finish up here so we can go home. If Thez asks me about the scariest thing that's happened to me I think I'll add that to the list."

On the way back to the car we hiked and talked. No need to track on the way back. The suspect had carefully led us on, obviously testing us. I didn't like the messages spray painted on the walls. They made me think we were being watched.

"I hope that was helpful to your investigation." I said as we walked along.

"It was and I'm not through with you yet. I know how you track. I want to know your impressions from this, too. You've got an idea what kind of a person we are dealing with here."

"This guy is used to the desert. He's had survival training. He has an attitude. He's too proud. You'll catch him. I know that just because his attitude is too flaunting. He's leading you on and trying to show off and it's just that attitude that will eventually be his big mistake."

"Do you want to try another site?"

"Another one? How many are there?"

"There's three in all, confirmed. There are others we are not sure of. This is the most recent. I brought you here because I knew the body had been found. But there are two others."

"How often does this guy hit?"

"So far, every couple of weeks."

"So the next site is two weeks old? There's almost no use even looking if the trail is two weeks old and he is as careful hiding his tracks. But it might be worthwhile to look the area over more carefully. Examine the area from the air to see if there are any shacks within a couple of miles of the site. Then, if you find one, we can hike in to it and see if he has done the same thing before. You know I'll try anything but I don't hold out much hope of following this guy's two week old trail."

"I know you tend to profile as you go along. Tell me the impression you got from this trail."

"He's taller than me, shorter than you. He's a little on the heavy side but I don't think he's fat. He is just heavily built. He walks with an odd rolling gait. I picture a guy walking, leaning into his walk, shoulders hunched. I'm willing to bet when you search this guy's house he has guns, ammo, a stockpile, outdoor magazines and catalogs stacked around. His place is going to look more like a bunker than a home. If I had to pinpoint his size, I'd guess five-ten, a hundred and ninety pounds. But, like I said, not fat."

"That's a lot of assumptions to make off a trail of footprints."

"Yeah, but I got a different impression when I tracked Silva, Peccati, and Kelly. Peccati always walked like he was strolling from one building to another in the city. Uphill or down it was the same strolling gait. I knew Peccati didn't live in a bunker. He was too used to the finer things in life. Off this trail, I'm getting the opposite. This is a killer from the other side of the tracks."

A few days later around lunchtime there was a knock on my door. I looked out the peep hole and Rusty was there, a cheerful but worn look on his face.

"Hey," I said opening the door wide, "what are you doing here? I thought you'd be hard at work."

He came in giving me a quick hug. "I was, unfortunately. That's what brings me to your house. I've got something you need to see." He held out a sheet of paper. "This isn't the original. The one we received at the station is being held as evidence. It wasn't addressed to any specific person but we kind of assume it was meant for you."

I motioned for him to have a seat and Shadow danced around his feet, barking, while I took the paper to the couch and sat down to read it. Rusty sat down in a chair and petted Shadow so he'd calm down and lie at our feet. The message was short. I read it twice.

"LITTLE GIRL, YOU'RE TRACKING DANGEROUS GROUND. I'D STAY HOME SAFE AND SOUND IF I WAS YOU. CONSIDER THIS A WARNING."

I noted the scratchy block letters and handed the paper back to Rusty. "Okay, I've been warned," I said.

"Cass, please be careful. This guy is not someone you want to mess with."

"I know. I'm always careful. Do you want to stay for lunch?"

"I wish I could, but I need to get going. I don't like the way this case is heading."

I walked him to his Explorer and watched as he drove away. As Rusty drove from the neighborhood, I noticed a large white pickup truck slowly cruise down the cross street.

Chapter 4

I wanted a trip to my camp before the next tracking call came. The following day I called Rusty at the station to check in. He knew I was familiar with the route, the wildlife, and that I had everything I needed for the trip.

"I just want a few days to track and stalk. I'll be back in four days. Two hiking days and two camping days. That ought to be enough," I'd told him.

I packed some backpacking food, threw in a new novel, a bottle of gas for my stove, and my hiking staple, trail mix. I packed a few scoops of dog food because Shadow was going along on this trip. Shadow happily jumped into the passenger seat, eager to be off. Most of the other items I needed were stored at the camp.

I drove up to Creekside Campground, passed through the camp and continued to the trailhead that started at the back of the campground. I parked, hung my Adventure Pass in the window, put on my funny looking hat and headed up the trail. I followed the trail beside a little creek that flowed down the canyon. Except for the heat the hike was pleasant. Usually heat will drive the animals into hiding but I saw an unusual number of squirrels and rabbits. Stellars jays flew from pine tree to pine tree. Ferns leaned out over the trail. It was good to be off alone again with good old dirt beneath my moccasins. The first two miles went quickly, Shadow heeling quietly by my side. He was used to this trail. It was our normal route and he had been missing these trips ever since I'd met Rusty. I felt more settled now, so the mountains pulled a little less harshly. Still, the city was beginning to get to me and the snake incident had left me a bit rattled. I wanted to relax.

I turned off the trail where two creeks came together. The next two miles would be a rough hike up a rugged canyon. I felt a need to focus on specific things during this hike. When I had to focus it helped to clear my cluttered thoughts, so I chose a route up the canyon that required a lot of rock climbing. Nothing major, just enough to make me focus and be careful. Shadow knew where we were going and found his own way, but always managed to keep tabs on me. He was a Shetland Sheepdog and keeping track of me was a job he took seriously. I was his flock, his one lonely sheep.

One rock led to another and I made my way up the canyon one handhold, one foothold at a time. It was relaxing. The creek tumbled down the rocks beside me. It was mid afternoon when I reached a tall, lonely pine tree and a large flat rock beside the creek. I was home. My hideout.

I'd made the camp a few years before and came here frequently on hiking trips because it was away from the tourists. I loved the creek and the ruggedness of the canyon. There were caves to explore in the canyon walls and refreshing little pools in the creek. I could find deer in two small meadows, one at the top of the canyon and one on the way up. Then one day I discovered a spot where two trees had fallen and been caught between two other trees. I saw the layout as a perfect setup to make a shelter. The next time I returned with a huge tarp and draped it over the leaning trees, then cleared the floor area. I piled branches over the outside to hide it and protect it from the weather. It was like a hidden cave made from branches. The forest had grown up around it and now it looked like a very wild patch of forest. Only someone who was shown the way could find the entrance. There was no door. To gain entry I needed to lift a corner of the tarp that was usually hidden by weeks of fallen pine needles and other forest litter. The inside was warm, snug, and watertight.

I searched for the corner of the tarp, lifted it and then crawled in with Shadow following me into the dark hidey hole. I felt around for the lantern, bumping into his soft, furry side.   I turned it on and looked around. Everything appeared to be in good shape. I pulled the sleeping bag from a dusty corner, removing it from a plastic trash bag. After rolling it out onto the hard-packed floor I laid down and stretched out. I relaxed, savoring the feeling of the earth against my back. Finally, quiet and nature again. I needed to stalk, track and climb to work out all the kinks the city threw my way. I didn't want to worry about bills or shopping or murders. This was my time, my place where things worked right, where I was comfortable. I unpacked the extra food I'd brought, adding it to the ammo box of food I kept in the hideout. The new novel was added to my stash of reading material. Occasionally when I was stuck up here by rain or fog the books came in handy.

Leaving the hideout I checked the area for signs of wildlife and found tracks of chipmunks and squirrels. One track, heading up canyon, looked like a coyote but it could have been left by Shadow. I studied it more carefully. It wasn't Shadow but it wasn't a coyote either. The track had been left by a domestic dog but one much larger than my Sheltie. I tried to gauge how old the track was, hoping the dog was no longer in the area. I never worried about the wildlife; it was the non-wildlife that could be dangerous.

I lit my stove, then heated water for a meal. Good old backpacker food. It was tempting to live off the trail mix but I'd soon tire of that. Maybe I could snare my next dinner and have some real meat. Maybe tomorrow. I'd be out in the game trails tomorrow anyway and get a better feel for things then. Today it was arroz con pollo backpacker style. I tore open the pouch, added boiling water and folded the top down to let the food cook. At least this was easy. No fuss, no mess, quick clean up; my kind of meal.

After dinner I hiked down to a small clearing below my camp to check out the deer population. I explored the wall of the canyon, looking for interesting places like caves or nice boulders for rock climbing. I'd been to this canyon dozens of time but always saved areas for further exploring so it never got old. Shadow followed along. When he brought pinecones to me I would throw them in a game of fetch. This was his play time, too. At home we used an agility course, and that was Shadow's job. He was a smart, working dog and needed to keep busy. Out here, his work changed to keeping track of me and investigating all the smells and animals.

As the sun dipped below the side of the canyon I headed back to the hideout. This was not a place for wandering around at night. It was rugged, so I kept close to camp after sunset. I slept when it was dark and got up with the sun in the morning.

The next day I awoke to scurrying noises on the roof of the hideout. Obviously a chipmunk or squirrel had taken up residence in the branches covering the tarp. I went outside to greet my new neighbor. I sat quietly on the flat rock, my eye on the hideout. Sure enough, out popped a chipmunk. He poked around in the bushes and then carried something into the branches and disappeared. Pretty quick he was back at it again. I went back inside, brought out my trail mix and hid some under a nearby bush for the chipmunk to find. When he had located that stash, I left out the open bag for him to discover. I was sensitizing him to this new food using different locations. After he made a few trips to the bag I took it and lay down at the base of the hideout. I put some trail mix in my hand and found a comfortable position that I could maintain for a long time, and then lay quietly, stilling my breathing. Be still, Cass, quiet. I relaxed and felt a shift in my attitude and I was settled in, ready for the long wait.

The chipmunk scurried around, then froze at the site of me. Still, I thought, stay still. The chipmunk stepped forward, froze, stepped forward. It wasn't sure about this new addition to the forest bearing food. I must have moved a bit because the chipmunk hurried up a tree. I laid beneath the tree for over an hour letting the chipmunk get used to me. You can't hurry nature. It moves on its own clock. I started getting hungry and realized I hadn't eaten yet but remained in place willing the chipmunk to come down. I could see him spiraling down the tree, stopping to sniff every few feet, nose twitching, tail flicking. He landed by my head at the base of the tree. Still, stay very still. Don't blink. The chipmunk inched towards my outstretched hand and placed his two front paws on the ball of my thumb. He quickly darted forward and snatched a piece of fruit then dashed up the tree. I lay there still as a stone as he spiraled back down and found another treasure in my hand. It was hard to stay still with a critter on my hand. I was enjoying the company so much I wanted to visit with him but I knew to do that meant I would lose the chance. I wished Rusty was here to try this. With his fast reflexes he'd probably flinch at the touch but it would still be fun to watch him try it.

Finally I had lain on the ground as long as I cared to. I put a stash of trail mix where it could be easily found and went on my way. I heated water and made oatmeal and hot chocolate, my normal camping breakfast. I didn't really like oatmeal but it packed and cooked easily and it lasted until lunchtime so it's what I ate.

For some odd reason I was developing an unsettling feeling. I began watching the woods around me with a critical eye, but couldn't pinpoint the source. Just a feeling that I wasn't alone up here. I changed my way of looking at things and started watching for odd colors or movements but continued my actions like normal. I called Shadow and we headed up the canyon, once again exploring the walls of the canyon for interesting places. When I found a rock that looked fun to climb I judged it by size. I wasn't willing to take a tumble of more than eight or ten feet when I was by myself so I only took note of the longer climbs. Occasionally I would find a shorter climb that I could try myself. Shadow didn't like me climbing rocks. He wanted to follow, but going straight up was not an option for him, so he watched me and whined and sometimes he would find a way to the top, only to watch me turn around and climb back down. I hoped he would eventually learn to wait at the bottom, but even after two years he still persisted in following me as closely as possible.

I climbed up a rock and looked at the country beyond, more boulder-strewn mountainside stretching up, up to the top of the peak. These boulders were not the eroded sandstone rocks so typical of the area. These boulders were just piled up haphazardly. How had that happened? I could understand the tilted sandstone of Vasquez Rocks. Wind and rain had eroded them. Earthquakes had tilted them. But these rocks looked totally foreign to their environment.

I was tempted to keep climbing but decided to save it for later. Even when I was alone I felt Rusty's watchful eye on me and it kept me in check. Maybe it would even keep me out of trouble. I climbed back down into the canyon again and continued following the walls, climbing and exploring the nooks and crannies. Rock climbing was slow going, and before I knew it the day was waning and I hadn't had lunch. Returning to camp, I rehydrated a pouch of lasagna flavored noodle stuff and washed it down with hot chocolate. The unsettling feeling persisted as I watched the canyon walls for signs of life. Walking around camp I searched for any footprints left by other people but only found my own. I circled the camp looking for sign but didn't see anything definite. Maybe my mind was playing tricks on me.

Night fell and Shadow and I slept in the hideout, waking to the scurrying of the chipmunk in the branches overhead.

I had not intended to spend the entire previous day rock climbing, so I headed down to the clearing to see the deer in the early morning. I didn't see any deer in the lower clearing so I headed up canyon to see if they were in the clearing above my camp. Although unusual for them to be in the upper clearing, they'd been there before and I was looking forward to stalking them.

When I reached the clearing the deer were very wary. I could sense tension in the air as though something had been after them recently, making them flighty. I had little chance for successful stalking under these conditions but I was determined to try. If I could get into the herd in their agitated state it would be quite an accomplishment. I started walking cautiously towards them, but noting my presence they began to dance around with pricked ears, watching me. I stood still, giving them a chance to accept my presence as nonthreatening. Taking a cautious step, I felt Shadow beside me and gave him the down/stay signal. He found a shaded spot and lay there waiting for my go-ahead signal. I stepped closer. Inching my way into the herd, I couldn't help but get the feeling something was brewing. The deer expected trouble and I wondered what it could be. If it was predators then I didn't need to worry because they would be after the deer. Although I hated to see one come down I knew it was just nature taking its course. I automatically felt for my pistol but remembered I'd left it home. I then felt for my knife. I brought a hunting knife; not for protection but in case I had to live off the land. A good knife was necessary for cutting things to make snares, and if I caught something, it was also needed to clean the animal. I had lived off the land before but lately I preferred watching the animals to eating them. It now took a day without food to convince me I better think about snaring something to eat. Thankfully I still had a few days of backpacker food at camp and wouldn't go hungry tonight.

Suddenly Shadow broke from his down/stay and raced across the clearing scattering the deer, his focus on a dark brown blur in the brush. The only thing I could think of that was dark brown up here was an occasional elk or bear, however it wasn't noisy enough for either animal. I heard Shadow's deep growl and when I found him he stood glaring and snarling at a large junkyard dog. It was a motley mix of large dog breeds and it was skin and bones. My temper flared because I knew someone had abandoned it to survive in these hostile mountains.

"Shadow, heel!" I commanded. He didn't budge. I approached the emaciated dog. I'd have caught and fed it and brought it back to town, but as soon as I stepped forward Shadow rushed it, nipping at its legs, sheepdog style. He thought he was protecting me but Shadow was a herder, not a fighter. The other dog attacked Shadow with a vengeance but only managed to grab a ruff full of fur. Shadow thrashed, paws scrambling around in the loose rocks and sand, trying to get his footing and run away. I stepped forward and this made Shadow even more frantic. The two closed in a huge snarling mess. I wasn't going to let this dog kill Shadow. Shadow suddenly broke free and dashed behind me. The big dog lunged. I raised a hand in front of my face to block the dog's charge and it latched onto my arm. I didn't pull back. To pull back would mean losing a pound of flesh. I felt the teeth biting in and instinctively followed the dog down. I found a spot with my free hand where I thought I could try to pry at his mouth but the huge jaws wouldn't budge. Shadow came racing back snapping at the dog from all sides. He was fast and this distracted the dog long enough that he loosened his grip. I pried again and was given just enough room to pull my arm out. I jumped back, pulling my hunting knife from its sheath. Shadow rushed the dog again trying to drive it away from me. The dog lunged again, this time latching onto my leg just above the ankle. I stabbed at it with the knife, causing the dog to pull back and rip my leg. I stabbed again feeling red-hot anger, not at the dog but at some inconsiderate person who had driven a good animal to be so dangerous. The simple act of turning a dog loose had now turned into a deadly battle. I hoped to be the winner. I had to. I thought about who would come looking for me up here. Rusty first. He knew where I was, but I wouldn't do that to him. I was going to beat this dog. I was going to haul it back to town and find out if it was micro chipped and I was going to find the owner and… and what? First things first, Cass. Go for the jugular. This knife is sharp, you can beat this dog. Just do it! The next time it lunged I brought the knife down and sliced up as hard as I could. I felt the blade bite and drag and the dog stumbled back and dropped, looking at me with sad eyes. I looked back, just as sad for having beaten it. I couldn't watch. I turned away as the dog died there on the mountainside.

I examined the damage to my leg. I was really in trouble this time. It was definitely a case for stitches. My arm had been bitten in a long arched line of puncture wounds, but my leg appeared to be worse. It was bleeding freely. I thought back to the first aid classes I had taken while in the Marines, but I didn't have much to work with up there on the mountainside. Applying pressure to the wound, I waited for the bleeding to slow. A large flap of skin left the muscle exposed. I needed to bind it, stop the bleeding, and hike out with the dead dog. Looking at the large dog, I didn't think I could do it. Even in its starved condition the dog weighed half as much as I did. I used the knife to cut the legs off my pants to shorts length, and then shredded the material into wide bandages. I pulled out my cell phone but there was no reception. I tried calling Paul at the ranger station anyway because all the rangers there knew me.

"Paul, this is Cassidy. I don't know if you can hear me but I have a problem. Can you send someone up here? Directions: go up Creekside trail two miles and then head up the canyon where the two creeks come together. I need a first aid kit and some muscle." I didn't know if anybody heard my message, which meant I was still on my own. I pulled the flap of skin over the wound and then bound the area tightly with the strips from my pants legs. All this took hours to do. The fabric of my pants didn't tear or cut easily. That's what I got for buying sturdy camping clothes from Army Surplus. They had weave that went in multiple directions so they didn't tear. By the time I finished wrapping the wounds I noticed the sun was dipping. I'd spent time hiking, stalking, fighting, bandaging and I'd somehow used up a whole day. I pushed myself to my feet trying to figure out what to do about the dog when pain shot up my leg. Oh great, this was going to be one painful hike out. I tried walking but it was too much. I searched the dog for a microchip. If the dog was dead it wouldn't be hurt by my search and I still meant to contact the authorities about it. Hauling it out wasn't an option in my present condition.

The more I moved, the more my leg hurt. I finally set my sights on just reaching the hideout again. There were other hungry critters out here and I didn't want them smelling the blood on me. After dealing with the dog I wasn't ready to face a bear or mountain lion. The hideout was the best place for me and if worst came to worst I would be stuck there for two nights. Okay, the hideout first, Cass, then tomorrow the trail.

"Shadow, heel," I commanded putting him in working mode. I stood to hike down the mountain and my leg buckled. Shoot. Hiking was out. I looked around for a branch to make a crutch but none of them looked like they would work, and I didn't have time to sit around whittling. I inched my way down the mountain any way I could without putting weight on the bad leg. Sometimes that meant crawling, sometimes hopping along. I put my weight on it occasionally but the pain quickly stopped me. Darkness fell and I was still a long, painful distance from the hideout. I got out my cell phone again and tried Rusty's number. Reception or not, I had to try something.

"Hello Rusty? Can you hear me? Please say you can hear me. If you can, then please call Paul and see if he got my message. If he got it don't do anything. He's got it under control. If not I could really use some help up here. Don't try to hike the canyon at night. I'll try to get to the hideout tonight and then make the trail in the morning. I need a first aid kit. If you can get your hands on some painkillers I'd appreciate it. I can't believe I'm asking a cop to bring me drugs."

Shoot. I sure didn't want to do that to him but I was beginning to doubt if I was walking out of here. I could deal with the pain once I was on the trail but getting to the trail was going to be hard. In the starlight I crawled along until I met a drop off. It was a rock I'd climbed up easily on the way up. Now it looked insurmountable. Going down was always harder than going up and it was night. On the bright side, rock climbing was more feel than sight. I just wondered if this was a rock that I could descend with only one good leg. Nope. The more I thought about it the more convinced I became that I couldn't rock climb to get down. It would mean hanging by my fingers until my good foot found a hold. I searched the area for an easier way down but every place I looked had a long drop off. I was stuck for the night. In the morning maybe I'd be able to follow Shadow's route down.

I curled up with my back against a large rock, my hunting knife in my hand. I tried to sleep but the binding hurt my leg and I worried about what I would be facing the next day. I wondered if anybody knew I was out here needing help. I couldn't count on it. I had to keep going until I got to the Jeep. I'd do that first thing in the morning. Then I'd have to drive the Jeep. That would be painful too. Shit and double shit. I was deep in it this time. Shadow found a place to curl up and slept where he could see me. I really wanted him to lie beside me because I could have used the warmth but Shadow never was very cuddly. I slept fitfully. I awoke in the night shivering but it wasn't dangerously cold so I just tolerated it. When I could see well enough to make my way down the canyon I headed out again.

"Let's go home," I told Shadow hoping he'd go into automatic and lead me down the canyon. He showed me the way he got past the large rocks. I sat and scooted down a trough worn through the rocks by thousands of small flash floods. My leg screamed at me with every movement. I looked down the canyon for the pine tree that marked my camp. Yes, I can do this, I thought. Just head for the lone pine tree.

Thirst drove me to the creek but the detour cost me. The way down the canyon was rougher around the creek, so I lost precious time. I made my way back to easier terrain and forced myself to walk downhill. When the pain became too intense I hopped and then crawled until at last I stumbled into the clearing by the flat rock. I army crawled into the hideout and collapsed. Shadow pushed his way in with a concerned whine. I was hungry but I didn't have the energy to cook. I grabbed the bag of trail mix, a bottle of water and drifted off to sleep. I awoke thinking I should go to the creek and take off the bandages and wash the wound but gave up on that idea. The creek, thirty feet outside my hideout, felt like a mile away. The trail to Creekside might as well have been on the moon. I drank the tepid, bottled water then drifted off again.

When I woke up I was determined to try and make it to the trail. It was becoming apparent that nobody had gotten any of my messages. While feeding Shadow I wondered how many meals he had missed. I had missed the same meals, but I had no appetite. I was feeling feverish and dull headed but decided to set out. Small goals, that's what I needed. Just make it to that rock, I thought. And when I felt the rock beneath my hand I would pick a tree. Just make it to the tree, Cass. One goal at a time. I was reduced to crawling before I lost sight of my camp. The next big rock loomed ahead and I headed in that direction.

Darkness fell again before I reached the trail so I found another out of the way crevasse to shelter in as I shivered all night long, drifting in and out of sleep. I awoke to Shadow's barking and noticed the sun was already high in the sky. Shoot. I'd wasted the best time of day for hiking.

"What is it boy?"

I heard a voice calling in the distance: "Where is she? Where's Cassidy?"

I pulled myself up and headed towards the voice but my leg buckled again. Whose voice was that? I knew that voice, but it wasn't Rusty. I tried again, determined to just ride out the throbbing in my leg. When I expected the pain I was able to tolerate it, at least that's what I told myself. I was clutching a tree for support while choosing my next goal when Kelly Green appeared. When he saw me shock flashed across his face. He took one look at me and rushed forward. I didn't want to think about what I looked like. Bandaged leg, dog blood, scrapes and tears from crawling over sharp rocks. He looked at the bite marks on my forearm and the makeshift bandages on my leg. He gently helped me to a sitting position and then urgently started unwinding the bandages.

"No!" I yelled. I didn't want him to see it. I knew the injury looked bad and that it would hurt like hell once air hit the wound.

"I have to, Cassidy. We need to know what we're dealing with here."

"It's not as bad as it looks, just painful."

"What did you run up against up here?"

"A dog, just a dog, but it was abandoned and it was starving and it couldn't catch the deer I was stalking. It attacked Shadow and then it turned on me."

"Did you shoot it?"

"I didn't have my gun, only a knife."

The last layer of blood soaked bandages were sticking together. I poured water on it trying to get the bandage to unstick, wincing with every touch. As the last layer came off, I didn't like what I saw. The six-inch patch of skin did little to hide the deeper wound beneath. The edges of the skin were dry and curled. There was swelling and discoloration. The concern in Kelly's eyes deepened. He took off his daypack and brought out a first aid kit.

"How did you know where to go?" I asked him.

"Rusty called. He said you were a day late coming out of the mountains. I got a description of where you went and headed out."

"He worries too much. I don't know what I'm going to do with that guy."

"By the looks of things here he doesn't worry enough."

"I tried to call for help, this time, but I couldn't get through. I called Paul and Rusty both. I don't know if anybody got my messages. But it's not stuff like this that concerns me. When I said he worries too much I guess what I mean is he has been worrying too deeply. Rusty is scared of something and I don't know what it is. It isn't that he's afraid something will happen to me. He sort of expects things like this to happen to me. This is more of an emotional thing."

Judging from Kelly's expression it looked as if he understood, but this wasn't the time or place to worry about Rusty. He had a medical situation that needed to be dealt with first. He returned his focus to his work and examined the wound, his touch sending needles of pain slicing up through my leg.

"If you dull the pain I can walk. It just hurts like hell. How far is the trail?"

"We're nearly on the trail. How far did you come like this?"

"We're on the trail? How could I not know that? That was the longest three miles of my life."

"Three miles? What were you doing trying to hike out of that canyon in this condition?"

"I didn't know if help was coming. I had to do what I could. I just need to get to my Jeep and I'll go have this looked at."

"You can't even drive the Jeep like this. Besides, your Jeep is worse off than you right now. Looks like a bear thrashed it. Did you leave any food in it?"

"Not that I know of. I never saw bears at Creekside before."

He disinfected the gash and bandaged me up again. Every touch sent pain through my leg. I hardened inside, determined to keep up a tough front.

I wasn't sure what he'd done but the pain had eased a little. He disinfected my arm although it seemed to be healing already.

I stood and tried putting my weight on the bad leg. "Let's go while it feels better. The trail ought to be easier than the canyon. We should make it out today no problem. Just two more miles."

"Cassidy, I'm not letting you walk on that."

"Then we have a problem because you're not carrying me either. Let's go. If I can make it down the canyon I can make it down the trail."

"Where's your gear? You came up here with something, I know that."

"It'll be safe where it is. I don't need it. I didn't want to deal with the weight so I just took water. It'll be okay."

I rose and tried out my leg. Limping badly, I headed down the trail. Kelly followed keeping a close eye on me.

"Nice shorts," he said trying to be funny. I felt the torn edges. Gosh, how short had I cut them?

"I was trying to get bandage material out of my pants legs."

"I'm not complaining."

"So," I continued, "do you know what's going on with Rusty? This all started when I went out to a plane crash to help track down a missing passenger... Rusty was irate. He wasn't going to let me go even though it looked straight forward and safe... I've never seen him like that. I know it had something to do with the fact that it was a plane crash but that can't be all there was to it... He just seemed different somehow. This just all feels so foreign to me somehow and I don't know what to do about it."

"You're getting to know him better. Just give him some space when he's like that."

"But I *had* to go on the search. It wasn't optional and he knew it. But he was trying to stop it anyway."

"You know he can't stand to see you get hurt..."

"No," I interrupted, "this had nothing to do with me. This wasn't the tough cop watching out for the poor defenseless girl. This was something inside him."

My leg was throbbing again but I pressed on. We hadn't even made a quarter of a mile so I couldn't stop now.

"Look, Cass, this is something that Rusty has to deal with on his own. If he thinks you should know about what's going on with him he will talk to you about it."

"This reminds me of that time at the ranch, remember? It was when my sister wanted to know how we met and Rusty told me that my family should know how we met, that they should know what all had happened to me so they could understand why I am the way I am now."

"And you think you should know something about Rusty?"

"Yes. There's something, I just don't know what it is."

"I'll talk to him," he said, "but I can't promise anything."

The more I walked the more my leg throbbed until the pain started shooting up my leg again. I looked down. The red stain had worked its way through the fresh bandage. I found an easy way down to the creek and turned off. Kelly turned off, too, knowing not to push. I found a rock beside the creek and stretched out, my leg slightly elevated. Shadow made his way down to the water and I heard him noisily lapping.

"Kelly, do you have any food along? I've only had a handful of trail mix since this happened." I still didn't really feel hungry but I needed the energy. He quickly dug around in his pack and came up with some beef jerky and energy bars.

"Sorry, no stroganoff pudding."

"Thanks," I said, taking one of each.

"How long ago did this happen to you?"

I had to think for a minute. Time was weird there for a bit.

"Well, I spent a night out in the open trying to get back to my camp and I stopped at camp to grab some trail mix and feed Shadow. I'm not sure how much time passed while I rested there. Then I started out for the trail and spent the night where you found me. If I'd known how close I was to the trail I would have kept going but I was pretty scatterbrained by then. I thought the trail was a half mile further."

"You spent two days up there like this? Here, take the rest." He handed the whole bag over. I sat back trying to relax, willing the pain to ease.

I poked at the bandage to see if the pain was any less and felt red-hot needles with the touch. This was going to be one long walk.

"This isn't helping. We might as well press on."

Kelly gave me a hand up so I wouldn't have to use my bad leg to do it. I braced myself for the shock of the first step and headed back to the trail.

It wasn't far to the trail but I was ready to rest again when we reached it. I bent over waiting for the pain to pass when my gaze fell upon the trail. The tracks jumped out at me. These were not the usual hiking-up-trail type tracks. These were hurried tracks. They were distressed tracks, tired of trudging uphill but determined to do it anyway. And they were Rusty's tracks. I'd recognize those tracks anywhere. I headed up trail.

"Uh, Cassidy, wrong way."

"Kelly, Rusty came through here. We couldn't have been down at the creek ten minutes. Can you catch him?"

Kelly took off jogging down the trail. After a while I heard a piercing whistle that I assumed Rusty would recognize. I sat down next to the trail to wait. I opened the energy bar, thinking I could use some energy to get through this hike. It didn't take long for the two men to return, walking quickly and talking in hushed, worried tones. I struggled to stand without using my bad leg and Rusty gathered me into a hug.

"Babe, when I saw your Jeep... I didn't know what to think."

"I didn't even know about the Jeep until Kelly found me. We're just taking it slow trying to get back to the campground."

"Yeah, because she won't take any help from me," Kelly interjected.

I braced myself for the pain again and stepped out heading down the trail. Rusty took one look at the short shorts, blood soaked bandage and quickly made his own conclusions. He came up next to me.

"Well, I can tell I'm the odd man out now." Kelly said. "I'm going to hike out and come back with something more helpful. What'll it be?"

"Crutches?" suggested Rusty. "You know Cass, she's not going to get wheeled out or carried out."

"You got it," Kelly replied. He took his canteen, handed the pack over to Rusty and took off at a fast walk. "Make sure she eats something."

"Kelly," I called out, "Thanks!"

I limped down the trail, pain searing each step.

"Cass," Rusty said following me. "You've got to stop. You're in no shape to hike out."

"I've made it this far. I'll make it to the trailhead," I replied, knowing I was being stubborn. "If you saw what I've been through you wouldn't doubt it."

"What did happen up here?"

I told him about the dog and the hike to the trail. "I called. And I tried to get back on time. I just couldn't do it."

"How did you know I'd passed you on the trail?"

"Your tracks. You think I don't recognize your tracks by now?"

"Guess I shouldn't be surprised."

I was watching the landmarks and the half-mile marker went by slowly. We were talking less. I hoped Rusty didn't notice I was quiet because I had to concentrate to keep walking. My mind was fuzzy again. I felt hot, so hot. I knew it was summer in California, but still, this was a different kind of heat. It dragged me down. In a way the fuzziness helped. I didn't feel as much pain, but after a while I started feeling nothing at all and pitched face first into the dirt. Rusty turned me over.

"It'll pass," I said, "I need to rest."

He scooped me up and started walking and I didn't have the strength to protest. His arms felt good and his shoulder made the perfect pillow. I wanted to feel more but the fuzziness took over and I drifted off again.

After a while I felt some light bumps and the ground beneath me and gentle shaking.

"Cass, babe, you're scaring me again. Come on. Talk to me. Wake up."

More shaking. I opened my eyes. "I had to stop. Your leg is dripping through the dressing."

"First aid kit," I mumbled, "In the pack." I tried to sit up but I couldn't. Rusty dug around in the pack.

"Here," he said handing me a water bottle. "Drink, you need it."

I took the water bottle and took a drink. It wasn't enough but maybe I'd have more energy in a minute. I felt the bandages unwinding and felt the sting as the air hit the open wound.

"It's not as bad as it looks. It'll just need stitches." I mumbled.

I cried as he worked. He was as gentle as he could be but the nerves felt like they were all exposed and the pain took over everything.

"Cassidy... Cass..." A damp cloth, coolness. Yes, I could use some coolness. I opened my eyes again. "You're burning up. Here, drink again. You have to keep drinking. You need the water. Come on."

I drank. I held up a hand to stand but he just shook his head. "No way. You're not walking anywhere. I don't know how you walked as far as you did. It's all infected. We've got to get you out of here. Drink. Come on. Drink."

I drank until the fuzziness cleared and Rusty looked at me with less concern. I searched in my pocket for an energy bar but I'd already eaten it. I motioned for the pack and he handed it over. I found another energy bar in there and fumbled with the package until it opened.

I finished the energy bar and put the wrapper in the pack. Pack it in. Pack it out. It was a backpacker rule. Leave a wrapper behind and the Head Backpacker would get you. If the head backpacker was real strict that even went for number two but I guess he must be a fairly easy going guy right now because I'd never had any visits from him.

I struggled to stand, braced myself for the pain and almost went down again. Rusty took it as a good sign though and he put on the pack and scooped me up.

"Rusty, don't do this to yourself. You can't carry me all the way down this trail."

"Who says I can't? Babe, I need to do this for you and if you weren't so stubborn, you'd see it isn't any hardship for me."

"You better be careful," I said playfully, "I might start enjoying this." I put my arms around his neck. He kissed my forehead.

"How far do you think we are?" he asked.

"Did we pass a blasted out tree? Looks like it was struck by lightning and burned."

"Yeah."

"That's close to the one mile mark. Is Shadow still with us?"

"Yup, Kelly should have taken him. I don't know what we will do with him at the hospital."

"Oh, no, Rusty, do we have to? I don't want to go there."

"Cass, trust me, you have to. This isn't a couple of stitches you're looking at. You shouldn't have walked on it at all."

"You still owe me a race."

He laughed, "I'll take a rain check on that. Let me know when you're ready."

He seemed content that I was staying alert and I felt awful about him carrying me but I had to admit the physical closeness felt good.

"For a little bit up there I didn't know if I was going to make it out. It wasn't really a scary thing though, just a really tough puzzle to work out. Two nights out in the open. I was a little worried that a coyote or mountain lion would be drawn by the smell of the wound. I'm going to carry my 9mm from now on. This was too close and I could have avoided it, if I could have shot the dog."

The trailhead finally came into view and Rusty set me down. I looked at my Jeep and hopped towards it. My poor Jeep.

"Kelly said it looked like a bear had thrashed it but a bear didn't do this." I said, "Bears don't intentionally flatten all four tires. They might shred a canvas top but they get target fixation and go for food. Someone purposely did this just to be mean."

"We'll have to come back for it later. I want to get you to town."

"What about Kelly? We need to tell him we don't need the crutches anymore. If we don't call him he will take off down the trail looking for us."

"He'll see the Explorer is gone but I'll try to call him when we get to Wrightwood."

We stopped at a convenience store to call and Kelly swung by in his ranger truck and traded the crutches for Shadow. Rusty drove quickly to Joshua Hills.

The hospital was a nightmare. I was poked and prodded and asked a million questions. I must have told them a hundred times there was no way to recover the dog. Even if there was someone willing to hike to the top of the canyon, the dog had surely been found and devoured by scavenger animals. They wanted to start rabies shots and I assured them the dog seemed healthy, just starving and emaciated. They ran tests and it wasn't until the next morning that I was whisked into surgery for my "few stitches". I watched on a TV screen as they opened up the wound but I had to turn away once they started the more serious work. Someone gave me a shot and soon I drifted into a light sleep. I woke up in recovery, groggy, my leg heavily bandaged and elevated but feeling better. An IV still snaked from my arm, but all in all I felt pretty good. I sat up, shifted around to find the bed controls, and tried to get an idea of how much strength I had. I wanted to get out of this hospital as soon as I could so I could return to Creekside. I would have to put new tires on my jeep and drive it home where I could do some real work on it. I was mad at the people who had vandalized it and I was mad at people who turn pets loose in the woods to die. But mostly I just wanted to be doing something. After a while a nurse came in to draw blood and a little later I was moved into to a regular hospital room. I tried to argue against that but they said I couldn't be discharged without doctor's orders and they couldn't do anything about it.

"Besides," said the nurse, "If I had a guy like that waiting for me I'd *march myself* upstairs."

"They wouldn't let him in Recovery?"

"Only family members."

"But he *is* family, or at least the closest thing I've got." And I realized it was true. Rusty was more family than my real family. It shocked me a bit to think how far he had worked his way into my heart.

The nurse pushed in a wheelchair and raised the footrest. She hooked the IV to a pole on the side of it and helped me into the chair. I didn't feel like I needed any help, but it was her job and I let her do it.

"Can we swing by the waiting room?" I asked.

"Sure, anything to get to meet this guy. Where'd you pick him up?"

"Umm, I was carjacked. I don't recommend that way to meet guys though."

We swung by the waiting room and Rusty launched himself out of the chair.

"They won't let me go yet. I told them I was fine but they don't believe me," I said.

"The only thing they will believe are the results from your tests," the nurse said. "As soon as your tests say you can go home, they will boot you out the door. It won't be long. The way you're acting I bet the paperwork is just sitting on some busy doctor's desk waiting to be signed."

Rusty smiled, glad to see my old attitude showing through. The nurse sighed.

"So, where to?" Rusty asked, commandeering the wheelchair.

"Upstairs," the nurse answered.

We all crowded into the elevator and it whisked us upstairs. I hopped over to the bed and sat down.

"We gotta keep that foot up," the nurse advised, adjusting a sling over the bed. "You keep the foot up and cooperate and I bet you're out of here today."

The nurse was right. Late in the afternoon a doctor came in and ordered me to stay off my foot for a week. He gave me a large prescription for pain pills and antibiotics and I was discharged, with orders to visit my regular doctor in ten days to have the stitches removed.

At home I was determined to eat some real food. Four days of nothing but energy bars and hospital food had taken its toll and my weight had plummeted. I needed meat, fruit, vegetables and cheesecake. I headed for the kitchen only to be derailed by Rusty.

"Go sit down, you're supposed to stay off your foot for a week."

"I *am* off my foot. I just want to fix an early dinner and then I will relax. I haven't had any real food for a week."

"What have you been eating?"

"Backpacker meals to begin with but after the dog attacked me I only had a handful of trail mix until Kelly found me. Then I had a few energy bars. I only got a light breakfast and lunch at the hospital. So can't I just cook something easy? If it'll make you feel better I'll let you help."

I got out a package of steak and defrosted it in the microwave. I mixed up some five-minute marinade and put it in a casserole dish and added the steak to it when it was thawed out. I stabbed the marinade down into the steak and felt little stabs of pain go through my leg with the movements. I sat sideways on the couch while the steak marinated.

"What can I do?" Rusty asked.

"Look in the vegetable bins and see if anything survived the week. I bet I need to clean all that out, but it's worth a look."

He found a bunch of broccoli that had survived and it looked like enough for both of us so he cut that up and put it in a steamer pot. I had him measure out rice and water and start the rice cooker. I stabbed at the meat some more and we started the grill. Rusty played grill master and before long we had dinner on the table. It wasn't fancy but it felt good to be doing something normal together. It was comfortable. I didn't want him to leave.

"I see the wheels turning. You're not going anywhere tomorrow. Not to the grocery store, not to the Jeep, you're staying home and you're keeping your foot up and you're going to wait for me to bring breakfast."

I sighed. How did he know? I was planning to buy new tires and drive up to the Jeep and change them and then find Kelly's house and get Shadow back. I was just trying to work out how to fit four tires in a BMW Roadster when he'd interrupted my thoughts. How I'd drive the car with a bum leg was a puzzle, too.

"What am I supposed to do at home? Everything I have to do requires activity. I'm not a sitter. I have to be doing something."

"Tomorrow you're going to be a sitter anyway. You have to give the muscles a chance to heal or you'll just make things worse."

As it turned out I had to sit the next day anyway. After the pain medication from the hospital wore off I could barely move. When Rusty came in with breakfast he brought me a pain pill too. I didn't want it.

"Just enough to keep you functional," he said.

Over the next few days the pain eased and I slowly stopped using the crutches. I carefully drove the BMW around the block without any problems, so I went home to get dressed for the gym. I didn't have to walk much at the gym to use the machines, and I was tired of doing nothing. I left a note for Rusty, in case he came for lunch, and then took off. Things were looking up again.

Later in the day I was bored and puttering around the house when the doorbell rang. I looked through the peephole and then opened the door with a smile.

"Rusty called and said you were ready to take this critter back," Kelly said as I motioned him in.

Shadow raced through the doorway and leaped up, knocking me over. I sat on the floor and petted him while he danced around excitedly. When he had finished his greeting I said the magic word "outside" and he ran to the back door to check out the squirrel population. I slowly pulled myself up using my good leg and hobbled off to open the door.

"That dog is just about as normal as you are," Kelly said. "The first time I fed him I put the food down and he just sat there. I came back a half hour later and he was still sitting there, just looking at me. I thought something was wrong so I went over and talked to him. I was asking him if he was mixed up because you weren't there and told him it would all be okay. As soon as he heard the word 'okay' he went for the food."

"I should have told you that he's obedience trained. 'Okay' is his release word. When I feed him I put him in a sit/stay and he stays until I say 'okay'. I'm sorry you ended up with him all this time. I would have been up to get him but I just drove the car for the first time today. I thought Rusty might want to go Saturday to pick up Shadow and the Jeep. We took a look at it and I don't think a bear ransacked the Jeep. It was vandalized. All four tires are flat. It's been sitting there so long the tires are ruined so I'll have to replace them. At least I know how. I won't have to call a tow truck. I sure miss my Jeep."

"I can't believe you. You just spent five days out in the woods, almost got killed by a stray dog, almost died trying to hike out and now you want to go back *and work on your car*?"

"Yeah, I miss my car. It's a lot like I am. We see eye to eye. I feel bad leaving it behind all torn up like that." I paused. "Kelly, thanks for coming out there for me. You knew Rusty would be hiking in. You didn't have to go but you did anyway. And if you hadn't found me where you did I might have missed the trail. I was beginning to lose hope. I wasn't even looking at the ground anymore, just aiming for the next tree or rock, whatever small goal I could find. If I'd have passed the trail nobody would have known where to look."

"Hey, you gave and risked a lot more when you went after me. When Rusty called it was all I could do to stay on the line until he'd finished telling me where you were. We both knew if you'd been able to hike out the fourth day, you would have. I couldn't stand to think of you out there without the help you needed. Who knew what you had run into? I had to find out."

"Speaking of things I ran into, I met your mean old cousin."

"My mean old cousin?"

"Yeah, Mojave Green."

I told him about the shack and getting cornered by the snake. He was used to dealing with snakes in the campgrounds. Still, he looked on in surprise when I told him about it.

Saturday Rusty and I went to retrieve my Jeep. We stopped by a garage where I bought four new tires which were loaded into Rusty's blue Explorer. We drove up to Creekside Campground. I pulled a lug wrench from the Jeep and started loosening the lug nuts. Rusty just shook his head knowing better than to try and stop me. He went to the Explorer and pulled out his lug wrench and went to work on the other side. Rusty had three tires done by the time I got one loosened. I pushed and pulled and yanked on the wrench while he slowly gave each lug nut a steady, firm pull and it came loose. I limped and hopped my way around the Jeep. Rusty could tell this was wearing on me. I got out the jack, hoisted up the front of the Jeep, we changed the tires and then switched the jack to the rear. We changed the back tires and lowered the Jeep. I let Rusty tighten all the nuts to make sure they were really secure. While he worked I lifted the hood and poked around in the engine. Using an old paper towel I checked the oil. I dropped the hood shut and started removing the torn canvas top. I'd have to buy a new top and seat covers. It needed a good washing, too, but that was a little hard to do without a top on it. Oh well, a little dirt never hurt a Jeep Wrangler.

I drove the Jeep down from the mountains and parked it in its usual space in my driveway. Rusty followed me, concerned the shifting would give me problems. Guess he didn't know I'd driven the BMW already.

Moving the tires around and doing things at weird angles had forced me to use my leg in ways it wasn't used to yet. When I got home I curled up on the couch and put my foot up.

"You're not cooking dinner," Rusty said as he walked in the door. "I'll call in an order and we can eat in tonight."

We ended up having Chinese food and watched a baseball game on TV. The Dodgers had pulled ahead by a point when I fell asleep, still curled up on the couch. Rusty shook me gently after the ball game had ended.

"Hey, babe, wake up. Time for me to go home."

I didn't want him to go. Being together had felt so comfortable that I didn't want it to end. "Do you have to?"

He knelt by the couch and looked me in the eye, his eyes smiling but his manner serious. "Is this an invitation?"

"Yeah," I said reaching out to him, "this is an invitation."

Chapter 5

The night was amazing. I wasn't sure what to expect, inviting Rusty to spend the night, but I knew what the invitation could include. He'd spent the night at my house before but it was in the role of a protector; he'd slept in the guest room. This, however, was an invitation to join me for the night. Why I suddenly chose a night when I could hardly move I'll never understand, but he knew I was hurting and so it was a very caring and tender time. Although my leg begged for a pain pill, the rest of my body didn't want to be dulled to his touch. Pain and pleasure mingled in an odd combination that left me wonderfully and totally exhausted. During the night his arm drew me closer and I sleepily rejoiced in his touch.

Morning dawned and I went through my doggie duties, my leg screaming with every step. I was still tired so I climbed back in bed. Rusty stirred, pulling me close.

"I could hold you like this forever," he said.

"You could hold me other ways too. I could tell last night," I said playfully. "Just wait until I can move again. You haven't seen anything yet."

"What I see is amazing." He kissed me tenderly.

When hunger finally drove us to the kitchen I started limping badly again.

"Cass, we could have waited."

"Maybe, maybe it was just right. It felt right to me."

"Well, sit for now. I'll make breakfast. What do you have to cook?" He started poking around in the refrigerator, pulling out breakfast ingredients. "I'm not much of a cook but I can do breakfast."

I heard cupboard doors opening and closing. "Where's the cinnamon?"

"Left hand cupboard above the stove, second shelf up." What kind of a guy uses cinnamon for breakfast?

Dozing on the couch with my foot propped up on a pillow I listened to the sounds of cooking from the kitchen. It was soon followed by the noise of Rusty setting the table. By the time he came to get me for breakfast my leg felt better and I was able to walk again. He'd made French toast and even whipped up honey butter to go on top.

"I'm impressed," I said. "This is really good. I'll betcha a six-pack you can't do dinner."

He laughed, remembering the circumstances of how we'd first met. I had been the unfortunate victim of a carjacking and as a detective he'd arrived at my door to investigate the robbery that had sparked the carjacking. I was being held at gunpoint, though, and needed more time. I silently managed to communicate my plan and he returned later impersonating a neighbor. He had used the ploy of asking for instructions on how to prepare a dinner to impress his girlfriend. He said that she'd bet him a six-pack that he couldn't cook dinner. His actions had provided just enough time for me to stall the carjacker and then make my escape. Once the carjacking was over and I'd asked how his dinner turned out he confessed that he didn't have a girlfriend. I hadn't believed him and it was still hard to believe he wasn't taken yet. Every day I spent with him I was more and more thankful for that. If it took a carjacking and beating and getting shot at to meet Rusty Michaels it was worth every minute.

We ate a leisurely breakfast, showered and then got ready to start the day. I dressed in khaki shorts and a brown tank top, hoping to spend a quiet day out and about.

"Bad news, babe," he said seriously, "the station called. I've got another ATM case out in the foothills. They've got a team out there right now. A girl disappeared just this morning. She was making an ATM run in preparation for a road trip. Usually we don't take missing persons calls until they're a week old, but this one fit in with the pattern so they put out an all points bulletin and her car was found just a little while ago. I've got to get out there."

"Can I go too? If it's like last time I'll need a fresh trail. I'm always afraid the police are going to cover the tracks in all their investigating."

"No, this is too new. This guy could still be out there on site. We could run into trouble. Plus I know your leg hurts. I can't send you on a long hike in the desert when you can barely walk."

"I'll take my crutches. I'll stay off it as much as I can. And if there's nothing to track, I'll sit in the car out of the way. Did you get any details?"

"Small car. If the pattern holds true that's all we will find. But if not, there's a body out in those hills somewhere."

"I know it's not what you want to find but it makes my job easier. If there's a body he had to move it. If he dragged it or carried it, it would be harder for the guy to hide his tracks. If there was a struggle maybe I can piece it together for you and you can get a better idea of how this guy's mind works. If you need a tracker and the guy is out there, how are you going to find him?"

"Cass, I know how your mind works. Even if I took you out there and you promised to stay in the car you'd start putting things together and as soon as you figured out something to investigate you'd be out of that car and off on some wild goose chase. I can't take that chance. This is the best break we've gotten so far…"

"And it could amount to nothing if you can't follow this guy."

He turned away in frustration. He knew I was right, but he knew he was right, too.

"Okay, you can come. But you'll wait in the car until I say you can do something. Bring your crutches, but don't move from the car until I come get you. If I catch you outside the car or away from me I'll handcuff you to the steering wheel. And you'll need to change clothes. You'll only be a distraction to the guys in that outfit."

I changed into khaki hiking pants and a sand-colored t-shirt. Although I'd learned to not push the combat look around cops I still needed the ability to easily hide in tense situations. I fed Shadow just in case we'd be working all afternoon. Grabbing my crutches I followed Rusty out to the Explorer. We hightailed it for the station to pick up a car, and then drove, lights flashing, to the foothills of the mountains.

The scene at the victim's car left me doubting I'd find any tracks on site. Four squad cars, with their lights flashing, were positioned around the scene. Six uniformed officers were milling around. I recognized Landon Wilson. Rusty dashed off to get caught up on what they had found.

I waited in the car like a good girl. I got out when it became apparent there was no immediate danger; I limped around the car, then stood leaning against the side of it. When Landon noticed me he walked over. He glanced in the back of the car, taking note of my crutches lying on the seat.

"What happened to you?"

"Dog attack on a camping trip."

"If I'd have been there you wouldn't have gotten hurt."

"You wouldn't have been there. Because I went out alone."

"If I'd had a say you wouldn't go out alone."

I limped around the car again. I didn't need this.

"So, what're you doing here?" he asked.

"Staying out of trouble. I may get a little tracking in if Rusty will let me."

"Why do you let him run your life?"

"He doesn't. He's just a little over protective."

"That's why you're sitting here at the car waiting instead of out there where you belong?"

"I'm sitting here waiting because I don't have any authority to go looking around their crime scene… and so I don't get handcuffed to the steering wheel."

"And Michaels doesn't run your life."

"Right. I think he was just kidding about the handcuffs."

"Yeah, right."

"Landon, why are you trying to undermine Rusty? It won't work."

"Ah, I bet you wise up to him eventually. When that happens let me know."

"Why? So you can gloat?"

"Maybe a little. Mostly I'd just like to take you out and show you a thing or two." Rusty, help, I've got a Level 4 Situation here, I thought.

"You already have. It doesn't take a whole lot to show me a thing or two."

About then he figured he better back off and thankfully he made his exit.

"See ya around?"

"That mostly depends on Lou."

"Yeah, right, okay."

Unfortunately, now I saw Landon in a completely different light. He was proud and arrogant and he didn't mind stepping on others to get what he wanted. Was I rude to him? Maybe, but I felt I needed to be. I definitely didn't want to encourage him.

After a while Rusty jogged over. "Here," he said, "put this on. I want you to see something; I think we already know what happened but I want you to see what we are dealing with here."

He'd handed me a bulletproof vest.

"I can't take this. Someone else might need it."

"He won't need it. Victor and Landon are staying here. You're not going anywhere without it."

I put on the vest awkwardly. I didn't like it and I felt restricted in it but if it was the only way to move forward I'd do it.

I got out my crutches and made my way over to the car. I glanced around on the ground. It was difficult soil to read but, still, the message was clear. The girl had tried to bolt from the car. She'd slipped and scattered the fine gravel that covered the hard soil, leaving deep gouges in the dirt. In her haste to escape the girl slipped and scattered a wide swath of gravel. The killer had fired a handgun, bringing her down, then stomped off after his victim. He yanked her to her feet, leaving the drag marks plain to see. He'd then pushed the girl towards some bluffs a couple hundred yards away. From the tracks I read that she had fought but he'd only pushed harder. The desperation was clear in the girl's footprints. I knew what she was going through, and it made me feel sick inside. I turned away for a second, trying to clear my head.

"Rusty, have you followed this through? Do you know where it ends?"

"Only half of it."

"Do you want me to tell you what happened?"

"I think we pretty much know."

"Do you want me to finish this?"

"Come here," he said and started off towards the bluffs.

I crutched off after him, but gave up and jogged to catch up, carrying the crutches. He stopped and glanced back.

"Sorry," he said and slowed down.

This time the messages were spray painted on the rocks of the bluffs. The one that bothered me most said *I'm watching you.* I stood beside the message and looked around. There were several possible vantage points and a shiver went up my spine as I thought about the murderer sitting up in the rocks watching the grim scene below. Rusty had brought me up there before they removed the body from the shallow grave, but the police would soon begin their grizzly work.

"He's out there somewhere," I said. "Is this the first half of the trail that you know about?"

"Yup, it's the other half we aren't sure about."

"And?"

"Are you sure you want to try this? This is the freshest trail we've had. This is only hours old."

"I'll do anything I can, you know that."

"That's what I'm afraid of."

I looked for the tracks leading from the grave, trying to keep a distance from the scene. At first there were too many police tracks, so I widened my circle until I was left with a single trail of tracks leading away. I knelt and examined them carefully. So far, so good. They appeared to have been made by the same person we had tracked from the van. Different shoes, but the stride, height and weight looked about the same. These shoes were more like hiking boots, which meant we could be in for a long hike or rugged terrain. I'm always using clues in the tracks to look ahead and didn't like what I was seeing. Every time I read this guy's tracks he seemed very prepared for what he intended to do. He was a planner, had a calculating mind and was very dangerous.

At first it didn't appear as though he was trying to hide his trail. This gave me a general direction to follow and when the murderer went into stealth mode it was in an area where his choices were obvious. They were the same things I would use if I was walking in stealth mode so I looked where I would walk and slight clues verified his passage. Unfortunately the tracks ended at the bottom of a large rock. The rock went straight up a short ways and then curved over ending at the top of the bluffs. It wasn't a difficult climb but I didn't like the situation it put us in. I walked around the bottom of the rock looking for any indication that he may have taken another direction but didn't find one. With a groan I set aside my crutches and examined the rock face. Finding a handhold and foothold I started climbing up.

"Cass, no, you can't go there."

"It's where the tracks lead. I've got to see what's up top," I said, still climbing.

"Wait then."

He started climbing and as he drew even with me I continued up. My leg was not ready for rock climbing. Each time I put my weight on the bad leg the pain made me quickly search for a way to get off it. Nearing the top Rusty drew his weapon, ready in case of trouble. We inched over the top of the rock and I had just stood and begun casting around for new tracks when I heard a *thwap! thwap!* I just had time to see Rusty tumble down the rock and a jerk sent me to the bottom, too. I fell over backwards and did a back flip off the top of the rock, tumbling, tumbling until I reached the drop off and felt a sudden *thump* as I hit the dirt. No! I thought and I was on my feet, running, looking around for Rusty. He was laying very still several yards away from the bottom of the rock. Uniforms rushed past and Victor and Landon closed in. Victor began working on Rusty and Landon brought me up short when I tried to rush over. I struggled but he held tight.

"Let Victor work. He'll be okay. He was wearing a vest too. He's just stunned."

Maybe, but I was beyond stunned. I'd never seen Rusty like this. It was scary. Seemed like my list of scary things was growing by the day. But this was the worst. I'd rather do anything than see Rusty hurt. My heart was racing a mile a minute and I fought the urge to hit Landon and make a break. When Rusty started coming around, relief flooded me, but so did the urge to be with him. I struggled again. I didn't like being so close to Landon. I had felt safer with the rattlesnake. My place was with Rusty. He'd always been there for me and now this jerk was holding me back.

"Wilson, you let me go, *right now*, or they are going to have to arrest me for assault!" I cried.

Victor glanced towards us, ready to come split us up if there was a dispute. Landon laughed and that was a big mistake. I brought my good foot back and raked it down his shin and stomped on his instep. Then while he stood there shocked I whipped around, socked him in the jaw and quickly jumped away. I ran over to Rusty, forgetting about the pain from my leg. I could see his anger, even in his dazed condition.

"I'm sorry, Rusty, but I did warn him," I said apologetically.

It was Victor's turn to laugh. Landon stalked over and it looked like a power struggle was in the making. I stood ready for the face off. I didn't know what to do. This wasn't a power issue to me, but if it was to Landon, that forced my hand. I tried backing down without backing up.

"Look, I know you were just doing your job. You keep things running smoothly while Victor works. I understand that. But you can't do anything, not physically, not mentally, not verbally to pry Rusty and I apart or I will clean your clock. And don't think I can't. I'll give up working with the team if that's what it takes but I'm still hoping we can work together."

Unfortunately, I got the distinct impression that Landon enjoyed a challenge. I was willing to bet he was already plotting round two.

Rusty was looking better. He was sitting there shaking his head like he usually did when I surprised him in some way. That was a good sign. Victor and Landon figured their job was over and backed off. Victor was talking to Landon as they walked away to continue their work elsewhere.

"You scared me half to death!" I said. "I didn't know you were wearing a vest too!"

"You didn't tell me you were having trouble with Wilson."

"I wasn't until today. This is only the second time I've ever seen him. He works fast."

"Yeah, it usually takes three for four calls before he makes his move. Will you talk to me before you clean his clock?"

"I don't want you to get mixed up in this, but, yeah, I'll talk to you first."

More police cars were heading up the dirt road. This was going to become a very busy place. A helicopter could be heard in the distance.

Rusty looked at my vest. There was a neat little indentation in the upper right hand shoulder. Rusty had taken one square in the chest.

"It's a little ironic that this is Landon's vest," he said.

The hunt was on, but Rusty wasn't joining in and that bothered me.

"Are you sure, you're okay?" I asked. "I thought you'd be off trying to bring this guy in."

"I'm way behind now. If he's going to be caught someone in the front lines will do it. I should be down with the cars though, listening to the radio."

As we sat with the cars, listening to the radio, I could picture the killer's moves whenever I heard a snatch of communication I was able to understand. I pictured him in stealth mode, hiding behind trees and rocks, staying just out of sight from the police. I hoped they isolated the guy's truck before he reached it. I wanted him caught. Anybody who enjoyed terror like this guy did should be removed from the streets. When I read the tracks leading from the car to the bluffs I had felt his taunting and the power struggle between the girl and her killer. He liked the fact that this girl had fought back. He had enjoyed the struggle.

It had been a disappointing day. We'd been so close and yet there was still a killer on the loose. I arrived home drained. I fed Shadow and then took a long shower. Tomorrow would be a better day. But the struggle I'd read in the sand near the bluffs still bothered me.

Chapter 6

To get my mind off the murder I went out tracking the next day. It was a simple thing I wanted to do. The morning was pleasant and the hills were calling so I drove out into the desert. I did this frequently. I would drive out to a remote place, park the Jeep, find a trail of footprints, and follow it until I find the animal at the end. It was practice. It was a challenge to follow a track crossing the differing terrains that coyotes traveled through. I would track anything that left a trail: coyote, ground squirrel, snake... it didn't matter. That day it had been a coyote. I followed, eye to the ground studying and taking my time on my sore leg. Finally I spotted a tawny back behind some brush and I froze. Surely the coyote knew it was being followed. I didn't want to disturb the animal, but it was always tempting to see how close I could get. I crouched, hidden behind a bush and then silently stalked the animal until it grew impatient and ran off seeking other parts of the desert.

The day had turned blistering hot and when I got low on water I headed back to the Jeep. I drove along peacefully enjoying being out on my own when the road crossed an arroyo and I slowed a little too much in the soft sand. I kept my foot on the pedal trying to keep a steady pace through the sand, but the tires started spinning and the sand started flying. Shoot. I didn't want to get stuck out here. It was too hot to get stuck.

I stopped the Jeep and got out, sinking ankle deep in hot, soft sand. I surveyed my predicament. Okay, I thought, so far so good. It wasn't too deep yet. I got back in and put the Jeep in reverse, hoping a different direction would work better than just pushing forward. At first I thought it would work. The Jeep moved a little but then the sand started flying again. I rocked the Jeep back and forth trying to ease it out but each reverse just made it sink a little deeper into the sand. Time for Plan B. I got out my camp shovel and walked to the short, scrubby brush nearby. I planted the edge of the shovel against a branch and stomped down, severing it. I did this a dozen times before gathering up an armload of branches. I stuffed the branches beneath the tires of the Jeep hoping for more traction, but the branches couldn't get any more purchase on the ground than my tires had.

The arroyo felt like an oven. I could feel the heat burning up through the sand and into the thin soles of my moccasins. I used the camp shovel again trying to create a path for the Jeep to follow up and out of the sand. However, the more sand I shoveled away, the more sifted in until the Jeep was sitting in a hole. I tried driving out again hoping for the best. I started the engine and eased it into gear, then gave it a little gas. The Jeep eased forward a foot or two, only to bury itself once again. The more gas I gave it the faster it sank.

I looked at the road ahead and then down at my half full water bottle. Yup, right now it was half full, not half empty. No use getting all pessimistic about it. I needed to keep a positive attitude about my situation. So I pulled out my crutches, just in case, and set off walking down the dirt road. My leg was nagging at me and the temperature was hovering about a hundred and five degrees. It was going to be a long, hot walk to the road followed by another long, hot walk to a building. My best guess put me four miles from pavement. Maybe I could flag down a car from there. I didn't really want to hitch a ride but the temperature might make it necessary. This desert was a killer. One thing at a time, Cass, just hike this road. We'll worry about the next step when we get there.

I started out at a brisk walk and felt like I might be getting somewhere but pretty soon I was dragging. My leg hurt and the road looked endless. Just keep walking, I told myself. You can't stop. It isn't an option. The pavement is your only hope.

Ahead of me the heat waves blocked my view. It was all I could see, but I kept walking, feet dragging, and sweat dripping off of me, all the while taking the tiniest sips of water that seemed to do any good. I knew not to be too conservative. People had died with a full canteen, so I drank. Sparingly. Time dragged on as the desert inched by. It all looked the same. How could I judge my progress when everything looked the same? My leg finally drove me to try the crutches. The sore leg felt better with the crutches but progress became much slower.

With alarm I wondered if I might be going in the wrong direction. I glanced around nervously and saw mountains ahead over the heat waves. Okay, south, south is good.

I lost track of time. How long had I been out here? I tried to figure it out, keeping my mind busy, but I was having trouble focusing on any one thing. If I walked two miles an hour I'd reach pavement in two hours. Just one hour was too long to walk in this heat. Still, I'd been in worse predicaments than this. At least this time there weren't any land mines. Last time I'd done this I'd been overseas with the Marines. If I could pull that one off, surely I could do this, too. Of course, in Afghanistan I'd been better equipped. I'd had a hydration pack and a firm goal. The helmet, which I hated at the time, had helped too. I was hobbling along thinking and kicking myself royally when the highway appeared in the distance. Yes! I thought, goal one met!

Finally, I stood on the shoulder of the highway. Cars zipped past at seventy miles an hour. I wasn't yet desperate enough to hitchhike but I walked backwards hoping for a patrol car. This highway was heavily patrolled because it was a deadly section of road, so I held out some hope that a police car would come by. I walked and noted each car as it approached. Red car, nope. Heavily loaded Chevy truck, nope. The cars were never ending. And fast. Short breaks separated groups of cars and then I noticed a group of cars approaching decidedly slower than the other groups. Yes! Only one thing slowed traffic on this road. I stood on the shoulder of the road and waved my hands over my head, my nearly empty water bottle in one hand my crutches in the other. A black and white Ford Bronco with lights on top zipped by but pulled off after he passed me. I limped down the shoulder of the road as it backed towards me. The officer stopped and got out. He was young and sharp looking, proud to be doing his duty serving the public. And here I was, sorry looking Ms Public in person.

"Car trouble?" he asked.

"Yeah, you could say that," I replied. "More like dead tired and needing some water trouble."

"Wait a minute," he said, looking me up and down. Khaki T-shirt, camouflaged pants, moccasins. A layer of desert sand covering every inch of me. Short, blonde hair, blue eyes. "You're Rusty's girl. Aren't you?"

"Umm," I stammered. "I guess, but how would you know?"

"His screensaver. It's got your picture on it."

I was dumbfounded. His screensaver? "You're kidding," I said, wondering if I looked like this on the screensaver. Windblown hair, sunburned face, covered in dirt. Come to think of it, I looked like this more often than not.

"Ben Tomlin," he said extending his hand.

"Cassidy Callahan," I replied, shaking it.

"Hey, I picked up a celebrity! Did you know you're still talked about at the station from when you found Kelly Green? Where are you going?"

"Just the next watering hole or to Joshua Hills if you were heading back anyway."

"No problemo. Can't just drop Rusty's girl off anywhere or I'd be in deep shit. So," he said, "how'd you do it?"

"Do what?"

"I don't know. Rusty has just been different. He was serious and depressed for a long time and then something came to a head and when that was resolved he settled down and his temper evened out. He just seems different somehow. More at ease. I just thought maybe you had something to do with his turnaround."

"I don't know what you are talking about. I've seen him change a little bit over the past few months, but I haven't known him a long time. We met last spring."

"So, how much has he told you?"

"Told me? I don't think he's told me anything, the way you're thinking. Is there something I don't know?"

"Not if he hasn't told you."

Now that was curious. I had always wondered why Rusty wasn't attached yet, and then I wondered if he had some deep dark secret. I'd also wondered what made him so protective of me. Now here was this bait dangling in front of me but nothing was going to make Ben crack. Rusty would tell me when he was ready.

I gave Ben directions and he drove me home. As we pulled into my neighborhood I glanced warily down my street. Oh shoot! Rusty's blue Explorer was sitting in front of my house.

"Ben, can you skip over my street?" I asked, but it was too late. We'd been spotted.

"No way am I going to miss this!" he said cheerfully. He pulled up in front of my house and Rusty got out of his truck. He moved slowly and I wondered if he was still sore from his tumble down the rock.

"What did she do this time?" he asked Ben.

"I picked her up on the 138 walking down the road."

He looked at me, "Want to tell me about it?"

"My Jeep is stuck in an arroyo. I'll go back for it later."

"How stuck? Where?"

"Level 4 stuck. Very. Out in the middle of nowhere."

"How are you planning to unstick it?"

"Well, since you found out about it, I guess maybe you could pull it out. I was hoping to do it myself so you wouldn't add this to my list of stupid, dangerous stunts."

"Ben would have pulled it out. Why do you think he drives this thing?" I looked at the Bronco. It had a winch on the front and would have had the Jeep out in just a few minutes.

"I didn't want word of this to get back to the station, especially after Ben recognized me. So I just accepted a ride. I'll call a tow truck if you're busy."

"No, I'm off for the day. We can go get it."

"Thanks, Ben," I said. "Next time drop me off at the next watering hole."

He got back in his Bronco and drove away leaving me with a worried Rusty.

"What are you doing sitting out here in this heat?" I asked.

"I haven't been here long. What were you doing out in the middle of nowhere in this heat?"

"Tracking, and digging. And walking, and walking some more. Please, don't get angry, I didn't mean to get stuck."

"I never get angry with you. Worried sick, maybe, but never angry."

"Well, at least come in. I need something cold to drink and a little time under the cooler. Can I get you something?"

"I'll take whatever you are having."

"It's just ice water. It was a long, hot walk."

When Rusty saw my Jeep later in the day he just shook his head.

"How did you get it *that* stuck?"

"*You* can see what I did. I tried reverse first. Then I tried rocking it out. I tried sticking branches under the tires. Then I started digging it out but the sand went on forever and it just sank worse."

"How did you move all that dirt?"

I showed him the camp shovel.

"You've got to be kidding," he said.

"No, I used this. I've had a lot of experience digging with camp shovels. If it had been winter I'd have dug it out but the heat was too much. I had to stop. I had to choose between digging and walking and walking won out."

"You walked all that way, on that leg, with half a bottle of water, in the summer. Why didn't you call?"

"I don't like to worry you and I thought you'd be working."

"Cass, you were very lucky today. You can't rely on luck. One of these days it isn't going to come through for you and I'd rather be inconvenienced than have it be that one time."

He pulled a tow strap from the back of his Explorer and backed up to the edge of the arroyo. He latched the two vehicles together and slowly pulled the Jeep free of its sandy trap. I thought it was funny that he now carried a tow strap too. I knew he hadn't bought it for his own use. He never got stuck.

"I really need to buy a winch. Every time this happens I swear I'll buy a winch."

"Looking around, I don't think it would have helped this time."

I looked around too. No bushes more than knee high. Joshua trees off in the distance. No large rocks. I guess he was right.

Chapter 7

After pulling the Jeep out of the sand we were both hungry so we made plans to meet later for dinner. I went home to shower and change clothes. I wished I owned something a little more appropriate than jeans and a blouse but my closet only contained tracking clothes, jeans and one fancy dress. I was determined to go shopping and buy some better clothes, especially something Rusty would like. For now, jeans would have to do. I curled my hair, put on some make-up and placed my wallet in a real purse, then I met Rusty for steak. I never could eat a whole steak but I've never met a guy who didn't like a good steakhouse. The restaurant was pleasantly rustic and I could sprinkle on my own pepper, so I was happy.

"Your leg is almost healed. When do we get to try that race?" he asked, not really expecting an answer.

"What kind of race did you have in mind? A speed race, a distance race, or an endurance race?"

"Well, since the last time we were at the gym I thought we could just see who's able to finish a mile or two the quickest, but I don't think they would appreciate all the noise that goes with that so maybe we should rethink our plan."

"Are you chickening out?" I asked.

"No, we'll probably end up with a tougher race if we don't use the gym."

"We could race to the hideout," I suggested. "That would be two easy running miles and two endurance miles. Or we could just do laps of my neighborhood. Or we could pick a destination neither one of has tried before. There are lots of possibilities. If you really want to rough it we could race from Piney Point to Elk Meadows and have Kelly pick us up."

"Nope, I still cringe whenever I think of you on that trail."

"Rusty, a trail is a trail. Now that Peccati is out of commission it's as safe as any other trail in the forest. It has some challenging spots but mostly it's just a long hiking trail."

"The hideout is no fair. You know all the different ways up the canyon and I only know one that takes lots of rock climbing."

"We'll figure something out."

The next day I did something totally out of character and decided to go to the mall. My mother would have been proud, and I wished that she or my sister could have joined me but they lived miles away. I just needed cash for lunch and then I would be set. Pulling up to the bank I locked the Jeep, went to the ATM and inserted my card. After checking my balance I withdrew enough money for lunch at the mall. I took my card, cash and receipt and stuffed them in my wallet to sort out later.

When I got back to the Jeep, something felt wrong. I looked in the back seat. It would be kind of dumb to carjack this vehicle. No top. I wondered why I had bothered to lock it with the top off. Still, I felt uneasy so I looked first. I got in, turned the key and nothing happened. That was odd. It had been working fine a second ago. I got out of the Jeep and popped the hood. I looked around and saw a cable disconnected from my battery. Red flags waved furiously in my brain as a young man strolled up. I noticed his walk and more red flags waved. I looked at his shoes. Yikes. I couldn't be sure but maybe they matched the prints just outside the van door. I wished I could see the tread. I tried to notice if there were any blood spots on them.

"Need a jump?" he asked. Now why would he assume I needed a jump so quickly? A hundred things could go wrong with a car, especially one as beat up as mine.

"No," I replied, "I'll just call for road service. They will only be a minute."

I dug out my cell phone and brought up Rusty's cell phone number with a few clicks. He answered on the second ring.

"Hello?" he said in a distracted tone of voice.

"Hello," I said matter of factly. "This is Cassidy Callahan. I'm at the bank on the corner of Foster and Main and my car won't start. It worked fine when I got to the ATM machine and now suddenly it won't start. Can you send a guy out?" I pulled a business card from my wallet and gave a bogus account number. I pretended to correct him on the last three digits.

"Yes ma'am," he said, suddenly alert, "someone will be there shortly."

I pretended to hang up but I just slid the phone in my pocket so Rusty could hear the guy's voice if he spoke.

"Someone will be here soon. I don't think you have any reason to wait."

"It's okay," he said, "I'm in no hurry to go anywhere. You shouldn't go places alone. Too many kooks out there. No telling what could happen."

I looked at the man standing before me, taking mental notes about his appearance. Five ten, heavy set, blonde spiky hair, blue piercing eyes, freckles, rounded shoulders, worn work shirt and Dickies, work boots, maybe steel toed. He tended to slouch like he'd bent over many car engines in the past. I thought he probably knew a lot about cars. He could easily disable a car with just a loose cable or a pulled wire.

"Really," I said, "I'll be fine. They will figure out what went wrong and I'll be on my way in fifteen minutes. I'd rather find out what's wrong with it than just do a quick fix and get stranded again."

"Have you ever called this company before? They can take hours. You want to go in the coffee shop? We could get a cup of coffee while we wait. You can watch your car from the window."

"No, thanks," I replied, "I'll just wait here."

"You sure? I'll buy. It's pretty hot out here."

"I'm fine thanks. I just want to get on my way."

"Where are you going? I could give you a lift."

Over my dead body.

"I'm sure road service will be here soon."

When a police car suddenly pulled into the parking lot the guy became very agitated watching its movements. As the car approached he wandered off and lost himself in the busyness of the lot. The officer pulled up and got out of his car.

"Don't worry about my car. I'm more worried about the guy that pulled the battery cable off. Blue work shirt, black Dickies, heavy set, spiky blond hair, blue eyes, freckles. He wandered off that way when he saw you pull into the parking lot."

I pulled the cell phone out of my pocket. "You still there?"

"Yeah," he answered, "I'm just around the corner."

Rusty pulled up a minute later.

"I'm lucky I know a little about this case," I said as he got out of his car. "If I'd have gone along with him I'd be a goner. We need to go see the sketch artist."

He walked up to my car.

"Don't touch it," I said quickly. "He pulled the battery cable loose, then just set it there to look like it was connected. I got suspicious because he assumed before he looked at the engine that I'd need a jump. I know it's a common thing to go wrong with a car but he spoke just a little too soon."

"Are you sure?"

"I installed that battery, so I know a loose cable when I see one. I do a lot of work on my car. I check the oil, change brake pads, and rotate tires. I can do most of the basic car maintenance."

"Is there anything you don't do?"

"Yeah, skydiving. I gave up skydiving. It was a big letdown."

He wasn't laughing. He was thinking how close this could have been if it had in fact been the same guy. We drove around the parking lot looking for him but the guy had melted into the busyness of the shopping center.

Rusty drove me to the police station where I was introduced to the sketch artist, Takashi Hakuta. Using a computer program he brought up different facial features on the screen. I then told him how to adjust each feature until the picture looked like the man who had approached me.

"Angular jaw, okay that's close, add a few pounds to his weight. Blue eyes, nope, too round, make them more squinty. Not that squinty, more like piercing. Straight eyebrows, darker than his hair. Blonde spiky hair, might be bleached. Straight nose, no, longer, a little wider. Thin lips. Freckles, no not that much, even less. Okay. Rounded shoulders, dark blue work shirt."

We pieced the drawing together and when we were through the guy could have stepped out of the screen. It was creepy.

"Were you able to pick up any of the conversation after I pretended to hang up?"

"Yeah, that was pretty smart of you to keep the phone line open."

"I thought it couldn't hurt for you to be able to recognize his voice if you heard it again. It's funny how he wasn't so eager to help when the police car drove into the parking lot. He didn't even say goodbye." Rusty was being unusually quiet. "I think I'll drive the BMW for a while. The doors lock automatically and it's harder to break into. Anybody can get into the Jeep now that the top is off."

"That's a good idea. What are you up to today?"

"You wouldn't believe me if I told you."

"Uh oh, you want to give me the coordinates so I can just show up and pull you out when you're done?"

"Very funny, I'm going to the mall."

"Really? I've never known you to go there voluntarily. What's up?"

"Nothing! A girl doesn't have to have a reason to go to the mall!"

"But you do."

"Rusty! I'm just shopping! Is there something wrong with shopping?"

"No, I'm glad to see you going shopping. I hope you find something you like."

"Are they going to try and take the fingerprints off my Jeep? If so I'll need a lift back to my house."

"I'll give you a ride home and I'll make sure your Jeep is dropped off later."

"Thanks."

I walked into the mall totally lost. Rusty was right, I never went to the mall without a specific reason. And I had one this time, I just wasn't telling him what it was. It was even hard for me to admit to myself that I wanted to buy some pretty clothes.

I wandered around a department store, lost in a sea of fashion. I didn't know what I was looking for. I needed help. Suddenly a tall thin black woman with a store nametag stepped around a rack and greeted me.

"May I help you?" she asked.

"Yes!" I said, "I'm a fashion klutz and I need an outfit."

"Just my kind of a customer," she said enthusiastically. "What's the occasion?"

I blushed, I wasn't sure. I was embarrassed to admit I was shopping for Rusty.

"Oh, that kind of occasion!" she exclaimed.

"Yeah, that kind of occasion."

"Oh good for you! Anybody who dresses like you and is out shopping for date clothes is in love, girl! I tell you. You are sunk. Congratulations! Okay, here we go, we are going to find you *some clothes*!"

I followed her to the petite section of the store and was shown several dresses and pantsuits. She sent me into the dressing room admonishing me to try on everything.

"You never know when something unexpected is going to be just perfect so you don't want to miss it. If you need a different size just holler and Lavene will help you."

I found a room and tried on the dresses one by one. I was feeling totally foreign to this whole shopping experience. The dresses were pretty, though, and that was the problem. I wasn't used to pretty. After trying on each one I'd leave the dressing room to see how I looked in the big mirrors outside the rooms. Lavene commented over each dress.

"That's a definite no, it clashes with your skin tone. That one makes you look like a school teacher. You're not a school teacher, are you? Don't worry, this is a work in progress. Every dress you try on reveals to you something else about your taste and choices, but eventually we'll find something."

Sounds like tracking, I thought. Tracking down the elusive perfect dress. Some of them made me feel stiff, some made me feel dumpy, some were okay but just not the right thing. I was surprised how easily Lavene was willing to criticize the store merchandise. I thought she'd encourage me to buy anything. I tried on one thing after another until I was about to give up. I had several dresses on the *maybe* rack and many dresses on the *no way* rack, but no dresses on the *Yes!* rack. Lavene took away the dresses on the *no way* rack and came back with another armful. I groaned. I took the first one and tried it on and put it on the *no way* rack, but the next one was cute! It was a little white sundress with big colorful sunflowers all over it. It looked like a clear summer day and it felt like a breeze. It looked like something Skipper would wear. Maybe that was what I should watch for: *what would Skipper wear?* I was elated, though. Lavene was, too.

"Oh, girl," she said, "that dress is da bomb! That there is *your* dress."

I agreed. I had to get this dress. It was written in the Shopper's Law.

"Do you have any others that are the same style?"

We found two more, a blue one with romantic styled flowers and another summery one with colorful palm trees, beach chairs, and tropical drink pictures on it. It looked like a dress to wear on a Mexican cruise.

I didn't like admitting it, but I needed shoes too. I hated buying shoes but dresses called for shoes. All I had at home were tennis shoes, moccasins and hiking boots so I needed shoes as well. And I especially hated it because everybody expected me to buy heels and I never would. I paid for the three dresses and headed for the shoe department. I found some low-heeled shoes that matched the two summery dresses and made do with one pair. I walked out of the store a happy shopper. I had actually planned on buying some things to go with jeans, too, but I was all shopped out.

As I walked through the mall looking for the food court I passed the bank. Something caught my attention and I didn't like what I saw. As a tracker I tend to notice behavior patterns and although everyone seemed calm something was wrong. The fear in the teller's eyes spoke volumes. The man in front of her was glancing around, antsy and impatient.

Cass, it's just money, I thought. Don't you dare go after that guy. It's not worth it. But then the other half of me said it wasn't just money. It was some jerk who thought he could do whatever he wanted despite what was right. He was no different than that murderer we were trying to catch. Maybe I couldn't catch the murderer but I could catch this guy. I looked around. I seemed to be the only one outside the bank who could see what was going on.

I set my purchases over the back of a bench, and got ready for action. The man grabbed a bag, darted from the bank, and started running down the mall. I quickly took off after him. He was dodging and weaving while I closely followed in his wake, catching up quickly. Suddenly he was blocked by a group of people walking slowly from the opposite direction. I leaped for him and grabbed his ankles, tripping him up and sending him crashing to the marble floor. The group of people he had run into scattered, the women shrieking with fright. I hung on for dear life as he struggled to free his feet. Pulling a gun from his pocket, he took one look at me and hesitated, a sheepish expression crossing his face. Two security guards closed in, their pistols aimed and ready. They disarmed the robber, cuffed him and hauled him away. I got up, brushed myself off and did my best to disappear into the crowd. I returned to the bench to reclaim my purchases and then located the food court. It was hard to be hungry after the tenseness of the chase so I bought Chinese food to go and headed back home. I hoped Rusty wouldn't hear about this. I'd never live it down. I go to the mall shopping and end up involved in a bank robbery. I wondered if anybody would think to rob the bank there if I'd decided to stay home.

I entered my house, greeted Shadow and then plopped down on the couch. It hadn't been my favorite way to spend the day, but I was happy. I ate my Chinese food, saving half of it for lunch the next day.

That evening I got a call from Rusty.

"Turn on your TV," he said.

"I'd rather not," I replied, turning it on anyway.

Oh, no. There I was in all my black and white glory running down the mall and quickly tackling and "subduing" the bank robber. I'd been caught by the security cameras. Everybody wanted to know the identity of the mysterious shopper who was willing to chase down a bank robber. Shoot. It wasn't just that I'd been caught by Rusty. Now the bank, the mall, and half the city wanted to know who I was.

"Rusty, help! I don't want them to know that was me. What am I supposed to do?"

"How about you quit chasing down bank robbers?"

"I tried. I really tried to talk myself out of it but I just couldn't. I was the only one outside the bank who knew what was going on so I had an advantage when the guy left. I was on top of it."

"Cass, that guy was one second away from blowing your brains out!"

"No he wasn't. I saw him. He couldn't do it. If I'd have been a guy he would have, but he wouldn't shoot me."

"That's supposed to make me feel better?"

The story was replayed on the ten o'clock news and I watched it so I could know what to expect. I wasn't interested in my tackling of the bank robber but was more curious of the reactions from the other shoppers during the chase. This time I closely studied the background of the picture. It appeared that most of the people had just stepped back in shock. They seemed unaware of what had happened and were more irritated by the bank robber and me for running in the mall and being pushy. But one man was different. He hid behind a pillar watching the scene intently. My blood froze. Oh, man. I didn't want to see this. I really, really did not want to see this. I'd love to be blissfully unaware but there he was. I snatched up the phone and called Rusty. He answered on the fifth ring.

"Did I wake you up?" I asked, my voice heavy with tension.

"Barely, why?"

"We need to get our hands on those security tapes from the mall. I have to show you something."

"They're at the station. Why?"

"When can we look at them?"

"Cass, what are you so worried about? It has to be something important or you wouldn't have called this late and you wouldn't have brought up the tapes at all because you'd like me to forget about the robbery. So something is up."

"When can we look at them? I mean, right now? Could you get your hands on them right now?"

"I might be able to. It's not my case so I'd have to find the person in charge of it."

"What I have to show you doesn't have anything to do with the bank robbery. It applies to your case. Rusty, I really need to show you what I saw happening in those tapes."

"Okay, I'll meet you at the station but I can't promise anything this late."

Rusty's drive to the station was further than my own so I spent a few minutes getting ready before leaving. Shadow didn't like it when I left the house after he'd gone to bed but this time I didn't care. I was too shook up by the image on that tape.

Even after giving Rusty a head start to the station I was still the first one there. I sat waiting in my BMW in the parking lot until he strolled towards me. Getting out of the car I carefully looked around, examining both the parking lot and streets around the station. A few homeless people walked by and a police car cruised down the empty street but other than that the city looked particularly calm. I wished I could be that calm.

"Come on," I said rushing up the station steps. I dragged him to his office knowing he'd make me wait there while he tracked down the tapes.

"Cass, it would really help if you'd give me a hint here."

"I think the ATM guy was at the mall. I think he followed me there."

That got his attention. He left the room for a while and came back. Then he got on the phone. I was tempted but made a point not to listen. He took me to a viewing room and then disappeared again. When he came back he brought up a view of the area outside the bank on the screen.

"Can you find the segment that was on the news?" I asked.

"That was pieced together from two cameras. This one just shows you running. The other one shows you bringing the guy down."

"Well, start it. I only saw the guy for a second on TV and I couldn't stop the action. That's why I wanted to see it here."

He fast forwarded the tape and stopped at the scene where the guy exited the bank.

"Don't look at the robber or at me in these pictures. Look at the crowd behind the action."

"Okay…" He advanced the scene slowly and it showed me setting down my bags and moving into position, then the guy exiting the bank running to the right side of the screen, and me taking off after him. "Looks like you had good luck shopping," he said.

"Yeah, I always get more than I bargain for when I go shopping. Bank robbers, carjackers… Stop! Okay look at the guy behind this pillar," I said pointing. "Watch carefully in slow motion."

The guy peeked from behind the pillar and edged his way around it as my angle to him changed. He stepped out in the open as I ran off the screen and his side profile was clear.

"Stop it there. Do you have that composite sketch?"

He opened a folder and took it out. The resemblance was eerie.

"Start the tape again. Let's see what happens while I am off screen. I know what I did. This is the guy we need to watch."

The guy stuck close to the pillar and watched the scene unfold. There was no surprise in his actions. He was calculating, observing me. After a while I came back into view to retrieve my bags and he slipped behind the pillar again. As I searched the mall to find the food court he followed, hunched over, looking as if he'd been working on car engines too much, and walked with an odd rolling gait. He stayed at a distance and used barriers and planters in the mall to break up the view between us, then he disappeared off screen.

"Can you get the other tapes? If we can follow him to the parking lot maybe we can get a description of his car."

"I'll try. I'm more worried about you. He seems to be fixated on you for some reason."

"I wonder how long he was watching the investigation at the murder site the other day."

"The whole time."

"Do you think the guy who approached me when I went to the ATM was the same guy?"

"I sure hope not. But it'll be safer to assume that he is."

"How would he have known who I was or what car I drove?"

"If he was watching, he saw you tracking. All he'd have to do to identify you is look up 'tracker' in the local newspaper on the Internet and it would have told him your name. From there he could probably find out a lot more about you."

"He would have had to follow us from the bank, to the station and waited for us to do the sketch, then follow us to my house. If so, he saw that I switched cars and then he followed me to the mall. This is creepy."

"It's worse than creepy. It's extremely dangerous. I don't want you to stay at your house tonight. You're not going to the hideout. The mountains are out. That would be baiting him if you went out there. You need to disappear for a few days."

"If I'm not going home, or to the mountains, or to the ranch, what am I going to do? I really don't want to hide. I don't want to go to the ranch because I might be needed here. I want this guy caught and I want to help do it."

"You know you are always welcome to stay at my place. It would be out of sight. You could lay low and still be around."

"Rusty, I don't want to lay low. If it takes being visible to catch this guy I'll do it."

"No, you won't. You are *not* going to be his next victim. Even if we tailed you and closed in when he tried to take you, it would turn into a hostage situation. We are not going that route."

"Okay," I said, with obvious resignation. It wasn't that I didn't want to stay with Rusty, but more that I didn't want to have to sort out the living arrangements and the relationship changes that were involved in this. We were treading new ground here.

"It's late. Tomorrow we can try and get the rest of the security tapes from the mall and try and learn something from those. Let's go to your house and pick up the things you need. Shadow can come too. You'll be better off with him around. Are you okay with this?"

We drove to my house and I chose an armful of clothes and packed a small suitcase. I remembered to take the bags I still hadn't unpacked from the mall trip. Rusty put Shadow's crate and bin of dog food in the truck. I packed a leash. There would be no agility course at Rusty's house. My Jeep looked abandoned as we drove away.

It was one o'clock in the morning by the time we reached Rusty's house and we both felt beat. He only had one bedroom but he had a large couch. He didn't want to pressure me but it was awkward.

"Rusty, just let me crash on the couch tonight. We'll figure things out better in the morning. I'll be okay out here. Any place that isn't open ground would be great right now."

"You can have the bed. I don't mind the couch."

"No, I'm not going to kick you out of your own bed. I don't even need a blanket. I'll be fine."

He left me to crash out and so that's what I did, clothes and all. When I awoke in the morning there was a blanket over me and a pillow left where I could easily find it. I got up and took Shadow out then came back in and fell asleep again. Pretty soon Rusty came in and sat on the floor next to the couch.

"Hey babe, I'm off to work."

I opened my eyes. "Do you want breakfast? I can make something for you."

"Nah, I'll get something on the way, like I usually do. I want you to stay quiet today. If it's okay with you I'll take the BMW and I'll leave the keys to the Explorer. Take a look around and see if you need anything and we'll get it later. I don't want you to drive the BMW for a while. It is too recognizable. If you go out take the truck."

"Okay, I'll pick up some groceries and cook dinner tonight."

"Take care, call if you need anything."

"Okay." I got up and walked him to the door and waited while he drove away. I closed and locked the front door and turned around. Rusty's house. It didn't feel right for me to be here. I felt like I was intruding. I knew Rusty didn't feel that way, but I still felt like a foreigner here. He came to my house frequently but we never seemed to have a reason to come here. Part of that was because even Rusty didn't seem to spend much time here. I went to the kitchen to see what I had to work with. There wasn't much. It looked like Rusty didn't cook for himself. The counters were clean, the stove was clean, the refrigerator was clean. The only way a kitchen stays clean is if you don't go in it. Another odd thing: no dining room. No dining table. I looked at the floor plan and saw there was space for a dining room table but the living room took over the spot. A small bathroom was next to the stairs and I went in. No towels, no shampoo, a bar of soap on the sink. Everything clean and stark. I tiptoed up the stairs and looked in the bedroom. It was the only room where he had splurged. The bedroom was huge and a king sized bed filled one end of it. With Rusty everything was brown. Brown couch, brown bed. But it suited him. The room was masculine, tasteful and comfortable. Blackout curtains covered the windows and recessed lighting made the room glow without the glare of lights. The master bathroom was off the bedroom. It made me wonder what Rusty had in mind when he bought this place. There was a large glass shower, garden tub, double sinks, and brass fixtures. It didn't look like a bachelor's bathroom. It was luxurious. There was an office off a small hallway and it was much like his office at the station. A computer on a desk, stacks of folders, bare walls. I found extra towels in a closet in the hall. I decided showering in Rusty's bathroom felt intrusive so I showered and dressed in the little bathroom downstairs.

After my shower I padded around the condo in my bare feet, feeling very much a stranger. I looked out the back door. There was a small charcoal grill off in a corner and a tiny patch of green grass surrounded by a narrow flowerbed that didn't have any flowers in it. A condo sized yard just big enough to get a little sun.

I went to the grocery store and bought a few days worth of groceries. I bought fruit and colorful things to make the kitchen look lived in. I should have looked through Rusty's pots and pans before I left. I bought a Texas skillet because I doubted Rusty had one. I remembered to get a large bag of charcoal.

When I got back to the condo I unloaded the groceries and put them away. I started the chicken marinating in the sauce. I put the fruit in a bowl on the counter.

The phone rang but since it wasn't mine I didn't know if I should answer it. The ringing stopped and my cell phone rang.

"Hello?" I said.

"It's me, just checking to make sure you had lunch. You probably figured out I don't eat at home much."

"That's an understatement. I went to the store and got some groceries."

"You okay for lunch?"

"Yeah. When are you going to want dinner?"

"Six?"

"Okay, six is good."

I spent the day trying to determine what Rusty didn't have but may eventually need. He didn't have many kitchen items but on second thought I decided they were things that he didn't really need. They were just cooking essentials that I was used to using: a rice cooker, a junk drawer, cooking utensils. He had the bare necessities, but they all looked unused. Other things surprised me. His dishes had a flower pattern. His kitchen curtains were sunny and quaint. The kitchen towels had never been used and matched the curtains. Somehow I doubted he had chosen them. I felt as though I had been dropped into some stranger's house where I didn't belong. The day was full of surprises, but none of them were pleasant.

I started the grill and let the charcoal burn until there was a good bed of coals. I raised the grill so the chicken would cook slowly and then put on the meat. After making rice and steamed vegetables I cut up a salad. I turned around, ready to set the table, but there wasn't one so I set the coffee table instead. I was checking dinner cooking on the stove when I heard the front door open. I came around the kitchen wall to find Rusty quietly standing there.

"Just a second," he said quietly, then climbed the stairs quickly two at a time. I took up the chicken so it wouldn't burn, setting it on the counter. I waited, paced and then spent time looking through his bookshelf noting that none of the books looked read. Half an hour later Rusty was still upstairs.

I tiptoed up the steps to check on Rusty. I found him sitting on the bed with his back to the door.

"Rusty?" He was so still. I sensed walls going up. "Nope," I said, "don't do that. Can you tell me about it?"

He shook his head.

I sat down on the bed next to him.

"Did something happen at work?"

He shook his head no.

"Don't worry about it."

"I have to. Everything that affects you affects me."

A long pause.

"It's been a long, long time. I didn't know it would hit me like this... As soon as I could smell cooking in my house... I knew it was impossible..."

"Hey, it's okay. Whatever it is, it's okay."

Another long pause.

"Have you ever seen someone and when they turn around you thought they were going to be Jack?" Rusty asked.

"I used to. I know how it feels."

"Do I do that to you?"

"No, never. You and Jack are about as opposite as they come."

He stood and motioned for me to come to him. He wrapped me in a big hug and held on for a long time.

"I'm sorry if I did that to you," I said softly, "I didn't know."

Dinner was cold by the time we went downstairs but I warmed everything in the microwave. We sat on the living room floor and ate at the coffee table.

"I guess I could use a table and chairs," Rusty observed. "I had a set once but I gave them away when I stopped eating at home. I think I gave it to Kelly when he was first married. He and Rhonda didn't have much."

"Did you get those tapes from the mall?"

"Yeah, do you want to see them? We were able to follow the guy to his truck but we couldn't get a fix on the license plate. It was a big white pickup truck."

"Jacked up? Big mud tires?"

"Yeah."

"Sounds like the truck that forced me off the road on Mount Pacifico. Was there a clearer picture of him in the later tapes?"

"Not really. He was keeping out of site, avoiding the cameras, avoiding being spotted by you. If you hadn't chased that robber and distracted him he would have been almost invisible to the cameras. At least we have a vehicle to watch for. How was your day?"

"Boring. I hate being trapped inside. I went to the grocery store."

"The bank at the store didn't get robbed did it?"

"Very funny. No, it didn't."

I was a little worried when nighttime fell. I knew I'd end up sleeping in Rusty's room eventually, but now I was worried that I would trigger unwanted emotions. He sensed my hesitation so he guided me to the stairs. I couldn't help it; I stopped midway up the stairs.

"Cass, what is it?"

"I don't know, I guess I just need to know that I'm me again. I feel funny thinking I could be someone else to you up there."

His eyes smiled. "You are definitely you and I'm glad you're here. Every minute I spend with you chases the gloom away."

Even wrapped in his arms I felt the gloom I'd seen earlier. He didn't seem to feel it anymore but it hung over me now. I guess that was okay, I'd rather I have it than him and I knew it would fade.

"Something is still wrong," he observed. "Talk to me."

"I'm just trying to figure out what I can do here to make this easier for you. Would it be better to go out for dinner? Would keeping busy help? I could invite Kelly and Rhonda over."

"You can't go tiptoeing around my emotions. Remember when you went to the plane crash and you said we would just deal with the consequences?"

"Yeah, but that was me, this is you."

"No, it wasn't. It was both of us, in different ways."

I paused, thoughtful. "I guess I knew that. I still don't understand it, though."

"There's just a few things I need to deal with so we'll deal with them and we'll come through this."

"Okay. What do you want to do for dinner tomorrow?"

"I tell you what, I'll buy dinner but you have to do something as hard as cook it."

"What's that?"

"Wear what you bought at the mall."

I turned around to face him, "Okay, it's a deal."

He kissed me and I knew it was really me he was kissing.

The next day passed quickly. I went to get my hair trimmed, then bought hose, make up and a curling iron at a discount store. I thought it would be better to just buy what I needed rather than return home for them. I trusted my instincts and they told me not to go home alone.

In the afternoon I curled my hair, put on make-up and slipped into my new dress. I felt cute and feminine, and realized how weird being cute felt for me. I had time and I didn't want to get the dress wrinkled so I did things standing up. I put Shadow through some obedience exercises in the living room. I thought maybe I could teach him something new before Rusty came home so I heeled Shadow over to the stairs and put him in a sit/stay. I gave him a moment to focus and to become alert for a command. Then I called out, "Go UP! Shadow, go up!" He knew this command when he did the A-frame so I thought it might work for stairs. He looked at me. I went up a few steps. "Go UP!" I said. Shadow climbed the first few stairs. "Good boy! Good UP!" I said. "Go UP!" I encouraged him all the way to the top of the stairs and then we turned around. "Shadow, go DOWN!" I commanded. He trotted down the stairs. For some reason up had been easier than down on the A-frame. Maybe Shadow felt more in control on the stairs. We tried it again. "Shadow, go UP!" He went halfway and looked down at me. "Go UP! All the way UP!" He went to the top and I praised him, "Good boy! Good UP!" and he immediately ran down and jumped around. Okay, so we needed to work on the stay at the top. I stood at the bottom. "Go UP!" I said and started up the stairs. Shadow went up. He beat me to the top so I immediately commanded, "Shadow, stay." He paused. "Good boy! Good stay!" I had him hold the stay for a few seconds and then commanded, "Shadow, DOWN!" he ran to the bottom. "Shadow, sit!" He sat. "Okay!" I called, using his release word, "What a good boy, good dog!" He jumped around excitedly; glad to have done a good job.

Rusty came home earlier than I expected but this time he seemed to be in good spirits. Maybe the promise of a surprise waiting for him at home had helped. I had placed a yardstick between the coffee table and the couch and Shadow was jumping over it when Rusty walked in. Shadow rushed around the couch in greeting.

"You didn't plan on your house becoming an agility course," I said putting the yardstick away.

"Come here," he said holding out his hands to me. I blushed slightly at his look. I stood before him and he turned me around. The dress was suggestive in a cute sort of way. The back was cut low and with a tie across it. He traced the line, his finger sending shivers up my spine. The skirt swung around in a springy way when I moved.

"Do you like it?" he asked.

"Yeah, I like it."

"Me, too. I'm glad you decided to buy something like this."

We had a wonderful evening with no ghosts of the past hovering around.

The night was warm so we decided to dine at a restaurant with an outdoor patio. A band was playing and the atmosphere was festive. We didn't talk much; we simply listened, enjoying the activity of the restaurant. The festivity carried over after we left and I felt wired.

"You look like you're ready for that race we keep talking about."

"Not in this outfit, and it's too late. But I think my leg is better. I haven't even felt a twinge for a few days. I need to find out when the next academy is and start working up to it."

"It's in August."

"Yikes, I need to get busy. While we are out and about why don't we drop by my house? I'll pick up a few cooking things. It's amazing the number of little gadgets I assumed everybody had."

We pulled up to my house and went to the front door. I unlocked the door and Rusty went in first, hand on gun. I felt it, too, a sense that something was not quite right.

"Wait here," he said and went through each room. I stood at the open front door looking for the thing that had set off my mental alarm bells. I couldn't identify it, but it was definitely there.

"Look around," Rusty said when he returned. "Somebody has been here. Is anything missing?"

"There are two things people look for when they go through a house, valuables and information. I'll check those places first." I didn't have much in the way of valuables. I didn't keep stashes of money. I didn't wear expensive jewelry. I didn't even have a big TV or a fancy stereo system. I looked through my bills basket and pulled out a few that needed my attention. I looked in the filing cabinet. Things were awry but I couldn't tell what was missing. I checked the bedroom closet and the guns and ammo were missing. Well, at least now I knew for sure. My home had been violated.

"This looks like the work of the ATM guy," I said. "It has his name written all over it and everything that is missing fits my profile of him. The only things I can identify as missing are the guns and some vague papers that he might have wanted information from. I don't even know what the papers would be, but the file cabinet has been gone through. I bet he covered his tracks, too. I bet you won't find a fingerprint in the house."

"What about the garage?"

"I hope he did take some stuff from there. He's welcome to it. It's all stuff I haven't even unpacked and if I haven't unpacked it I bet I don't need it."

"Take a look anyway."

The garage had been searched too but I couldn't find anything missing.

Guess I don't lead a very interesting life to a murderer.

Rusty went outside to search my Jeep. I looked it over too: in the glove box, under the seats, the undercarriage, inside the fenders, under the hood, in the nooks and crannies of the body. One thing about a Jeep Wrangler, there were a lot of places to hide something. Rusty may have thought I was looking for something missing but I was checking for a tracking device. Somehow this guy had known where he could find me when I drove the Jeep. I wasn't planning to drive the Jeep soon, however I wasn't taking any chances.

I loaded some kitchen utensils and gadgets into one of the many boxes in my garage: rice cooker, mixer, blender, whisk, large mixing bowl, large cutting board, anything I used a lot but hadn't seen in Rusty's kitchen.

"I need to stop by the station and report those missing guns," Rusty said on the way out. "No telling when they will be put to use with this guy."

While Rusty was at work the next day I decided to pay the bills I had picked up from my house. I opened the first few, looked them over and then wrote out checks. I opened the third one and stopped in shock. Folded up in the envelope with the bill was a letter. A short letter, handwritten, to me. I didn't want to read it. There was only one person who could have left a letter for me in that basket and I didn't want to know what he had to say. I put the letter down, forgetting the unpaid bill, and started pacing around the house. I wanted to call Rusty but first I had to read the letter. I took a paper towel from the kitchen and used it to smooth out the paper and to avoid touching it with my bare hands. It read:

Cassidy Callahan, time to watch your back. Now it's your turn to be tracked. It's nice to find a challenge. I like a girl who uses her head. You got away once. You won't do it again. You got three strikes against you, helping the police is strike one and two. Eluding me is strike three. You're out. I want to make your police friends squirm so we'll have fun together. Lookin forward to it.

It wasn't dated but it had to have been left in the past two days. The two days I was at Rusty's house. I called Rusty's work number.

"Hey you," he said cheerfully, "what's up?"

"I've got something here you need to see."

I could feel the tension seeping through the telephone line.

"What is it?"

"It's a letter."

"Do you want to bring it down here or do you want me to come home?"

he asked.

"Were you watching for a tail last night?"

"Of course."

"And?"

"I couldn't see anyone. Traffic was light. It would be hard to stay out of sight last night."

"What car do I have here?"

"The Explorer, but don't leave. I'll be right there."

"No, Rusty, if he's watching for the BMW he'll follow you here. And I have reason to think he could be watching the station."

"I'll take an unmarked car."

He almost exploded through the front door, making me jump.

"How did you get this?" he asked brusquely.

"It was folded in with my bills. When we were at the house I picked up a few bills that needed to be paid. When I get bills in the mail I open them, take note of when they're due and drop them in a basket. So the bills are all open in there. He could easily add a letter to one of them knowing I'd be paying it before it came due. He could have even written it while he was at my house. It's just computer paper. It's written with the pens I like to use."

"The station got a letter, too. Yesterday."

"Well, at least he is doing things to make himself more visible. That's always a good sign on these cases, right?"

"I guess that's one way to look at it. It also means he's ready to act again and I don't like the sound of that."

He took the letter and went back to the station, admonishing me to stay home.

Chapter 8

Later in the day my cell phone rang. It was Lou Strickland.

"Cassidy, can you meet me at the station in half an hour? I've got a team forming to go out after a lost kid."

"Ummmm," I said, "I'd love to. Can you give me some facts? I'm kind of being stalked by a murderer right now and I'm hiding out."

He paused. "If anybody else said that I wouldn't believe them. What did you do this time?"

"Nothing much. I helped Rusty track this guy a couple of times and then he tried a dumbass trick to carjack me and I didn't let him. Now he's trying to send the police a message by threatening me."

"Stay by the phone. I'll call right back."

I hoped that he would call. I wanted to get out and do some tracking. Anything to get out of this house. I really wanted to find this kid. Although the searchers could probably find him, I would be able to locate him more easily and much more quickly. I wished Lou had given me some facts before he hung up. How old was the trail? Where was the search? The phone rang and I snatched it up.

"Hello?"

"Can I pick you up in half an hour?"

"Sure, you know where I am?"

"Yup."

"I'll be ready."

I looked through the clothes I had brought to Rusty's house and realized I didn't have any of my normal tracking clothes. I changed into old jeans, an old t-shirt and hiking boots. I looked around for a place where Rusty might have stored a day pack or camping gear but couldn't find anything before Lou knocked on the door.

"I don't have any gear here and I can't go home. Do you have any water? I'll be fine for the day if I just have water."

We stopped at a convenience store and I bought a six pack of water bottles and a box of granola bars. I stuffed a few bars in my pocket, just in case.

"Can you fill me in a little before we get there? How big is this search? Where are we going? How long has the kid been missing?"

"For right now, it's just you and me. Everybody else is at work and will join us after they get off. I've talked to Lansky and Wilson. They'll set up base camp when they get there so we can hit the trail. The kid disappeared yesterday. The parents weren't concerned until darkness hit and then they thought nobody would go look in the dark. Then they searched by themselves before calling in help.

"How old is the kid? Does he have any woods sense?"

"Eight and I doubt it. This is going to be tricky, not from a tracking standpoint, but because we have so little to work with."

"What do you mean?"

"You'll see when we get there."

"Where is our starting point?"

"Coon Creek."

That was good news. Coon Creek was next to a small lake. There were only two ways out of the area of the campground. Lou didn't act like it was good news, though. He sounded pessimistic.

We left the desert behind and started up into the junipers. Coon Creek was not up in the pines. It was a little dusty place nearly in the desert. I wondered why anybody would choose to camp there when Creekside was close by.

We pulled into the campground and Lou chose a camping spot two spaces down from a large RV.

"Have patience," he admonished me.

We got out of the car and walked over to the RV. There was a large group of Asian people gathered around the picnic table. More people walked into and out of the RV.

Lou greeted them and explained that we were there to find their son. We were met with only blank stares. A young woman stepped forward.

"You find boy?" she asked.

"Yes," I answered.

"You no find boy. Go back city."

"Mrs. Chang," Lou said, "This young lady is perfectly capable of finding Lee, if you will just do as she says."

She looked at me suspiciously.

"She no find Lee. You find Lee," she said to him.

"Okay," Lou replied. "I'll find Lee. Can you answer a few questions for me? How old is Lee?"

"Eight."

"How tall?"

"Small."

"How small?"

"Small, small, like small boy."

Now I could see what Lou meant. Not much information here.

"How much does he weigh?"

"Way?"

"How big?"

"Small."

"Shoes, ask her for a pair of his shoes." I whispered to Lou.

"Do you have a pair of Lee's shoes? Can we see them?"

"Shoes? Why you need shoes?"

"To find Lee we look at the ground. We see tracks. Tracks of Lee's shoes. We need to know what tracks to look for."

"You no look ground. You look for boy."

Okay, now my patience was wearing thin but I forced myself to stay calm.

"Please, Mrs. Chang, just show me a pair of Lee's shoes."

She shot us an irritated look and disappeared into the RV. She reappeared with a small pair of sandals. I took them from her and measured them against my hand so that if I found a footprint I would have a guide to go by. Lee *was* a small boy.

"Lee no wear shoes," Mrs. Chang said.

"You mean he was barefoot? In the woods?"

"Lee no wear shoes. Lee go lake. Like water. Lee like walk water."

"Clothes," I whispered.

"Can you describe Lee to us? What was he wearing when he disappeared?"

"Lee small boy, black hair, brown eye."

"And his clothes? What color?"

"Blue."

"And where did you last see him?"

"Here, camp."

"And where was he going?"

"Lake."

"When?"

"Lunch, yesterday."

Lou looked at me. It wasn't much to go on but I didn't know what else to try and pry out of them. Lou was right, this was going to be tricky. There were dozens of people in camp and most of them had gone to the lake. Many had gone to the lake barefoot. Many small kids had also gone to the lake barefoot. Where could I start?

"One more thing," I added, "Ask them about Lee's frame of mind when he left."

"Mrs. Chang, when Lee left yesterday, was he happy? Mad?"

"Lee always happy boy. He…what is word?"

Lou looked at me. Always happy? What was a tough word for always happy?

"Do you have a picture of Lee?" Lou asked.

"Yes, me have picture," she said smiling, "Me have many picture."

She disappeared into the RV again and brought out a billfold. She leafed through pages of photographs and then held one up.

"This Lee," she said tapping the picture. "And this."

We looked at the pictures and then exchanged glances. Lee was a Downs child. This search just took on a whole new meaning.

"Thank you, Mrs. Chang. We'll find Lee."

I walked away from camp shaking my head.

"What are we going to do? There are thousands of barefoot footprints at the lake. He could even be *in* the lake." I didn't like that thought. I looked at the ground, trying to get any kind of fix on the multitude of tracks I saw. Small barefoot prints were everywhere.

"You no look ground. You look boy!" We heard behind us.

"Okay, if you were a small boy at a lake, what would you do? I'd head for the water. Bad tracking there." We went down to the water and looked around. "Okay, now what? I'd either circle the lake or check out the creek coming into the lake. The reeds on the far side could have caught his attention. Let's circle the lake around the far side. There's too many prints to be of use on this side. After we circle the lake we'll examine the creek."

We walked around the lake while I examined every inch of ground. I measured several footprints but they were all too large. The area around the reeds showed no sign of small barefoot prints. We continued around the far side of the lake and the footprints faded out. Not many people ventured over this far. It was a small lake but the near side held more appeal. A small snake slithered past and I reached out and picked it up.

"Have you seen a small boy?" I asked it. Lou looked at me like I was nuts. "I'm just kidding," I said. "Can't hurt to ask."

"I've just never met anyone who would willingly pick up a wild snake before."

"It's harmless and it's just a baby. Guess you haven't talked to Rusty much recently. There's a snake story making the rounds of the station."

"I talked to him before I called you back. You knew that though."

"Yeah, I figured that's what you were doing."

"He thought you'd be better off out here than in town."

"He was right. I just wish I had something to go on here."

"What's this about a snake?"

"Oh, I had a tangle with a rattlesnake. I seem to be the subject of a lot of storytelling at the station."

We reached the creek and a trail. We followed it a short way and then the trail petered out. I examined the creek side in minute detail. I looked at the trail with a side view. Nothing looked odd. Nothing jumped out at me. Nothing even remotely looked like a small boy had played here. Or maybe it looked like a thousand little boys had played here. But none of them had *Lee* stamped on them. We followed the creek a little further but there was no sign of a small boy. The woods revealed nothing.

"Okay, sit down a second. I gotta think. The only thing we have to go on is that Lee liked the lake. Doesn't mean he went to the lake. It just means they thought he would have started out there. What did we see around camp that would draw the attention of a small boy?" I wracked my brain. This wasn't a camp I came to frequently. I mentally went through everything I remembered of the campground. "You think we should circle the campground? Maybe we can catch a trail leading out of it."

We started at the lake and chose a borderline around the campground where the land changed from campground dirt to wooded forest. This border would be the most likely place to pick up a trail. We began circling slowly and eventually something finally caught my eye, the tracks of a dog. A large dog, but domestic. I was guessing a very large Husky or a Samoyed. What was odd however was a faint drag mark next to the animal, like a stick being dragged along. I looked at the tracks and then at Lou.

"What?" he asked.

"Run back to the camp and ask the Changs if they have a large dog. If they do ask them if the dog would be with Lee."

He disappeared and I followed the dog's trail slowly into the woods. I didn't want to lose Lou but I had a hunch this dog had something to do with Lee. He came trotting back half an hour later.

"Bingo. It's an Akita, big dog, Lee loves it and it kind of watches out for him."

"So, we follow the dog. What is it with me and critters these days? Tigers and rattlesnakes and dogs. I hope this dog is nicer than the last one I ran into."

I focused on the tracks again. Animals are much harder to track than people. People are not careful when they walk in the woods. They are heavier and clumsy. Animals are lighter and move with an easy grace. People are predictable. Animals are more consistent but less predictable. I followed the dog as it wandered up the hill out of the campground traveling in a relatively straight line, which was helpful. After a short way the trail changed, turning into two trails. One set of tracks was the dog and the other was just a vague flattening of the grass. Lee was walking now. I knew there were dogs big enough to ride but I'd never seen one that could support a kid for any length of time. This was one huge dog.

I followed Lee's tracks, or rather the broken grass where Lee had walked, while keeping tabs on the dog's tracks too. Lee's trail was plain but it didn't reveal much. Usually a lost kid's tracks would show fear but Lee's tracks just ambled forward. He tended to waddle and drag his feet. I still wished he had worn shoes however I was grateful to have something to go on. The helpless feeling I'd felt in the presence of too many tracks and the total lack of tracks was gone. I could do this.

After about half a mile the dog's behavior started changing. He would circle around in front of Lee and I pictured the dog trying to push Lee to turn around. Lee would change direction but the adjustment in direction was small. He would grind his feet in frustration with the dog, then become distracted and wander off in a new direction.

Lou followed. I wasn't quite sure why he was on this job but I felt better with his presence. I got the feeling it was one of those "Can't let the girl go wandering in the woods alone" things but it may have been more than that, too. Maybe he was the search commander and right now this was all there was to command. Maybe it was a little of both.

The dog continued to prod Lee back in the direction of camp and I became determined to bring the dog back, too, whether he turned on us or not. Lee needed this dog.

"Lou, are you armed?"

"Of course, why?"

"If the dog gives us trouble, do your best to not shoot. Lee needs this dog. It's trying to steer him back to camp. If it acts aggressive we need to try and work with it. I sure wish I spoke their language. The dog may not understand English."

"First you talk to a snake. Now you're talking about the language the dog knows."

"Okay, so I knew the snake wouldn't answer. I was just thinking aloud. But the dog might know several key words if we just knew what they were. My dog knows at least ten commands and obeys them quickly. This dog is used to people. It must have good manners around people or they wouldn't tolerate him. So he must know some common commands."

We followed the tracks and it appeared Lee was tiring. I found flattened spots where it looked like he had sat for a time. This was good news. The more he sat the more we would gain on him. At one flattened spot I noticed he had broken off a branch and tried to eat it. He'd spit out the offending taste. It was a harmless plant but I hoped he wouldn't try anything poisonous.

Lou's radio crackled. I continued tracking as he talked to Landon, who had just arrived at the campground.

"We've got the trail covered," I heard him say. "You and Lansky stay at the camp in case we need medical help. If anybody else shows up, send them home."

"Lee hasn't had any water but he doesn't know how to find any." I observed. "We need to step up the search." I quickened my pace. I should have thought of this little twist earlier. Dehydration was a killer.

Lee toddled on while the dog continued with its effort to guide him back. I had to give this animal credit for being so patient. Then Lee's tracks disappeared again and I wasn't sure what to do. Was he riding the dog? I could follow the dog but I didn't want to leave Lee behind. The dog's tracks headed in a different direction than Lee's had been going. I circled the point where Lee's tracks vanished. He had definitely gone with the dog. I saw nothing to indicate otherwise. I followed the dog again. I was glad to note it was headed back toward the campground. It would stop and start and stop again. Something odd was happening. There was a battle of wills going on. In this case I trusted the dog more than I trusted Lee. The dog knew what lurked in the forest. It had sharper senses and instincts that protected it from predators. I hoped the dog was behaving this way because of Lee and not because of some danger.

I was relieved to find the single line of tracks ending in a flattened out spot next to a log. Lee had walked around a little in the small clearing but he was obviously either disoriented or coming to a decision. I pictured night falling and the boy trying to decide whether to press on or to sleep. I found the tell tale circling paw prints of the dog as it settled in next to Lee's flat spot. Our search was half over. Lee's progress the next day would be slower. I continued on. We had an hour or two of daylight and it was crucial that I find Lee tonight. Another night in the woods would be too much for the kid.

When Lee awoke the next day he didn't start moving quickly. It took him a while to leave the little clearing. The dog followed his actions and finally Lee chose a direction, the dog again nudging him towards camp. The boy ground his feet with frustration and took off running away from the dog. The dog again followed easily, falling in beside Lee. I tracked this battle of wills around a hill and then we finally spotted them, Lee sitting on the ground, his head resting on the side of his large protector, the dog sitting there patiently being used as a prop. When we came into view the dog rose and the child almost fell over. Lou rushed forward. The dog gave a low growl.

"I'll take care of the dog," I said. I wanted to save this animal. It deserved all the rewards it could get. I approached the dog and it checked me out head down, ears back. It was a beautiful white dog with large black and brown patches, thick fur, straight ears and that alert Akita look. The animal's tail curled over its back but wasn't wagging. It was a *huge* dog and probably weighed more than I did. I held out my hand so he could sniff it. I stalked it in a friendly way, waiting until it was ready to accept the next step. When I stood directly in front of him, he gave another low threatening growl, then took a step forward ready for action.

"It's okay boy. We're friends. Come on. Let me touch you. Come on. Just a pat." I reached out and set my hand on his massive head. I gave the dog a scratch and made the final step closer, then petted it with both hands. Lou came forward and the dog stepped between him and the boy.

"Hey, pooch, it's okay." I grabbed the dog's collar and tried to pull it away but the dog weighed as much as I did and appeared determined to stay put. "Lou, let me try something." I stood in front of the dog and in a firm voice said, "Dog, SIT!" I used the universal *sit* motion with my hand. The dog looked at me. A slight recognition crossed its face. The words were wrong but the motion was clear. "Dog, SIT!" I repeated.

Lee said something in another language and the dog sat.

"Dog, DOWN!" I commanded using the *down* signal.

Lee said another command that sounded like gibberish to me but the dog laid down.

I crossed the clearing and faced the dog. "Dog COME!" I commanded.

Lee repeated the command for me. The dog rose, walked in front of Lee and then sat down. "Dog COME!" I called again.

Lee repeated the command in his foreign language. This time I caught the basic sounds and repeated them in a commanding tone. The dog took a few steps in my direction.

"Good dog!" I called out. "Good come!" I encouraged him to come to me until he no longer blocked Lou's path. I then put my hands through the dog's collar, petting and praising him while still holding on firmly. I caught sight of my arm, still bearing the tooth marks from my last canine encounter. Lou knelt down next to Lee to check him out. This really was a small, small boy. I doubted he was much bigger than Patrick, my four-year-old nephew. Lou removed a new water bottle from his pack and handed it to Lee who drank eagerly. He then handed Lee some granola bars which he ate happily. Lou picked the small boy up while I tested the dog, ready to grab hold again should the dog lunge. Since Lee was happy with these strangers the dog accepted us and followed us back to camp. Lou got on the radio to update Landon who then called in an ambulance. The young boy appeared to be fine but he had gone too long without water and would need fluids. As we hiked along, Lee chattered away in his foreign language, unconcerned that we didn't understand him. We walked into camp and were greeted to an enthusiastic welcome. The family all surrounded Lou chanting, "You find

Lee! You find Lee!" I backed off and was immediately sorry because I nearly backed into Landon.

"Nice work," he said. "Makes me want to get lost in the woods. Would you come find me?"

"I've tracked murderers and found mean old snakes so I guess I'd track you, too, if you really needed it." I said it jokingly, but really meant what I said.

"Oh, I'll be sure to need it bad," he said with a pained voice.

Yeah, right, I thought.

I was glad to let Lou be the hero of the day but I felt like a skunk. Why was it I couldn't be nice to Landon, no matter what? I enjoyed watching Landon explain to Mrs. Chang why Lee needed to go to the hospital. And I was glad when Lou and I were finally able to head for home.

Lou dropped me off at Rusty's house, no questions asked, and waited for me to get in the door before taking off.

"Hey, babe, guess you found your man again?" Rusty said as I entered.

"I sure did," I replied, smiling. He was standing right in front of me.

Chapter 9

We spoke over dinner that evening.

"This latest search convinced me I need a little camping gear handy in case Lou calls again. I was lucky this time. The search was short but if it had gone into a second day I would have needed more gear. I should keep both backpacks handy and full of gear so I will be ready for anything. I better carry a few days worth of food, water, and the stove and matches, and probably just bring whatever the guys would pack. If I have to go out tracking with them, they will have trouble letting me sleep out in the open when they have a tent and sleeping bag. I might be used to sleeping out in the open but they never seem to see that as a good thing. Can we go to my house and pack up some gear?"

He seemed amused by my observations. "Sure. Tell me about the search."

I told him all about it, leaving out any references to Landon. It made a decent story, but nothing bad had happened. What I really wanted Rusty to understand was that problems were not a constant in my life. Sometimes my life was almost normal.

After dinner we left to pick up the camping supplies. As we pulled up to my house my heart fell as I stared in amazement at what I saw. Spray painted across my Jeep was, "You can run but you cannot hide."

"My poor Jeep," I lamented. First it had been thrashed, then neglected and now spray painted. Despite the warning I felt sorrier for the Jeep than for myself.

There was a bullet hole through the front door of my home, obviously another warning.

After Rusty checked the house, I packed my camping gear, an armful of clothes and grabbed the rest of the bills from the basket. Then I picked up the mail from my mailbox down the street.

"Let's ask your neighbors if there has been any odd activity around your house," Rusty said.

We went next door. Dirk Sykes didn't even wait for me to speak. He was mad. "Cassidy, you've got to do something about these kooks around here. Spray painting your car, shooting at your house!"

"Did you hear the shot?" I asked. "When was it?"

"I didn't hear the shot. I saw the guy do it but I couldn't hear it. I called the cops but he was gone by the time they got here."

"You could see the guy shoot but you couldn't hear it?"

"Yeah, the TV was on and I was just closing the curtains last night before going to bed when I saw him. Must have been around eleven o'clock. Just stood on your sidewalk, aimed once and pulled the trigger. I was relieved you weren't home at the time."

"Have you seen any strange cars or trucks on the street lately?"

"Just the maniac who shot at your house. Sometimes his white truck is parked on Joshua where he can watch your place."

"Thanks for telling me. Sorry to bother you so late. If you see the guy or his truck again don't approach him, just call the police. He's wanted for murder and he's very dangerous. Can you spread the word to the other neighbors too?"

Rusty handed him several cards to pass around and said, "Please call me if you see anything."

As we drove back to Rusty's house he calmly noted, "We've got a tail." He got on his cell phone and continued driving normally but changed his route. I could see him watching the other car's moves, trying to catch the guy's license plate number. I watched in the rear view mirror but it wasn't set right and I didn't want to turn around and gawk. I figured that would put me in line for a bullet and I'd had my share of being shot at. Pretty soon a cruiser pulled in and the car vanished. Rusty continued home, his mood grim.

At Rusty's house I unloaded the backpacks and distributed the supplies between the two packs. I needed more backpacker food. I wanted to pack light for tracking. The necessity of packing a tent and sleeping bag was a pain. I decided to go to the sporting goods store the next day to see if there was a smaller tent available. Wearing the big pack with the tent and sleeping bag attached was bulky and it always took me time to adjust to moving right in it. If I could limit the bulk I'd be able to pack it better.

The store was busy the next day when I arrived. Taking my time I studied all the tent choices and read the boxes, noting weights and pack sizes. Although tents had improved a lot over the years, I doubted I could find one I liked better than my old one. I needed one more packable though, and decided to look for backpacker food while I mulled over my tent choices. When I returned to the tents a bearded man was looking at the display. He was dressed in khaki pants, black boots and a weather beaten camouflage jacket. I chose the tent I wanted and headed for the checkout counter. The man, in a nonchalant manner, started following me. Although not taking the same path as I did, he was obviously closing in on the same place. He inconspicuously made a point of keeping track of my movements. I looked around the store, weighing my options. Losing this guy in the store was going to be impossible because there were mirrors encircling the top of the room. He'd spot me anywhere. Anywhere, I thought, except the dressing rooms. At the clothing racks I chose several items I might buy and took them to the dressing room, leaving the backpacker food and tent outside the door. To prevent being overheard I entered the last dressing room and pulled out my cell phone. I then scrolled down to Rusty's number and hit the call button. The curtain was thrust aside.

"When you try to escape, try choosing a women's only dressing room. That might help."

I hid the phone. The man was blocking the doorway and the room was small. Behind the beard I could make out the face of the ATM murderer. What did he have under that jacket?

I didn't think he would kill me here. His goal was to make the police squirm so he wanted to take me alive. I heard Rusty answer his phone but I covered the speaker. I had to get some information across without using the phone.

"Who are you?" I said loudly.

"Like I'm really going to tell you that. You know enough who I am."

"Aren't you supposed to be lurking outside banks, watching ATMs? What made you come after me, here, at GearUp! 4 Adventure?"

"I don't care where I pick up my victims. I came after you because I like you. You think like I do. Now, I want you to walk out of this store and get in your car."

"No. If you thought like I did, you'd know I wouldn't cooperate with you."

"No? You think you will leave this place alive if you refuse?"

"You're not going to kill me here. It would cause a scene and you'd get caught. You can't intimidate me with fear. All I have to do is stay put and you can't do a thing."

"There's lots of things I can do without killing you. There's plenty of things that I can do quietly. Besides, this place is as good as any for a standoff. I don't really expect to get out of this alive but I wanted to take you with me. Teach the police a little lesson. How about you? You want to help me teach the police a little lesson?" He stepped into the dressing room and pulled the curtain.

"You're nuts," I said. "I hope you don't die because you need to be locked up for a long, long time. Some *families* need to see you locked up and I am going to see that happen."

Okay, Cass, I thought, you're going to have to make a scene, big time, and now's the time to do it. I slipped the phone into my pocket. I set down the clothes and looked around. I tried to remember what lay beyond the dressing rooms. This guy was a lot bigger than me but I was building up enough adrenaline to make up for that. I readied myself and launched myself at him sending him staggering through the doorway. The curtain ripped as he fell through it. I squeezed past and looked for a door or opening. Anything but the main showroom. Preferably not a break room full of employees. He grabbed me from behind and put an arm around my neck. He started dragging me into the dressing room again. I fought and squirmed, doing anything I could to make things more difficult for him. I punched at his face but the angle was wrong and the hits were ineffectual. I tried to elbow him in the side but he held on to me too tightly. He let go of my neck and spun me around to face him. He was smiling so I socked him right in the middle of that smile and threw another punch into his stomach. I had to get past him. Surely someone outside the dressing rooms could hear a scuffle. Someone should be showing up any second. I jumped up on the bench at the back of the room and aimed a kick at his head. He jumped aside but I followed the kick past him and dashed out of the opening. He grabbed at me as I passed him but he only caught some fabric and I yanked it loose. I dashed through a random, unlabeled door, yanking it shut behind me, and ran smack into the back of a closet. Mops and cleaning supplies came clattering down around my feet. SHIT! I turned around and grabbed the door handle. He yanked on the other side of the door while I pulled with all my might. A stab of light appeared in the door. What the heck!? Realization dawned and I hit the floor. I heard scuffling outside and the door started to open. I lunged, pulling it closed again.

"Open up! Security!" a voice bellowed.

"Prove it!" I yelled back.

There were several voices talking behind the security guard but I couldn't understand what they were saying. The guard slid a badge under the door. I couldn't see it in the dark but I felt it. I opened the door cautiously.

"Follow me, please," he said brusquely.

"Where's the guy who was after me?" I asked nervously.

"After you? He said you were after him."

"Do I look like I would be trying to gun *him* down? Look at the bullet hole! It was shot from the *outside* of the door. I was on the inside trying not to get killed. I hope you didn't let him get away."

They hustled me towards the manager's office and as we came out from the back several uniformed officers marched through the store's front door. A couple of them grinned at me in recognition.

"Big white monster truck! Use the same description, except add a beard."

I called in their direction. Rusty burst through them as he hurried into the store. He pushed his way through the onlookers flipping his phone closed and followed the parade to the manager's office. We entered the office, they closed the door, and I rounded on them. I couldn't help it. I was mad.

"You let a guy armed with a silenced handgun loose because he claimed some *lady* trapped in a closet was trying to kill him? How was I supposed to kill him being shot at in a closet?! Did it ever occur to you that women usually don't stalk men into dressing rooms? If we're going to kill someone it is *not* going to be on a shopping trip. We might be smart enough to choose our own territory to do our battles, but you don't have to worry about us shooting up your store!"

Rusty went in scared and angry but he couldn't help turning around so the manager and security guard wouldn't see him laugh at me.

The manager looked at the security guard.

"Why did the police turn around and leave?"

"Because the police are right here," I said, "And they know that guy is after me so they went looking for him."

"Miss Callahan, why don't you let me take care of this?" Rusty said, humor mixing with general weariness. "Finish your shopping and I'll get in touch with you later." I understood the formality but it still caught me by surprise.

I left the office debating whether to go to another place for the tent and backpacker food but decided in the end not to boycott every place I'd been attacked in. Pretty soon I wouldn't be able to shop in town. Plus, if I didn't buy it now I'd be leaving myself open while I went to another store.

Another problem was not being sure I should even leave. What if the guy was out there waiting for me? I looked outside the front windows for the white truck. He could be anywhere by now and I couldn't bring myself to drive home because I thought I'd be followed. I had to assume he'd followed me to the store, but how had he known?

I paid for my supplies then sat on a fold up chair in the entryway waiting for Rusty to come out. I watched for white trucks. Waiting was bad news though because waiting meant thinking and thinking usually got me into trouble. I was glad Rusty came out before I'd talked myself into anything drastic.

"I'm sorry," I said quickly as he came out the door. "I tried calling to tell you he was at GearUp! and that I was being followed, but then he surprised me and I couldn't talk without tipping him off."

He picked up my bags and I followed him to the car.

"How did he know you were here?"

"I don't know. I assume he must have followed me but he isn't supposed to know about the Explorer. I guess he could have just happened to be here."

"The car that followed us last night was just a kid paid to watch your house in an inconspicuous car."

I thought about what that might mean. "So he knows about the Explorer. And he knows I'm not coming home often or alone. At least he doesn't know where your house is. But I sure am feeling trapped right now. Every little piece he puts together traps me a little bit more."

"Cass... hearing you get attacked like that...each little noise that came through the phone gave me a ray of hope and a stab of fear. It meant you were still there, maybe. I never knew if the last noise I heard would really be the last or who made it. Silenced or not, I heard the shot. I knew that sound and I heard it come through the door at you."

We drove home and he waited until we were in the condo to pull me to him in what I now understood was a physical reaction to his fear. He needed to feel me close and know that I was whole. His big bear hugs were a comfort to me, too. His protective embrace left me feeling like I was treasured above all else to him. It encircled me from head to toe, his chin always resting on the top of my head. Whenever he had been working it meant I'd get lost in the folds of his sports coat, always soft, well worn, and smelling softly of him. I always wondered how he looked so sharp in his old worn sports coats and how he found so many different brown ones. These were precious times. We'd won a few more moments again. It was all we could count on sometimes and it made them valuable to us.

He released me reluctantly. "I have to get back to work."

"Okay."

"Will you stay home?"

"I think that's a good idea right now."

Rusty kissed me goodbye, a deep, tender kiss. He then looked at me oddly as he walked out the door, returning to the police car.

A moment later he was back. He went upstairs and changed into jeans and a soft camp shirt. "What were you going to do with the rest of the day?" he asked.

"I was going to load up the packs, take out the tent and set it up. I don't want to do it for the first time on a search. I need to know how to do it by myself so I don't look like a dunce. And I was going to cook dinner. A big, exciting afternoon. Why, what do you want to do?"

"Nothing, but that comes close enough."

"I thought you had to work."

"I changed my mind. I decided there were better things to do this afternoon."

We set the tent up on his tiny plot of grass and then lay inside talking.

Shadow poked his head in and walked around the tent wanting to play. I chased him around it a few times but the yard was too small to really play. Rusty watched, relaxing in the sun. We cooked dinner together and then ate at the coffee table. Stolen moments of peace in a time of trouble. How long would it last?

Chapter 10

It was time for some serious training and if academy started in August there wasn't much time. I wanted to improve my endurance. After my little scuffle at GearUp! I figured I could work on my arm strength. I used to be in pretty good shape when I had access to a punching bag but I didn't have one now. I suggested a trip to the gym and Rusty took me up on it. I'd have to deal with the jealous glares of all the women and silently gloat while they watched Rusty.

"Are you ready for our race?" he asked.

"To be honest, I doubt I could beat you unless we were out in the woods. You'd race me into the ground at the gym. But I'm willing to be beat if you want to try. I need something to shoot for."

All the women's faces lit up with interest when we walked into the gym. We headed for the treadmills. To keep this a peaceful competition and not jar the ears of the other members we started at a light jog. Each time I felt comfortable with my pace I upped it a couple of notches. Rusty upped his until he was comfortable, too. We continued until we were both sprinting, but not pounding the machines. We'd both put in two miles when I glanced at him. No sweat. I figured I could at *least* make him break a sweat. That was my goal; just give him a run for his money. I upped my machine and sprinted away. I upped it again, glad I had taught myself how to move quietly. Even when running as fast as I could, my feet landed softly. Mile three went by and glancing towards Rusty I realized he was smiling as he ran. I set my mind on the track at my parent's house. I'd used that track to train once after an accident. It was made for racing horses and I had run the sandy middle part of it to get in shape again. When Rusty came to visit me at the ranch, unbeknownst to me, he had watched me run, pleased to see me recovering. It was like that now. He was enjoying watching me push. He didn't care if he won or lost. He was just there to help me improve. Mile four went by. Generally when coming to the gym I jogged four miles. I thought my ultimate goal should be about ten miles. If I could jog ten miles I'd feel like I was ready for academy. If I could sprint part of that, so much the better. I never knew when I'd be chased by homicidal lunatics nor what a homicidal lunatic was prepared for. My mind had run ahead of my feet and I hadn't paid attention to the machine. I'd been thinking.

"Cass…Cassidy, you better quit, slow down."

I hit the slow button several times and almost overshot the machine. I'd lost focus. I set it to a slow sprint and regained my breath.

"Why?" I asked.

"I'm not chasing you with a gun. We're just running. Relax."

I looked at the machine and the numbers spun around. I grabbed the bars next to the belt and pushed up bringing my feet off the belt. I found the sides of the machine with my feet and hit stop. I stood for a second, waiting for the room to stop spinning.

"How far did you go?" I asked.

He hit the reset button and his screen blanked out and came up all zeros.

"It doesn't matter. How far did you go?"

"Five point six."

"And how far do you normally go?"

"Four, but I stop for a different reason."

"Then you won."

"You skunk, how far did you go?"

He smiled. He wasn't going to say.

"Why do you usually stop at four?"

I paused, letting my breathing settle down.

"Because if I do too much I waste away to nothing. I figure four miles is a nice round figure. But if I have to do more for academy then I'll do it. You should have seen me in boot camp. When I put on camouflage gear, a backpack, helmet and rifle all you could see were my eyes. We'd go on ten mile hikes with forty pound packs and eat MREs and I'd get thinner and thinner. I expect academy to take its toll but I'll bounce back and once I put on a little weight again I'll be better off for it."

"Cass, don't push yourself. You took me too seriously when I said they make you run till you drop. Go for five miles. That's what they test you on."

That was good news. Five miles I could do already. I decided to go for five miles out in the hills. Five miles over rough terrain would do the trick. Five miles in the gym was easy. Air conditioning, level ground, no rocks. I needed to train outdoors.

"Okay," I said, "Then for our next race I want to do the five miles in the desert. We can run around Saddleback Butte."

"Cass, you're nuts."

"Hey, I'm not kidding. I doubt the test is in a nice air-conditioned gym. I'll have to be prepared to do five miles outdoors."

"Let's concentrate on the first step. Have you applied?"

"Yes! I applied as soon as I found out it was required."

"Are you going to get into the August academy?"

"I can't be sure. There's so much to do."

"How are you going to get to all your exams and physicals and interviews if our cars are all targets?"

"I'll just have to be careful."

"Were you careful today?"

"No, well, as careful as I normally am, but I thought the Explorer was safe."

"Babe, you can't assume anything is safe anymore."

I winced and looked around. Twenty pairs of female ears had heard him call me babe. Now they knew. I wondered if I'd just acquired twenty new stalkers.

"I did notice I was being followed before leaving the store. At least I was that observant."

We finished up our gym routines separately. I felt the glares of the other women. They were torn between watching Rusty and shooting warning glares at me. This was getting entertaining.

The woman next to me on the ab machine asked, "How did you meet that guy? I've been dying to talk to him."

"I got carjacked. I don't recommend it as a way to meet guys."

"And?"

"And I really don't recommend it, especially now. You have to be careful out there. There's a killer on the loose."

Her eyes got big.

As we got out of the Explorer at home Rusty informed me, "You are not going running by yourself. It's too easy to get picked up."

"What if I go armed?"

"Cassidy, don't press your luck. This guy is starting to make some really dumb moves. Only the stupidity of the store manager kept him from being caught this last time. It bothers me that he is not expecting to get out of this alive. It means he is willing to risk everything. He's got a mission and he's set on it and it includes you. Don't tempt him by going out by yourself."

I was pacing the condo, bored to tears. I'd put Shadow through the paces, jumping over the yardstick, running up and down the stairs with stays at the top and bottom. This was all well and good for Shadow but I was bored and had cabin fever. I was itching to get out but I didn't have a good enough excuse to actually go. I was pacing, trying to come up with a good excuse when my cell phone rang. I picked it up and answered, "Hello?"

"Hey Cass, where are you? Are you busy?"

"I'm at your house, bored stiff. What's up?"

"You're at home?"

"Yeah."

"Then what's your Jeep doing at the station?"

"It's not at the station. It's at my house."

"Babe, I know your Jeep. It's unmistakable and it's sitting right here in front of me in the station parking lot. You want me to run the plates and make sure?"

"No, I know it's unmistakable." Thanks to the spray paint job. "Any idea how it got there?"

"Nope, it was just sitting there when I got to work this morning."

"Do you want me to come down there with the keys?"

"Not yet, I..." And I heard a loud *BOOM!* A sharp noise that rumbled and echoed off the walls of the buildings, rattling windows a block away... I'd seen car bombs in Afghanistan. I knew what they could do. My heart stopped.

"Rusty! Rusty are you there?" No answer. Oh, please, oh, please be okay. "Rusty?"

I dashed for the car keys and took off running for the Explorer. I jumped in and screeched out of the driveway praying for green lights, speeding all the way. When I neared the station I couldn't get close because four patrol cars were parked out front. Officers were directing traffic around two fire trucks. An ambulance stood to one side. I pulled into a parking lot behind the realty office across the street and ran for the station. I was dashing in and out of firemen and rescue people looking for any familiar face when two hands reached out and pulled me up short. I spun around. Half of me prayed it was Rusty and half of me feared it was the ATM murderer. I didn't know whether to hug him or slug him. It was Landon. Okay, I thought, I'll slug him, but I didn't. He saw the desperation in my eyes and steered me in the right direction. I took note of the grip on my arms. Gentle. Gentle was good news. If Rusty were truly hurt Landon would be prepared to restrain me and I knew he could do it. The crowd parted and there he was, sitting next to the rescue squad, eyebrows and hair singed, skin bright red. I didn't know what to say. I was so relieved, I was speechless. I felt tears coming. He started to get up but I rushed to his side and knelt beside him. I was afraid to hug him. I didn't know how painful it was and I didn't know if it was kosher to hug a detective in front of his station. I just knelt there, tears running down my cheeks and when his eyes got so sad that I couldn't look at them any more I sat beside him as close as I could. He put his arm around me. Landon stood there for a minute taking in the scene, knowing love when he saw it. He gave me a wink and turned on his heel and joined the crowd. When the paramedics were finished Rusty picked up his coat and we went to the station. On our way in he dumped his coat in the trashcan. We went to his office for some much needed peace and quiet.

"Rusty, I was so scared…. I've seen car bombs before. I helped find body parts. I couldn't tell one person from another…. When I heard the explosion I couldn't think…. You were gone. And I didn't know how gone you were…."

He pulled me close. "I know. I lost the cell phone in the blast. I would have called you as soon as I could but everything turned to mayhem and I was right in the middle of it. We were very lucky this time. A few pedestrians were knocked flat. Several cars were damaged from falling debris. The fire was contained fast. At least the blast was just meant to destroy your car. It wasn't meant to take out a whole city block."

"What about you? Are you okay? You're missing your eyebrows, you need a haircut and you look like you've been roasted."

"I'm okay. I just got a quick flash from the explosion."

"Does it hurt?"

"How bad does it have to hurt for you to kiss it and make it better?"

I smiled and he bent down for his kiss. I poured all the relief I felt into that kiss.

The next few hours were spent completing paperwork, and he had a lot of it to do. Fortunately, most of it could be done on his computer. People came to his office door to talk and then went on their way again. I filled out my report by hand. I needed to file a police report so I could inform my insurance company of my Jeep's unfortunate demise. If they had known how many close calls it had before being blown up they would have yanked my insurance anyway. I swore up and down that when I got that check in the mail I was going to buy a Jeep with a winch on it. Somehow, some way, I would end up with a winch on my Jeep.

After filling out the forms it finally sank in that my Jeep was really gone. I had owned that Jeep before I was married. It had taken me on adventures in the woods and had been there for me when Jack died. It had taken me on many grief filled flights into the woods and it had always been there when I hiked out.

I remembered some of those trips. I needed to get my mind off the grief so I'd go into the woods. No food, no water. I'd force myself to only think about survival so I wouldn't think of my loss or the loneliness. After two or three days of only living on what I could catch, I'd drive home to recuperate and would appreciate civilization again until the next wave of grief sent me running. It was a rough time and I'd only broken out of that cycle for a few weeks when I'd met Rusty. I knew too many of those trips would take their toll on me but Rusty had somehow managed to pull me back to reality without knowing he was doing it. I'm still not certain how it had happened but with each day I felt better able to cope and I started looking forward to the next.

I looked at the forms in numb silence. Rusty sat at his computer but he wasn't working. He knew something was going on inside me. I thought he was telepathic or something.

"Cass, I'm sorry about your Jeep. I know you really liked it." Okay, so he wasn't telepathic.

"I did, but the Jeep was nothing compared to the thought of losing you. I'll be okay without the Jeep. I wouldn't make it without you. I just got to thinking how much you've done for me. You've done even more than you know. And just the part that you do know about is beyond what could be expected of any one person. You helped me escape from Silva. You saved me from a fire. You stuck with me through thick and thin and stuck with me when trouble came over and over again.

"But you've done some things without knowing about it too. Before we met I was in a cycle of grief that would have killed me eventually. I'd get so full of sorrow I'd go out in the woods with nothing. No food, no water, no tent. I'd snare rabbits and eat dandelions and berries. I even went once in the winter, snow shoeing and building snow caves to sleep in. I was hoping I'd freeze out there. But my survival instincts wouldn't let me. I'd wander the mountains in search of something, anything. Well, actually, mostly food, but searching for food took my mind off of the grief. I'd hike out and find my Jeep before I starved to death and go back to civilization and start the whole thing over again. My parents never knew this was going on. I'd write and tell them about my 'camping trips' and they thought I was having fun. I thank Silva every day for helping me to meet you. I'd just spent two weeks in civilization and the mountains were calling again when I got carjacked. When you called it gave me a reason to stay home. I looked forward to your calls even though you seemed to just be checking up on me. I stuck around just to hear your voice and eventually I was able to break free of the cycle I'd put myself in."

He looked at me dumbstruck. What? What had I done? He walked around the desk and sat down in the chair next to me. He seemed to have trouble putting together what I'd said and I wasn't going to repeat it. It was hard enough to admit the first time.

"Cassidy, you really went through all that, even before I met you?"

"I wouldn't say I went through it. I chose it. It was just my natural reaction to grief, to run to the woods. I learned a lot about survival. On one of my outings I'd heard you could collect water by making a still so I brought a sheet of plastic, a jar and a piece of plastic tubing up onto a remote mountain and I made one. I dug a big hole, put the jar in the center of it, arranged the plastic in a cone shape so the tip was just over the jar and put the tube from the jar to the edge of the cone. There wasn't a creek or spring for miles but I had water. The still collects ground water and it drips off the plastic into the jar. You can drink right out of the jar without taking the still apart. That was one of my easier trips.

"Maybe I should have told you about all this earlier. Maybe if you'd known about it you would have been more comfortable letting me go after Kelly. It was a time of my life I had just put behind me and I was just starting to look at what was ahead of me. I didn't want to call up the past again. I wanted to do something that would count in the future. That's why visiting Kelly in the hospital was so rewarding. I'd done something right, something that would last.

"Rusty, don't look so sad. I didn't tell you this to make you sad. I wanted you to see how much you'd done for me. I wanted you to see how thankful I am."

"I just can't imagine you up on a mountain, alone, trying to find something to eat, having all that grief. It was too much. How could you make it through all that? What did you bring along? What kept you alive?"

"My hunting knife, and a magnesium stick. I wasn't *totally* stupid."

He seemed amused that I thought a knife and a magnesium stick could keep me alive, but they had. I used the knife to make snares to catch food and I used the magnesium and steel stick to make fires, tiny fires, only enough fire to cook what I caught. Then I'd immediately put the fire out and find a place to sleep away from the food smells. I ate when I had food and I slept when it got dark and I searched for more food when I didn't have any. And I was always hungry and I was bone thin and I couldn't have kept up that life. When I compared my life then to what it was now, all I felt was total thankfulness towards Rusty. And now I'd made him sad.

"What can I do to cheer you up?" I asked. "I didn't want to make you sad. Just try and focus on today and not a year ago. Today is much brighter."

"Your car just got firebombed and you have a murderer stalking you and today is bright?"

"Yes, today is wonderful, now that you are still here. I'm ready to celebrate."

He smiled. "Celebrate? Celebrate what?"

"Anything, another day together. It doesn't matter."

"Let me finish up a few things, then I need to see what's going on outside. Maybe we can go see about a haircut."

"That's better."

He felt his hair in the front where it had burned short. "You've never seen me in a flat top."

"Have I ever seen you with a haircut?" Of course I had. I just couldn't tell a new haircut from his normal appearance. Rusty always looked the same to me. His sandy brown hair was always nearly collar length in back and always long and windblown looking in the front. He would comb it up and within minutes it would fall down. The only time I'd seen his hair stay in place was at my birthday party and he'd been dressed up in a black suit and tie. He must have used a ton of hairspray to get it to stay up that long. I laughed at the thought of Rusty toiling over his hair. But, no, Rusty didn't toil over anything. I think he normally didn't mind the windblown look and I was glad. It suited him.

At last we were free of the station and my Jeep was towed away to wherever Jeeps go when they die. I thought with amusement that it ought to be the *Jeep heap*. And I thought of it sadly sitting there alone, no more camping trips, no more getting buried to its axles in sand… I led Rusty to the Explorer and we drove to the barbershop. The shop was only a few blocks away and the barber was glad to get news of the commotion down the street. He'd had customers come in with all kinds of stories and speculation about it, but no one had actually been there. He looked at Rusty's hair.

"The usual?" he asked.

"I don't think the usual is going to work this time, Tony. Just do what you can."

"Ya tell me what ya want, I'll do it."

"What do you think, Cass? Flat top? Spikes? Mohawk? Just extra short?"

"Don't look at me! It's your hair, except I doubt you could get away with a Mohawk at work. And I doubt if your hair will stay up after it's been down so long. But you can *try* anything."

I walked out of the barbershop with a different person. The short haircut gave Rusty a more angular look. His features looked harder.

"What do you think?" he asked.

"If you're looking to intimidate criminals, it's the look to go for." I answered.

"What, you don't like it?"

"You look great. You just look… tougher. I feel like I have a bodyguard. I just need to get used to it. I need to see your eyes smile and see the real you behind the look." He smiled and his eyes smiled, too. That's better, I thought. "If you really want to know what people think of the hair cut, go to the gym tonight. You'll get 20 instant opinions. I bet they all faint and when they come to you *will* have to play bodyguard because they are going to mob me. They'll either try and kill me or ask for your phone number."

"Cass, you're exaggerating this whole gym thing. Nobody pays any attention to what you do at the gym. It's common courtesy. You let everybody work at their own pace and know everybody there is improving themselves so you leave them alone to do it."

"And they are all watching you wondering how you could possibly improve. Are you telling me you don't watch cute girls at the gym? Because I don't believe that for a second."

He smiled again. He wasn't going to dig himself in any deeper than he already had.

"Tell you what," he said, "I've got a new look. You wanted to celebrate. Let's both take our new look out and celebrate."

"That sounds like you want me to put that dress on."

"You can wear what you want. I need to change out of these clothes."

I slipped the romantic blue dress over my head and felt big strong arms come around me from behind.

"Maybe we should stay home and celebrate in a different way." He kissed my neck. He traced the lines of the low cut back of my dress and turned me to face him. The hardness of his features caught me by surprise but the longing in his eyes pulled me in. It was always the eyes that did it. And then the touches. I always wondered how hands that big could be so gentle. They slid and caressed and I melted under his hands.

"You said something last time we did this," he reminded me.

"What's that?" I asked softly wondering what he remembered.

"You said that I hadn't seen anything yet."

"Mmm, I did. Didn't I?"

"You sure did."

"And we *are* celebrating another day together. So we ought to make it special," I replied, unbuttoning the top button of his shirt.

His hands wandered looking for a button or a zipper. Another button and he started looking around. His hand slid up my thigh. I unbuttoned each button slowly, letting him sweat it out. When all the buttons had been undone and his shirt hung open I kissed him. I stepped back and started pulling the dress over my head. He took over and it came up in one fluid movement.

I like to think of making love almost like reverse stalking. Instead of staying invisible and calming, the goal is to build tension, just a little bit at a time. Leave them longing for more. A look here. A touch there. A touch… oh yeah, right there… right there. Back off. It's like teasing a tiger, only you want the tiger to attack. And so I stalked Rusty right into his bed and into his arms and into those luscious touches. It was a celebration of another day together and we took pleasure in every moment and movement. We fell asleep all tangled up and we awoke the next morning in each other's arms.

Chapter 11

The next day was bright and I was ready to take on the world except for one small problem. There was someone in the world looking to take me on, too. I was trapped but didn't want to waste my good mood or excess energy.

"I need something to do," I announced. "I don't care what it is, cleaning, fixing something, planting flowers. It doesn't matter what, but I need something to keep me busy and I don't know what I can do at your house."

"Cass, you can do whatever you want, just as if this were your house. I know I haven't done much around here. It's because I used to spend as little time here as possible. It was a crash pad. But now that the place is being used more it needs some attention. Go ahead and plant flowers. Find us a dining room table and chairs."

"That's what you want me to do? Really?"

"Yeah."

"Okay, but it'll mean being out and about."

He paused at that.

"Tell me what you need to do to stay safe."

"Watch my tail. Lock the car. Keep an eye out for anything unusual. Watch the people in the stores. Choose places that are open and where I can see around me. Keep the cell phone handy. Ummm, anything else?"

"Watch for big white trucks and call me if anything happens. Remember the bullet in the box. Little things can have big consequences."

"Rusty, I'll be fine."

I drove the Explorer to the home improvement store that was closest to the condo. I debated whether to go across town to one with a more open floor plan but I thought time on the streets was just as bad as time in a crowded store. I bought flats of colorful flowers. I didn't know what grew well so I looked at parking lots on the way and bought what I noticed the landscapers had planted. I figured they bought plants that took minimal care and would withstand the desert heat, and that was what Rusty needed. I didn't feel right picking out Rusty's furniture for him so I saved the dining room table project for later. Maybe I should ask him to look at some store ads to get a feel for what he liked.

I was working my way around Rusty's little yard, elbow deep in dirt and my cell phone beeped at me from the house. I brushed off as much dirt as I could on the way and picked it up in a huff.

"You okay?" Rusty asked.

"Yeah, I was just outside and the phone was inside so I had to run for it. Everything's fine."

"Well, everything is not fine here."

"Where are you?"

"Next to a car out in the desert."

"Did you break down or do we have another victim?" I asked nervously.

He paused, uncertainty clear in the silence. We had another victim and it was bad news. Or risky. Or both.

"Cass, I don't want you to do this. But it's serious. And it might be a trap. I don't see any sign of a trail. What I've got is a car with a note in it. The note says, 'She's alive. IF you get there on time.' He's baiting us and he hid his tracks so I'd have to call you in."

"Do you know if there really is a victim?"

"Yes, he left a picture so we'd be sure. The car is registered to a woman, thirty five years old, went out this morning and hasn't been seen since. Plus the car tip was phoned in anonymously. It wasn't an ignorant passerby that called it in. It was a very serious sounding tip. Serious enough to send me out here right away. Now we've got this note and picture."

"Does the handwriting on the note match the one that I found in my bills? Scratchy block letters?"

I listened while he fumbled for the note. The silence changed tone and I knew it matched.

"Rusty, I'll come out there if you want. We'll find her. We have to."

"I've got backup on their way out. They'll have a vest for you. Cass, are you sure? I'm not. I don't want you anywhere near this situation."

"Hey, I'll only be following tracks, that's all. I can't do anything else until I finish academy and that's six months away. And if this turns out to be as tough as the last time he hid his tracks I'm not going to be in plain sight much anyway. Tell me where you are."

He gave me directions but they were obscure. Just in case it was needed, I filled up my hydration pack with water and threw in a couple of granola bars. I drove south on Ridgeline Road six miles past the last subdivision then turned left into the desert and took the right turn three miles away from the left. Then the dirt road went through an arroyo and up the other side. The road split and I took the left fork. This was barren land again. This guy loved putting us in the most hostile places around. I saw a group of police cars and a new, yellow Mustang that had been driven off the road and parked haphazardly.

I got out of the Explorer, and made my way to the scene. Rusty held the police tape aside, so I could get close to the tracks. Once again, I was faced with hard ground and very little to go on. To make matters worse, the first footprint, usually the most easily read after exiting a car, was placed neatly in the middle of a small, scrubby sagebrush.

Rusty handed me the note. Same scratchy block letters.

I circled the car looking for signs of two sets of footprints. I didn't even see one. Here we go again. Rusty handed me the vest and I put it on and pulled a loose camp shirt over the top of it. I hated these things. I couldn't move in them. But one had saved me from a shot once before, so I didn't fight it.

I looked around me. Six burly police officers waiting on little old me to find some invisible clue in the sand that they couldn't see. And a woman somewhere was counting on me to see something they couldn't. I pictured her being knocked around like Silva had knocked me around and my determination set in.

I focused on the squashed bush and the area a few feet around it. If the first step was uncertain maybe the correction for it would be clear.

"If this turns out to be the woman at the gym I'm going to kill her myself," I muttered under my breath.

"What woman at the gym?"

I looked up with surprise not realizing that I'd spoken loudly enough to be heard.

"It was after our race at the gym. You said I was exaggerating the women's reactions to you. But one woman asked me how I met you. I told her I got carjacked but that I didn't recommend it as a way to meet guys." Some of the officers snickered and Rusty looked slightly embarrassed. "She looked scared enough not to try it."

Rusty exchanged glances with another officer. "Did she look like this?" he asked as he pulled a Polaroid picture from his shirt pocket. I looked at the photograph with relief. It was a different woman. The picture was disturbing to me. It showed the carjacked woman. She had been thrown against the side of the car and she lay on the street beside the vehicle crying. She'd been struggling. Her hair was a mess and her clothes were twisted around. She had grass stains on her knees and one of her shoes was untied but she was beyond caring.

"No," I said, "this is a different woman." I took a last look at the photo and then handed it back to Rusty. Something was wrong with that picture, I thought. It was disturbing, yes, but something else niggled at the back of my mind.

"So, Michaels, who won the race?"

"He did," I said confidently "But he pushed me past the 5 mile mark and that was the goal. Next I want to try it out in the desert."

It was time to focus on the tracks. Come on, Cass, you've got to find something here. You've got six skeptics, Rusty, and one scared woman counting on you. Not to mention one crazy murderer. Was he counting on me to follow this track? Did he want me to find what was at the end of his trail? This was why I preferred to work alone. I liked to keep the tension and the waiting to a minimum and I'd deal with whatever was at the end of the trail. I didn't like bringing a bunch of other people on what could either be a wild goose chase or a dangerous situation.

Focus, Cass, find a track. I got down on my belly in the dirt and looked at the area from ground level. Nothing. Shoot. I walked around the car again. Nothing. I made my circle wider and I thought I caught a faint clue. I got down again and glanced at it sideways. Maybe. I looked at the car and looked at the light scuff. I examined the scratch marks of the tiny pieces of gravel and determined a direction. I remembered this guy had a long stride and went to the next spot where I expected a track to be. Rusty walked up with a pair of gloves.

"I hate wearing gloves," I complained.

"You're not going to blister yourself like you did last time."

I felt silly; t-shirt, Kevlar vest, camp shirt, hydration pack and now gloves, too. And it was a hundred degrees in the shade. Even worse, they were Rusty's gloves so they were twice as big as my hands. I couldn't work with these on. I put them on anyway and tried to get back to my job.

I went back to the scratch marks and followed the direction to the spot where the next track should be. I studied it at ground level. More faint scratch marks. I looked for the next track or the next spot I would have attempted to hide one and tried to ignore the group of men waiting for me. This could be an all day job here.

No, Cass, this is a trick. This guy is just testing you. He doesn't want you to spend all day at it. He wants to see the results and he isn't patient so this won't take all day. Just follow the tracks. I followed the clues. I couldn't really call them tracks. The ground was hard and tracks didn't show up. A few scratch marks, a few bent grasses were all I had to keep me going but I followed it belly down in the dirt one step at a time. The guys watched me from the cars until I started fading from view. Only Rusty stayed with me.

The clues meandered through the desert and suddenly stopped. No shack, no rocks, nothing. I stacked up a few rocks to mark the ending point. I circled the stack and broadened the circle and broadened it again. As I was walking around and around the stack it occurred to me that I was also circling a large Joshua tree standing next to the rocks. I went over to the tree. I glanced around in its bizarre, oddly shaped branches and a spot of white caught my eye.

"Can you reach that white thing up there?" I asked Rusty.

He strained but it was out of his reach.

"Give me a boost up then." I stepped into his hands, he lifted me up, and I grabbed the thing. It was caught by a length of string in the prickly branches so I had to tease it loose. "Okay, just drop me. It's okay, I've jumped from higher." I landed with legs bent. I unrolled the piece of paper in my hand, read the scratchy block letters and then kicked the tree. "Let me see that picture again," I demanded, and snatched it from his hand to examine it more closely. "Damn," I said, "I should have noticed this sooner. Look, in the background. Above the car's roof. The thin line that shows the building behind the car. I knew there was something about that picture that I should see but was missing. I knew it! And now we've spent hours tracking down a Joshua tree to only get this!" I handed him the paper and he looked at it, then back to me, his expression blank, which meant he was surprised and worried but didn't want to let on. The note on the paper didn't say much. It was just an address. My address. The faint line of background above the car in the picture had been my house and I hadn't even seen it.

Rusty and I jogged back to the group at the cars. Rusty fired off orders and they all raced away. Two officers stayed behind to secure the area.

"Go home," he ordered me, "I mean to my house. I don't want you anywhere near your house when we do this."

"Rusty!"

"Nope, you're not going. I'll tell you about it when it's over."

"It's my house and my stalker," I said. Okay, it even sounded dumb to me and I knew I should stay away. But I was worried and not just for the woman or what might have happened to my house. I didn't want Rusty to walk into yet another trap. But, it was his job and his case and he had to go whether I liked it or not. I couldn't keep him from it just like he had to let me go to the plane crash.

"Okay," I said in defeat "I'll go home. I'll go finish planting flowers while you go walk right into a trap and get shot at and…"

He pulled me to him and gave me a long kiss.

"Be careful," he said.

"You too."

"There won't be anything for me to do if I don't get going. Those guys are worse than a hound on a chase."

I had promised to go to Rusty's house, and had started to, but I couldn't help but swing by my neighborhood on the way. Then I saw the mob of lights and had to drive by. Not too close, just around the neighborhood. I glanced down my street. Oh, man, I didn't like what I saw. The three police cars, an ambulance and a large fire truck filled the street and beside it all the smoking ruin of my house. There was nothing in there that I needed. There was nothing I particularly valued. But I felt violated nonetheless. I went to Rusty's house but I couldn't plant flowers. All I could do was wait in tense anticipation.

As the sun set and the day cooled off and my mood settled down, I was able to go outside and plant some more. I could at least make things pleasant out there for Rusty. When darkness fell I turned on the porch light and kept working, planting color all around his yard except for the corners. I thought I could find some ornamental trees or bushes to put there. I took the remaining flowers to the front yard and planted them in little groups next to the sidewalk in his entryway.

It was very late when Rusty came in the door. I'd forgotten about dinner but I didn't care. He came in dejectedly, not wanting to tell me about the rest of his day. I wasn't sure I wanted to hear it either, but I wanted to know if the woman was okay. I didn't expect the murderer to be caught. He wouldn't hang around my house waiting for me to walk in with the cops. Nope, he had other plans and I feared the woman he kidnapped had been left as a message to me.

He sat on the couch and stared at the floor. I knelt facing him, feet dangling off the edge of the sofa.

"Cass…" he paused, unsure where to start or how much to tell me.

"The house is a loss," I said. "Don't dwell on it. What about the woman? Did they find her? Is she okay?"

"We found her. She'll be okay. She's traumatized and hurt but it's nothing that won't heal."

Relief flooded over me. "Good, that's what counts."

Silence stretched out between us.

"Look, Rusty, I know the house is gone. I know the girl is okay. I know she was left there with a message for me. And now I know you don't want me to hear it. But I have to hear it. And I doubt it surprises me. Anything I can come up with would be worse than what he said. So what was it?"

"We got a name."

"A name?" Now that *did* surprise me!

"I looked it up in the computer." He looked through his pile of papers and handed me a printout. There was a mug shot, so he was a repeat offender.

"Tyrone Trent," I read, "looks like he is doing his best to spend his life in prison."

"Hates police, hates society, thrives on violence. You're right, his house is a bunker and he was in the military. Got kicked out. Knows explosives.

Right now his main goal is to use you to teach the police a lesson."

"Why did he kidnap the woman? Why didn't he just kidnap me?"

"He'd tried, you didn't cooperate so he was sending you a message."

"And he thinks I'll cooperate more now?"

"He wants you to be scared."

"Guess he doesn't know he has competition in the Scare Cassidy Contest. I'm just about all scared out. I'd go knock on his door and tell him to try his best but he stole my gun."

"There's one more thing you should know. He gives you forty-eight hours. Two days."

I sat, still, letting the message sink in. "Well, what should I do? I'm supposed to go to orientation on Thursday. I'll be in L.A."

"What?" This took him by surprise.

"Reserve Academy Orientation meeting."

"Cass, it's not that important. They do those once a week. You can go to another one."

"You'd rather I stay here than go to L.A.? Seems like I'd be harder to find in L.A." I tried another topic. "Okay, tell me about the house. Is it a total loss?"

"Structurally. They managed to save a few things."

"How did it happen?"

"It was booby trapped to explode when the front door was opened."

I gasped.

"Fortunately the bomb was planted in the kitchen and all the action was in the living room. But, you know how that house is built. Take out that central part of the house and the rest goes fast. Everyone got out okay. I think the fire hit *me* worst. All I could see was your whole life going up in flames."

"Hey," I said, anger on the inside and comfort on the outside. "Don't dwell on it. There was nothing in that house that can't be replaced. And I was thinking of moving anyway."

"Where? Where will you go?"

"I don't know. I hadn't gotten that far. I wanted a place in the hills where I could keep Shasta. He's used to company so I'd probably need to bring two horses from the ranch. I wanted a place where I could hike and ride back into the hills. Rusty, what's wrong?"

"You want to move away?"

"No, not away, away. I'd still be close." This didn't seem to calm him for some reason. "Rusty, the house was the result of a decision that has long ago changed. It wasn't the house I'd have chosen for myself. It was part of a plan Jack and I had and since that plan is no longer valid the house is just a reminder of a good plan gone bad. It's time for me to make my own life. It's what I should have done in the first place."

"He's taking everything from you. Your car, your house, your safety. He's stripping you down."

"No, no he isn't. He can't touch me through all these things. There's only one thing he could take from me that would really hurt. Only one, and you're it. As long as you're here I'm okay."

Finally, I'd said something that resulted in just a little calm.

It was Rusty's turn to have nightmares that night. He tossed and turned. I tried to shake him gently but it was like moving a brick wall. It was a scary dream. I could tell. Emotions were boiling and I thought I was going to get slugged when I woke him up. He awoke startled, frightened and grasped me so tightly that I couldn't breathe.

"Hey, it's okay, it was just a bad dream," I said reassuringly. He got up to pace the room, came back to bed and lay there wide awake. Then he pulled me to him again. We lay there for a long time waiting for peace to settle in.

"What is it?" I asked gently. "What has you so uptight that you can't go back to sleep?"

"It was just a nightmare. It's one I used to have a lot. Usually I just recognize it for what it is and forget about it. I guess it's too close to reality tonight. It could happen again and I'd be just as powerless as I was the first time."

"Then this dream really happened?" I felt the walls go up again. "You're blocking it in again. Rusty, don't do that. You think I won't understand but I promise to try. Ask Kelly, ask Ben, ask Lou or Landon. I've been trying to figure out for a month what you've been hiding and they won't tell me. I've been kind enough to your past that I don't pry but I really want to understand this. It's part of you and it shows, but not enough that I can get a glimpse. I just get these odd behavior changes that I don't understand. You're allowed to have a past, you know. Life didn't suddenly begin when you knocked on my door this spring. Do you remember what you told me when Jesse wanted to hear how we met?"

"I said that they could tell you had secrets and it would be good for them to know what happened so they would know why you had changed."

I said with as much kindness as I could muster, "Rusty, you're changing on me. I can tell. But I don't know why. And I want to understand."

"Kelly called me and told me this was coming. We talked for a long time. We nearly argued about it and he nearly told you himself so I know he was serious. Kelly doesn't get serious unless he thinks something is pretty important. He cares so much for you. He'd do anything for you, even come to blows with me. He thought you should know and I've been too chicken to bring it up."

"It's not chicken to hold onto your past. It's natural. But there's a time to let it go too. And I won't judge you for it. It's past. It's gone and what you are today is what counts. It might be hard to put the past and the present together again but we'll get through this together."

I could feel the battle inside him. It emanated from him in every way it could. His arms tensed and his eyes got hard and I wished his hair was long again so that look would soften just a little. Okay, Cass, you've got to take charge here.

I sat up so he could see he wasn't dealing with an enemy here. It was a little Skipper look alike who cared the world for him, who just wanted to understand him.

"You need a starting point. Tell me what happens in your dream."

He paused and I could see him relax just a little.

"It's a car chase. We'd been chasing this guy through town, out of town. He'd nearly run over a few pedestrians, side swiped a parked car. I'm tailing this guy and the goal is to box him in and direct him into a barricade so he can be stopped. I'm tailing him behind... Gina is boxing him in from the side. The guy points his gun out the window and fires. Gina's squad car drifts off the road and hits a bridge support..." A deep breath, "and I can't stop. I can't go back. I've got to stay on this guy's tail. I know there are other guys behind me that will stop but it doesn't matter. That's when I wake up, when I should go back but I can't... In real life I followed the guy and we did catch him at the barricade. He took out two patrol cars and nearly killed himself. By the time I got back to the accident scene, she was gone. She was gone and there was nothing I could do. And I wasn't there when she needed me."

I lay back down and wrapped my arms around him, just being there. "Rusty, I'm sorry. I'm sorry you had to go through that. How long ago did it happen?"

"It's been years. It's why I'm a detective now instead of in uniform. I couldn't do first response calls anymore. If it was a crash I'd turn into a basket case. I couldn't look at a wreck without having flashbacks. So Schroeder had me take the test to become a detective so I wouldn't be first on the scene. So I'd have cases assigned to me and he could pick them."

"Is that why it was so hard for you when I went to the plane crash? I remember you told Lou that you couldn't ask me to do something you couldn't do. That was one of the things that triggered my curiosity. And somehow I knew just from that one line that it was a plane crash." He nodded in the dark. "Thank you. Thank you for watching out for me. It worked out. Just like you will work this out... Tell me about Gina. What was she like?"

"Cass, I can't do that. It's like comparing apples and oranges..."

"You're not comparing anything. Just tell me what she was like. She was on the force. That tells me something about her right there."

"She was pretty in a serious way. She was dark, dark hair, dark eyes and she was serious on the job. She felt the competition from the guys and tried everything she could to beat down their comments. That only seemed to fuel the rivalry so she was always pushing for tough cases and proving she could do it right. But she had another side and not very many people got to see it. Her family, maybe some best friend that I never met, and eventually me. She never felt competitive towards me for some reason. She used to sneak into the condo and cook for me. That's why that first night you were here hit me so hard. It was like Gina had snuck in while I was away. I never knew how she got in. She never would tell me. The doors were always locked... Why would you want to know these things?"

"Because they are part of you. And I need to know some of what you are. I hardly know you at all even with all the time we've spent together. I don't know if you have a family or if you were ever married or where you grew up or when your birthday is or how old you are."

"I didn't realize that. I know so much about you, but the bare facts I got from files. Your name, age, birthday, Jack. That was all stuff I could look up."

"I remember you called me by name when you came to my door when Silva was there. I assumed you got it from DMV records but I always enjoyed the fact that you called me by name before we'd even met. Do you still miss her?"

"No, that part has faded, unless something unusual triggers it."

"She picked out your dishes and curtains and towels."

"And set up the kitchen with basics. She was appalled that I didn't have things to cook with. I think I had a little frying pan in case I needed a quick breakfast. I had a refrigerator that only cooled eggs and beer. And a freezer that only froze ice and ice cream."

"And when she was there your crash pad felt like a home again. Don't be afraid to talk about her. She is part of who you are. And I thank her for being there for you. Did you get married?"

"No, although we might have eventually. She was a lot harder to get close to. That was part of what made her death so hard. I'd lost her before I could even get a handle on who she was. All I knew was I couldn't let her go and then she was gone."

"How old are you?" He was calming down now. He could see the thought of another girl in his life didn't scare me and we were treading safer ground now.

"Thirty, does that matter?"

"In what way? I'm not going to take off running just because you are a little older than me. I've always felt you were older. Maybe it's because you are more stable and stability is something I tend to be short on. When is your birthday?"

"In November."

"That's appropriate, that you were born in the fall. Your clothes are brown. Your furniture is brown. It suits you and now even your birthday is in the fall when everything is turning brown. I'm glad I didn't miss it. I was worried that I'd missed your birthday but always wondered what to get you even if I knew. You don't seem to have any interests. All I know is you go rock climbing."

We chatted like this for what felt like hours but eventually we tired again and fell asleep.

Chapter 12

I basically spent Wednesday under house arrest. I was ordered to stay home and at random times uniformed police would knock on the door. After a few of these visits I figured Rusty was sending them to check up on me and to also keep Trent from trying anything. I made cookies for something to do and it gave the officers a reason to sit and chat for a little while. We didn't talk about much. I pried a few interesting stories out of them. I found out the snake story had made the rounds. And the dog story. And the ATM story. And, of course, my fight at GearUp! For some reason I didn't mind being the comic relief at the station. They needed a reason to laugh. Their jobs were way too serious and the stories broke that up. They started reminding me of the hands at my parent's ranch, always looking out for me but waiting with eager anticipation for my next mishap. And they didn't seem to look at the mishaps in a dangerous way. It was more like I'd become indestructible to them. It was like watching super hero cartoons, knowing the hero was going to survive and just watching to find out how they would do it this time.

I met some of the officers that I'd wanted to meet. Schroeder stopped by. I'd never met this friend of Rusty's. He reminded me of Lou but a little more serious, more of the drill sergeant and less of the grandfather. I could see him as a mentor for Rusty.

After the first two came by and I started my cookie baking they all left with a little bag of warm cookies. I was probably ruining my reputation but, hey, a trouble magnet is allowed a few cooking skills, too.

Once the cookies started making their way to the station I got more visitors until I had to start a second batch. I never baked so much in my life. But I was enjoying the day and it was keeping trouble at bay.

My cell phone rang and I picked it up, "Hello?"

"Hey, you better be saving some of those cookies for me. No one will share."

I smiled. "I will, I can always make more. How many guys work at that station? And what have you started? I thought you sent them to check up on me but now I think they are just here for the cookies."

"I didn't start anything. You started making the cookies. You should have known better."

"I was just trying to be nice."

"Hey, you can't blame them. Cute girl, in danger, all alone, making cookies. What cop could resist?"

The door bell rang.

"Here we go again."

"You'll survive, I'll be home in a couple of hours."

I answered the door and there stood Landon, in uniform, with another officer. He looked sharp in the uniform but he wasn't fooling me.

"What're you doing here?" he asked.

"Hiding from a stalker," I said. "What're you doing here?"

"We just came to make sure you were all right," Landon's partner replied.

"Yeah, that's what they all say. Then they head for the kitchen."

"Okay, so we heard you were handing out cookies. And I couldn't pass up some cookies. So, what are you really doing here?"

"I told you, I'm hiding from a stalker. Then my house got blown up."

"That was your house?"

"Yeah. As soon as Trent is out of the picture I'll find a new house."

"Trent? Not maniacal, suicidal, cop hater Trent?"

"Tyrone Trent."

His concern deepened.

"And you're sitting here making cookies while Trent is after you?"

"Hey, it's been working great so far."

"I rescued him from a wreck once. If I'd have known him then like I know him now I'd have arrested him on the spot. I pulled him out of his truck and he high tailed it into the hills. After he disappeared we were loading his truck onto a tow truck and found all these guns and explosives in the cab. You don't want him to be after you. What's Michaels doing about this?"

"As much as I'll let him. I'm not very cooperative when it comes to sitting around and doing nothing. That's why I started making cookies. I'm not staying home tomorrow, though. I have plans."

"You better cancel them. Have yourself locked up. Shit, Cassidy, you'd have to be nuts to go out with Trent after you."

"I'm just going to an orientation meeting. It's required to get into academy. It's in L.A. I figure I'll be safer in L.A. than I would be here. And I'll have one more step in the process done."

"You're starting academy? Trent will love that. That's like giving him an invitation to torture you. He won't let you become a cop."

"I don't want to. I just need to go through the academy so I can work search and rescue. I'm not joining the force."

"I'm telling you, you shouldn't go. Academy or no academy. Trent is no one to mess with. I've been digging up the bodies. I know what he does."

"Landon, you can't scare me. I've seen too much to be scared. I'm to the point of just being wary. I'd be armed but he stole my gun. He stole my gun, he blew up my Jeep, he blew up my house, he shot at and nearly blew up Rusty. I think he better be careful how close to me he gets. The last guy that came after me ended up dead. I didn't shoot him but I had him in my sights."

"How'd he end up dead if you didn't shoot him?"

"I was holding him at gunpoint until Rusty could arrive with help. Rusty showed up with backup and he was talking to me, trying to get me out of the line of fire. When I turned to give Rusty the rifle the guy went after me and the police fired." I shuddered. "Can we change the subject? I can still see that dead face staring at me. I can still hear the gunfire... So you see, it kind of takes a lot to scare me now. Trent doesn't scare me. If something happens I'll just deal with it, whatever it turns out to be."

"Michaels should..."

"Don't even start. I meant what I said, Landon. I will defend Rusty with my last breath. I will... I don't even want to think about what I am capable of for that guy. I've walked into traps to keep Rusty from it. I've been fired on to keep Rusty from being fired upon. He might not know it but it's true. We've been to hell and back again and, and..."

"Cassidy, I know I'll never have your heart. But can I have some cookies?"

I was so keyed up I could have slugged him. I went over to the couch and sat trying to get my head on straight. He came over, cookie in hand.

"I won't give up easily. I see something in you. I don't know exactly what it is yet. But I'll figure it out. And I know when I do I'll love you to the ends of the earth. In the mean time, I want to protect that something. So you have no need to fear me. And I won't come between you and Michaels. We better be going."

I put several cookies in a bag and sent them on their way.

When Landon was gone it was time to wind up the cookie baking and begin dinner. I started some meat cooking, added seasoning and cut up vegetables to add to it, then made Spanish rice and heated up beans. I left the meat and vegetables to simmer when the doorbell rang again. I went to answer it and two more officers stood at my door. I invited them in and the aroma of cooking wafted into the living room.

"I heard you were baking cookies but it looks like we showed up in time for dinner."

I gave them each a cookie.

"Is this second shift? Or did you guys just get word late?"

"We got word late. Thought it couldn't hurt to stop by..."

I packaged up a sack of cookies for each of them.

"So, why in the world is Tyrone Trent after little Suzie Homemaker here?" one of them asked.

"One: I refuse to be kidnapped. Two: he hates the police and he saw me tracking his crime scene. I think he also said he enjoyed a challenge."

"The part about refusing to be kidnapped sounds like a good idea. You okay here?"

"Yeah, I haven't been alone for five minutes. Everybody wants cookies."

"They're good. I know what I'm going to ask you to bring to the Christmas party."

"You guys work pretty cheap. Two double batches of cookies for a day's protection. Sounds like a good deal to me."

"What're you making tomorrow?"

"Sorry guys, I'm going to L.A. tomorrow."

They looked at each other. Oh, no, not them too. The front door opened and Rusty came through, looked around and headed for the cookies.

"You're real popular at the station. Everybody kept coming in with big smiles and little bags of cookies. Then who ever hadn't gotten any quietly sneaked out. How many cookies did you make today?"

"I quit counting. This is the last of two double batches. So what would you like for dinner? Fajitas or cookies? We got both."

He walked around, cookie in hand, and stood at the sliding glass door leading to the backyard.

"The flowers look nice. Flowers in the back yard, cookies in the kitchen, dinner on the table. A guy could get used to this. All we need now is a dining room table and a hammock in the back yard."

"I'll help you find a table as soon as I can. I'll look but I don't want to pick one. You should choose your own furniture. You need to get something you like, not what I like."

He looked disappointed. I was getting the feeling that he didn't want me to leave. First he got upset when I talked about moving. Now he wanted me to choose his furniture for him? He'd also been using words like *us* and *we* a lot. This sounds serious, I thought to myself.

The two officers shifted around uncomfortably, excused themselves and slipped out the front door. I wondered how this little exchange would get twisted around in the station gossip.

We ate fajitas at the coffee table, the tension mounting between us. We'd gotten through the first day.

Thursday might be tricky. I still thought it was safer to go to L.A. than stay in Joshua Hills. I even thought that Trent probably knew where I was staying if he'd been watching the station. He seemed tuned in to any odd behavior and having each and every one of the officers at the station quietly head for Rusty's house would have piqued his curiosity. So I was determined to get out of Dodge for the day and the meeting in L.A. seemed a good way to do it. When I got back to town, I'd go directly to the station so I wouldn't be out by myself for long. I thought the easiest way to sneak out of town would be the early morning rush hour. I could make my way slowly over the pass in a camouflage of suburban commuters. There's more than one kind of camouflage. A BMW on the freeway to L.A. only stands out when it's doing eighty or better. In bumper-to-bumper traffic it is just like any other car: stuck.

I got up at five a.m. Rusty noticed the activity right away and paced the condo nervously. I was ready to go by six.

"Wait," Rusty said. He went to the phone and made a quick call. "Just wait."

A few minutes went by and he received a call on his cell and after another short wait an officer was at the door. A quick conversation ensued and the officer left.

"Babe, be careful out there. You know what to watch for?"

"What was that all about?"

"I had them check the neighborhood for anybody sitting in a car. I just needed to know you were at least getting a clean start."

"Yeah, I know what to watch for and I promise to be careful. My cell phone is charged and handy. I'm taking the BMW. It looks more like a commuter car. I don't have to be there until nine but I wanted to get away before Trent gets up and about. And I thought I could blend in with the early morning crowd. I'll come straight to the station when I get back to town."

He wrapped me in one of his worried hugs. I knew this was hard on him but I really thought it was for the best. I gave him a goodbye kiss and went out to the BMW. I stood there for a second taking a big breath of courage and went to face my next twenty-four hours. I squared my shoulders, adjusted my attitude and got in the car. I started it up and pulled out of the driveway. As I left the neighborhood an officer in a patrol car waved a tense goodbye and then pulled out. He followed at a distance until I exited onto the freeway and joined the crush of cars headed south.

This was something I usually avoided at all cost. Going to L.A. and driving in rush hour were both foreign to me. If I ever left town it was to go camping, for the peace and quiet of nature. Traffic flowed well down the 14 until it hit Acton and then the press began. It was comforting in a way to be surrounded and hidden by cars. I took note of the colors and types of cars around me so I'd be sure to spot someone following. If that happened though, I didn't really expect it to be on the way to L.A. Nope, Tyrone Trent, was after the Joshua Hills police. They were the ones that cared about me. In L.A. I was just another civilian. Thanks to the whole cookie thing yesterday almost everyone in the station knew who I was. I hadn't planned it that way but that's how it had worked out. Now I worried that I had accidentally drawn them into the situation.

The traffic inched along the 14 and then crawled into the 5, everyone jockeying for position as the 210 and the 405 split off. I stayed on the 5 as it crawled along towards downtown L.A. There were spots where the pace picked up but it was bumper to bumper all the way with no unusual activity to suggest I was being followed. I reached the parking garage of the building where the meeting was to be held an hour early and waited, feeling like a sitting duck. Sitting for an hour was not good for me. It gave me too long to think about the trip back.

What would I do if I *were* followed? If that was the case then going to the station would be out. It's just what Trent would hope for: a big standoff in front of the police station. Nope, if I were followed I would call Rusty and pass along my location. Then I'd drive around, letting the police close in and surround Trent. If they could get between the white truck and me they could bag him. If I was followed I'd take the situation out of town. No use endangering the public. I'd find open roads where I could take advantage of the BMW's speed and maneuverability. If worse came to worse, I'd head for a place where I could find cover on foot. I was confident I could lose him in the woods but I preferred to avoid that. It would be harder for the police to catch Trent if I let him loose in the woods. I'd only do that if I thought it was my only chance.

While I sat waiting I went through the car, taking inventory. I was glad to find an old camping pack in the back floorboards. I opened it and found the usual contents: backpacker food; an old, stale water bottle; old, stale trail mix; a stick of beef jerky; and a hunting knife. Not much to rely on if I had to face Trent but better than nothing. I replaced the contents except for the water bottle and the knife. I placed the knife out of site next to my seat. I brought the water bottle into the meeting with me to refill it with fresh water at a drinking fountain.

It was the usual orientation type meeting with warnings about what to expect and the time needed to complete the course, the educational, physical and mental aspects of the job. I think they were trying to weed out the weak, the squeamish, and the uncommitted. After listening to all the warnings, I was skeptical myself. I was committed to completing academy but I wasn't sure if I wanted to be the person they intended to produce.

They instructed us on what to bring, how to dress, and what to expect on the first day of academy. They outlined what would be taught but I didn't see how anybody could get through it all in five months. I hadn't been to school since my days in the Marines, and even then I'd opted for the more physical aspects of the military. I'd have codes, regulations and procedures to memorize but I didn't expect to use that much in tracking. By the time I left I'd filled in all the forms they needed me to, I had several pages of notes, a sheaf of handouts, and my head was buzzing with new information.

I approached the BMW with trepidation. I was well into my last forty-eight hours and Trent could be ready to try something. I decided to eat lunch before heading back. No use meeting Trent on an empty stomach. I pulled off the freeway at a place that looked busy enough to have hotels and restaurants. I found a big, bustling, family-style restaurant and settled in for a slow meal. I took my time and worried about the drive home. Morning rush hour was over and the next wouldn't start for hours, so I'd be more visible on the way home. I looked around the restaurant for an odd man out, or someone watching me.

I could take the mountain road home, through Glendale, then up and over the mountain. But that would be dangerous if Trent knew where I was. If I drove over the mountain, I could stop in at Kelly's house or the ranger station. I'd feel better with a couple of stops on the way. But the high, mountain road still intimidated me. Normally I would enjoy the drive over the mountains but being forced off that road was more dangerous than the flats. Nope, the drive over the mountains was out for me this afternoon.

Cass, I thought, you need to change your attitude here. You can't let Trent get to you. You have to take charge. Just drive to Joshua Hills, and then drive to the station and everything will be fine. Just do it. But watch circumspectly. Keep an eye way ahead and an eye on your tail and it'll be fine. Yeah, right. To be safe I called Rusty before I hit the freeway.

Traffic going home was fast. I didn't have the cover of other commuters and I felt vulnerable. I zipped down the freeway hoping to get pulled over, but no such luck. I exited the 14 at Angeles Forest Highway to avoid Trent possibly staked out at the usual exit. I took surface streets into the foothill communities and took a long and winding route to the station.

The station was two blocks up and I was waiting at a red light when the door of my car gave a snap. It was locked and wouldn't open but I was startled by the sound. I turned to look and the first thing I saw was the barrel of Trent's silenced handgun inches from my face. I glanced at traffic, hit the gas and hung a right as a bullet tore through the convertible top of the BMW. How could I have been so careless! Where was he? Where was the stupid, big, white truck? I took the narrow residential streets too fast but I needed space. I needed distance!

This was the worst time to call Rusty, too, I needed my hands to shift and steer. I couldn't call until I was able to relax a bit. Remember the bullet in the box, Cass. He wanted to know. He needed to know. The police needed to jump on this. They needed to jump on Tyrone Trent's sorry ass and haul him to jail. I looked in my rear view mirror. The white truck was barreling down the street after me. I had to think. I had to find a way out of town with minimal traffic and lights. I needed to find a place where I could get the car into gear and not need to shift. All the major streets had lots of traffic. I'd get caught at a stop real quick taking those streets. Staying on the little residential streets risked life, limb and property not to mention the risk of accidentally stumbling into a dead end. I fumbled with the phone. Found Rusty's number and hit call. When he picked up I yelled, "I can't hold the phone! I need to shift! Just listen!" I put the phone on the seat and started a tense monologue. "Trent surprised me two blocks from the station! Put a bullet through the car top. I am going south on a little street called Glover and I'm fixing to hit Sierra. I gotta get this guy away from downtown. He's crazy!" I looked up. The truck was tight on my bumper. I couldn't stop at Sierra. I'd have to run the stop sign. Tires screeched as I came onto the larger, more open road. I stayed on it until I came to Liberty Blvd. There were very few cars around so I looked both ways and ran the light, turning left. "I'm going east on Liberty. Shit, this guy is stuck on me. I can't shake him." I came to an intersection that was packed with cars and I had to stop. I picked up the phone. "Rusty?"

"Keep him going. Choose a place you can lead him to."

"Shoot the light changed. I gotta go."

Traffic started moving and I weaved in and out of the traffic just as I hated other people to do. Trent dropped back a few car lengths.

"I'm still on Liberty. I don't know where to go. Where can I lead him? I can't hear you. The phone's on the seat."

The big, white, truck came up on my left and the lanes were merging. Trent laughed at me. I hit the brakes and let him go ahead. I pulled to a stop and let traffic flow around me and then flipped a U turn.

"West on Liberty," I said. "I'm going west now." I hit the gas, shooting forward. I picked up the phone. "Okay, I can listen for a bit. I need some advice. He'll catch up eventually but tell me where I can go."

"Two cars are closing in on you. Don't worry about your driving. They know what you're trying to do."

I felt a crunch and looked behind me to see the truck breathing down my neck, ramming the back of the car. I didn't want to lead Trent back into town again so I ran the light at Sierra again and headed down to another less populated street.

"I'm back on Sierra. Going south. I see lights behind us." Two squad cars closed in on Trent but he was right on my bumper. I needed to give them space to work. "Rusty, I need a goal here! Where do I lead him? How do I get him off my tail?"

"The white van. Do you remember the way to the white van? The road runs along the foothills. Don't get off on the dirt roads. We need a little time. Work with the guys behind you and then head for Foothill Road."

I turned on Palm, which led out to the desert. I hit the gas, weaving in and out of cars that were doing the legal fifty miles per hour. The monster truck stuck to my bumper like glue. I had some space with no traffic so I tried braking and then hitting the gas. Anything to create some distance. It didn't work. Trent had the reflexes of a fighter pilot. When I finally left the city traffic behind and I had a straight shot I floored it. How fast would this car go? I knew it would go faster than I was willing to drive.

"I'm doing ninety and this guy is right on my tail! I'm no racecar driver. I don't like this! How fast will that truck go?"

"Where are you now?" Rusty asked.

"Way out on Palm Drive. I have space out here but I can't lose him. And I'm scared to go faster. I can't do anything at this speed except go straight. I have to slow down to do anything! I don't know how far this road goes and I don't want to hit the end of it at ninety!"

I came over a low hill and met a slow moving tractor. I hit the brakes and skidded this way and that trying to control the car. Trent bashed into the back of the car again nearly sending me off the road. The police cars jostled for position. I zipped around the tractor, Trent on my bumper. A squad car pulled up beside Trent and Trent fired at it, shattering a window. The officer shot back and Trent hit the gas nearly colliding with me again. He pointed the gun in my direction and squeezed off a shot. The bullet tore though the top and landed with a *thunk* in the dashboard.

Give them some space, Cass. Let the police get between you and Trent. I hit the gas again, accelerating suddenly. Eighty, eighty-five, ninety. Nothing worked.

I picked up the phone. "Tell me what to do. I can't get space between Trent and me."

"We're setting up. Make a wide circle and come out at Foothill Road. Come in from the west."

"What do I do when I come to the set up? I need to know what to expect."

"Just drive through it. Try to slow down. If Trent won't go through it it's even better. He'll be boxed in from behind."

"Drive through it? What is it? Okay, I see a turn I gotta go."

I slowed down and hung a left, starting a big circle that would end on Foothill Road. I climbed back to ninety and there was a small gap behind me. That was encouraging so I hit the gas again and shot up to a hundred. A car appeared on the road ahead. It jerked to the side of the road when it saw me coming, Trent behind, followed by police cars, sirens wailing, lights flashing.

Having a goal helped me think and I was feeling a little more in control now. Trent was still there but he seemed to be waiting for something to happen. I think he *wanted* to meet this roadblock and he was looking forward to this standoff with the police. He had earned his fifteen minutes of fame and his only goal now was to take me with him.

I started going through scenarios. What would Trent do if I just pulled off and the police were still on his tail? He'd pull off and I'd be a hostage. What would Trent do if I just hit the brakes and rode out the consequences? He'd take out the car and then me. Plus it would involve the police cars chasing us. Nope, both of those were out. I didn't have many options so I headed for the barricade.

I saw the foothills of the mountains ahead and they quickly grew closer and closer. I slowed down watching for the turn. I came to Foothill Road and turned left.

"Okay, I'm on Foothill Road but I'm still a few miles away. I'm not sure how far out you are."

I cranked the car back up to eighty but the road started winding around the hills and I had to slow down. I doubted the car needed to but I wasn't comfortable taking the turns that fast. I looked behind me and saw the grill of the truck planted firmly on my bumper. I gave the car more gas but he stuck to me. The road straightened and I could see a faint dot on the horizon. The police.

I hit the gas, trying to put any distance possible between Trent and myself. I almost panicked when he pulled up beside me. There was more firing from the police cars as they spread out to fill the road and close the gap. The monster truck suddenly swerved into my lane. I hit the brakes and wrenched the steering wheel to the side to avoid him. The wheels of the BMW dropped off the pavement and jerked the car to the side. There was no shoulder on the road and I felt the car tipping and then rolling. I hung onto the steering wheel with all my strength as the car tumbled across the desert floor, filled with air bags. Everything was crashing noises and confusion and dust until the car settled, top down.

I looked around but couldn't see anything except airbags. My only thoughts were of Trent and that he was after me. Police or no police, he wanted to take me down. I punched at the airbags. I found the knife I'd hidden next to the seat now on the roof of the car in a pool of blood. I knew the blood had to be mine but I was too shocked to take stock of things. I was in flight mode and the blood would just have to wait. I used the knife to stab at the airbags until I could find a door handle. The doors wouldn't open! I was trapped! Looking out of the window all I could see was a cloud of dust. I put myself in action mode. Think, Cass, think. He'll shoot you if he gets to this car! He'll shoot you and you won't be able to avoid it!

All my exits were blocked. I had doors that wouldn't open. I had the floor of the car above that I couldn't get through. I had the roof. The roof! I had the roof! I took the knife and cut the convertible top of the car, thankful that I kept the knife razor sharp. There had been other times when my life depended on it. I slid through the cut I'd made, flattened myself against the ground and used the knife as a digging stick. It was sandy, like the car had landed in an arroyo. The sand moved around and I was able to lie under the car, almost invisible. Nearly killed by one arroyo and now saved by another. I pushed the sand aside until I was looking out the backside of the car. I took in my surroundings, hidden under the car. It *was* an arroyo. It ran under Foothill Road and up into the hills. It was about three feet deep and narrow. I slipped out from under the car and crouched in the shadow of the arroyo wall. Trent had left his truck and was running for the car, determined as ever to get at me somehow. I crouched and ran up the arroyo keeping to the wall and cover. I felt sand stuck to my face and reached up to brush it away but it was stuck in blood. The grit scratched at me. I left it alone, thinking I was just making it worse.

I heard gunfire behind me. I ran up the arroyo until I couldn't run anymore. I had a stitch in my side and the crash was catching up to me. I started getting shaky and out of breath. I looked over the edge of the arroyo and realized that I was up in the hills. It was summer in the desert yet I trembled so much it was almost like shivering. I was so scared. Okay, I thought, so Trent really could scare me. I sat trying to catch my breath. I looked around and saw trees. Yes! I could lose myself in the trees! So I dashed for cover and went into stealth mode hiding from the direction I last saw Trent. Hiding my tracks. Hiding in any way I could until I collapsed beneath an area of dense brush.

I couldn't run anymore. Why couldn't I run? I didn't know. I just couldn't. I was too weak, scared and shaky. I pulled leaves up around me, hiding me from the casual observer. I hid, knife in hand, waiting for whatever came my way, waiting for some strength to go on.

I heard leaves crunch and froze. Did I fall asleep? Pass out? I felt the knife being taken from my grip. No! I clutched at the knife, raising my hand defensively, tensing, backing into the brush. An iron grip closed around my wrist. I pulled with the knife hand and swung a punch hard with my left. It connected and I felt my fist slide through sticky blood. I gathered my feet beneath me and sprang forward, knocking the man over backwards. I yanked my knife hand free and forced my way out, stumbling out from under the brush, leaves flying. I turned, ready to face my attacker. I heard scrambling noises, crunching leaves and running feet. He crawled out from under the brush and stood, rubbing his jaw and looking at me, a mixture of shock, relief, and concern. I stood there, knife in hand, ready for the next move. Everything hurt, from head to toe. There was blood everywhere. My hair was stuck down in it. My hand was covered in it. Leaves were stuck in it.

"Back off, guys. Cassidy, stop. Please stop. You don't need to fight anymore. There's no need to run. Be still. Come on, babe, just be still." He stepped forward. I looked to the trees. I gripped the knife tighter, tensing. I was still in flight mode. "Trent's gone. You don't need to run." I took a step towards the trees just hearing the name. "It's over. No one is after you anymore. Come on. Look at me. Cassidy, look at me. Please don't run. You'll only hurt yourself worse."

As the words made their way through the tension and fear, I realized this wasn't Trent... it was Rusty. He stepped forward as he saw recognition settle in. I turned to him needing his strength, needing some peace. He took my hand and I felt the sticky blood give way as the knife was peeled from my palm. He handed it to an officer. He put his arms around me and I felt a deep relieved breath as he checked his emotions.

I looked around. Police cars were parked down the hill, lights flashing. My car had been pulled out of the arroyo. The white truck was loaded on a tow truck. The white truck. I turned away from the white truck, ready to bolt again. Trent. He's gone. Rusty said he was gone. I looked to the hills again and felt Rusty's gentle hands on my shoulders. "How did you find me?" I asked shakily.

"I tracked you up the arroyo. That part was easy.. You made things hard after that."

"Sorry, I wasn't hiding my tracks from you."

"I know. At least you didn't get far. And now I know you really do know how to hide. It took us hours to find you after you started hiding your tracks."

"Rusty, I hurt so bad."

"Will you let the guys help you now?"

"Yeah, I think I better."

Landon and Victor came forward. Leave it to Landon to be there. Didn't he have a normal job? Before I knew it I was on a stretcher being carried across the desert. I didn't like it, but I was hurting enough that I couldn't fight it. When we got down to the lights it was confusion again. They took my pulse and blood pressure and put an IV in. I felt gentle hands feeling for broken bones. Everything started blurring together again. I fought it.

"Cassidy," Victor said, "stay focused here. Talk to me. You need to focus."

There was a long pause while I tried to gather my thoughts.

"Was it you?" I finally asked. It was the only thing I could think of to say to Victor.

"Was what me?" he answered.

I carefully formulated the question in my head before I spoke. "Did you lay the test trail for Lou when he was going to talk to Rusty about a tracker?" It was a long question. I almost didn't get through it.

He paused in his work. He looked at me weird. "Yeah, it was me."

"I thought so."

He and Landon looked at each other. They both looked at Rusty.

"What made you decide it was me?"

"It just had you written all over it. I thought it was you by the end of the helicopter ride."

"You had barely met me but you matched my tracks to me?"

"I just get a feel for these things. I just wanted to find out if I was right."

They were working as they talked and the talk helped. But pretty soon everything started running together again.

"Where's Rusty?"

Landon said, "He's right here, just like he always is. He knows the drill."

"There's too much, too much going on. I can't separate things out."

"Then look at me or look at Rusty. Just look at the small picture and let the rest just happen."

"I don't want to be down again. I have academy to start. I have a race around Saddleback Butte to run. I only have until August."

"Knowing you, you'll make it to academy in August. I think it's a miracle that you came out of this at all and now here you are talking about starting academy."

"I was hoping it would keep me focused enough to stay out of trouble. But trouble seems to stalk me." A wave of dizziness hit me. "I'm fading. I hate that feeling. Don't let me fade."

There was poking and prodding and disinfecting. They strapped me down to a backboard. Just in case, he said. A bandage was wound around my head. I ached from head to toe.

"All right, here we go."

There was a clunk and a clatter and then the sound of people climbing in.

I looked around. I'd never ridden in an ambulance before. I thought of Lee. Lee had probably enjoyed the ride. He was happy and curious. He'd have thought of it as an adventure. I wasn't enjoying it. It was like ICU again. Then I remembered that wasn't true. I *had* ridden in an ambulance. I just hadn't known about it. I was glad I hadn't known.

"Rusty, talk to me, please talk to me. It's not as bad as it looks."

"You haven't seen yourself yet. You don't know how bad it looks."

"I know it looks bad because of the blood but I don't even know where the blood came from."

He took my hand and held it up "Look at your hands. Just looking at your hands makes me hurt for you."

I looked at my hand. It was covered with small cuts and was purple and swollen. I flexed the other one and felt gauze bandages. I didn't want to think what the rest of me looked like.

I was drifting again. Gentle rubbing. Concerned shuffling about in the ambulance. "Cassidy, come on girl, talk. You need to stay with us here," Victor said.

"Cass, tell me a story," Rusty said, "think of something you did and tell me about it."

I gathered my thoughts but I couldn't organize them. A story? Okay, a story. I couldn't sort out all the stories so I just started on the first one that came to mind. I started out weakly, hoping I was going to make sense, "When I was little, probably about eight, my dad sent me out to fetch Steve. I went out to the corrals and picked up Steve's boot prints in the yard and I followed them to the barn. Then I followed his horse's tracks out the back of the ranch." I paused gathering my thoughts. "I didn't know it but Steve had lit out after a colt that had been missing for days. It was a yearling with plenty of spirit and it had taken off at a gallop. It had plenty of energy so it was way off in the hills. I tracked Steve's horse until darkness fell and then I didn't know what to do. I thought I was closer to Steve than I was to the ranch so I spent the night sleeping with my back to an old tree. You know the old trees there."

"Yeah."

C'mon Cass, think, think…

"The next morning I still thought I was closer to Steve than I was to the ranch so I kept after Steve's horse. It was easy following a horse, no real tracking involved. Steve had gotten back to the ranch and he didn't know I was looking for him so he went about his chores. It wasn't until I'd missed dinner on the second day that people really got worried. They were used to me forgetting about dinner and I'd find something to eat later so they didn't worry that I'd missed one meal, two was a different story. Steve took off after me and found me just before dark the second day, still tracking his horse. Just goes to show you how stubborn I can be. Eight years old, tracking a horse for two days. Funny thing was, he didn't run up all relieved when he found me. He circled around in front of me until he found his trail and then he acted like I found him, just like I was trying to do. He let me accomplish my goal, so I told him Dad wanted to talk to him and he gave me a lift home on his horse. He went to talk to Dad and I got some dinner. It wasn't until my mom found out I was home that I knew they were worried. Dad wasn't worried. I was just out tracking Steve. But Mom knew how long I'd been without food and you know how moms can be."

I took a deep, trembling breath.

"And you were only eight?"

"Yeah, probably."

"What about water? There's no water out there."

"I thought Steve would have some. I wasn't worried about water. I thought I'd find him around the next curve or over the next hill."

The ride to the hospital turned quiet again and as the silence slipped in I could feel it slipping into my brain.

"Rusty?"

"What is it, Cass?"

But it was too late. I was drifting and couldn't drift back.

I woke up to quiet. Everything was too quiet. And white. And fuzzy, but the fuzziness was clearing. When things felt better I moved around a bit, trying to feel how strong I was. I couldn't move much. It hurt to move.

I sensed movement beside me and Rusty appeared.

"Shhh, just stay still. It's okay."

I wanted to say something but I couldn't think of anything to say so I just lay there hoping something would come to me. I went over the day in my mind. When I got to the car chase I couldn't help it. I tensed. The car. I'd lost the car. I felt for Rusty's hand, not because I needed it. I felt a need to be there for him. Images flashed in my mind of what I thought it had been like for him. The car crash. Seeing the bullet holes. No way in…

"Cass, babe, shhhh. Be still." But I couldn't. "What is it?"

"I'm sorry," I cried, "I'm so sorry, Rusty."

"Shhh, you have nothing to be sorry for. You didn't do anything wrong. What could you have to be sorry for?"

"I lost it. I'm sorry I lost it. I didn't mean to."

"Lost what?"

"The car, I didn't mean to."

"Don't worry about the car. You can get a new car."

He wasn't understanding and I was in no shape to try and explain it to him. But I couldn't let it go. The images flashed through my mind like a slide show. Rusty coming up to the car. The fear. The flashbacks. The bullet holes. The shredded airbags. The locked doors. Waiting for something to pry the doors open with. The puddle of blood in the roof. No Cassidy. The relief. The new fear. I cried quietly and he sat there beside the bed, not knowing what to do.

I'd needed a dozen stitches, five to close a gash across my head. That must have been where the blood came from. I was guessing the long cut down my thumb was from digging with the knife. A deep cut on my foot was probably from walking on glass. I was a mess. I was one big bruise. The doctors and the police both thought it was a miracle. They kept me a day to prove to themselves I was really going to live. Once I had enough fluids, painkillers, and antibiotics into me, and the x-rays and lab tests came out clean, they let me go home.

Unfortunately, I didn't have a home to go to. I didn't have a car. All I had left to my name was a very worried Rusty, a very bored dog, half my clothes, and a few kitchen gadgets.

I pushed myself out of the wheelchair, painfully climbed into the Explorer, and Rusty took me home. I hobbled into the condo and sat on the old brown couch but was too sore to sit so I lay down instead. I couldn't shake the images that rolled around in my head. I couldn't focus on anything. I wouldn't talk. I just lay there trying not to cry, trying to think of a way tell Rusty how sorry I was.

Rusty went out to get lunch but I couldn't force myself to eat. As evening wore on he began to worry. He knelt by the couch. "What is it Cass, what's eating at you? You've hardly spoken for two days. Please talk to me." But the images just flew by faster when I tensed enough to try and talk about it.

"Tell me about it." I finally managed to say.

"What do you want me to tell you?" He was being very careful, knowing he could lose this chance, but not understanding what it was that I needed to hear.

A long pause.

"The crash…" I was really trying. But I couldn't ask him to do that. I couldn't ask him to relive it again like I was. But I wasn't reliving reality and I knew it. I was just reliving what I imagined it was like for him. So I was reliving what it would be like for me. And it hurt so bad. "If you can."

He froze. All the care and concern vanished and was replaced by… what? Fear?

"No." he replied flatly. Not 'I can't.' or 'Don't ask that of me.' Just 'no'.

"Okay," I said, even sadder. I curled up on the couch, willing the images to go away.

Dinnertime came. I stared at my food, not willing to put in the effort of lifting the fork. Rusty picked at his food. He watched me, concerned.

"Cass, you have to eat something."

He ate just enough to assuage his hunger and carried me up the stairs to the bedroom. He set me on the big soft bed and handed me a pillow. I bunched it up, hiding in the folds, the soft pillowcase caressing my face.

"Cass, this can't go on. Please talk to me. At least tell me why you can't talk."

I caught the oxymoron in his words and almost laughed. How could one little statement break down a wall of fear and guilt and sorrow? It all came crashing down around me again but that tiny break gave me enough comfort to try.

"I can't make them stop," I said.

"You can't make what stop?"

"The images, I can only imagine and they are too big."

"What are the images?"

"What the crash must have been like for you. I don't have reality to go by so I keep imagining it and it's too big. I can only hurt when I see them and..."

Understanding was finally coming through for him. I could feel the walls go up. He was guarding that memory and it made the sadness in me grow.

"Rusty, please, I need some reality so I can deal with it. I can't grasp a piece of imagination and deal with it. It just grows."

It was his turn to retreat. He lay down on the bed and gathered me into his arms. It hurt to be hugged but I wasn't going to stop him.

After a long, patient, sorrow-filled wait I felt him give in. "I could only hear it," he said so softly I had to strain to hear him. "I was at the roadblock so I could only hear it on the phone. The screeching brakes, the sound of the car rolling. Then the radio talk started. The officers pursuing Trent got in a tangle trying to slow down and park. Trent went off the road right after you did. He came to a controlled stop in the desert and took off after you. I heard the quiet after the car settled... then I could hear noises. I couldn't figure out what they were. They were active noises, though, so I had hope that you were okay. I jumped in a car and drove down there as fast as I could. On the way I heard the shots, first Trent's silenced shots going through the car." A long pause while he gathered his thoughts again. "After... after the shots I realized I didn't hear noises through the phone anymore." He squeezed tighter causing me to squirm. "I could only imagine what that meant. I thought I'd lost you. Babe, I really thought I'd lost you... I heard the gunfire that brought down Trent. I could have killed him myself right about then... It took four guys to restrain me and it took forever to get your car up out of the ditch and open a door. You should have seen all the guys. No one wanted to go in that car. No one could stand the thought of pulling you out of that mess... I was trying but no one would let me go." It hurt to think of the raw emotion that would make Rusty that uncontrollable. "Wilson finally crawled in. It felt like an hour had gone by but I know he wasn't in there a minute. A lot of thoughts and emotions can fly around an accident scene in a minute... And he crawled out smiling. I was so messed up I could have squashed him right then and there. 'She did it again.' he said, 'She's not in there.' Schroeder gave the guys the okay and they let me go. I dived into the car. I looked around, found your phone. I was drawing a blank, though. I couldn't imagine how you escaped. I looked at the car and there was no way out."

My heart was pounding as he told me about it.

"Did you notice the roof? I cut the roof of the car with my knife and slid underneath."

"Is that how you did it? I looked around where the car had landed. I saw the dirt had been disturbed but I thought it got that way hauling the car out of the ditch. I picked up your trail. I found your footprints in the arroyo but I could just as easily have followed the trail of blood. You were bleeding so bad. I thought I wouldn't find you in time. Then when you left the arroyo you did something, I don't know what. Maybe the blood got lost in the weeds, but we didn't have anything to go on anymore. And I didn't know if you were running or hiding or... dying or what... It took us hours to find you and all the time I was thinking there was no way you could make it, through the crash, through the escape, losing all that blood. When I found you and you weren't moving... at first I couldn't move either. I crawled under the bush, hoping, just hoping I had gotten there in time. I tried to take the knife, knowing if I didn't I could end up cut to pieces, and I almost was. I was never so glad to be clobbered in all my life. That's quite a left hook you have there."

"I'm sorry. I still thought you were Trent."

"It's okay, I was relieved you had that much power left in you. Then I was worried you were going to take off again..."

"I'm here," I said, "I'm here. And I'm sorry I put you through all that. I didn't mean to. Even as it was happening I was kicking myself for putting you through the one thing you couldn't face.... Can you forgive me?"

"Forgive you? Cass, there's nothing to forgive. We did face it. We made it. We're still here, together, that's all that counts."

Finally, I could begin to find peace. Trent was gone. Rusty had faced his fear and come out on top. I fell asleep in a sea of pain and hurt, but at least I could relax enough to sleep. When I woke up Rusty was still there finding his own peace, soaking up the fact that we were still there together.

Chapter 13

I was trapped in the condo again but it was okay because I was so sore I wouldn't have gone out. A few days later I was still sore. It felt like the ache just settled deeper and deeper. The doorbell rang and I looked out the peephole. Tan uniforms. I opened the door and there stood Lou and Schroeder. Lou looked at me with his grandfather look. I invited them in and hobbled to the couch. They sat down, suddenly uncomfortable. They handed me a box and I took it with my purple, stitched up hands. I hefted the box and I couldn't help but smile.

"From the guys at the station," Schroeder said. "They heard you like cheesecake."

"Can you tell them all thanks for me? And that I'll send cookies as soon as I am able."

I got up to go get plates and share. I rattled around in the kitchen and brought out three plates and napkins. I settled back down and then remembered forks. Schroeder jumped up and came back with them. I opened the box and served up three pieces of cheesecake. We all took a few bites, the guys looking uneasy.

"So what's up at the station nowadays?" I asked.

They weren't going to beat around the bush. Lou asked, "Are you really trying to make it into the academy in August?"

"Sure, I'm not going to let a little thing like this stop me. As soon as the bruises heal a little it's back to the gym."

"A little thing?... What if I said 'no'?" said Lou.

"Then I'd have to go for a different reason, I guess. You could keep me off the search and rescue team. And Schroeder, I know you have the authority to stop me from helping Rusty. But you can't keep me from learning what I need to know."

"What if Rusty said 'no'?"

That surprised me. I wasn't sure what I'd do if Rusty tried to talk me out of attending.

"Rusty might be a little apprehensive about it. I'll grant you that. But I don't think he would forbid it. For one thing, he knows that if I don't do this I'll be up in the woods. He can't go with me because he has to work. So I'd be up there alone. It's something he doesn't like me to do. I don't mind it. I've hiked almost every inch of those mountains with gear, without gear, in rain, sleet, snow, fog. I need to be out in the woods. If I don't do it on a search then I will do it on my own. I'd just prefer to look for kids like Lee and people like Kelly. Sure, I'll still get cabin fever and head for the hills and get my Jeep stuck in ditches and end up hiking out. That's all normal for me. Hell, it's impossible to keep me from getting into a little bit of trouble. The best I can hope for is a minimum of suicidal murderers after me. If we can just cut back on those guys I might live to see some good come out of my life and that's my aim. Just to see some good come out of it."

"You don't need the academy to do tracking," Lou said.

"No, I know, but I won't be on call and available on a regular basis until I graduate from academy. So I need to go through it."

"You tracked before," Lou said.

"Yeah, but it was just recreational tracking. I doubt if any of the deer or wolves or other critters needed me to track them. Are you trying to talk me out of academy? Is Rusty having second thoughts? He talked me into this in the first place. He thinks I can get my outdoors fix in safer if I join the team."

"Kelly Green needed finding. Lee Chang needed finding. We want you to track. We want you to use your talent for good. But, Cassidy, you have come this close to losing your life not once, not twice, but several times. You've already experienced more danger and hardship than most people see in a lifetime. I know war veterans who have seen less action than you."

"And you think I'd get into less trouble bumbling like I have been instead of getting the training I need? You guys are not making sense. If I go through academy that is a full time job right there. I'll be out of trouble for five months. Just think, five months of not worrying. It worked for four years in the Marines."

They seemed amused by that.

"When I graduate you still don't have to use me. I'll just be qualified if you need me. And I'll know all the procedures, codes and policies. I'll be able to go out on the searches armed.

"Schroeder, what happened to Trent? After my car rolled all I knew was there were two patrol cars on his tail. I couldn't count on them catching him before he got to the car so I took off. What happened?"

"He got to your car in time to empty his clip into it. He reloaded and then he turned on the guys."

"And they shot him," I said.

"Yeah," he said slowly, "they shot him. And then they checked out your car. You know, it's not easy for a guy to watch you get gunned down and then have to go remove the body. These guys have been around. They knew what they'd see. And then Rusty got there. He'd only heard the crash through your phone, then he heard Trent shooting at your car. Then all the other shots…"

"Schroeder, stop. I know what I did. Tell me what I should have done."

"I can't. You did what you had to. Given the fact that Trent ran you off the road, you just did what you could."

"And what do you think I would do if I'd been through academy? If I'd been through academy and I had killer on my tail, I'd have been armed. I'd have taken Trent out myself and saved you all a lot of heartache. We might have been able to prevent the whole car chase and crash. If I'd just been armed I would have risked jail time to bring Trent down. He'd killed four people and he would have killed more. Eventually he would have found another way to make a stand against the force and it would have come to bloodshed then, too. I'm not afraid to take a stand. I just need to know where to draw the line and academy will show me where to do that. It'll fine-tune my judgment calls. It'll prepare me if this ever happens again and at least postpone it for a while. So why do you want me to back out?"

They didn't have an answer for that. We'd kind of forgotten about our cheesecake so I got up and got them something to drink and we finished eating in silence.

After they left I went up to the bedroom and lay there thinking. I realized that Schroeder could easily keep me from academy. One phone call would do it. That's it. One phone call and they wouldn't accept me and then what would I do? I could think about this so much better if I were at the hideout. Thinking about my future in Rusty's bedroom was getting me nowhere. It would be a tough hike the way I felt but I could take it easy. I had enough food stashed up there and I had a pack ready in case a search came up. But I was in no shape to backpack. I packed the bare essentials: trail mix and a bottle of water. I made sure the house was orderly and then called a cab. I left a note for Rusty saying I'd be back in two days tops.

I put on jeans, a t-shirt and hiking boots, then grabbed the daypack and was off. The cab dropped me off at the trailhead and I started walking. I took it very easy, just walking, not hurrying. I had most of the day to get there. The stitches in my foot pulled and felt irritated but that wasn't what slowed me down. I was still very sore. Movements were all slow. At the canyon I found the easy way up. I only climbed the rocks when I was tired from the hiking. I stopped frequently because I really did need the rest. I wasn't ready for this hike but I needed to come to a decision and I needed to be where I could cry. I really needed a good cry and I didn't want to do it with Rusty there. So I came to my hideout where I was free. So many tears had been spilled in these mountains. So much toil and sweat had been poured out here.

I reached the hideout at dusk and immediately cooked up some dinner so I could have everything cleaned up by dark. I was glad I kept a stash of backpacker food up here. The hideout was a mess. I'd left in some haste after the dog attack. There was dried blood on my sleeping bag from the attack. I'd wash it out tomorrow in the creek and the sun would dry the bag during the day.

I lay awake that night, listening to the coyotes howl. They sounded as mournful as I felt. What was I going to do? I had no home, no car, and no chance of that changing for six months. I couldn't stay with Rusty for six months. That was pushing his hospitality too far. I should move out now that Trent was no longer a danger. But where would I go? What would I do? Could I buy a house without the insurance money? If the insurance fell through how would I make payments? I needed a job and I needed to get through academy but the two didn't work together. I couldn't handle both. Just give me a trail, I thought. Give me a trail and a pack and let me go and I'll find my way. But here I was, trail and pack and feeling totally lost and lonely. I couldn't do this anymore. I couldn't just take off. Now that I had Rusty I only felt lonely in the mountains. And when I was in the city the mountains called me. I was stuck. My heart and my feet were at odds with each other.

I fell into a restless sleep and later woke with the sun to scratchy, scampering noises on my roof. I then remembered the chipmunk who made his home there. I brushed my hair and crawled out of the hideout. The chipmunk dashed up the tree and hid on a branch, staring down at me. I started up the little one burner stove and made oatmeal and hot chocolate. I sat on the flat rock next to the creek. Every bone in my body ached from the crash. Sleeping on the ground hadn't helped either. After breakfast I washed out the cup and the pan and packed up my stove again. I got out the trail mix and found a spot next to the hideout. I lay down on the ground with my arm stretched out in a comfortable position where I could see the chipmunk if it ventured onto my hand. I lay there for a long time thinking and watching the chipmunk's progress. He spiraled down the tree and shot back up again several times before he got brave enough to investigate my hand. It took him a long time to get used to me. I spent the whole morning there but that was okay. I didn't have the energy to go out and hike or rock climb or stalk. This was the only stalking I was going to do today. Finally, the chipmunk ventured out onto my hand and sat there eating and picking out his favorite nuts. I had to admonish myself to stay perfectly still and I was laying there thinking, keeping still when I saw Rusty's sandy brown head appear as he made his way up the canyon. When he saw me lying there alarm crossed his face, but he backed off once he saw I was at peace with the chipmunk contentedly eating from my hand. He stepped quietly behind a tree where he could watch out of sight. I lay there for a few minutes more, letting him see me be content in my mountain hideaway, then I moved my hand and the chipmunk dashed up the tree. I put the handful of trail mix where the chipmunk would find it. I started to get up and all the aches and pains clamored to be felt at the same time so I just sat. Rusty came over and sat next to me. He knew he was intruding in my private place and he was waiting for acceptance.

"I needed time to think," I said. "I'm not doing anything outside of camp. I won't get into any trouble. I don't feel up to it."

"Okay, so think."

"I haven't gotten very far in the thinking department yet."

"Then think out loud and maybe I can help."

"Rusty, it's something I have to decide on my own."

"And what do you need to decide on your own?"

"I'm still deciding that, too."

"Cass, you've just been in a major crash. You're physically and emotionally drained. Now is not the time to make major decisions."

I shifted around until I found a way to stand up. I held out my hand to him and he pretended I was helping him as he stood.

"I want to show you something."

I walked slowly across the canyon, wincing in pain as I hopped over the creek. I led him to the wall of the canyon and then followed it to the rock I'd discovered with Shadow. I climbed the rock slowly and stood on top of it, waiting for Rusty to make his way up. I showed him the mass of boulders. They looked like a giant had just tossed them onto the mountaintop. Huge boulders on top of other boulders. Boulders ten, twenty feet tall, stretching from the canyon wall all the way to the top. I stepped onto the first boulder.

"Cass, wait," Rusty said, alarmed that I was going to try a climb like that in my condition.

"How do I get to the top of the mountain without climbing the first rock?"

"You don't have to climb this mountain."

"Okay, say my life is this mountain. Something is at the top and I want to see what it is. How do I find out?"

"Then you have to climb the first rock."

"What if there's a rattlesnake or a bank robber or a suicidal murderer hiding up there? I still have to climb the first rock. And when I climb that rock, there's going to be another one. And every time I climb a rock I don't know what's going to happen. Anything could be lurking down there. I just have to climb it to see what's at the top."

"Cass, what are you trying to tell me?"

"I want to know what's at the top. I don't need to know what's lurking in those rocks. I'm willing to do the work of climbing up there if it's worth the trip. Right now that rock is finding a job, this rock is finding a house, that big rock about three weeks up the mountain is academy. I'm willing to climb but I need to pick a path and I don't know how to choose. I don't know what my options are. I know I can't stay with you forever. I should be out looking for a house but I don't know what I can afford. And I need to buy a new Jeep whether I can afford it or not. I need to find a job and if I find one I need to decide between it and academy. If I choose the job then I'm trapped in suburbia. And if I choose academy I have to find a way to get along for the next six months. And I need to train for academy. I need all these aches and pains and bruises to go away. And…"

"Cass, stop. You're taking on too much. Don't look at it all at once."

"And now Lou and Schroeder don't even want me to go to academy. I'm fighting an uphill battle here and I don't have anything to fight with."

"You don't have to fight anything. Come home. All you have to worry about right now is getting better."

"I don't have a home."

"Yes, you do. You always have a home with me. Cass, you think I didn't know what was going through your head? You have a puzzle to work on with a million pieces and you think you have to figure it out right now. But you don't. I don't want you to go. Please stay with me. I can't bear the thought of you leaving. At least give it a try while you do academy. It'll give you some time to figure the rest out."

"You don't want me to go?"

"Babe, I could hardly get through the night."

"And you want me to do academy?"

"If it's what you want to do. I'm not going to push you into it. It has to be your decision."

I didn't know what to say. My heart did a little flip flop. He didn't want me to go. And I realized I didn't want to go either. In fact, now that I thought about it, it would break my heart to go.

I looked at the sky. "It's after noon. I can't hike out today. It took me all day yesterday to get up here. Do you have to go back today?"

"Nope, but I didn't bring anything with me but a bottle of water. I just took off at first light."

"It'll be a chilly night. We only have one sleeping bag. We can use it for a ground cover. We've got plenty of food if you don't mind backpacker food. We can take the trail mix when we hike out. Are you okay with that?"

"I'm okay. I'm more than okay."

"Someday, though, when we are both feeling good again. Can we try to climb this mountain? I really would like to try it. I found it the day before the dog attacked me and I wanted to show this to you. It looked like fun and it looked like something I shouldn't try to climb by myself."

"I'm glad you didn't try it by yourself. Maybe Kelly would like to try it, too. Do you mind if Kelly comes up here?"

"He won't arrest me for squatting on national forest land? Will he leave the camp alone here for me? Even if I never come back, it's a comfort to know it's here."

"He'll be just as amazed by it as I was, and he'll leave it. It's not hurting anything. You can't even tell it's here. We don't even have to show him the hideout. You can't tell this is a camp."

"Kelly will know. Even without seeing a tent or a fire ring. He will be able to tell."

"How?"

"Camps just have a feel to them. So do places where animals regularly bed down. They feel comfortable."

"Let's climb back down. We'll remember this place and we'll come back when we're ready to tackle it."

I turned to descend the rock but got that eerie feeling again. I turned, examining the woods and the rocks around me. Someone or something was out there. Whatever it was, it was subtle. It was used to the woods and it seemed peaceful, so I tried not to worry. We climbed down the rock again. I was stiffer and sorer and the climb was exhausting.

"How did you get the squirrel to eat out of your hand?"

"Patience. Do you want to try it?"

"I don't know if I have that much patience."

"It's like stalking except you don't move at all. All the stalking is internal. You have to find a position you can hold perfectly still for a long time. Then you make yourself become as still as possible. You try to meld with the forest and still your mind. Eventually, if you have something they want, they get used to you and they will come to the food source."

"Do you think I could do it?"

"I think you'd have the patience for it. But you shouldn't be disappointed on your first try if you don't succeed. It takes a lot of self-control to not flinch when you feel little claws on your hand. Then, when you have them on your hand, it is hard to think without giving yourself away. You need to learn a new level of thinking to stay that way and not scare the critter."

"How does thinking affect it? Can't you think without moving?"

"Hmmm, maybe. It's the thinking, though, not just movement that gives you away. You know how an animal can sense if a person is afraid of it? Well, it's like that only more subtle. That's my guess anyway."

We had backpacker food for lunch and again for dinner. I'd have to buy more before my next trip up here. The night was chilly but not as cold as many nights I had spent on these mountains. It was warm with a different kind of warmth… the warmth that comes from two. And as we scooted closer in the night, we knew it was right for us to be like this.

In the morning after breakfast we set out slowly, easing our way down the mountain. As long as I walked gently I did okay, but hiking was out. It tired me quickly. When we stopped to rest, it hurt to bend and so we mostly just walked. We reached the trailhead, found the Explorer and drove into town. Rusty stopped at the kennel to pick up Shadow. I'd left in such a hurry I'd counted on Rusty to take care of him.

"I didn't know how long I'd be gone," he said by way of explanation. "I knew you wouldn't just leave him unless you were upset so I didn't know what it was going to take to bring you back."

"But you came anyway. How did you know where to bring him?"

"I asked around. You were on file and they knew Shadow."

"Detective work."

"Yeah, detective work."

The condo felt different when I walked into it that evening. It felt more settled. It still needed a yard, and I still didn't know what to do with Shadow here, but we'd be okay until the next step became clear.

Chapter 14

Over Rusty's protests I went back the gym. I took things slow at first and my bruised muscles complained the whole time. I came home exhausted and took long naps.

We bought a small dining room table that we both liked and rearranged the living room to make space for it.

I bought a new Jeep. Tan, four-wheel drive, soft top, with a winch and air conditioning. I didn't replace the roadster.

My trips to the gym gradually got easier, and then progressively harder.

I had the stitches removed, thankful most of the scars were hidden. The long thin scar on my thumb would fade.

Rusty and I settled into a comfortable routine, which, of course, grated on me within a few weeks. I was back in a rut again, ready for change.

I added shrubs to the backyard and a hammock big enough for two.

I made cookies and sent them to the station.

And suddenly it was August. When the first day of the month arrived I noted it in stunned silence. Only a few more days.

August is an awful time in the high desert, especially for running five miles. I ran in town. I ran in the desert. I ran around Saddleback Butte and thought I was going to die. I ran at the gym. I did pushups, chin ups, crunches and aerobics, anything to build endurance and strength. I knew my size was going to be a disadvantage so I built up in the strength department.

I needed to do some shopping before academy started. It was going to be almost like going back to school. I needed a binder, pens and exercise clothes in the right colors, including some clothes in "business attire" to wear until we were issued uniforms.

I entered the mall a little more confident this time and headed straight for Lavene's department.

"Hey there, girl!" she greeted me. "How'd it go with the dresses?"

"I love them," I answered.

"But what did *he* think of them?"

I laughed, "He loved them too."

"Right on! That's what I love to hear. What are you looking for this time?"

"I need clothes that are 'business attire'."

"And are these 'business attire' clothes meant to attract the same young man?"

"No, I'm attending a school where I need to dress right, just until we get uniforms. Slacks and blouses ought to work. I'll need to be able to move around in them but still look nice in the classroom."

"Business attire is all relative these days. Business people wear all kinds of things."

"No dresses, no shorts, no sandals."

"What kind of school is this?"

"Reserve police academy."

"No shit? You trying to catch yourself a cop? Girl, I thought you was smart. You know what it's like being married to a cop? Worryin' night and day…"

"Yes, I know what it's like. And I'm not really trying to catch him, per se."

"Then what's a kid like you doing in police academy?"

"I'm a tracker. And I'm not a kid."

"*You*, a tracker? You mean you follow footprints on the ground and look for people?"

"Well, yeah, but that's not all there is to it. Anyway, I found out that to help in search and rescue in any official capacity I need to graduate from reserve academy, so that's what I'm doing."

"I never met a tracker before. No wonder you had trouble finding a dress."

"Hey, trackers are allowed to look pretty once in a while too."

"You wear those dresses out tracking and you won't need to track, all the guys will be *following* you."

Lavene was a good saleswoman. Not only did she help me find slacks and blouses but she handed me "this little number" and an outfit "designed just for me" so I tried on everything she brought out. I left the store with three days worth of business attire, another dress, a pair of jeans that fit just right and a little plungey top that was supposed to go with the slacks but I knew I'd never wear it in the classroom. I didn't even know if I'd wear it at home, but it was cute.

"Thanks, Lavene," I said as I left the checkout counter. "If you ever get lost in the woods look me up and I'll track you down."

I stopped at a discount store for a white t-shirt, socks and black sweat pants, the standard workout wear for academy. Maybe I'd switch to shorts once I'd proven myself, but for now I didn't want to draw attention to the scar across my ankle.

Rusty was home when I walked in the door. I took my purchases upstairs and laid them on the bed. I moved stuff around in my section of closet to see if there was space. He picked up the items one by one. He'd been to academy. He knew what it all was, except for the little plungey top. Oops. And the dress. Shoot. I'd been caught.

"We aren't going to see much of each other once school starts." I said. "I'll have to be in L.A. by six so I'll need to leave by four and I won't get home until midnight."

He held up the dress. "Did you have something planned for tonight?"

"No, but I could start planning."

He held up the little plungey top. "And exactly what were you going to start planning?"

It seems like transition times always drove Rusty and I together for some reason. The thought of long separations or the possibility of change or danger brought us extra close. Neither of us wanted to admit that we didn't know how much time we had left together. It was an unspoken feeling that hung in the air, a dark and stormy cloud, so we took refuge in each other. I wore the little plungey top and the jeans that fit just right and we went out to a fun place and laughed and talked while he filled me in on what to expect at academy. He was so much fun to watch, his expressions lively and his mind sharp, his body relaxed and well muscled. I was glad to see the man I knew behind the tough look again. He was a man with the kindest and most dedicated heart. The gentlest person I had ever met hidden in this powerful and very dangerous cop, ready to take on whatever came at him. Every move he made delighted me. The more I watched, the more I thought the thing that was likely to come at him next was me. My body was ready to go home and my heart wanted the evening to last forever.

For some reason evenings never last forever, no matter how long we try to stretch them out. Dawn came and we reluctantly rose to meet it. The first day of academy. It was hard to leave the big, soft bed. I didn't have to go anywhere until late in the afternoon, but I didn't want Rusty to go to work without a good send off so I got up and made breakfast and we enjoyed a leisurely morning.

I walked him out to his Explorer.

"Don't wait up for me. I'll be late."

"Drive carefully," he admonished.

"Okay, I always feel like a kindergartener on the first day of school when I do things like this. Getting on the plane to go to boot camp was the same way."

He gave me a big hug and I felt even more like I was five years old again. If he told me to be good and listen to my teacher I was going to scream.

This was going to be an odd schedule to follow. About two o'clock I started cooking dinner so I could eat and get on the road by four. I cooked just enough for two and made up a plate for Rusty. I changed clothes, feeling stiff and uncomfortable in the slacks and blouse. I ate dinner and hit the road. Traffic was easy. All the commuters would be coming the other way shortly and the drive into L.A. went quickly. I pulled into the parking garage at the training center and located the room where we were meeting. How did I get myself into this, I thought. Commuting to L.A., going to school. What was I thinking? But it had been my choice and here I was.

We were a class of seventy-seven. Seventy-seven eager police reserve recruits. Well, most of us were eager. I was more like nervously optimistic. I was here to do a job, a bit uncertain what it would entail, but it had to be done. Six were women. It was a man's world here and it felt like it too, but that was what I was used to, raised like a son on a ranch full of men, then marching off to join the Marines. Only meeting Rusty had tuned me in a little to my feminine side, a side I was now beginning to explore, and I found pleasure in both worlds.

I got along great with the physical aspects of academy. Our first day was mostly taking stock of our physical abilities. I was pleasantly surprised to find out that running in L.A. was much cooler than running in the high desert. And academy was in the evening so running was very literally a breeze. I enjoyed it much more than running in the desert or gym. They started the class out on a one-mile jog so I was confident I could keep up with the physical part of academy. The exercises were all ones I was used to. The one physical thing I worried about was the body drag. A hundred and sixty-five pounds of dead weight and me a measly hundred and fifteen pounds.

The classroom part of academy was going to test my patience and my brain. There were so many things to memorize and read. Ten-codes were no problem. We'd used those in the Marines. Penal codes, regulations and procedures were going to be tough. Everything seemed to have a specific procedure linked to it. I knew these procedures were tested and proven to work in law enforcement, but whatever happened to just using your head when a situation arose? As it turned out, procedures were a protection to the officer. If procedure had been followed, the officer was in good standing. If procedure had been ignored, he could be in trouble. And in a group situation everybody followed the same plan towards a common goal. Hoo boy, so we do things by the book or not at all. Okay, I could deal with that. In fact I felt for Rusty and even for Landon, going by the book and having to deal with me.

I ran, I exercised, I climbed walls, I ran through an obstacle course. I sat through hours of instruction and felt like I was drinking out of a fire hose. I finally was dismissed and made the long drive home. There was very little traffic on the freeway and I was relieved, but this drive was going to grow old very fast. I pulled into the driveway a little before midnight. There were lights on downstairs. Rusty was in his office working when I stepped in.

"Hey, there. It's late. You didn't have to wait up."

"I know, but I just got back from the gym a half hour ago and I wanted to see how your first day went."

I sighed. I didn't mean to but it just escaped. "Well, no big surprises so far. It's going to be a lot of work. The procedures are going to be the hard part for me. You know I never was one to follow instructions very well. Lou has already questioned some of my actions but I didn't have anything to go by at the time."

"You'll catch on. You'll practice them and write about them and answer questions about them until they pop into your head automatically."

"That's what I thought about my self defense classes in the Marines. Then when Silva carjacked me, something told me not to use it. What do you do if instinct and procedure disagree?"

"Then it's time for statistics. How many people will be affected by each decision. You protect as many as you can."

"I've given you lots of practice with statistics. Seems like I am always going against procedure. Can I use your computer on Thursday to write a paper? I need to get a new email address, too. My mom and Jesse are probably wondering what happened to me."

"You didn't tell them about the fire?"

"I haven't talked to them. Besides, what will I tell my mom when she asks what I'm doing now? I can't tell her I'm living with you. She'll start bugging me about getting married."

"And you don't want to get married?"

I slammed on my mental brakes. Quick, Cassidy, backpedal as fast as you can and get out of this. "I didn't say that. I don't know what I want. I just don't want to be pressured *by my mom* to get married."

"After academy, would you think about it?"

My heart went from zero to sixty in two seconds. Butterflies waged war in my stomach. Think about marriage? I couldn't think about marriage. When I thought about marriage to Rusty I got shivers up and down my spine and broke into a cold sweat. There wasn't anything I wanted more, and that was what scared me.

"Is this a proposal?" I asked.

He looked at me seriously. "Yeah," he said. "It wasn't the way I would have chosen to do it but, yeah, this is a proposal. But, I know it's not a question you can answer right now."

I was stunned. I didn't know what to say. My heart said, "yes, yes!" And my head said, "no, no!" So I stammered, "Rusty, I'll never want anyone else, ever… But you don't want to be stuck with me for the rest of your life. It wouldn't be fair to you. I've already caused you so much heartache. Every time trouble strikes all I can think about is your reaction to it. And it hurts that I put you through so much. Yet you're always there. I don't want to put you through a life time of trouble."

He looked sad. No, he didn't, he looked lost… and broken.

"Babe, you're no trouble to me. I need you. I really, truly need you. Even if it only lasts a day. I want that day with you. I want every minute you'll give to me. When I hiked to the hideout, I was terrified. I didn't know if I could get you back. And what would I do if I couldn't? I didn't know what I would do. I'd be lost. I'd be totally lost and you'd be the only one who could track me down… but I didn't know if you would."

A long pause. I got a big lump in my throat. "I would. I couldn't stand for you to be lost."

"Then marry me and I won't be. I won't be lost as long as I know we've got each other."

With tears in my eyes I softly quoted one line of the old marriage vows, "I will never leave thee nor forsake thee as long as we both shall live."

He thought about my words and gathered me in his arms and held me for a long, thankful time. He was at peace again. He wasn't lost. And… and I'd said yes.

Chapter 15

Each day of academy we were thrown a few more curve balls. I soon began to think of life as a series of curve balls, sinkers, sliders, change ups, fast balls. In a way I was glad that they all happened in academy these days. Maybe that was a good thing considering the unpredictable nature of law enforcement. Sometimes the curve balls were different for me than for most people. When we were issued our uniforms I put mine on, but not with the proud dedication of most cadets. I wondered what Gina had looked like in her uniform and worried that I'd cause flashbacks or stir up more memories for Rusty.

As I drove home that day I was trying to think of an easy way to break in the new look to Rusty. I was coming up to a bridge when a man in dark clothes climbed over the side and sat watching the traffic. It was hard to make out what he was doing. It was night. The guy was dressed in black. He leaned forward and I started a frantic merging toward the shoulder of the road. I was on the shoulder as I eased under the bridge and then parked on its backside where the man couldn't see me. I called 911 and reported a man on the side of the bridge for unknown reasons. I ran back, climbed the bank, and stalked over to the edge of the bridge. I crouched behind the bridge railing, watching the man because there was no good reason for him to be out there. He was either up to no good or he was a jumper. If he was just up there spraying graffiti it wasn't worth the risk of catching him but if he were jumping I had to do something. He stood gripping the top of the bridge looking shakily at the cars zipping by. No spray can. He leaned forward.

"No!" I yelled, "You don't want to do that."

I sprinted out onto the bridge. I edged over the top of the old stone railing and eased down the side where I could see him.

"Get back!" he yelled. "Get the hell back!"

"Okay," I said, "I'll back off if you won't jump. You don't want to jump down there. It hurts. I've fallen that far before and it didn't kill me but it sure as hell hurt a lot."

"Yeah, right," he yelled back tense and threatening. "Sissy, white, cop, girl. When have you ever been away from your mama? You don't know what it's like to be me. You got no idea what I got against me. If you been through what I been through you'd jump too. Even if the fall don't kill me the cars will. I've thought this out."

"One: I'm not a cop. Two: I bet I can top any sob story you can throw at me. Three: I'm not a mama's girl. Four: if you jump from this bridge you aren't just killing yourself. There's a whole line of cars that are going to come around that bend. The first one will try not to hit you. He'll go swerving around the freeway taking out another car or two. He just might kill you but he might die doing it. The guy behind him might, too. After the pile up starts you could have a long line of people to deal with at the pearly gates and they'll all be blaming you. And what about the ones that don't die? What about the ones you cripple for life? What about the *families* of the people you kill simply by being selfish?"

"Shut up! Just shut the hell up. You don't got the cops after you. You aren't looking at jail time."

"Jail time is not worth killing yourself over. Plenty of people have led happy lives after jail. I haven't had the cops after me but I've had worse. I've been hunted by rifle carrying drug dealers determined to kill me."

"Ha, yeah right. You think I'm going to believe that shit?"

"Does the name Mario Peccati mean anything to you? It was his men after me."

This got a look. He was interested in this. A squad car came up and two more parked under the bridge. Pretty soon the place was crawling with cops.

"You had Peccati men after you? Shit, what did *you* do to piss off Peccati?"

"I discovered a drug lab he had hidden up in the mountains. I knew too much. He sent his goons after me. Look if you'll just climb back over the bridge I'll tell you all about it."

"No! You aren't tricking me like that. Even if I wasn't going to jail I got too much against me." The police were closing in. "Get back!" he screamed at them.

They backed off a few steps. "Let the girl go!" one of them yelled through a bullhorn.

"I'm just trying to talk him down," I yelled back. "He's not doing anything but trying to jump."

A news van pulled up on the street leading to the bridge.

"You got family?" I asked.

"I got a whole shit load of family just fucking trying to kick me off the family tree. I been getting into trouble so long they don't want nothing to do with me. Guess they think I get into the wrong kind of trouble. Shit, they always in trouble but they don't like *my kind* of trouble."

"Well," I said, "you can wave and say 'hi'. Looks like you're on TV. Bet they get a helicopter in here, too. How'd you like to be on national news? You think the whole country wants to see you bash your head open on the asphalt below. I don't think so. It isn't a pretty picture. Just think, all those kids sitting beside mom or dad, watching the news. You don't want them to see you do that."

The police were now expending as much effort on fighting off the press as they were in trying to help me. I noticed cars were no longer driving under the bridge.

"Look, you're kind of in a bind here. Your plan is unraveling fast. They've blocked off the freeway so no cars are going to finish you off. Now you have miles of angry drivers waiting on you to decide your fate. But all you will do by jumping is make every bone and every muscle in your body ache for weeks. Maybe you'll break a leg. About the most you can hope for is to break your neck and end up an invalid, but I don't think you're going to kill yourself."

I was inching over bit by bit. Stalking the inattentive jumper. Each time he checked on the location of the police I took a tiny step closer. Each time I took a tiny step closer the looks on the faces around me grew more concerned.

"I'm not going back!" he told me, "They'll have to shoot me to bring me in. I don't got a job, don't got money unless I rob someplace, my girl friend dumped me, my family dumped me."

"It can all change," I told him. "You can change. I know all about change. If I can do it anybody can. And the worst situation you can think of can be the turning point to a bright future. I know that, too. I've lived it. You can turn this around and use it for good. You can battle back from desperation and you can win over it. You don't want these guys to shoot you. It hurts to be shot. It hurts to jump off a bridge. If you go out violently it'll only be worse for you. If you come quietly it'll go easy. These guys don't want to shoot you. They all have hearts. They want to see you win, too. They want this to end peacefully."

I was right next to the guy now. I waited until he glanced away and I grabbed the back of his black sweatshirt. I wound my hand around in it, gripping as hard as I could.

"Now, look what you've done. You can't jump without taking me with you. The one person who was willing to come out here and stop you. I care if you jump. I really do. So if you still want to hurt yourself that way, go for it. If not, then come with me."

I started slowly climbing back over the bridge railing, keeping hold of the guy's shirt. His eyes held a desperate, scared look. He lunged for the edge but I held on tight. He didn't have enough leverage. As I clung to the bridge and to the guy's shirt, I heard the collective gasp of thousands of TV viewers across the country. The police ran forward and hauled him over onto the bridge, forcing him to spread eagle on the street.

I sat down on the curb away from the action, watching it happen all around me. I wasn't sure what I was supposed to do. Did I have to hang around and talk to the police? Did I need to file a report?

Next thing I knew there was a mob of reporters after me. Oh, shit. If there was one thing I didn't want to do it was talk to the press. They crowded around, firing questions at me.

A reporter shoved a microphone in my face. "Why did you stop?"

"Because I could see from the freeway what was happening."

"But, why stop, why not keep going? Hundreds of other people didn't stop. A single man on a bridge. What tipped you off that he was a jumper?"

"Suspicious behavior. Something just didn't feel right."

"You stopped on the freeway, in downtown L.A., at night just because something didn't feel right?" she asked, disbelieving.

"That's right."

"How do you feel about the outcome?"

"I'm glad he didn't jump. I'm glad he didn't force the police to shoot. I hope he straightens up his life and gets back on track."

"Some people would hope one of L.A.'s most wanted criminals *would* jump. Many people would like to rid the world of people like him. Why did you save him?"

Most wanted? "One: he was just a person to me. He told me the police were after him but I didn't know he was any different from any other person. To me, he was just a very depressed man. Two: I'm not going to judge which person lives and which person dies. If there's a chance to save a life, I choose to save it no matter who the person is."

"You are very young. How long have you been with the force?"

"I'm not an officer. I'm training at the reserve academy. I just happened to be at the right place at the right time."

I started inching out of the press of reporters and finally broke free. They gave up and put their star reporters on the air to review what had happened.

I climbed back down to my Jeep and noticed there was a parking ticket on it. Thanks guys, just what I needed.

I started the Jeep and began the long commute home again. So much for worrying about Rusty seeing me in uniform. Surely someone had recognized me and told him to turn on the TV. There were some disadvantages to having the whole Joshua Hills police force know who I was.

I pulled into the driveway at nearly three in the morning. I peeked into the condo before entering. It was quiet. The lights were on but... Rusty appeared at the top of the stairs wearing boxers and a t-shirt. He folded his arms across his chest in that all too familiar way that told me I had a lot of explaining to do. On the bright side, he didn't seem freaked out at the sight of the uniform.

"I think in the next academy class they need to teach us the procedure for talking to reporters," I said.

He descended the stairs, took a seat on the couch and motioned for me to sit.

"Do you know who that guy was?"

"No, I didn't think to ask his name. I was just trying to get him off the bridge."

"You did a good job on that count. When you are working in that situation, always try to get the guy's name. If you use it later, he will respond better if he hears his name."

"Okay, so who was he? A reporter described him as one of L.A.'s most wanted but it didn't mean much to me. To me he was just a man."

"He was Ramon Peccati. He was Mario's nephew and the family screw up. He was probably armed and very dangerous. You were lucky you caught him on a bad day."

"I wasn't trying to catch him and I wasn't even thinking about a jumper possibly being armed. If I were going to jump off a bridge, I wouldn't put a gun in my pocket first. It hurts to fall on a gun."

As usual, my logic didn't quite register with Rusty. He grinned at the naivety of it. I guess I couldn't blame him. I should have considered that possibility.

"So, what spin did the news put on the story?" I asked.

"You're a hero. You saved a life. You apprehended a dangerous criminal. You're a young, dedicated cadet and the world needs more like you."

"Yeah, right," I said, and tossed the parking ticket onto the coffee table. "While I was busy being a young, dedicated cadet they ticketed me!"

In class we try to stay on top of things and since the bridge incident was still fresh in everyone's mind they took class time to talk about crisis negotiation.

"Callahan, come up here." Oh, no. I went to the front of the room. I stood straight and as tall as my five foot four inch frame would stand. "For those of you who don't know, Callahan met with a little bit of trouble on her way home last class. Tell the class what you learned from your experience on the bridge. What did you do right? What did you do wrong?"

"Well, sir, I learned that if you park to help in a situation, you need to park legally." This drew a few snickers from the class. "I learned that I should have asked the guy's name while I was engaged in negotiations.

Using a person's name can make crisis intervention easier in that a person will be more cooperative if they hear their name. They will be more inclined to listen to you if you call them by name periodically. And it will be helpful to identify a person later if you can get his or her name. I also learned that even bridge jumpers could be armed. I didn't even think about the jumper possibly being armed and I should have considered that."

"And what did you do right?"

"I succeeded in my goal. I didn't know my goal was to catch a criminal. I was simply talking a jumper off a bridge and the jumper did not jump, so I consider that meeting my goal."

"And? You must have done something right if you succeeded in your goal."

"Sir, I really didn't know what I was doing. I just talked to him. I tried different things to see what might be used to talk him out of jumping. I even ended up contradicting myself and, in the end, I only managed to create enough time for me to edge close enough to get a good grip on him. Then I held on until the police took over. I didn't do things by the book. I just did what seemed logical at the time."

We then examined minutely the proper steps to crisis negotiation. I found the class interesting. I tried to fit what I could remember of my conversation with Ramon Peccati in with the steps to crisis negotiations and found I came up short. And some of the things I did right I'd done right accidentally. Establishing a common ground was one of the steps. How was I to know the common ground we had was his uncle Mario? I'm glad I didn't tell him I was responsible for his uncle's death.

One of the things I was very good at in academy was target practice. I'd been through sniper school in the Marines and had kept in practice with my 9 mm until Trent had stolen it. It was now sitting at the police station as evidence against him, but I would get it back eventually. In the mean time, at academy, we did target practice in a range and I found it a good way to keep my mind from the things that distracted me. I was dismayed when we started out with shotguns at close range. How could you miss with a shotgun at four feet? Eight feet? Twelve feet? But it didn't take me long to progress, four feet at a time, from shotgun to rifle to pistol. Then I was in my element. I'd always preferred pistols, probably because of my size. I just liked the fact that they are quick and simple to operate and it was what I was most accurate with.

We had two shooting ranges. One was simple target practice using paper targets with outlines of people on them. The other was a range with moving targets, some of them criminals, some of them civilians. We had to decide who should be shot and who should not. It was an exercise in quick reflexes and that was where I excelled.

I also enjoyed the physical aspects of academy. Running in L.A. was cooler and more pleasant. The obstacle course was similar to others I had run. Once the obstacles were familiar I set little goals for myself to complete it as lightly and quietly as possible, practicing for getting through the woods with grace and ease. No hauling myself over walls. It was a leap, a push and a drop on bended knees, ready to go again. I adapted what I could at academy to my life in the woods. I imagined a bed of dry leaves on the other side of the wall. How would I land without noise?

I didn't like learning how to subdue a suspect with a baton. I didn't like the drills in capture and arrest. I just didn't fit in with the aggressive parts of police work. I tried to psyche myself up, thinking that if I'd known these things when I went against Mario Peccati I could have avoided a lot of problems.

In the classroom I tried my best to apply what I was hearing and reading to what I would be doing. I trudged through writing papers, taking tests and examining situations.

The drills became more and more complex. We had a simulated shootout. Since I was good at being invisible I was rarely a target, yet I was a good shot. Figuring out exactly when to shoot and when not to was tricky. It wasn't a case of shooting all the bad guys. Some of the bad guys needed to be shot while some of them we were to be captured and arrested. Deciding which was which was a puzzle.

Chapter 16

One day during a break in activities I was talking to Sergeant Stafford.

"Callahan, what are you going to do after you graduate? Are you going to come back for a Level One?" he asked.

"No, the plan all along was simply to graduate from Level Two so I can work search and rescue in Joshua Hills. That's one reason I have trouble applying myself to the technical aspects of police work. I am simply a tracker trying to use my talents where possible and now I'm here in this totally police oriented school. I'm not sure I belong here, but I need to graduate to do what I really want."

"You're a tracker?"

"Yeah."

"We are going to have a few classes in tracking. How good are you?"

"I can't really say, sir. I feel confident of my abilities. I've followed some very tough tracks. I've followed week old trails. I've followed people who were hiding their tracks. I've tracked murder scenes and a car accident. If you want to know from an officer's point of view you can talk to Rusty Michaels or Lou Strickland at Joshua Hills. I seriously doubt you can come up with a trail for class that I can't follow. However I do look forward to learning more about tracking in the city. That's one thing I've never been called on to do. I think it would have to be attacked from a different point of view, more of a psychological perspective. Once I had to track a man from my house to a trailer park and some of that was over asphalt and residential yards and I basically just looked at what I thought the man would do and confirmed that he did it as I went."

"Why would you need to track a man from your house? Something tells me you lead a very interesting life."

"That's an understatement. Interesting doesn't even come close. I was tracking a man who had carjacked me. After I escaped from him, the police busted into my house to arrest the guy, but they lost him. I had an idea how he got away so I tracked the guy and led Detective Michaels to where he was hiding out. You see, I can be useful to the force. I just need to complete training so they can call on me more often. That's why I am here."

"Well, now I am looking forward to our tracking classes."

"Me, too."

When our first tracking class came up we were taken to a vacant lot and spent an hour just tracking. There was very little lecture to it. We were told how tracking fit into police work and the basic principals involved, including reading primary and secondary signs. Primary signs are the actual tracks, while secondary signs are things like evidence, broken branches, and items found on the trail. Sergeant Stafford asked the class who was particularly interested in tracking and the six who raised their hands were sent to work with me. I guess he had talked to Rusty or Lou because I doubted this was standard procedure.

We were told to follow the trails laid out in a vacant lot. I followed my trail with no problem. It was a simple walk through various surfaces. Then I went back to my group and helped them where they were stuck.

"Look," I said pointing, "the soil has a small mound on this side of the track, which means it pushed against that direction, so if you look in the other direction you should be able to find the next track. Did you take note of the length of the stride? If you did that, it would tell you how far away from this track the next one should be."

I went to the next person.

"I don't see anything!" he said.

"Try different angles. Try looking for something other than a track. Look at the rocks. Are the rocks disturbed? Are there bent or crushed plants? Sometimes you aren't looking for footprints."

Every time I came to a stuck tracker I could see what they were missing. This was beginning beginner stuff. It was what I did when I was six, tracking the ranch hands around when my dad sent me to fetch someone.

I went on the next person in my group.

"The trail turns here. Don't assume the trail is going to go straight. See the twist to this print? It signifies a turn. You have to be ready to follow in any direction."

"My trail merges with another trail. What do I do?"

"Take note of the tracks you are following so you know them and can tell them from another person's tracks. Then you will recognize them even from partial prints. Note the tread. Note the size. Note the wear patterns on the sole. Just follow the partial prints until you can see whole prints again and then compare to make sure you are still on the right set."

I made the circuit again.

"What kind of motion would produce a track like that? Look at the track and picture the person making it. What are they doing?"

I tried not to give them straightforward answers but to get them to think differently, to look differently. I guess it was working. The group overheard my comments and would try out my instructions to other people on their own trails. People started using different angles, they started picturing the physical motion that went with the track and they started piecing together the easy trails before them. Sergeant Stafford noticed we were finished and barked out instructions for me to start a new lesson. I took my group to another part of the vacant lot and had them wait while I ran, walked, turned, twisted, backed up. I just laid out a varied trail so they could gradually compare one kind of track to another.

"Compare. Look at the running tracks. Take note of the way the track pushes back." I pointed at a particularly good example. "If you are tracking a lost person or a person who is fleeing from the police, it'll look like this. Lost people often will panic and run off through the woods. You should be able to recognize a run. It tells you a lot about the mindset of the person you are following. People don't usually run without a reason. Now compare the running tracks to the walking tracks. You will notice after you track a while the different ways people walk. Toes pointing in or out should be noted when tracking. The walking tracks are harder to read than the running tracks, but you can get a better feel about the person as a whole if you follow them walking. Here's a turn right, see the twist to the soil? See how it mounds a little from the action? And the same thing happens on the left turn." I led them through the trail I had laid out, explaining everything that I could think of. When we finished, I found a piece of sand and laid the softest track I could. The imprint was too easily read for my liking so I made a print with my hand in the sand, invisible from above.

"When you lose a trail try looking at it from different directions. You may have to get down on hands and knees to see some tracks. You may have to get down to ground level. Do you see the footprint and the handprint I put down? If you have trouble seeing it from above, look at it from the side, like this." I got down on hands and knees and showed them the side view. They all tried it and noted that they could see from the side what was invisible from above.

"I tracked a man a half mile and all his tracks were about as distinguishable as these two tracks. I spent a half mile on my hands and knees, face down in the dirt, but I found the end of the trail."

The other groups had finished their trails and we had run out of time, but I felt confident my group had come out with a little more information than they would have otherwise. At least they came out of it with more tools.

The second tracking class took a different turn. They brought a tracker in from San Diego, Charles "Chase" Downing, and he led the class through some exercises. We did a simulated pursuit. We pieced together the path the "suspect" had taken to get away from a "hit and run accident". I let the others contribute as much as they could and I stepped in when they got stuck. At one point the tracks were hidden below grasses and then followed a ditch. I pointed out the direction that the grasses leaned and bent them aside to show the class the tracks below and how the tracks matched the bend of the grasses. When the tracks came to the ditch, I showed them a smudge that was a footprint leading into the water and I followed the ditch downstream until I found sign of the trail coming out the far side. It went into some rocks and I asked an individual from my group if they wanted to take over. I could make out definite sign that the cadet could clue off of and he needed the experience, so I backed off. Downing even threw in a little stealth mode to the tracking and I stepped in again, showing the class where the tracks were hidden and why. Roots, rocks, hard pack, brush, water... all these things were useful for hiding a trail.

Later, Downing took me aside. "Stafford told me about you. You're pretty sharp. Why did you back off? You knew all the answers."

"They wouldn't learn as much if I gave them all the answers. It takes too much practice to get good at tracking for them to get it all in just a few classes. They need to practice while they can. I try to teach them how to think and how to look at things, but it really boils down to years of observation. I'll be glad to put in my two cents worth when we study urban tracking. I'll be just like the rest of them. Actually, they might do better than me, since they are more pursuit minded than I am."

Urban tracking was a whole different ball game. It involved extensive profiling. Looking ahead. Figuring out what the person would think to do. It was more searching than tracking. Building evidence that points to a certain direction. Basically, it was detective work boiled down into one big search. It was a puzzle, and since I always think of things like a puzzle anyway, I found the classes fascinating. The pieces fit together in so many ways but usually only one direction jumped out at me from the evidence in class. Perhaps the lessons were designed that way. Maybe it was my observation and puzzle solving working in a different way. I'd have to wait until a real life search presented itself to find out for sure. Downing made it sound like urban searches were a fairly common thing. Finding runaways, Alzheimer's patients who wandered from home, suspects that had gotten away, prisoners who had snuck away from work groups. All these fell under the heading of urban tracking.

Another long day was behind me and I drove the long and winding road home. Home. It seemed strange to think of Rusty's condo as home. I hadn't done anything to change it except plant a few things in the back yard and help Rusty choose a dining room table. Still, the condo seemed to accept me and I seemed to accept it, at least for now. Rusty always managed to wait up for me. Shadow always greeted me at the door. He and Rusty had come to a truce. He obeyed Rusty and didn't jump up on him, so they got along. I wished he didn't jump up on me.

"How's school going?" Rusty asked as I came in the door.

"We've been doing a little tracking."

"Yeah? How did it go?"

"Mickey Mouse stuff. But I was surprised that Sergeant Stafford assigned a group of cadets to me. He let me work with the ones that showed more of an interest in tracking. So I got to do a little teaching, not just tracking. How did you do on tracking when you were in academy?"

"I passed. It was nothing compared to what I've seen you do and that's what I told Stafford when he called."

"We talked about urban tracking today. I bet you're better at urban tracking. It's more detective work."

"Speaking of detective work, your mom's been doing a little of that. You need to call her. She called asking why your telephone's been disconnected. She's been worried about you."

"What did you tell her?"

"I told her you were fine, and I'd pass the message along next time I talked to you."

"That's all?"

"I thought you should choose what to tell her."

Sigh, "Okay, I'll call her tomorrow."

I picked up the cell phone reluctantly. What should I tell her? How much should she know? Should I stress the positive? Ignore the negative? I sure didn't like these kinds of conversations.

The phone at the ranch rang several times before Martha picked it up. I knew to let the phone ring. The ranch house was huge and it took a while to get to a phone unless my sister Jesse was there. When we were growing up Jesse was the official phone answerer because nearly every call was for her.

Martha greeted me enthusiastically and made small talk until she tracked down my mom.

"Cassidy!" my mom said brightly. "Where have you been? I've been trying to reach you for weeks! Your phone's been disconnected. Are you okay? Are you having trouble? You should have called if you were having trouble."

"Mom, I'm fine. Why didn't you call my cell phone? Everybody calls my cell phone now."

"I tried, but you didn't answer."

"I'm sorry, I have to turn off my phone while I am at school. You must have called while I was at school."

"You're going to school now? That's wonderful! What are you studying?"

"Umm, it's not your typical school. I'm in Reserve Police Academy."

"Cass, what are you *thinking*? That's like *asking* for trouble to get involved in police work. Next thing you know some criminal will be after you just like that Peccati man." Been there, done that, thanks Mom.

"I'm not going to academy to get into police work. I need to graduate from academy so I can do tracking for the search and rescue team here. The reason my phone doesn't work is because I moved. Do you want my new address?"

"Of course!"

I gave her Rusty's address. "Don't pass it around. It's unlisted." A long pause.

"Cassidy, you're not telling me everything. You wouldn't sell your house and you have no reason to have an unlisted address unless you are in trouble."

"Mom, I swear, I'm fine."

Another long pause. She wasn't going to buy it. Hoo, boy! Here goes.

"Mom, how do you know these things? Okay, my phone is disconnected because my house burned down. The address I gave you is Rusty's. It's unlisted because all the police have unlisted numbers. I'm doing fine. I'm staying with Rusty until I finish academy."

Shocked silence. "How did the fire start?"

"Like usual, a murderer was after me."

"Cassidy! What do you do to attract murderers?" she asked, incredulous.

"The good news is the murderer has been caught. I have had very little trouble since school started and I'm due to graduate in January if I pass all my exams. Will you and Dad come down to the graduation ceremony?" Stress the positive, Cass.

"Of course! If you want us to."

"Good, I'll let you know if I pass. It's a tough exam. There's a psychological test, a physical test, a shooting test, and a written exam. So there's plenty of chances to mess up."

"Back up a bit. What did you mean by 'very little trouble'?"

"Mom! I wasn't in danger. I was driving home from school and I saw a bridge jumper. I just talked him off the bridge and the police arrested him and everything was fine. I was on the news. I'm glad you missed it."

"Cassidy, I don't hear from you for several weeks and then I find out a murderer was after you, your house burned down and you have rescued criminals from bridges. I need to call more often! Is there anything else you aren't telling me?"

"Mom! Oh, all right, I was in a car wreck, both my cars are totaled and I'm driving a new Jeep. Rusty and I are unofficially engaged. There, that's it, I promise! Don't mention the engagement. We aren't making it official until I graduate from academy."

"Are you sure that's all?"

"Mom! That seems like enough to me!" Oops, I forgot the dog attack.

"How did you total *two* cars?"

"The murderer blew the Jeep up to make a point to the police. I wasn't there. I was fine. Rusty nearly got roasted. I rolled the BMW trying to escape from a car chase but I'm fine, I promise!"

"And now you're going to school and you and Rusty are engaged?"

"Right, but don't start planning anything yet."

"Well, that sounds wonderful!"

"You're really glad?"

"Of course, dear. Rusty's a great catch and you have always enjoyed tracking."

"Thanks, Mom."

"Now that I've caught up on the news. I was trying to call you to see if you could come home for Thanksgiving. I thought if I called early enough you could plan better. Everybody misses you and we'd love to see you again."

See how common trouble is in my life? Now that I've caught up on the news... Like I'd told her it rained yesterday or that I bought new kitchen curtains.

"Can Rusty come too?"

"Of course, Rusty's almost family. He's always welcome here."

"I'll talk to Rusty and I'll let you know in a few days. He might have other plans for Thanksgiving."

Whew! I did it. I talked to my mom and she thought everything was wonderful. How did I manage that?

It suddenly dawned on me that November was just around the corner. Time flies when you're buried in homework and classes. What could I do for Rusty's birthday?

When Rusty came home for dinner he gave me the *Well, did you do it?* look.

"What?" I asked.

"Well, did you do it?" Ha, I knew it.

"Yes, I did it."

"And?"

"And she wants to know if I'll be home for Thanksgiving."

"And?"

"So we better get out a calendar and look at the month. We have a lot going on."

"Cass…"

"Okay, she pried almost all the news out of me. The fire, the cars, academy, our engagement."

"And?"

"She thinks it's wonderful."

"Wonderful?"

"Yeah."

"Are you sure you were talking to your mom?"

Halloween had arrived before I knew it. Rusty never stayed home for Halloween, but I couldn't disappoint the kids. I took a look at the neighborhood, estimating how many kids were in it, and bought a truckload of candy, some pumpkins, and lights to string around the door.

Rusty came home to find his front stoop decorated with pumpkins and orange twinkle lights. Yellow and orange mums were planted along the walkway. When he walked in I was up to my elbows in pumpkin guts. He grinned.

"Grab a Sharpie and draw a face on that one." I said pointing to a squat pumpkin covered with warts. A twisted stem protruded out the top and curled around.

"You want *me* to draw something?" he asked.

"Sure, it doesn't have to be a face. Draw what you want to carve."

"You want me to *carve* something?"

"It's not hard. I like to carve fall leaves around my jack-o'-lanterns. The kids usually like when I do black cats. One time I did one of a wolf face but all the kids thought it was supposed to be Shadow. If you like this pumpkin better you can have this one. I like to buy pumpkins with character."

"Pumpkins have character?"

"Of course! That one over there looks like an old man. It needs a serious face on it. Or a spooky picture. This one is friendlier. Which one would you like?"

He looked like he was going to protest but went upstairs and changed into jeans and a t-shirt. He sat cross-legged on the floor with a pumpkin in his lap and puzzled over what to draw. I wished there was a camera handy. After I had finished gutting my pumpkin, Rusty was still puzzling. To help him get started I took a sheet of paper and drew several possible pumpkin faces, then handed it to him. Next I took another piece of paper and drew the basic outline for a black cat with an arched back, and a second cat sitting with its tail hanging down. I cut out the cat shapes and used the pattern pieces to trace cats around my pumpkin. I found the little saw I'd bought for pumpkin carving and went to work, carefully cutting out each cat and trimming the sides so the picture would be nice and crisp when the jack-o'-lantern was lit. Rusty had chosen a face and done a decent job of drawing it on the pumpkin. I handed him the saw.

"Work slow, it's easy to put too much pressure and bend the saw or overshoot your cutting lines."

He overshot his cutting lines. His pumpkin was missing a tooth. Oh well, the kids would never know. I added a candle to both jack-o'-lanterns and placed them on the stoop, ready for lighting.

"I hope you're not setting a precedence here. Will I have to be home for Halloween from now on or risk a toilet papering?"

"Hopefully you'll learn to enjoy Halloween and you'll want to stay home. Should I be Skipper or a biker chick? It's the only looks I can pull off on short notice."

"Guess."

Sigh, he wanted me to put on the cute little summer dress and be Skipper. I went upstairs and changed clothes, curled my hair and then brushed it out to maximum volume. I put on tons of mascara and some green eye shadow. I added pink lipstick. Rusty grinned when he saw me.

"You pull off Skipper pretty good. When do I get to meet the biker chick?"

"You go tracking with the biker chick. I wear camouflage pants, military boots, a Harley t-shirt, a bandana and glue on temporary tattoos."

Darkness fell and I turned on the lights and lit the pumpkins. Before we knew it there was a constant flow of kids at our door.

"You look like Barbie's little sister." I heard over and over. Rusty looked over my shoulder as I handed out a couple of candy bars to each kid.

"Hey," one little girl exclaimed to Rusty, "Are you Ken?"

I laughed out loud. Rusty never intended to look like Ken but I guess he was as close as he could get. His hair had grown out again so he resembled Ken a little bit.

I closed the door as a group of kids left to go on to their next stop.

"What do we do for dinner when all this is going on?"

"I usually end up calling out for pizza but I'll cook if you want to answer the door."

The doorbell rang again. I brought the bowl of candy bars to the door and opened it cheerfully. Kelly and Rhonda stood there, big grins on their faces. Rusty stood behind all the Halloween decorations and his little Skipper look-alike, looking very embarrassed. Kelly looked at his best friend and burst out laughing. A group of kids ran up behind them and Kelly grabbed a handful of candy, dropping one into each bag. The group ran off again. I handed him a Snickers bar and invited them in. I let Rhonda choose from the bowl.

"Oh, man, are you sunk! We were wondering where you were. The whole crowd is at Trujillo's and you're at home handing out candy. I should have known Cassidy had something to do with this."

"Rusty, you can go if you want to," I told him, "I wasn't trying to keep you from your plans. Go on with Kelly and Rhonda."

"We live at the end of a dirt road. No one ever comes to our house," explained Rhonda.

The doorbell rang again. I answered it cheerfully.

The kids all sang out, "Trick or Treat! Hey, you look like Barbie's little sister. Cool costume!" I handed them each a couple of candy bars.

"Thanks, you too. Have fun! Happy Halloween!"

"Rhonda, call Zeke's, we'll be back," Rusty called to us as he and Kelly headed out the door, then softer, "I swear, I never know what to expect out of this girl."

"It's okay. It's good for you," Kelly replied.

They got into the Explorer and drove away. Fifty kids later they were back with chips, dips, and beer. The pizza dude delivered three large pizzas. I paid him his thirty bucks and gave him four candy bars. Pretty soon we had a party going. By the end of the evening Rusty was answering the door too.

It seemed like trouble was taking a vacation. Since academy had started my life had been pretty much trouble free. Academy, homework and figuring out what to do for Rusty's birthday kept me busy. I looked around the condo, trying to find any evidence that pointed to interests or hobbies that Rusty might have. The only thing I knew for sure was that he went rock climbing with Kelly. I started looking around the condo for things that could be upgraded. I kept coming back to Rusty's office. His computer sat on an old metal desk that looked like it was snatched off the set of Dragnet. Folders were stacked in organized piles. Odds and ends filled the drawers. I wasn't going to take his office apart and put it back together. I knew not to touch that project. But I thought he could have a more pleasant place to work.

There wasn't much furniture in the room so there wasn't much to be careful of when I started my project. I found some police patches, photographs of the local squad cars and other things that were police related. I copied them and blew them up and framed them. Then I went to a home improvement store and bought wallpaper borders that matched the color scheme of the pictures. I hid everything then went shopping and found a professional looking, cherry wood computer desk. I made arrangements to have it delivered while Rusty was at work. I pulled his old desk to one side and had his new desk placed in the corner. I covered both desks with a sheet of plastic and hung the wallpaper borders. It was really a two-person job, but eventually I developed a system and put the border all the way around the room. I positioned the empty desk and hung the pictures. I looked around. The office still needed something so I decided to buy an ornamental tree, which I placed in the corner. Then the threadbare, old chair had to go, so I bought a new chair.

When Rusty arrived home from work I was cooking dinner determined not to say anything about the office. He came in and gave me a hug. He checked out dinner and then went upstairs to change clothes. He was gone for a long time. I finished dinner, set the table and got drinks for both of us. I put dinner on the table then went to call him to come and eat. I climbed the stairs tentatively. I peeked in the bedroom, not there. I peeked in the office and found him sitting silently in his new chair. I was almost afraid I'd done something wrong. He was so quiet. It seemed as though no matter what his reaction, the first thing Rusty did was become quiet. Was it a cop thing?

"Everything is just where you left it in your old desk. I didn't want to mess up your system."

He motioned me in, still quiet. He pulled me down into his lap and rested his chin on my shoulder. He was still for a long time.

"You did all this for me?"

"Is it okay? I was worried."

"It's fine... I just can't believe you would do something like this for me."

"Why? I would do anything that I thought would make you happy. This is the only thing I could think of. I wanted you to have a nice office, one where you could be comfortable. I didn't know if we were allowed to paint the walls so I didn't do that. The borders will be easy to take down if necessary."

"Don't touch them. It's perfect. I don't know what to say."

"You don't have to say anything. If you like it, I'll help you switch your stuff over after dinner. If you don't like it, we'll figure something else out."

Dinner was a quiet time. Guess he still didn't know what to say. I cleaned up the dishes and found him transferring things from his old desk to his new one. He'd pulled it out from the wall to run the computer lines and after pushing it back we started adding things from his desk drawers.

"You know what this room still needs?" I asked.

"What could it possibly need now?"

"After we take out the old desk we should put a comfortable chair in that corner. If you have people over they will have a place to sit."

"And if you're up here you can sit there and tempt me to quit working."

Chapter 17

Time was ticking by and I was watching the mountains. I had to get back up there before the first snowstorm. After the first snowstorm hit I would be trapped in the desert until spring. Sure, I could drive up into the mountains and spend a very cold night in a campground. I could snowshoe in, make a snow camp and freeze my buns off. I'd done that before. But the hideout would be impossible to get to. The canyon was too rough and quickly became impassable.

Academy was playing havoc with the other things in my life. I would have school on Rusty's birthday. Then Thanksgiving would be spent at the ranch. I had school the following Tuesday.

December weather was bearable in the mountains but I risked missing my last trip to the hideout. I circled the second weekend in December on the calendar.

Academy seemed extra intense for some reason. Maybe it was just because I was trying to get ready for a trip to the ranch, study, write reports, and keep up physically all at the same time. The class also seemed to sense our training time was becoming more limited. Our schedule would get thrown off by the holidays and before we knew it January would be here. Would we be ready? Everybody wanted to be ready. Nobody wanted to fail, although it was very common to have several cadets not pass. We all knew we could be one of those that didn't quite measure up this time around. So I pushed, I studied, I read the policies and procedures manual. I ran the obstacle courses and fine-tuned my shooting.

I had academy the Wednesday before Thanksgiving, so Rusty and I had to drive to the ranch on Thanksgiving Day. We took off early in the morning and drove straight through after a quick breakfast. No use eating lunch if Martha was cooking dinner.

When we arrived I could smell pumpkin pies and Martha's wonderful cooking as soon as I got out of the Explorer. Everyone at the ranch was in a festive mood. There were hugs all around. Martha held me out at arm's length and looked at me with concern after she hugged me.

"Cassidy, you're wasting away to nothing. Betty, look at this daughter of yours, she's skin and bone."

"Mom, I'm fine. We just exercise a lot at academy. You know this always happens to me when I exercise a lot."

Mom said, "Rusty, it's good to see you. I'm so glad you could come."

I could tell Martha and my mom had been busy. There were fall decorations on the coffee table and fireplace mantel. Fall colors adorned the massive dining table where the whole ranch gathered for meals. Rusty and I took our suitcases upstairs and settled in. Our rooms had fall flower arrangements on the dressers. It was like staying at a bed and breakfast inn, except it was home. Rusty gave me a disappointed look as he went to his room, next door to mine. Don't worry, I thought, I'll find a way.

I went to my room and changed clothes for dinner. I put on the dress Lavene had convinced me to buy when I was shopping for academy clothes. I curled my hair and freshened my make-up and went downstairs feeling almost comfortable in the dress and pumps. My mom and Jesse looked at me strangely.

"Cassidy, are you sure you're okay?" asked Jesse.

"Yeah, I'm more than okay."

"She's in love!" Jesse exclaimed. "The only thing that could get Cassidy into a dress is love."

"Jess, I chose to wear this. Is that okay? It's Thanksgiving. I wanted to dress up a little for dinner."

"She's in love," Mom said.

"I would be too, if I was her," Jesse confessed.

Rusty came downstairs in his brown sports coat and tie. These were his typical work clothes, but he looked sharp. No need for him to get dressed up. He looked at me standing there in my new dress, glad I had chosen it without being asked.

When Martha rang the big triangle on the back porch everybody out and about headed for the house. We all gathered around the huge ranch table and my dad then stood to give a word of thanks, his booming voice filling the room.

Thanksgiving dinner didn't just mean turkey at our house. With a dozen people at dinner it meant turkey, roast, venison, and ham, sweet potatoes, mashed potatoes, stuffing, vegetables, fruit salad... the list went on and on, and for once I actually had an appetite. Jesse picked at her small portions while I heaped up my plate and dug in.

"How can you eat like that and be so skinny?" she exclaimed.

"Join the police academy. It'll do that to you," I explained.

The table instantly fell silent. I looked at my mom.

"You didn't tell them?"

"Well, no, I talked to your father but..."

"Okay, well, I'm attending reserve police academy in L.A. so I can do tracking for the search and rescue operations in Joshua Hills. When I graduate I'll be a Level Two reserve deputy. It means I can do whatever an officer can do as long as a Level One officer supervises me. But I really just want to track. I've already participated in a few searches."

"She found a kid lost in the woods," Rusty interjected. "And found a passenger that was missing from a plane crash."

"So Trouble, what kind of trouble have you gotten into since we saw you in the spring?" asked Steve.

I looked at my mom.

"You didn't tell them that either, did you? What about Dad?"

"No…"

I looked at Rusty.

"Actually things have been pretty quiet since I started academy."

"Amazingly quiet," added Rusty.

"Then watch out," said Randy, "because when trouble comes it'll be a doozie!"

"I think I can do without a doozie after what we've been through *before* academy," Rusty said.

This started the questions and the storytelling. I threw in the tiger story and the rattlesnake story for Patrick's sake. He always liked stories that included animals. I left out the dog story. For some reason I still felt badly for killing the dog. Even if it was in self defense, its death still bothered me. And I didn't want my mom to worry about my camping trips. I told them about academy and what it was like and all the different things we did.

The hands at my parent's ranch were Steve, Zack, Randy, James and Old Frank. Old Frank was more of a manager and the four younger guys were the hands-on nitty-gritty workers of the ranch. They did everything and anything from training horses for racing to doctoring to fence mending. They were all around cowboys, except for a lack of cows.

Jesse's my sister and she's married to James. They have two boys, four-year-old Patrick and three-year-old Wyatt. Patrick is a little worrisome because, well, he seems to take after me. No worries with Wyatt though. He likes to color and play with trucks and cars. Patrick on the other hand stalks rabbits out of the yard, makes friends with anything four footed, and follows tracks on the ground. So far he doesn't seem to be a trouble magnet but his curiosity leads him where it shouldn't.

My father, Big Wayne Gordon, is an old west buff. That's why we all have western names. I am Cassidy, named after Butch Cassidy. Jesse is named after Jesse James. Patrick is named after Pat Garret and Wyatt is named after Wyatt Earp. Maybe that's why I get into so much trouble.

Maybe it just comes with the name. James and my mom lucked out on having old west names. We credit James with also being named after Jesse James, and my mom with being named after Elizabeth Simpson Bradshaw, who brought her children all the way across the country in a pushcart and settled in Utah. Now my mom goes by Betty, but she still enjoys the little bit of heritage that goes along with her proper name.

It takes a group of hungry cowboys a while to finish Thanksgiving dinner and Martha makes sure there is plenty. After Thanksgiving dinner was over, we all retired to the living room and sat around, still catching up on my recent adventures. Martha served coffee and those with a little extra room left over had a piece of pumpkin pie. As the evening wore on and the talk came to an end, people got lazy and drowsy, then wandered off to the bunkhouse or home. Rusty and I went out to the porch swing, one of my favorite spots on the ranch. I could see the horses out in the pasture, the hands going about their evening chores.

Nighttime fell and a million stars came out. Nights at the ranch were spectacular. The ranch was nestled down in the hills off the main road and away from town so the air was clear and the stars shone brightly. There were times as a kid when I'd been caught away from the ranch after dark but the stars shined bright enough to light my way home.

The night air turned chilly but I didn't want to move. The porch swing rocked gently and the peaceful sounds of lazy horses drifted up to the house. It was the ranch at peace. I could have spent all night there but it was finally time to go to bed. Rusty followed me up the stairs and to our rooms. He gave me a good night kiss outside my room and went to his own dejectedly. I heard a door close down the hall.

I entered my room and gathered up the few things I'd need in the morning. Then I went to my door, checked to see if the coast was clear, silently crept down the hall, and finally into Rusty's room. He smiled as I closed the door silently behind me.

"Cass, your family…"

"Will never know and they won't see me leave."

It must have been all the storytelling. I don't know what brought it on but I drifted into nightmares. The car was tumbling again, but this time I couldn't find a way out. I could hear Trent's footsteps approaching the car and I fought the airbags just as I had in real life, but this time there was no way out. Trent was out there, and I was trapped. I heard him trying to open the car and saw his face peering at me through the windshield. He backed off, pointing his gun at the windshield. I flattened myself against the roof of the car, laying low, trying to be as small a target as possible as the bullets came through the windshield. Rusty shook me gently, talking quietly to me, rubbing my arms soothingly, bringing me out of the frightening dream. I awoke clinging to Rusty, still making myself as small as possible. He held me while the feelings settled down. He understood what it was like. His touch was so tender. Would the nightmares ever go away? Would I ever lead a peaceful life? One I would like to dream about?

I awoke early and showered in Rusty's bathroom. After dressing silently I crept back to my room carrying my boots. I slipped in, remade the bed, put my boots on and puttered around the room. I wore Levi's, a turquoise and red plaid western shirt and buckskin-colored riding boots. I left my bedroom door open as I headed for the kitchen. I scooped out a large helping of scrambled eggs, took a slice of bacon and ate quickly.

It was a cool, crisp, clear autumn day. I went down to the barn to visit with Shasta. I talked to him, catching him up on the news, just visiting. It had been months since I'd seen him. Did he even know he was my horse, or was I just a stranger who showed up periodically and rode him during my visit? I thought about what we could do together. Shasta was a very versatile horse. Since I got bored easily as a kid, I'd tried him at a variety of horse activities. He didn't do well at dressage, but that was more because I detested anything that involved formalities. If it could be done on the fly in normal clothes, I'd tried it. I put an English saddle on him and took him out to the corral, rolled the barrels around, and hauled out boards to make jumps. Rusty found me busily setting up jumps and helped me carry and set the boards on their posts.

I trotted Shasta around the arena and brought him at a lope to a low jump. I hadn't done this in years, so I was taking it slow. He cleared the jump easily. I wasn't going to try any really high jumps, but I was enjoying the ride and setting Shasta up for the jumps. I knew not to come at them from just any direction. I had to set the run up for a clean jump. Rusty settled in at the fence, watching me ride. He hadn't ridden enough to be comfortable in the saddle, so he preferred to watch me from the sidelines. Maybe I could get him to go on a trail ride later.

After I'd gotten the course settled in my mind, I took Shasta through it trying for more speed. Shasta came out of the second jump and I turned him to go into the next, but the speed threw off his timing. He tried to clear the jump and made it over but, with his timing off, he tripped on the way down, sending me sailing over his head. I hit the ground stunned, watching a thousand pounds of gray quarter horse rolled over the top of me. It felt like being run over by a steamroller. I felt myself get ground into the dirt of the corral, the air was pressed from my lungs. A hoof missed my head by inches. Shasta struggled to a standing position. He stood nearby as he'd been taught to do while I fought to breathe. I could get a little air, but I had to think about it to do it. Gasping for air I struggled to get up, but couldn't. I lay back, waiting for everything to settle down. Talk about being at one with the earth. I felt like I was now a permanent part of the corral.

"Rusty, no!" I heard shouted from the barn. Running footsteps. "Stop, I know how hard it is, but you have to give her time." Steve, leave it to Steve to jump in.

"You didn't see it," Rusty countered.

"Hey, I saw it and I've seen it before. I've seen worse. You just have to give her time. This isn't a first. Cass is made out of rubber or something. She's okay."

Rusty was angry. "She's not made of rubber! She's just like you or me. And she's hurt!" He started over to me but he kept Steve's advice in mind and knelt beside me.

Made out of rubber. Ha! I felt like a pancake, that's what I felt like. Nope, not even that. Pancakes rise. I didn't have any air to rise. I wouldn't say I was hurt. I couldn't feel much of anything except squashed. What does squashed feel like?

"Watch this," Steve said. "Cass, take your time. I'll take care of Shasta for you."

"Nope," I gasped, "you know the rule."

"The rule?" Rusty asked.

"Just wait," Steve replied.

Shit, the rule. Yeah, I knew the rule. As I gained control of my breathing my head cleared and as my head cleared I started taking stock of other things. Hands and arms, okay. Feet and legs, okay. I pushed myself up, no broken ribs. Broken ribs would hurt like hell. Okay, I thought, I was okay. I peeled myself off the corral and walked around, getting things back in working order. I scuffed my feet through the person shaped indentation in the sand of the corral. I brushed the dirt off my clothes. I pulled my pocket inside out and a hand full of dirt fell out. I emptied my boot and pulled it back on.

I looked at Rusty. "Yeah, the rule. The rule says I have to go back and complete the jump right, before I can call it quits. Think of it as ranch procedure. There's a reason for it even if you don't see it. I need to go do the jump again so Shasta and I both know it isn't a scary thing, that we can do it. I know what I did wrong, I just took the jump too fast, so now I need to go correct that. If I don't go back and take Shasta through the jump, it can lead to problems later. I don't want him to balk at jumps. With horses, training never stops. It's just part of the ongoing work."

I took Shasta and walked him around, watching for any signs of limping. I climbed into the saddle and rode in a wide circle around the corral, going through the gaits, watching Shasta for any sign of pain. Rusty backed away to the fence, shaking his head. I ran through all the jumps a little sloppily so we did them again with more grace and ease. We took our time, setting up the jumps carefully. By the end of the exercise Shasta and I both felt better.

I let Shasta wander in the corral while I put away the boards and barrels. Rusty helped carry boards again, although I didn't need him to. He kept looking at me like he expected me to keel over, but I didn't. I left three barrels out so I could try barrel racing later. Then I took Shasta to his stall.

"What do you want to do with the afternoon, now that we got our daily disaster over with?" I asked. "Would you like to take a drive? Do some stalking? Go for a ride in the hills? Learn how to do calf roping? Barrel racing?"

"Something a little less accident prone."

"Aw, come on, I got the accident over with. That means we can do anything we want to safely now. Want to go hang gliding? Sky diving?"

"I want you to do something for me," he said.

Uh oh, that means none of the above.

"Okay, what do you want me to do?"

"I want to go out in these hills and I want you to show me how to track you."

"What?"

I looked around. Steve looked up, interested.

"I want you to teach me how to track you. I want to know what you do when you don't want to be found. When I tracked you up the arroyo after the crash and you took off into the trees, I had no clue what to look for. So show me. I almost you lost you once. Maybe if you teach me what to look for…"

"Okay, I can try. It usually takes years to be able to track like that. And that's if you actually practice tracking. You haven't had time to develop the basics yet."

I went upstairs and changed from boots to moccasins. He'd only have to track me in moccasins or hiking boots, but I didn't bring my hiking boots along. We hiked up into the hills. I found a place that looked very normal to the untrained eye but held an abundance of track hiding tools: rocks, tree roots, young green plants that would spring back quickly, an old log.

"I'm going to lay a trail. Watch what I do before you try and follow it. Seeing the action behind the track helps. Later you will see the track and picture the action."

I took off just walking carefully, placing my feet in places where the outlines of my footprints would blend with nature. I found a rounded rock and used it to hide a track. I followed some brush where damp leaves would still be left looking like damp leaves. I followed a tree root and carefully edged around the trunk following another tree root in a different direction. I made sure to touch the ground every once in a while, for Rusty's sake, but I still wanted him to lose my trail enough to make him really think. I followed the dead log and moved in stealth mode over to a large tree that he could use as a landmark to finish the track. Then I slipped into stealth mode and made my way back to him, staying invisible, appearing out of nowhere beside him. He didn't startle when I appeared, but he gave me that pleasantly surprised grin that I now watched for.

"Now, you saw me do it. Find the evidence that supports what you saw."

He looked at the ground and had trouble right from the start. He'd seen me make the tracks, slowly, carefully and purposely, yet now they were invisible. How could that be?

"You let the watching distract you from the beginning of the trail. What was I doing here?"

"Just walking. It should be plain."

"I wasn't just walking. It might have looked like I was just walking but I was placing my footsteps carefully. If you were going to hide your tracks here what would you do?"

"It's just open ground. I wouldn't think to try and hide my tracks here."

"There's almost no such thing as open ground. The arroyo was open ground. Wide, sandy stretches are open ground. This is not open ground. There's many ways to hide tracks here. First, remember I'm hiding my tracks, and think what you would do if you had to hide yours. If you still draw a blank, try different angles. Remember what my shoes are like. They aren't going to leave hard lines. Look for soft lines."

"Mmm, I like that approach. Look for Cassidy's soft lines."

I laughed. "And keep your mind on the job."

He studied the ground. He really wanted to see what I had done, but this kind of tracking was too advanced for him.

I stripped off a handful of leaves from a nearby branch. "Here," I said, "I'm going to mark my foot prints. When you can make out the sign enough to go to the next one, then go on." I tracked myself through the trail and placed a leaf in each footstep. When I got to the rocks and tree roots I skipped those, leaving them as puzzles for him to figure out.

It took him all afternoon to track me a quarter of a mile, but he finally reached the tree.

"Now," I said, "I have two ways of walking when I'm in flight mode, which is what I was in when Trent was after me. One is where I am hiding my tracks. The other is easier to track because I am just trying to stay out of sight. That's what I did on my way back to our starting point. This trail you can take more from a logical point of view. Keep in mind where you were standing and look for things that block the view from that direction. Then follow the footprints using that kind of logic. If you were to track me from the arroyo, you'd remember that Trent would probably be coming from the direction of the car, or his truck. So I was hiding from that direction. When I was running from Peccati I was running from the general direction of his house. You can't count on that all the time. Tracks are rarely that straightforward but it gives you something to start from. One thing you can usually count on with me is that I do things logically, no matter what the situation. It is a puzzle and so I look at the pieces. Where is the threat? If you can identify the threat you can narrow down the choices I had to work with. Usually if I am being chased I use a combination of both stealth modes. You have to keep in mind that it is easy to slip between the two modes. I tend to switch back and forth a lot."

"You make it sound like this is something you do a lot."

"Well, I do practice it a little in all my hiking off trail. I always walk carefully, leaving few footprints. I use this kind of walking in tracking sometimes. I slipped into it when I was tracking the passenger. When I knew the tiger was loose, and particularly when I thought the guy was shooting at us, I slipped into stealth mode without even thinking about it. It's just normal for me. When I was a kid I even walked in stealth mode around the ranch."

When he finally reached our starting point again he looked at me worriedly.

"I sure hope I never have to do this again. I'm glad you are capable of hiding so well, but, Cass, I don't think I could do it again."

"It takes practice. Try just tracking me around the ranch, anywhere you know it's my tracks, and they will become more familiar to you. The quicker you can identify them in easy settings the quicker you will identify them in tougher situations. I'll wear my moccasins more so my tracks will be easier to distinguish from the boot prints around the ranch."

Saturday we went out into the hills again. This time we just went hiking, but Rusty followed me. I walked normally most of the time, but every once in a while I did something to hide my tracks and I'd feel him slip behind while he pieced together what I'd done. If he got stuck, he'd call a halt to the hike until I explained to him what I'd done. There were no trails through the hills so it was all cross country tracking for Rusty and it was good practice. By the end of the day, I was pleased to note that he was asking for help less and less. My tracks were getting familiar to him. My mannerisms were recognizable. All this practice on my tracks would pay off on other people's trails, too.

It felt good getting out in the hills with Rusty. I knew as soon as we got home I'd have to focus on academy, so the hills were a pleasant and relaxing way to spend an afternoon.

"Did you notice for part of our hike we were tracking some deer?"

"No, I was too focused on your tracks to notice any other tracks."

"What if you were tracking me and I was being followed. Would you notice that if you were tracking me?"

"If the other tracks got in the way I would. If they stayed off to the side I'd probably miss it."

"Trent knew enough about tracking, he would have been in stealth mode and off to the side if he had followed me. Sometimes it pays to see more than the tracks you are following."

We were walking back to the house after our long day in the hills when I heard the frightened cry of a young horse. There were shouts and swearing and the thud of hoofs on hard packed dirt. I ran for the small corral at the back of the barn. Steve and Zack were there with a colt dancing at the end of two lead lines.

"Cass, you want to try?" Steve asked.

"What are you trying to do?"

"Just get him to accept the blanket on his back. He freaks out whenever anything touches his back."

"Is this a new thing to him?"

"Yep."

"Okay." I stepped into the corral. "Back off guys, he knows you're the bearer of the evil blanket. Let me talk to him."

I took the lead ropes and walked over to the frightened colt. I talked to him in a sing song fashion, just making conversation.

"What's the matter, boy, did those guys try and put an evil blanket on you. Those bad guys, they should know better..." Crisis negotiation, horse style. I brought the rope down tighter as the colt settled until I was just standing next to a very agitated young horse. "It's okay, look, I don't have a blanket. It's just you and me. Come on, settle down. Easy, boy, easy..." I ran my hands over his blaze and down his neck. I felt the muscles tighten with the touch. I talked to him as I ran my hands over his neck and finally his shoulders. I talked constantly and gently as I worked, getting him used to the touch. It was like stalking. Friendly stalking. Closing in on the ultimate goal, to get a blanket on a calm horse. I ran my hands over his back and he immediately started bucking again. Hooves flew around my head but I let out the lead ropes and then gradually pulled them tighter, talking all the way back to a calm, then I started over. Talking, touching, working my way over to his back.

Rusty watched with interest until the colt reared and then it was all he could do to stay on his side of the fence. He didn't know what to do anyway, so being on my side of the fence wouldn't have accomplished a thing. Steve pulled him back to stand by the barn. There was an exchange of conversation that I couldn't hear because I was talking to the colt. I imagined Rusty was getting another dose of ranch procedure that he'd rather not know about.

An hour later the colt was calm again and I was able to touch his back without being in danger of losing my head. I ran my hands over his back, getting him used to the touch. I led him around the small corral until I found the blanket sitting draped over the fence. I put his back to the offending blanket and ran my hands over his back again, talking to him all the while. I deftly grabbed the blanket with one hand while touching his back with the other then substituted the blanket for my gentle touches. The colt tensed but the blanket wasn't that different from what he had felt before. It was just a different texture. I ran my hands over the blanket so the new texture felt a lot like the touches he was now used to. I led him around the corral, praying the blanket wouldn't slide, talking to the colt, running my hands over the blanket to keep the feeling familiar.

"Good boy, good blanket, what a good boy." I kept a constant motion with my hands, soothing the troubled colt, keeping him slightly distracted from the bad blanket, running my hands over the blanket to keep the feeling of familiarity, talking, always talking.

"Are we going for the saddle yet? I don't think he'll take the saddle."

"No, you're doing great." Turning to Rusty, Steve said, "She's been doing this since she was a teenager. The horses just respond to her for some reason. Whenever we had a tough case we'd call Cassidy in and she had the horse calm and accepting within hours. We tried not to call her in, though, because next thing we knew she'd try and ride the horse. She'd climb up on any horse old enough to be ridden."

The colt shied away from the male voice but I thought it was time for the guys to take over again. I talked to the colt while I moved the blanket. He shied away but he didn't startle again. I slid the blanket back and he shied again. He was relatively calm, so I left the blanket on him and tied the rope loosely to the fence. When I stepped out of the corral, the blanket was still on the colt's back.

We finished off the Thanksgiving dinner, including all the pie. I only managed to get two pieces of pie this Thanksgiving and was tempted to bake another one but didn't have time. I needed to hit the books. I spread out all my homework on the dining room table to put in some reading time. There were a few police reports to fill in by hand and then I needed to write a paper. I had to remember the drills we had done in class because the police reports were supposed to be about them.

Randy came through the house looking for my Dad and found me with the mound of books.

"Looks like you're back in high school again."

"Except this is harder. And there is a lot more physical work involved, too. I keep reminding myself that if I'd known all this when Peccati showed up, he wouldn't have gotten away when he came to the ranch. I'd know what to do now. So, see, this police stuff has its uses."

"Rusty says you aren't going to do police work."

"Well, the hope is I won't be doing any police work. I want to track. But I am finding out that everything I learn is helpful, even if I never do a lick of police work. I'll be a lot better prepared defensively after learning all this."

"Rusty told me some of the things that have been going on. More of a 'What am I going to do with this girl?' attitude. He knows what happens to get you into these messes but he can't seem to figure out how to prevent them. You've got to stop walking into these traps. He can see why these criminals have gone after you, and he can protect you up to a point. But in the end, you walk right into danger and Rusty can't stop you. He talked about the car chase and the crash. He still doesn't know how you survived the crash with just cuts and bruises. You need to find a way to keep trouble away, Cassidy. I'm afraid one of these days trouble's going to sneak up and finish you off."

"Tracking with a search team should be a lot safer. They thought it was funny that I chose search and rescue to keep me out of trouble, but then I told them a few stories and I guess they believe me now. Plus, a couple of the guys on the team have been working with the police when I ran into trouble, so they kind of see how it happens. I didn't do it on purpose, but somehow I've got quite a web of security around me now. Everybody at the station knows me."

Dad walked through the house and Randy remembered what he'd come in the house to do. He followed Dad to his office calling out, "Mr. Gorman" on the way.

I read through my procedures manual, wrote out the two police reports, and commandeered my dad's computer to write a paper. I was typing away when my Dad walked in to say dinner was ready.

"I wish you'd have been this serious about school when you were little. You were always day dreaming in school, taking off tracking whenever you hit the playground. I can't count the times I had to sign notes from your teacher about you following some trail off campus at recess and getting in trouble for it. Now here you are where there are plenty of tracks and you're hitting the books."

"Only so I can track, though, Dad. It's still the same old story. Only you won't see any notes from my teacher."

"That's too bad, I got a kick out of some of those notes. Jesse wasn't nearly as entertaining. All the notes from her teachers were about talking too much and passing notes in class."

It was our last evening at the ranch. Everybody knew in the morning it would be time to say good-bye again.

"Will you be home for the holidays?" my mom asked.

"I don't know. If I am, it'll just be for a day or two. I can't miss school, because it will be so close to graduation time. The further we go at academy, the more intense it gets."

"You missed so many holidays at home. It's good to have you back."

"If I pass all my tests you can come to graduation. That's just a few weeks after the holidays."

I finished up my paper, printed it out, then brought all the books up to my room to go through the reading once more. Seems like every time through it I noticed there was something else I should know for a test. Anything and everything could be on those final tests. The sheer volume of little facts, policies and procedures overwhelmed me.

Rusty knocked quietly and came in. He looked at the book I was reading.

"You're trying too hard again. When will you ease up?"

"January twenty-first, if I pass."

"You promise?"

"I might ease up earlier if I had a good enough reason," I said, closing the book.

Chapter 18

We said our goodbyes the next morning and drove home the quick way. Shadow loaded up into the Explorer reluctantly. On the ranch he had been free to run and investigate things and play with the other dogs. He didn't want to be trapped in a car.

We pulled up in front of the condo, relieved to be alone again. I spent Monday buried in the books, trying to get in gear for academy the next day. Rusty came home from work in good spirits. Everything seemed to be on an even keel again. Trouble was going to have to figure out a different way to get to me.

"What's the day circled on the calendar?" Rusty asked over dinner.

"It may be the last time I can get to the hideout until spring so I wanted to go up there that weekend."

"The last time?"

"Yeah, the canyon fills with snow and it's too rough and too steep to snowshoe in, so I have to go in before the first big snowfall."

"This is southern California. It doesn't snow that much in those mountains."

"Wanna bet? Why do you think they have ski resorts up there? It snows. It snows a lot more up there than it rains here in town. And I bet as soon as I graduate I get called on to track down lost skiers and snowboarders up there. If you can get the weekend off, call Kelly and see if he wants to try and climb that mountain."

"Okay, I'll try."

"Even if it doesn't snow in December, I'll be too busy with school and the holidays, so it's our last chance until March."

Academy was tough on Tuesday and Wednesday. It was hard to get back into the swing of things after being away. Ranch life was just different somehow; it seemed to run on a different clock. Academy time had a much faster pace and I was trying to catch up to it. I dragged myself into the condo at midnight ready to hit the sack and then slept in late the next morning. The weekend was even worse. I had to be at academy at eight a.m. and it was intense physical training all day Saturday and Sunday. We did drills. Quick thinking. Quick action. Go by the book drills. We broke down doors. We pursued and subdued criminals. We practiced self-defense. We practiced at the target range. When I returned to my Jeep I wanted to just pop the seat back and sleep in the training center garage. Only Rusty and the upcoming trip to the hideout made it worth that long drive home.

After keeping the hideout a secret for so long, I didn't know why I was so excited about taking Kelly there. It just seemed like the right thing to do and I knew he'd love the mountain of boulders to climb. He met us at the trailhead early Friday morning.

"You really like this trail, don't you?" he asked as Rusty and I got out of the Explorer.

"Yeah, I do," I answered. "It's my favorite. It's shady and follows the creek. It's just a pleasant hike. You brought backpacking gear for two nights, right?"

"Yep."

"I've got dinner covered tonight. It's my special first day of camp meal."

"The best steak I've ever had," interjected Rusty.

"Where's your gear?"

"Right here."

He looked at me skeptically.

"It's okay, I've got everything. If you want to lighten your pack we can repack so everybody has an even load. You've got a tent and sleeping bag. We can tie your bag onto my pack. We have a stove and we don't need two so you can leave that in your truck."

He let me take the sleeping bag and kept the rest. That was another Backpacker's Rule: the guys had to have heavier packs. Or at least it had to appear that they did. It was a short trip, though, so we didn't need a lot of gear. Everybody had a light pack.

The weather was wonderful for hiking and we made good time. The coolness brought out the animals and squirrels scurried across the trail ahead of us. We saw a rabbit bound away at our approach. We stopped at the creek to enjoy the water whenever we needed a rest.

When we turned to go off trail Kelly looked at me skeptically again. "You're a glutton for punishment, aren't you? You barely made it out of this canyon and now you're back for more?"

"This is a special canyon. You'll understand why when you get there."

We started up the canyon, hiking at first, then rock climbing where it was necessary. Kelly was getting into the swing of things. He liked the rocks so I focused the climb closer to the creek where there were more rocks and less hiking. The sound of water tumbling followed us up the canyon.

"I can't believe you hiked out of here after that dog attacked you. How did you do it?"

"There are easier ways down. I thought you liked the rocks so I brought you up the rocky way."

"Still... I don't know how you did it. You said it was three miles?"

"To the clearing where the dog was, yeah. We're only going two. See the big pine tree? That's where we're going."

We climbed the big rock next to the waterfall that marked the deer clearing, so I had the guys drop their packs. This was always a good place to rest and I knew Kelly would like to see the deer. I hopped over the creek and led them to the clearing. Three does were in the clearing, grazing contentedly. I was glad to see them calm again. We sat and watched for a few minutes and then went back to our packs. It was tempting to stop and stalk them but we had a camp to set up.

Several rocks and a couple of short hikes and we came to the big pine tree. Rusty and I shed our packs and Kelly looked around.

"Nice spot, tent space, water, shade. How did you find this spot?"

"I was just wandering around. I liked the canyon, and the creek. The canyon has lots of places to explore and I explore it a little bit every time I come up here. That's how I found the place where we will rock climb tomorrow. I like to stalk the deer in the clearing and if the deer aren't there they are usually in another one up canyon from here. There's a chipmunk here I've made friends with. Pick a spot and we can get you set up here."

"What about you guys?"

"We're all set up already."

Kelly looked around the camp for signs of a tent or other camping necessities.

"Just show him," Rusty said.

"Okay," I said, "follow me."

Kelly followed me to the wild patch of forest and stood watching as I looked around for the flap of tarp that served as a door. I lifted it and crawled through the small opening. I felt around for the lantern and turned it on. Kelly hesitated but eventually crawled through, too. He looked around, grinning.

"My mountain home," I said. "I come here a lot and I found these two trees that formed a good structure to build from. I brought up a huge tarp and cleared a floor and built this out of just a tarp and some forest branches. I call it my hideout. Rusty was the first person I ever showed it to. Nobody knows about it but the three of us. So you see, we really did have enough gear. I've got a stove, food, books, sleeping bag. There's water in the creek and a barbeque grill hidden in the woods. Rusty thought you'd like to see it and we wanted to take you to the boulders tomorrow."

"You really built this all by yourself? After climbing that canyon?"

"I came up here several times before I found the spot to build the hideout. It was just a favorite place to explore and then when I found the two trees I knew I wanted a permanent camp here, so I built one."

"This is amazing."

He crawled out and looked over the outside carefully. He started pulling a branch and I stopped him.

"No, don't do that. There's a chipmunk who lives in there and I don't want to disturb his home."

He grinned, "When will I quit being surprised by the things you do?"

"Never," Rusty said. "Every time I turn around she still surprises me."

"Do you want help with your tent?" I asked.

"No, it's an easy one," he replied, pulling the tent from its sack. "Just leave a little space for cooking and we'll be fine."

I left the guys to talk and set up camp while I put the mayo jar full of steak in the creek to keep it cool. I wandered up the creek, played in the water and looked for tracks. I wandered back, watching the guys working together with comfortable ease. It was comforting to see these two so at ease in the woods. I wished they could see nature through my eyes, see the game trails and the small life that exists where people simply don't notice. I wished they could see all the evidence of life around them.

"Rhonda could have come too," I said while washing the barbeque grill in the creek.

"Rhonda's kind of a flatlander. She likes the outdoors and wildlife. She just doesn't like to work to get at it. That's why we live up in the mountains. The wildlife comes to us and she has friends and neighbors. She prefers town life with a little wildlife thrown in. She would have given up at first sight of the canyon."

I put the grill over the tiny fire and waited for the flames to die down and the coals to form. I then added the steak and made backpacker rice. It was my standard first day of camp meal whenever I had time to prepare for a trip.

"What do you call this steak?" Kelly asked after the first bite.

"I call it mayo jar steak, but that's only because I pack it in a mayonnaise jar. It's really just teriyaki steak."

"You'll have to give Rhonda the recipe."

"There's nothing to it but you have to carry it around in the mountains for several hours. Maybe the creek has something to do with it, too. I don't know. I make the same thing at home but it doesn't taste quite the same as it does up here."

After dinner I put out the fire, erasing any evidence that it had existed. Kelly seemed curious about my thoroughness.

"I don't want the place to look like a camp. If someone wanders up this canyon I want them to think this is just another part of the forest. What do you think? Can you tell it's a camp?"

"Not at first glance. If I stayed here for long I'd probably pick up clues that it was used frequently, but I'd never guess there was a hideout in that patch of brambles."

The stars came out and we sat around talking in the dark.

"I have a lantern but I have never lit it outside of the hideout. Do you think it would be seen from the trail below? I won't do anything to draw attention up here. When I am alone I sleep when it gets dark and get up when it's light."

"We don't need a lantern."

"You know what we need, some music."

"Music?" they said in unison.

"Yeah, just a little bit." I walked over to the hideout and felt around in the dark for the flap. It was easier to find the second time. If it were still covered with pine needles it would be impossible to find in this darkness. I crawled into the hideout feeling around for my pack and then felt around inside it for my bamboo flute. I carried it frequently on backpacking trips but didn't have much occasion to play it. I felt the smooth wood marred by the teeth and claws of a bear then played a scale to make sure it still worked before bringing it back outside.

"I'm glad it survived," I said, taking my place back on the rock. "The bear got ahold of it when I was tracking Kelly. See the teeth marks in it?" I handed the flute over. They couldn't see them but the gouges in the wood could be felt.

After they handed it back I played a little tune I'd made up that sounded woodsy. The notes drifted away and occasionally we heard them echo off the walls of the canyon. I played a few familiar tunes that I'd picked out by ear and memorized long ago. The guys sat back, listening to the mournful sound, a lone flute deep in the woods.

"Anybody know any more tunes in E flat and only one octave?"

"See, she surprises me every time," Rusty said. "I need to show you my office."

After a few more tunes we all started yawning. We'd have a long day on the rocks tomorrow so we turned in. It was a cold night. I hoped Kelly brought a winter bag to sleep in. The hideout offered more insulation against the cold than a tent. Surely Kelly had the right gear for these mountains; after all, he worked in them every day.

We awoke to frost on the ground and kept moving in the morning, waiting for hot chocolate to warm our hands. Then we walked around with steaming cups until the powdered eggs were done cooking. We ate on our feet, pacing and talking quietly. Once the sun hit, things would warm up fast.

The guys could feel the rocks calling, and there were lots of them. With a warm breakfast behind us and the frost quickly melting, we headed for the canyon wall. Kelly was keyed up. He didn't know what he was facing yet. He knew it wasn't a long technical climb or Rusty would have brought ropes, but he knew the day would bring new challenges. He'd never seen these rocks before, even after working in these mountains for years, so he was anxious to see what was up there.

Rusty knew. He knew it was a long, rough climb.

I just looked at it one rock at a time. If I thought about tackling the whole mountain it was too big, but I could handle one rock at a time. I led the way to the canyon wall and climbed up the rock leading to the boulders. Kelly looked at the boulders stretching far and away up to the top of the mountain. Each would present its own challenge. Hopefully we'd have to employ a variety of climbing techniques to reach the top, and hopefully the guys could teach me a thing or two along the way. I had climbed many rocks in my time and I'd learned a few climbing techniques, but most of it had just been experimenting on my part.

"That's a lot of rocks," Kelly said.

We set off up the first rock. Unfortunately, getting to the top of one rock didn't necessarily get us closer to the top of the mountain. If we climbed up one rock we then had to climb down it to get to the next boulder. We realized that to make real progress up the mountain we needed to make our way progressively up between the rocks. So we ended up climbing in the cracks and gaps. We gave up our quest once the top of the mountain started looking less appealing than just climbing around on the rocks. We each picked a rock within hailing distance of one another and then explored on our own. Rusty and Kelly tended to stick together so they could talk about the technical aspects. I picked my way from rock to rock, choosing different ones from the guys because of my size. I wandered unconcerned, knowing the guys were enjoying the boulders and that we'd meet up eventually. I looked down into the rocks and found I was three boulders up off the ground. Rocks on top of rocks were down there.

Rusty and Kelly were off in the distance when I missed a foothold and went sliding down the rock. I managed to keep my footing while sliding downward, until I hit the next rock. That sent me tumbling off one rock after another until I hit the sandy floor of the boulder field. I tested my limbs, dusted myself off and looked up. I tried climbing back up but the upper rocks were too steep. Walking around beneath the rocks, I searched for a way up. It was interesting to be able to walk along under the rocks while the guys worked hard climbing the rocks above.

I weaved in and out of the boulders watching for a way up but was dismayed because the land sloped downhill. This didn't make sense. I knew the top of the mountain was before me but the ground sloped downhill even as the rocks continued up. I was getting worried. Did the guys even know I was gone? They would think I'd just dropped off the face of the earth but I couldn't find a way up to locate them again. As the ground went down and more rocks were above, the light began to fade. I began thinking it would be better to head back to where I could be found, but then I noticed something completely odd. It was a footprint. A very recent footprint. What was a footprint doing way down here? It was like Robinson Crusoe finding Friday's footprint on the island. Was this the person who had recently given me the odd feeling of not being alone in the canyon? Was there someone up here who knew about the hideout? Had they been watching me? I examined the footprint carefully. It was a bare foot, medium sized, made by a man. I followed the footprints through the maze of rocks. He was a tall man, comfortable in this setting. The light faded more and more as I descended until I realized that I was no longer on the side of the mountain. I was in a cave. Or a mine. No, I thought, it had to be a cave. All these rocks had been here much longer than any mine would have been. I turned to make my way back. I'd never had an occasion to track myself but was glad to be capable of it. I had turned my back on the puzzling trail when suddenly a strong arm yanked me back and dragged me deeper into the cave. I struggled, but the arm was like a vice. I pried at the arm fastened around me. I tried to bring my feet around to trip the man up but he grasped my upper arms, lifted me off my feet and held me face to face with him. I gazed into the grizzled face of the old man in the mountain. His gray hair fell down his back in ragged tangles. His beard was long and matted and his yellow teeth were rotting in his mouth. His tattered clothes hung on a scrawny frame but he was tall and powerful.

"What do you want with me?" I almost yelled.

"Just company, for now. I'll think about what else later." His voice was raspy like he'd smoked too much over the years. "Maybe you can shed some light on where I went wrong."

"You went wrong assuming I'd go with you. I'm not going with you. I need to get back. I've got friends who are going to start looking for me soon."

"They won't find you down here. They aren't trackers. They just know to look but they won't look deep in the mountain. The farthest they will look is in amongst the rocks. This place is about as safe as they come."

He set me down.

"You can't keep me here," I said. "I can be a royal pain in the ass if I want to be. You don't want to piss me off."

"I'm real scared. Come on."

"No," I said standing firm, "you haven't done anything to convince me I should trust you. I'm out of here." I made a dash down the tunnel but he caught me easily. Who was this guy? I felt the vice-like grip close around me again as he dragged me down the tunnel. The floor of the cave dipped, becoming darker and colder as we went. Where the cave ended there was a camp set up. A small fire had burned down to coals and a light, smoky haze hung in the air stinging my eyes. Part of the cave was used for cooking and part of it for sleeping. The bones of animals lay in a pile and stashes of assorted groceries lined a section of wall. He forced me to the ground and tied my wrists behind my back. Then he tied my ankles together. I wasn't scared yet. Even though I had not been treated kindly, I saw no evidence that he meant to do me harm, either.

"Who are you?" I asked.

"You don't want to know."

"Why? You can't be that scary a guy just by name. What name could you have that would scare me? It takes a lot to scare me these days."

"How about Trent? Does the name Trent scare you?"

"It used to."

He grew still. He came over to me, squatted down and looked me in the eye.

"What happened to Tyrone Trent?"

"How far back do you want me to go? He was stalking me, trying to kidnap me. He'd kidnapped three women, at least. I know he'd killed two of them. So I wasn't cooperating much when he tried to kidnap me. He didn't like that. Then he found out I had friends who were police officers and he wanted even more to get his hands on me. He said he wanted to teach the police a lesson. He followed me in his truck. He rammed my car repeatedly and followed me all over the valley. He was going to kill me if he could catch me. The police were on our tail and he forced me off the road. My car rolled into a ditch. I had to cut the roof to get away. Trent thought I was in my car so he filled it with bullets. The police caught up with him and he fired on them. They fired back. That's all I know. I wasn't told if he lived or died. I fled the scene of the accident and hid in the hills and I didn't come down until it was over."

He sat still listening and hung his head at the news. He got up and with a wild yell drove his fist into the wall of the cave.

"How did you know about Trent?" I asked. "How would you know he was linked to me in any way?" I needed more puzzle pieces to work with here.

"He followed you into the mountains after he saw you track. He was very interested in you. He'd never seen a girl adept at something he valued. He started keeping tabs on you everywhere and when he saw you come up here he had me watch your camp. I'd been looking for a place to lay low and so I came up and found a place I could live in where I could watch the camp. I always saw you in and around camp, but I never found the place you slept and that intrigued Tyrone even more. When he came up for reports, I talked to him. He never would listen. I told him he couldn't win against the cops. He came from a long line of family who couldn't get along with the law. His mother was killed in a bank robbery. We all found one way or another to get on the wrong side of the law. I got sick of it. I left. Tyrone still managed to find me. He still valued my opinion, but he had a temper and he liked power, so retreating was not an option for him." His voice had been calm, but then it turned eerily quiet. "You led my son into a trap."

"He left me no choice. He was going to kill me. And he *wanted* a standoff with the police. He made that very clear. He wanted to kill me and he wanted to do it with the police watching."

"You even killed my dog."

"That was *your dog*?" Now my anger flared. "That dog was starved to the point of attacking people. Why didn't you at least feed the poor thing? It couldn't find food in these mountains. It was trying to hunt deer and it didn't have a chance. It attacked my dog and when I tried to help him it attacked me, too. I still have scars from it. No dog should have to live like that, trying to hunt in these mountains. I know. I've tried to survive in these mountains. It's harder for dogs. They can't make snares, they can only hunt, and there's not enough things to hunt out here. I'd have taken the dog to camp and fed it but it attacked me. I had no choice but to kill it."

"I'm not blaming you. Not for Tyrone's death, not for the dog."

"Then what do you want? Why do you have me trussed up here?"

"Anger management. I'm sick of the world. I'm sick of people sticking their noses where they don't belong. What are you doing in these mountains? Why do you keep returning?"

"I need the mountains. I'm at home in them."

"These are my mountains now. Thanks to you, they're all I've got left. You're leaving and you're not coming back."

"The mountains don't belong to anybody."

"You're leaving and you're not coming back!" he shouted, kicking me in the stomach.

"If you want to fight," I said, "untie me and fight like a man. Don't just beat on me. It's what Trent would have done."

He picked me up and threw me across the cave.

"I said untie me and fight!" I yelled. "If it's violence you want you can sure have it. Or is beating up people who can't move what you prefer. You're going to have a hard time making me squirm like this. People take a number to do this to me. It wasn't your turn yet!" He picked me up again, his fingers digging into my arms, his face an angry red. I kicked at him with my bound feet, but it was awkward. I couldn't get any real power behind my kicks. He slammed me down and slugged me again, snapping my head back and leaving me dazed. I lay there quietly, waiting for things to settle down. Anger wasn't getting me anywhere. I closed my eyes, letting calm take over. I opened them slightly and saw Trent Senior pacing the floor of the cave. I worked my hands back and forth, trying to loosen the ropes. I felt the knots. The knots were big, but big ropes don't like sharp bends. It's hard to pull big ropes into tight knots. I worked and worked at it. Trent continued his frantic pacing. He seemed to be thinking.

While working at the knots, I glanced around the cave looking for anything that might work to my advantage. I felt behind me for pieces of rock that could be used to cut the rope. I didn't find anything. I then worked my feet to see if the knots were any looser and found there was a little give. I pushed off my boots hoping that would make my feet smaller and they could slip through the hole. Fortunately I'd worn bulky hiking boots and not my moccasins. As I slipped off the boots I felt a rope slide over my heel. Yes! Any little gain was a reason to celebrate. I slipped one foot loose from the rope. I located the back of the cave and then the opening of the tunnel. I tried to remember if there were any bends to the tunnel and decided there weren't enough to worry about. It was the rocks I'd have trouble with but maybe once I got to the rocks Rusty could hear me.

I looked back at Trent. He was sitting in the middle of the cave, head in hands. I tested my body. If I was going to make a dash for it I didn't want any surprises. I knew Trent was fast. I decided I could deal with the pain, and prepared myself mentally for a quick dash out the tunnel. The trick was to stand without use of my hands before Trent could cross the cave. I tensed, getting ready, but something told me to wait. I didn't know why. But listening to instinct had worked before.

It was hard to wait. I kept imagining Rusty and Kelly searching the rocks, thinking I had fallen, not knowing where, not knowing why I couldn't answer their calls. To take my mind off the outside world I concentrated on improving my odds. I worked my hands back and forth, turning the ropes this way and that, pulling at any pieces of the rope that I could reach with my fingers, watching Trent through nearly closed eyes. Eventually he got up and opened a can of food with an old can opener and ate the cold contents with a dirty fork. He paced the cave and then walked out, glancing at me to make sure I wasn't going anywhere. I heard his footsteps fade. Standing silently, I lowered my hands to floor level and stepped over the binding so my hands were in front of me. Pressing myself to the wall of the cave, I inched along until I came to a spot where it jutted out. I peeked around, making sure Trent was nowhere in sight and found my next hiding spot down the wall of the tunnel. I found a little niche that I could crawl into and pushed my way into it. I waited until Trent walked back in and I stayed put. He hurried back out, passing me by. Now what would I do? If I got out of the niche I'd be discovered and brought back. Just wait, Cass. Wait and you'll know when to go.

Time passed and I saw Trent go by me several times. Good, I thought, he's confusing my trail. I slid off my socks and stuffed them in the niche so that when I made my escape my tracks would blend in with his.

I was getting impatient. Waiting was killing me. But any time I left the niche it would be risky. I wished I could tell time. I didn't want to be trapped in the rocks at night. I'd never find a way up. I calculated the time that had passed. We'd been rock climbing a good hour before I fell, I'd spent another hour trying to find a way up the rocks before noticing I wasn't in the rocks anymore. I'd probably spent an hour or two in the cave, and was pretty sure I'd spent an hour in the niche. So I figured it was early afternoon. That meant Rusty and Kelly had been searching for several hours.

What would I do if I were Trent? If my prisoner escaped I'd check the tunnel. When I reached the rocks I'd check for tracks to see if the tracks exited the tunnel. If they hadn't, I'd know to look in the tunnel or the cave. So, Trent knew I was in the tunnel. If it were me I'd wait at the end of the tunnel and watch, but I knew he was somewhere at the cave end of the tunnel. I had to assume he was watching the tunnel and would see me if I tried to leave. Just lay low, Cassidy. While in the niche I worked the knots that bound my hands by rubbing them against the roof of the crevasse. I pulled at them with my teeth, anything to loosen the knots, but they held firm. It gave me something quiet to do while waiting.

The tunnel gradually grew quiet. Had Trent given up? Another period of unbearable time passed and I was getting to the point of wanting to do anything, even fight him, to get out of there. I moved around making sure all systems were still A-okay. I didn't want to get out in the tunnel only to find my foot was asleep. Silently scooting out of the niche, I crouched next to the wall and listened for movement before making a mad dash down the tunnel. I heard a blood-curdling yell behind me and pushed myself to run faster. I saw light ahead and ran for the rocks. As I came to a place where I could see the ground again I followed Trent's tracks but I couldn't track as fast as I could run and I had to give up following the tracks in favor of losing him in the rocks. I dodged in and out of boulders but I couldn't climb without my hands.

Off in the distance I could hear a long drawn out, "Caaaassidy!" being yelled, like people do when they are searching. I couldn't call back without telling Trent where I was, but headed for the sound. The rocks were confusing. I kept being turned in wrong directions and I was never sure where Trent might be. I kept to the general direction of the voice, hoping I was getting closer, watching for a rock I could scramble up without using my hands.

I could hear Trent moving in amongst the rocks and needed some distance in order to get away without being seen. I went into stealth mode but there was no way to hide my tracks in the sand. All I could do was constantly keep a rock or two between us.

At last I found a rock I could try to climb. It was actually two rocks set in a V, but I wedged my back against one and walked my feet up the other. I wriggled until my back was higher than my feet and then walked my feet up the rock. It was awkward chimney climbing. I'd done it easily with my hands free, and I'd rested in this position previously but I'd never climbed this way. Pushing against the rock with my back, I walked with my feet, pushed with my back, again and again. When I reached the top of the rock I waited, wedged high above the ground where Trent was looking for me. Now I had to figure out how to get out of this crack.

"Cassidy!" I heard being called closer.

"Rusty!" I called back, risking being heard by Trent.

"Where are you?"

"I don't know. Look for tall rocks with a V cut between them," I yelled back.

"Kelly! This way!" he yelled.

"It sounds like you're downhill from me," I called out.

"Wave your hands or something!"

I raised my hands but I couldn't wave much with my hands bound.

"I can't! My hands are tied!"

It took time but finally I saw him scrambling from one rock to another.

"Rusty, stop!" He froze. "Look to your right!" He turned, looking around, his gaze followed the mountain up and I saw his gaze stop at my hiding spot. He climbed toward my rock, looked around for Kelly, and waved his arms.

"Cass, what happened?"

"Trent's dad is down there. He's been watching the hideout for Trent. He didn't know Tyrone was gunned down by the police and wasn't too happy to hear the news. Can you untie me?" I pushed and walked with my feet and pushed some more inching up.

"You climbed this whole crack like that?"

"Yeah, it was the first rock I could manage without using my hands."

Rusty climbed to the top of my rock and lowered himself into the crack. He made his way to me in the normal chimney fashion until we were together. He then worked the knots loose, stuffing the rope into his pocket. I wiggled my hands around, getting the circulation going again and assumed a more normal position. Then we climbed down to a more stable rock surface where we could wait for Kelly.

"We need to get out of here. I don't know what Trent is up to. Last I saw him, he was chasing me around under the rocks, but he is savvy enough to find a way up. He's sneaky enough to listen and wait. I didn't see any weapons in there, but it was dark and they could have been hidden. We shouldn't go back to camp. He's been watching it. He'll assume we are going to go there."

"Talk to me. What are we dealing with here?"

"Well, given that we can follow creeks all the way, we should make it out fine even without a stop at camp. If Trent decides to stop us, we may have a struggle on our hands. Kelly ought to be fine. Trent blames me for leading Tyrone into a trap. And he'll blame you just for being a cop. He's generally not as violent as Tyrone, but he's on edge since he just found out Tyrone is probably dead."

Once Kelly caught up with us, we filled him in on what happened and then hit the trail. Unsure of the land we climbed back into the canyon choosing an open path where I watched for movements and tracks.

We reached the trail in record time. "Wait," I said, "don't touch the trail yet." I looked the trail over carefully before stepping out onto it. I walked down trail a little ways and then walked up trail. I didn't see any tracks, so I turned to give the guys the go ahead. Suddenly I heard a hoarse yell. I turned just in time to see the big mountain man run and leap from the cover of some brush beside the trail. I was quickly knocked flat and we fell with a thud into the dust. Trent straddled me, pummeling me with his fists, eyes blazing, driven by grief. I put my arms over my head, shielding myself from the blows. Rusty and Kelly pulled Trent off of me while he swung at them, struggling. A few good cracks and Trent went down. Rusty stood over him, pistol in hand. Never before had I seen Rusty so angry or even strike someone. Kelly hauled Trent to his feet while Rusty used the rope in his pocket to tie Trent's hands behind him. I stood up, wondering what we would do next. Rusty handed the pistol to Kelly and took me aside.

"Cass, are you okay?"

"Yeah, I'm okay. Really."

"What if I told you to hike out? Would you do it? I don't want you here tempting Trent to try anything, and I want you to call in some backup. I can't haul this guy in with the Explorer." He took his wallet out and handed me a card with a number to call. "Do you want Kelly to go with you?"

"No, I can do it and Trent's less likely to pull something with both of you here."

"Are you sure you're okay?"

"I'm sure. I even remember the codes for this."

I started for the trailhead.

"Cassidy! Where are your shoes?"

"In Trent's cave. Don't worry about it. I usually hike in moccasins anyway."

I jogged until I hit the rocky section of trail, then picked my way through the rough rocks, then jogged again. I made good time, thanks to my running at academy and the familiar trail. I tried the cell phone from the trailhead but it didn't work, so I jogged into the campground and knocked on the door of the camp host. I briefly explained that I needed to call the police and they put me on a landline. I took the card out of my pocket and the number brought me through to the station. The woman on the other end seemed confused about who to send to a call in the mountains, so I asked to be put through to Schroeder. He knew Rusty's cases and would know who to send. I explained the situation and walked to the entrance of the campground to await the police. After a while a black and white Ford Bronco pulled up and I flagged him down.

"I should have known you'd have something to do with this," Big John Jankowski said as I approached the Bronco. I recognized him from my day of cookie baking. "What happened to your eye?"

"I got into a little tangle with Trent Senior."

"Where is he now?"

"Rusty sent me ahead. Last I saw him they were two miles up the trail. I'll show you."

I hopped in the Bronco and pointed out the way through the campground to the trailhead. We parked and headed up the trail.

"A little tangle with Trent Senior? Not Trent who forced you off the road and filled your car with bullets Trent."

"His dad. He wasn't too happy with me."

"I'm surprised he's still alive if Michaels knew about this," he said, pointing to the purple mark under my eye.

"It's going to be a hike of a mile or so. There's creeks, but if you have water you might bring it."

I started up the trail and Jankowski stopped me. "You better wait here. There's no telling what the situation is up there."

"No way. Rusty's armed and he isn't alone with Trent. Kelly Green is with him. It'll be okay. Besides, if they did run into trouble I'll recognize it by the footprints on the trail. If Trent got away somehow, I know how to find him."

We set off up trail again. I had to keep to a walk this time because Jankowski didn't like me getting too far ahead. He was more of a slow and steady kind of guy.

Getting Trent out of the mountains was a long drawn out process. When we reached the group again there was some discussion. Kelly and I sat on the sidelines.

"I guess I'll hike back in tomorrow just to pack up camp. I'm sorry your rock-climbing trip got messed up. I'll bring your gear out."

"You can't bring all your stuff and mine."

"Then I'll bring your stuff and make sure mine is secure in the hideout. I'll just fill your pack with as much as I can carry and stow the rest."

"No way. Rusty won't let you go back up there alone tomorrow. I'll meet you at the trailhead at nine. We can go in, pack up and hike out."

So that's what we did, only Rusty insisted on going, too. We hiked in quickly this time and packed up camp. I stored all the gear in the hideout and tucked the door under so it would get covered with pine needles and become invisible again. Then I set my pack against a tree, took the lantern and a short climbing rope and headed for the canyon wall. I climbed the rock and then cast around for a way to the cave.

"Cassidy, what are you doing?" Rusty asked.

"I want to find the way to that cave. It could be full of evidence, my hiking boots are in there, and it is just plain interesting. I wonder how Trent found it. I only came across it because I fell off a rock. You need to see down here. You can walk around on the mountainside underneath all the boulders. It's really cool."

I climbed to the area where I fell through the rocks and found a way to anchor the rope. I rappelled down the rock face to the sandy floor below. The guys followed one by one. I tracked myself to the tunnel and led the guys in. I retrieved my socks from the niche where they'd been hidden. In the cave I stuffed them into my hiking boots. In the middle of the cave I turned on the lantern. The smoke blackened walls swallowed the light. We looked around at the filthy interior. It looked like Trent lived off of mostly canned goods and small animals. He had a cardboard container of oats and boxes of cereal, but mice had eaten through the cardboard and carried most of it away. We found an old 45 and a box of ammunition stashed on a rock ledge. So, I thought, he could have killed me if he'd been so inclined. I was glad he chose his fists first.

"You still haven't told me what happened to you here."

"Nothing we can find evidence of. Mostly he wanted to know about Trent."

"Cass, you know what I need. You've been writing reports for months now."

So I gave him a detailed account. I really didn't want to do it with Kelly there, but he asked for it. Both men sat there, grim and angry.

"He's lucky I found out about this now. If you'd told me this yesterday, I would have pounded him," Kelly said. "I'm surprised you got away from him. You could still be down here."

"I'm getting good at escapes. It takes practice. Creating distractions, slitting car roofs, untying bindings, hiding in dark tunnels. I'm multi-talented."

Chapter 19

The holidays were upon us before we knew it and academy had become increasingly intense. I took a ribbing my first day back when they saw the purple bands of bruises around my arms and my shiner of a black eye. I wondered how many times a person could bruise before their skin just turned a permanent shade of purple. If they were ever going to do a study on that I'd be the perfect candidate.

Sergeant Barrera took me aside, asking for an explanation about what had happened. In academy, we were required to maintain behavior befitting of the police force as a whole, and if I had done something unbefitting I could be thrown out of academy. Therefore I was careful to explain the whole back-story and how I came to meet up with Trent Senior, what he had done and why. I got the usual look of disbelief but the ribbing stopped.

Rusty and I got a Christmas tree and set it up in the living room. We made an evening out of the Christmas tree hunt, looking through all the tree lots until we found one we both liked. We strapped it to the roof of the Explorer and took it home. We bought all new ornaments. Rusty hadn't had a Christmas tree as a bachelor, and all my ornaments had been burned in the fire.

I wound fake pine branches and twinkle lights up the stairway and made Christmas cookies and fudge. I taped all our Christmas cards to the downstairs bathroom door, so they could be seen from the entry.

We couldn't go to the ranch for the holidays. Things were just too hectic and the pressure was really on at school. We were down to our last few weeks and everybody was stressed out trying to balance jobs, academy, holidays and family time. I only had a few things competing for my time, but I felt it too. The condo twinkled with holiday cheer, and almost quivered with tension. I studied nervously. I managed to shop and mail a box of gifts to the ranch hoping it would arrive on time. I was stumped on what to get Rusty. I knew this was going to be an ongoing problem. Twice a year for the rest of my life I was going to be stumped about a gift for him.

Christmas day was peaceful with no school, yet I was tempted to spend the time studying. We had a leisurely breakfast and then spent a peaceful morning relaxing around the house. However the computer and my books seemed to be constantly calling my name from upstairs. For Christmas I'd gotten Rusty a chair to go in his office and made a collage of photos that my mom had sent me of our Thanksgiving weekend. He hung it in his office.

As soon as New Year's Day passed, the pressure was really on. We were down to the last three weeks and testing began in earnest. I went to my post at the firearm test feeling more nervous than usual. This was the real thing. I would pass easily if this were normal practice in class. If only I could settle my nerves. I tried to look at the tension in a good light. Edginess or tension was all right and actually helped. Nervousness or anxiety tended to throw off my accuracy. I chose to call this feeling edginess to give me some confidence. Edgy was how I felt in tense situations when things tended to happen fast, and edginess made me think and react quickly.

Load, wait, aim, squeeze, aim, squeeze. The pistol jerked in my hand. Slight, controlled jerking. Aim, squeeze. I felt each bullet leave the gun, and each bullet flew home. Like a baseball player can feel the way the ball comes off his bat and knows where the ball was going to land, I felt each shot and knew they hit true. If a shot was off, I'd feel it.

With each test, our class got a little bit smaller. Every time someone failed a test, they were quietly called to the office. Each loss was felt by all. We knew we could be next, so it just made us strive harder. I studied night and day for the POST test and the Criminal Justice test. It was the written ones I was the most worried about. It was the bookwork, the regulations, the procedures, the codes, the thinking part of police work. I had to force myself to look at only one question at a time. I couldn't let the big picture overwhelm me. As long as I took one question at a time, I did okay. After the Criminal Justice test was first aid and CPR. My dummy survived, so I did, too. One thing led to another, and with each test we dreaded the call to the office. When all was said and done, we were down to sixty-nine.

We lined up at the front of the room, all sixty-nine graduates of the Reserve Police Academy. We'd gained a ton of knowledge and lost almost a ton of weight. The group standing at the front of the room was not the same group who had started academy. We were all changed somehow. We'd all made it. I looked out over the crowd and found my mom and dad sitting next to Rusty, Kelly and Rhonda. Steve and Randy sat behind. Landon stood along an outside wall, like he'd just stepped in to check things out and he would be on his way soon. In another part of the room Lou and Schroeder sat, serious expressions on their faces, whispering things between them like, "Now what are we gonna do? She actually made it. Good luck pal, you're gonna need it. Me? What about you? What about Michaels?"

Ya, I thought, what about Michaels? As they handed me my certificate I wondered what kind of adventures the next year would bring. I had a place as a tracker. It should be safer. It should be happy. If only trouble would stay away. Yeah, right.

Within days of graduation I was trudging through the snow, looking for a lost snowboarder on the backside of the ski resort. I was glad to be out in the snow, glad to be up in the mountains, glad to be serving a purpose. After a mile of shuffling, it started changing to trudging, and now here we were, the three of us, trudging through the snow. Temperatures were falling and the light was fading. There was no way back to base camp that night so we continued searching, following the snowboard's track to the bottom of the mountain. Then we followed the kid's desperate lunge through the deep snow. If we could find him that night we'd be in good shape.

We all had gear for a night on the mountain. Our main concern was getting the kid to shelter before night fell. Landon, Rosco and I were beat. Climbing around in the mountains cross country on show shoes was exhausting. The kid went downward, ever downward, which meant to get back to base camp we'd have to climb ever upward unless we needed to call in a helicopter. The forest was thick here, though. A helicopter might not be an option. At night it was even less of an option.

This was mostly a training mission for me. Landon and Rosco could have found the kid without me. There was only one set of tracks to follow and they were three feet deep. Unless it snowed before we made contact, the trail was easy to follow.

The sun dipped behind the mountain and darkness fell with it. At last we were forced to get out headlamps. Normally I only track in the daylight hours but when the tracks are deep in snow they show up under headlamps, so we trudged on. We would keep trudging until something made us stop. We could be at this all night. An hour after nightfall we heard a cry.

"Hey!" we heard. "Over here!"

"Keep yelling," Rosco yelled back, "we can't see you."

The calls came from the mountainside to our right and we headed in that direction, zeroing in on the voice. We found the kid bedded down in a shallow snow cave next to a fallen tree. He'd used his snowboard as a scoop or a snowplow to hollow out a sheltered place, prepared to spend a frigid night on the mountain. Rosco quickly unpacked his tent and Landon opened his pack, ready for a quick physical examination. Hands and feet were a major concern.

"I th-thought I'd freeze to death out h-here," the guy chattered.

"Well, you won't freeze to death but we're still stuck out here. Let's take a look at you. What's your name?"

"T-t-thomas P-parker."

That got my attention. "Not Thomas Parker the Boy Scout who got lost up here two years ago?"

"Yeah, so what?"

"Thomas, you've got to find a way to get yourself out of these messes. Take an orienteering class or something."

"I did, but t-trouble just seems to follow me whenever I h-head for the woods."

I could identify with that. Still, how many times did I have to find the same person? I remembered Rusty, always there no matter how stupid I'd been. Okay, so I'd track down Thomas Parker again.

"Come on, Thomas, let's get you checked out here," Landon said.

"No chance of getting out of here tonight?" I asked.

"No way, no serious injuries, too dark, storm rolling in, bad pickup terrain, maybe in the morning."

Rosco got on the radio and, in a mixture of codes and words, the staccato transmissions fired back and forth.

"Ten sixty-five found." Missing person found.

"Forty-five?" Condition of patient?

"Forty-five A." A was good, B was serious and C was critical.

"Advise weather conditions."

"Weather poor."

"Arrange pickup?"

"Affirmative."

Rosco checked the GPS and fired off coordinates. Rats, we weren't walking out. Now that the situation was under control I wouldn't mind a little snow shoeing in the woods. I sighed and started setting up camp. I shed my pack, found a flat spot a ways away from the guys and set up my tent. I rolled out my sleeping bag and I was set for the night. After they made Thomas comfortable Landon set his camp up, too. I got out my camp stove, fired it up, and made hot chocolate.

"Got cookies?" Landon asked as he held a steaming hot cup in his hands.

"How's Thomas?" I asked.

"Frostbite on three toes but he'll be okay. You okay out here?"

"Yeah, sure, I've camped like this before."

During the night another four inches of new snow fell. I loved waking up to fresh snow. Rosco looked at the beautiful sight and groaned. Landon, too, just saw the snow as more work. I made hot chocolate again and heated water to make oatmeal. A hot breakfast always makes a cold winter morning better, even if it is only oatmeal. I was pleased to note the guys were prepared with their own food. They didn't force me to be camp cook, but they accepted my hot chocolate. That seemed like an agreeable compromise to me. Maybe next time I *would* bring cookies.

We cleaned up camp, radioed Strict, and shuffled to the nearest clear spot in the forest to await pickup.

Later, I tromped into the condo cold, wet, tired and totally jazzed.

Rusty walked up grinning at me because I could barely be seen under all the paraphernalia. Grinning from ear to ear, I dropped the snowshoes and pack by the front door and slipped off my hiking boots. He took off the sunglasses and I shed the heavy winter coat. A quick kiss and I went upstairs where I took off the thick ski pants and thermal shirt. A fast, hot shower erased a lot of the weariness and I came downstairs in a t-shirt and shorts. Curled up on the couch next to Rusty, I thought, yes, this is the life. I can do this.

www.ingramcontent.com/pod-product-compliance
Lightning Source LLC
Chambersburg PA
CBHW020321260626
47156CB00004B/1325